Cindi Myers is the author of more than fifty novels. When she's not crafting new romance plots, she enjoys skiing, gardening, cooking, crafting and daydreaming. A lover of small-town life, she lives with her husband and two spoiled dogs in the Colorado mountains.

Tyler Anne Snell genuinely loves all genres of the written word. However, she's realized that she loves books filled with sexual tension and mysteries a little more than the rest. Her stories have a good dose of both. Tyler lives in Alabama with her same-named husband and their mini "lions." When she isn't reading or writing, she's playing video games and working on her blog, *Almost There*. To follow her shenanigans, visit tylerannesnell.com.

DEPUTY DEFENDER

CINDI MYERS

THE NEGOTIATION

TYLER ANNE SNELL

MILLS & BOON

First Published in Great Britain 2018
by Mills & Boon, an imprint of HarperCollins*Publishers*
1 London Bridge Street, London, SE1 9GF

Deputy Defender © 2018 Cynthia Myers
The Negotiation © 2018 Tyler Anne Snell

ISBN: 978-0-263-26593-4

0918

MIX
Paper from
responsible sources
FSC™ C007454

This book is produced from independently certified FSC™ paper to ensure responsible forest management.

For more information visit: www.harpercollins.co.uk/green

Printed and bound in Spain
by CPI, Barcelona

DEPUTY DEFENDER

CINDI MYERS

For Gaye

Chapter One

Yellow was such a cheerful color for a death threat. Brenda Stenson stared down at the note on the counter in front of her. Happy cartoon flowers danced across the bottom of the page, almost making the words written above in bold black ink into a joke.

Almost. But there was nothing funny about the message, written in all caps: BURN THAT BOOK OR YOU WILL DIE.

The cryptic message on the cheerful paper had been enclosed in a matching yellow envelope and taped to the front door of the Eagle Mountain History Museum. Brenda had spotted it when she arrived for work Monday morning, and had felt a surge of pleasure, thinking one of her friends had surprised her with an early birthday greeting. Her actual birthday was still another ten days away, but as her best friend, Lacy, had pointed out only two days ago, turning thirty was a milestone that deserved to be celebrated all month.

The message had been a surprise all right, but not a pleasant one. Reading it, Brenda felt confused at first, as if trying to make sense of something written in a foreign language or an old-fashioned, hard-to-read script. As the message began to sink in, nausea rose in her throat, and she held on to the edge of the counter, fighting dizziness. What kind of sick person would send something like this? And why? What had she ever done to hurt anybody, much less make them wish she were dead?

The string of sleigh bells attached to the museum's front door jangled as it opened and Lacy Milligan sauntered in. That was really the only way to describe the totally carefree, my-life-is-going-so-great attitude that imbued every movement of the pretty brunette. And why not? After three years of one bad break after another, Lacy had turned the corner. Now she was in school studying to be a teacher and engaged to a great guy—who also happened to be county sheriff. As her best friend, Brenda couldn't have been happier for her—and she wasn't about to do anything to upset Lacy's happiness. So she slid the threatening note off the counter and quickly folded it and inserted it back into the envelope, and dropped it into her purse.

"No classes today, so I thought I'd stop by and see what I could do to help," Lacy said. She hugged Brenda, then leaned back against the scarred wooden desk that was command central at the museum.

"I can always use the help," Brenda said. "But you're putting in so many hours here I'm starting to feel really guilty about not being able to pay you. If the fundraising drive is successful, maybe there will be enough left over to hire at least part-time help."

"You already rented me the sweetest apartment in town," Lacy said. "You don't have to give me a job, too."

"I'll never find anyone else who's half as fun for that garage apartment," Brenda said. "At least if I could give you a job, I'd still be guaranteed to see you on a regular basis after you're married."

"You'll still see plenty of me," Lacy said. "But hey—I hear Eddie Carstairs is looking for a job."

Brenda made a face. "I seriously doubt an ex–law enforcement officer is going to want a part-time job at a small-town museum," she said.

"You're probably right," Lacy said. "Eddie certainly thinks highly of himself. He's been going around town telling everyone Travis fired him because he was jealous that Eddie got so much press for being a hero, almost dying in the line of duty and all." Her scowl said exactly what she thought of her fiancé's former subordinate. "Obviously that bullet he took didn't knock any sense into him. And as Travis told him when he fired him, Eddie wasn't on duty that day and he wasn't supposed to be messing around at a crime scene. And he wasn't a full deputy anyway—he was a reserve officer. Eddie always fails to mention that when he tells his tales of woe down at Moe's Pub."

"Is Travis as upset about this as you are?" Brenda asked. She had a hard time picturing their taciturn sheriff letting Eddie's tall tales get to him.

"He says we should just ignore Eddie, but it burns me up when that little worm tries to make himself out to be a hero." Lacy hoisted her small frame up to sit on the edge of the desk. "Travis is the one who risked his life saving me from Ian Barnes."

"And anyone who counts knows that," Brenda said. Ian Barnes—the man who had killed Brenda's husband three years before—had kidnapped Lacy and tried to kill her during the town's Pioneer Days celebration two months ago. Travis had risked his life to save her, killing Ian in the struggle.

"You're right," Lacy said. "And I'm sorry to be unloading on you this way. You've got bigger things to worry about." She glanced around the museum's front room, comprising the reception desk and a small bookstore and gift shop. Housed in a former miner's cottage, the museum featured eight rooms devoted to different aspects of local history. "How's the fund-raising going?"

"I've applied for some grants, and sent begging letters to pretty much every organization and influential person I can think of," Brenda said. "No response yet."

"What about the auction?" Lacy asked. "Are you getting any good donations for that?"

"I am. Come take a look." She led the way through a door to the workroom, where a row of folding tables was rapidly filling with donations people had contributed for a silent auction, all proceeds to benefit the struggling museum. "We've gotten everything from old mining tools to a gorgeous handmade quilt, and a lovely wooden writing desk that I think should bring in a couple hundred dollars."

"Wow." Lacy ran her hand over the quilt, which featured a repeating pattern of squares and triangles in shades of red and cream. "This ought to bring in a lot of bids. I might have to try for it myself."

"My goal is to make enough to keep the doors open and pay my salary until we can get a grant or two that will provide more substantial funds," Brenda said. "But what we really need is a major donor or two who will pledge to provide ongoing support. When Henry Hake disappeared, so did the quarterly donations he made to the museum. He was our biggest supporter."

"And here everybody thought old Henry was only interested in exploiting the town for his rich investors," Lacy said. "I wonder if we'll ever find out what happened to him. Travis won't say so, but I know since they found Henry's car in that ravine, they think he's probably dead."

Henry Hake was the public face of Hake Development and Eagle Mountain Resort, a mountaintop luxury development that had been stalled three and a half years ago when a local environmental group won an injunction to stop the project. Brenda's late husband, Andy, had been a new attorney, thrilled to win the lucrative job of representing Hake. But Hake's former bodyguard, Ian Barnes, had murdered Andy. Lacy, who had been Andy's administrative assistant, had been convicted of the murder. Only Travis's hard work had freed her and eventually cleared her name. But then Henry had disappeared. And only last month, a young couple had been murdered, presumably because they saw something they shouldn't have at the dormant development site. Travis's brother, Gage, a sheriff's deputy, had figured that one out and tracked down the couple's killers, but the murderers had died in a rockslide, after imprisoning Gage and schoolteacher Maya Renfro and her five-year-old niece in an underground bunker that contained a mysterious laboratory. A multitude of law enforcement agencies was still trying to untangle the goings-on at the resort—and no one seemed to know what had happened to Henry Hake or what the young couple might have seen that led to their murders.

"I guess I don't understand how these things work," Lacy said. "But it doesn't seem very smart to base a budget on the contributions of one person. What if Henry had suddenly decided to stop sending checks?"

"Henry's contributions were significant, but they weren't all our budget," Brenda said. "When I started here four years ago, we had a comfortable financial cushion that generated enough income for most of our operating expenses, but that's gone now." Her stomach hurt just thinking about it.

"Where did it go?" Lacy asked. But the pained expression on Brenda's face must have told her the truth. "Jan!" She hopped off the desk. "She siphoned off the money to pay the blackmail!" She put her hand over her mouth, as if she wished she could take back the words. "I'm so sorry, Brenda."

Brenda had learned only recently that before his death, Andy had been blackmailing her former boss, Eagle Mountain mayor Jan Selkirk, over her affair with Henry Hake. "It's all right," she said. "I can't prove that's what happened, but probably. But if that is what happened, I don't know where the money went. I mean, yeah, Andy used some of it for the improvements on our house, and to buy some stuff, but not the tens of thousands of dollars we're talking about."

"Maybe Jan was giving the money to Henry, and his donations were his guilty conscience forcing him to pay you back," Lacy said.

"That would fit this whole sick soap opera, wouldn't it?" Brenda picked up a battered miner's lantern and pretended to examine it.

Lacy rubbed Brenda's shoulder. "None of this is your fault," she said. "And you're doing an amazing job keeping the museum going. These auction items should pull in a lot of money. Didn't you tell me that book you found is worth a lot?"

The book. A shudder went through Brenda at the thought of the slim blue volume she had found while going through Andy's things a few weeks ago. *The Secret History of Rayford County, Colorado.* What had at first appeared to be a run-of-the-mill self-published local history had turned out to be a rare account of a top-secret government program to produce biological weapons in the remote mountains of Colorado during World War II. Was that what had whoever left the threatening note so upset? Did they object to the government's dirty secrets being aired—even though the operation had ended seventy years ago?

In any case, Brenda's online research had revealed an avid group of collectors who were anxious to get their hands on the volume, and willing to pay for the privilege. Thus was born the idea of an auction to fund the museum—and her salary—for the immediate future.

"I still can't imagine what Andy was doing with a book like that," she said. "But I guess it's obvious I didn't know my husband as well as I thought."

"Whyever he had it, I'm glad it's going to help you now," Lacy said.

The local paper had run an article about the fundraiser, and listed the book among the many donations received. That must be where the letter writer had found out about it. Was it just some crank out to frighten her? Could she really take seriously a letter written on yellow stationery with cartoon flowers?

But could she really afford not to take it seriously? She needed to let someone else know about the threat—someone with the power to do something about it. "Can you do me a favor and watch the museum for a bit?" Brenda asked.

"Sure." Lacy looked surprised. "What's up?"

"I just have an errand I need to run." She retrieved her purse from beneath the front counter and slung it over her shoulder. "It shouldn't take more than an hour." She'd have to ask the sheriff to keep the letter a secret from his fiancée, at least for now. In fact, Brenda didn't want anyone in town to know about it. She had been the focus of enough gossip since Andy's murder. But she wasn't stupid enough to try to deal with this by herself.

She figured she could trust the Rayford County Sheriff's Department to keep her secret and, she hoped, to help her.

DEPUTY DWIGHT PRENTICE would rather face down an irate motorist or break up a bar fight than deal with the stack of forms and reports in his inbox. But duty—and the occasional nagging from office manager Adelaide Kincaid—forced him to tackle the paperwork. That didn't stop him from resenting the task that kept him behind his desk when Indian summer offered up one of the last shirtsleeve days of fall, the whole world outside bathed in a soft golden light that made the white LED glare of his office seem like a special kind of torture.

As he put the finishing touches on yet another report, he wished for an urgent call he would have to respond to—or at least some kind of distraction. So when the buzzer sounded that signaled the front door opening, he sat back in his chair and listened.

"I need to speak with Travis."

The woman's soft, familiar voice made Dwight slide back his chair, then glance at the window to his left to check that the persistent cowlick in his hair wasn't standing up in back.

"Sheriff Walker is away at training." Adelaide spoke in what Dwight thought of as her schoolmarm voice— very precise and a little chiding.

"Could I speak to one of the deputies, then?"

"What is this about?"

"I'd prefer to discuss that with the deputy."

Dwight rose and hurried to head off Adelaide's further attempts to determine the woman's business at the sheriff's department. The older woman was a first-class administrator, but also known as one of the biggest gossips in town.

"Hello, Brenda." Dwight stepped into the small reception area and nodded to the pretty blonde in front of Adelaide's desk. "Can I help you with something?"

"Mrs. Stenson wants to speak to a deputy," Adelaide said.

"That would be me." Dwight indicated the hallway he had just moved down. "Why don't you come into my office?"

As he escorted her down the hall, Dwight checked her out, without being too obvious. Brenda had been a pretty girl when they knew each other in high school, but she had matured into a beautiful woman. She had cut a few inches off her hair recently and styled it in soft layers. The look was more sophisticated and suited her. He had noticed her smiling more lately, too. Maybe she was finally getting past the grief for her murdered husband.

She wasn't smiling now, however. In his office, she took a seat in the chair Dwight indicated and he shut the door, then slid behind his desk. "You look upset," he said. "What's happened?"

In answer, she opened her purse, took out a bright yellow envelope, and slid it across the desk to him.

He looked down at the envelope. BRENDA was written across the front in bold black letters, all caps. "Before I open it, tell me your impression of what's in it," he said.

"I don't know if it's some kind of sick joke, or what," she said, staring at the envelope as if it were a coiled snake. "But I think it might be a threat." She knotted her hands on the edge of the desk. "My fingerprints are probably all over it. I wasn't thinking…"

"That's all right." Dwight opened the top desk drawer and took out a pair of nitrile gloves and put them on. Then he turned the envelope over, lifted the flap and slid out the single sheet of folded paper.

The capital letters of the message on the paper were drawn with the same bold black marker as the writing on the envelope. BURN THAT BOOK OR YOU WILL DIE.

"What book?" he asked.

"I can't be sure, but I think whoever wrote that note is referring to the rare book that's part of the auction to raise funds for the museum. It's an obscure, self-published volume purportedly giving an insider's experiences with a top-secret project to manufacture biological weapons for use in World War II. The project was apparently financed by the US government and took place in Rayford County. I found it in Andy's belongings, mixed in with some historical law books. I have no idea how he came to have it, but apparently it's an item that's really prized by some collectors—because it's rare, I guess. And maybe because of the nature of the subject matter."

Dwight grabbed a legal pad and began making notes. Later, he would review them. And he would need them for the inevitable report. "Who knew about this book?" he asked.

"Lots of people," she said. "There was an article in the *Examiner*."

"The issue that came out Thursday?"

She nodded. "Yes."

He riffled through a stack of documents on his desk until he found the copy of the newspaper. The article was on the front page. Rare Book to Head Up Auction Items to Benefit Museum—accompanied by a picture of

Brenda holding a slim blue volume, the title, *The Secret History of Rayford County, Colorado*, in silver lettering on the front. "How much is the book worth?" he asked.

"A dealer I contacted estimated we could expect to receive thirty to fifty thousand dollars at a well-advertised auction," she said. "I thought that in addition to the money, the auction would generate a lot of publicity for the museum and maybe attract more donors."

"People will pay that much money for a book?" Dwight didn't try to hide his amazement.

"I was shocked, too. But apparently, it's very rare, and there's the whole top-secret government plot angle that collectors like."

"But this note wasn't written by a collector," he said. "A collector wouldn't want you to burn the book."

"I know." She leaned toward him. "That's why I'm wondering if the whole thing is some kind of twisted joke. I mean—that cheerful yellow paper…" Her voice trailed away as they both stared at the note.

"Maybe it's a joke," he said. "But we can't assume anything. Has anyone said anything to you about the book since this article ran?" He tapped the newspaper. "Anything that struck you as odd or 'off'?"

"No. The only thing anyone has said is they hope we get a lot of money for the museum. A couple of people said they couldn't imagine who would pay so much for a book, and one or two have said the subject matter sounded interesting. But no one has seemed upset or negative about it at all."

"Where is the book now?" he asked.

"It's at the museum."

The old-house-turned-museum wasn't the most secure property, from what Dwight could remember about it. "Do you have a security system there—alarms, cameras?"

She shook her head. "We've never had the budget for that kind of thing. And we've never needed it. We just have regular door locks with dead bolts, and we keep the most valuable items in our collection in locked cases. But we don't really have much that most people would find valuable. I mean, antiques and historical artifacts aren't the kind of thing a person could easily sell for quick cash."

"But this book is different," Dwight said. "It's worth a lot of money. I think you had better put it somewhere else for now. Somewhere more secure."

"I was thinking of moving it to a safe at my house."

"That sounds like a good idea." He stood. "Let's go do that now."

"Oh." She rose, clearly flustered. "You don't have to do that. I can—"

"I'd like to see this book, anyway." He gestured to the door, and she moved toward it.

"I'll meet you at the museum," he said when they reached the parking lot.

She nodded and fished her car keys out of her purse, then looked at him again, fear in her hazel eyes, though he could tell she was trying hard to hide it. "Do you think I'm really in danger?" she asked.

He put a hand on her arm, a brief gesture of reassurance. "Maybe not. But there's no harm in being extra careful."

She nodded, then moved to her car. He waited until she was in the driver's seat before he got into his SUV, suppressing the urge to call her back, to insist that she ride with him and not move out of his sight until he had tracked down the person who threatened her. He slid behind the wheel and blew out his breath. This was going to be a tough one—not because they had so little to go on to track down the person who had made the threat, but because he was going to have to work hard to keep his emotions out of the case.

He started the vehicle and pulled out onto the street behind Brenda's Subaru. He could do this. He could investigate the case and protect Brenda Stenson without her finding out he'd been hopelessly in love with her since they were both seventeen.

Chapter Two

Brenda had come so close to asking Dwight if he would drive her to the history museum in the sheriff's department SUV. She felt too vulnerable in her own car, aware that the person who wrote that awful note might be watching her, maybe even waiting to make good on his threat. She shuddered and pushed the thought away. She was overreacting. Dwight hadn't seemed that upset about the note. And really, who could take it seriously, with the yellow paper and cartoon flowers?

She had always admired Dwight's steadiness. When they had been in high school, he was one of the stars on the basketball team. As a cheerleader, she had attended every game and watched him lope up and down the gym on his long legs. She had watched all the players, of course, but especially him. He had thick chestnut hair and eyes the color of the Colorado sky in a ruggedly handsome face. There was something so steady about him, even then. Like many of her classmates, he was the son of a local rancher. He wore jeans and boots and Western shirts and walked with the swaggering gait that came from spending so much time on horseback.

A town girl, she didn't have much in common with him, and was too shy to do more than smile at him in the hall. He always returned the greeting, but that was as far as it went. He'd never asked her out, and after graduation, they'd both left for college. She had returned to town five years later as a newlywed, her husband, Andy, anxious to set up his practice in the small town he had fallen in love with on visits to meet her family. Dwight returned a year later, fresh from military service in Afghanistan. Brenda would have predicted he would go to work on the family ranch—the choice of law enforcement surprised her. But the job suited him— the steadiness and thoughtfulness she had glimpsed as a teen made him a good cop. One she was depending on to help her through this latest crisis.

When they entered the history museum, Lacy was talking to a wiry young man with buzzed hair and tattoos covering both forearms. "Brenda!" Lacy greeted them, then her eyebrows rose as Dwight stepped in behind her. "And Dwight. Hello." She turned to the young man. "Brenda is the person you need to talk to."

"Hello, Parker," Dwight said.

"Deputy." The young man nodded, his expression guarded.

"This is Parker Riddell," Lacy said. "Paige Riddell's brother. Parker, this is Brenda Stenson, the museum's director."

Paige ran the local bed-and-breakfast and headed up the environmental group that had stopped Henry Hake's development. Brenda couldn't recall her ever mentioning a brother. "It's nice to meet you," she said, offering her hand. "How can I help you?"

Parker hesitated, then took it. "I was wanting to volunteer here," he said.

"Are you interested in history?" Brenda asked.

"Yeah. And my sister said you could use some help, so…" He shrugged.

"Well, yes. I can always use help. But now isn't really a good time. Could you come back tomorrow?"

"I guess so." Parker cut his eyes to Dwight. "Is something wrong?"

"No. Deputy Prentice is here to discuss security for our auction." Brenda forced a smile. That sounded like a reasonable explanation for Dwight's presence, didn't it? And not that far from the truth.

"Okay, I guess I'll come back tomorrow." Keeping his gaze on Dwight, he sidled past and left, the doorbells clanging behind him.

"What was that about?" Lacy asked Dwight. "He was looking at you like you were a snake he was afraid would strike—or a bug he wanted to stomp on."

"Let's just say Parker has a rocky history with law enforcement. I'd be careful about taking him on as a volunteer."

He sounded so serious. "Do you think he's dangerous?" Brenda asked.

Dwight shifted his weight. "I just think he's someone who should be watched closely."

"I'll keep that in mind." Brenda turned to Lacy. "Thanks for looking after things here while I was gone. You can go home now. I'm going to go over some things with Dwight, then close up for lunch."

Lacy gave her a speculative look, but said nothing. "We'll talk later," she said, then collected her purse and left.

Brenda crossed her arms and faced Dwight. "What's the story on Parker Riddell?" she asked.

He rubbed the back of his neck. "I probably shouldn't tell you."

"This is a very small town—you know I'll find out eventually. If anyone links the information back to you,

you can tell them I was doing a background check prior to taking him on as a volunteer. That's not unreasonable."

"All right." He leaned back against the counter facing her. "He got into trouble with drugs, got popped for some petty theft, then a burglary charge. He did a little jail time, then went into rehab and had a chance at a deferred sentence."

"What does that mean?" she asked.

"It means if he keeps his nose clean, his record will be expunged. I take it he came to live with Paige after he got out of rehab to get away from old friends and, hopefully, bad habits. And I hope he does that. That doesn't mean I think it's the best idea in the world for you to spend time alone with him, or leave him alone with anything around here that's valuable."

"Do you think he might have sent the note?"

He frowned. "It doesn't fit any pattern of behavior he's shown before—at least that I know of. But I can look into it. I *will* look into it."

"I can't think of anyone who would do something like that," she said. "I mean, anonymous notes—it's so, well, sleazy. And over a stupid book."

"Show me the book."

"It's back here." She led the way into the workroom, to a file drawer in the back corner. She had placed *The Secret History of Rayford County, Colorado* inside an acid-free cardboard box. She opened the box and handed the book to Dwight.

He read the title on the front, then opened it and flipped through it, stopped and read a few lines. "It's a little dry," he said.

"Some parts are better than others," she said. "Collectors are mainly interested because of the subject matter and its rarity."

He returned the book to her. "Maybe someone is upset that this top-secret information has been leaked," he said.

"The whole thing happened seventy years ago," she said. "As far as I can determine, most of the details about the project are declassified, and all the people who took part are long dead."

"A relative who's especially touchy about the family name?" Dwight speculated. "Someone related to the author?" He examined the spine of the book. "S. Smith."

"The research I did indicated the name is probably a pseudonym," Brenda said. "In any case, since the author was supposedly part of the project, he would most likely be dead by now. Since his real identity has never been made public, what is there for the family to be upset about?"

"Someone else, then," Dwight said.

"Are there any new suspicious people hanging around town?" she asked.

He shook his head. "No one who stands out."

"Except Parker," she said.

"I'll check into his background a little more, see if I can find a connection," he said. He turned to survey the long table that took up much of the room. "Are these the items for the auction?"

"Everything I've collected so far," she said. "I still have a few more things people have promised."

He picked up a set of hand-braided reins and a silver-trimmed bridle. "You've got a lot of nice things. Should net you a good bit of money."

"I hope it's enough," she said. "I don't suppose you have any hope of finding Henry Hake alive and well and enjoying an island vacation, have you? He was our biggest donor."

Dwight shook his head. "I don't expect any of us will be seeing Henry Hake again," he said. "At least not alive."

"I figured as much. So all we need is another wealthy benefactor. I'm hoping that rare book will attract someone like that—someone with money to spare, who might enjoy getting credit for pulling us out of the red."

"What will happen if that benefactor doesn't materialize?" he asked.

She straightened her shoulders and put on her brave face—one she had had plenty of practice assuming since Andy's death. "I'll have to find another job. And this town will lose one of its real assets."

"I hope we won't lose you, too," he said.

The intensity of his gaze unsettled her. She looked away. "Sometimes I think leaving and starting over would be a good idea," she said. "But I love Eagle Mountain. This is my home, and I'm not too anxious to find another one."

"Then I hope you never have to."

The silence stretched between them. She could feel his eyes still on her. Time to change the subject. "Lacy was telling me Eddie Carstairs has been mouthing off to people about his getting fired, trying to stir up trouble."

"Eddie's sore about losing his job, but Travis did the right thing, firing him. Any other department would have done the same. The fact that he's making such a fuss about something that was his own fault shows he doesn't have the right temperament for the job. You can't be hotheaded and impulsive and last long in law enforcement."

Dwight had never been hotheaded or impulsive. He

was the epitome of the cool, deliberate, hardworking cowboy. She replaced the book in the box and fit the lid on it. "I don't want to keep you any longer. I'll close a little early for lunch and you can follow me to the house—though that probably isn't necessary."

"No harm in taking precautions." He followed her into the front room, where she collected her purse, turned down the lights, then turned the sign on the front door to Closed. "After we secure the book in your safe, maybe I could take you to lunch," he said.

The invitation surprised her so much she almost dropped the book. Was Dwight asking her out on a *date*? *You're not in high school anymore*, she reminded herself. He was probably just being friendly. Her first instinct was to turn him down. She had too much to do. She wasn't ready to go out with another man.

Andy's been dead three and a half years. When are you going to be ready?

"Thanks," she said. "That would be nice."

He walked her to her car, and when his arm brushed hers briefly as he reached out to open the door for her, a tremor went through her. Why was she acting like this? She wasn't a schoolgirl anymore, swooning over a crush—but that's what being with Dwight made her feel like all of a sudden.

She murmured, "Thanks," as she slid past him into the driver's seat and drove, sedately, toward her home. She laughed at herself, being so careful to keep under the speed limit. Did she really think Dwight would suddenly switch on his lights and siren and give her a ticket?

The house she and Andy had purchased when they moved back to Eagle Mountain had undergone extensive remodeling, expanding from a tiny clapboard-sided bungalow to a larger cottage trimmed in native rock and including a detached two-car garage with an apartment above. Only recently, Brenda had learned that those renovations had been financed not by Andy's law practice, as she had thought, but with money he received from people he blackmailed, including her former boss, Jan Selkirk. The knowledge had made her feel so ashamed, but people had been surprisingly kind. No one had suggested—at least to her face—that she had been guilty of anything except being naive about her husband's activities.

She pulled into the driveway that ran between the house and the garage and Dwight parked the sheriff's department SUV behind her. That would no doubt raise some eyebrows among any neighbors who might be watching. Then again, considering all that had happened in the past three and a half years, from Andy's murder to the revelations about his blackmail and Jan's attempts to steal back evidence of her involvement in the blackmail, everyone in town was probably used to seeing the cops at Brenda's place.

Dwight met her on the walkway that led from the drive to the front steps. "You haven't had any trouble around the house, have you?" he asked. "No mysterious phone calls or cars you don't recognize driving by? Any door-to-door salesmen who might have been casing the place?"

"If door-to-door salesmen still exist, they aren't in Eagle Mountain." She led the way up the walk, keys in hand.

He smiled at her, and her heart skipped a beat again. He really did have the nicest smile, and those blue, blue eyes—

The eyes hardened, and the smile vanished. She realized he wasn't focused on her anymore, but on her front door. She gasped when she saw the envelope taped there—a bright yellow envelope. Like a birthday card, but she was pretty sure it wasn't. Her name, printed in familiar bold black lettering, was written on the front.

Dwight put his hand on her shoulder. "Wait before you touch it. I want to get some photographs."

He took several pictures of the note taped to the door, from several different angles, then moved back to examine the steps and the porch floor for any impressions. He put away his phone and pulled on a pair of thin gloves, then carefully removed the note from the door, handling it by the edges and with all the delicacy one would use with a bomb.

Meanwhile, Brenda hugged her arms across her stomach and did her best not to be sick in the lilac bushes. Dwight laid the envelope on the small table beside the porch glider and teased open the flap.

The note inside was very like the first—yellow paper, dancing cartoon flowers. He coaxed out the sheet and unfolded it. Brenda covered her mouth with her hand. Taped to the top of the paper was a photograph—a crime scene photo taken of Andy at his desk, stabbed in the chest, head lolling forward. Brenda squeezed her eyes shut, but not before she had seen the words written below the photograph. THIS COULD BE YOU.

Chapter Three

Dwight could feel Brenda trembling and rushed to put his arm around her and guide her over to a cushioned lounge chair on the other side of the porch, away from the sick photo. He sat beside her, his arm around her, as she continued to shudder. "Take a deep breath," he said. "You're safe."

She nodded, and gradually the trembling subsided. Her eyes met his, wet with unshed tears. "Why?" she whispered.

"I don't know. I'm going to look at the note again. Will you be okay if I do that?"

"Yes." She straightened. "I'm fine now. It was just such a shock." She was still pale, but determination straightened her shoulders, and he didn't think she would faint or go into hysterics if he left her side.

He stood and returned to the note on the table. The image pasted onto the paper wasn't a photograph, but a photocopy of a photograph. Dwight couldn't be sure, but this didn't look like something that would have run in the newspaper. It looked like a crime scene photo, the kind that would have been taken before Andy Stenson's body was removed from his office and then become part of the case file.

"Have you ever seen this photograph before?" he asked Brenda.

"I think so," she said. "At Lacy's trial."

Dwight nodded. Lacy Milligan had been wrongfully convicted of murdering her boss. At the trial, the prosecution would have shown crime scene photos as evidence of the violence of the attack.

"Who would have had access to those photos?" Brenda asked. "Law enforcement, the lawyers—"

"Anyone who worked at the law offices or the courtroom," Dwight said. "Maybe even the press. This isn't one of the actual photos—it's a photocopy. The person who wrote the note included it to frighten you."

"Well, they succeeded." She stood and began pacing back and forth, keeping to the side of the porch away from the note and its chilling contents. "Dwight, what are we going to do?"

He liked that "we." She was counting on him to work with her—to help her. "You could burn the book," he said.

She stopped pacing and stared at him. "And give in to this creep's demands? What's to stop him from demanding something else? Maybe next time he'll suggest I burn down my house, or paint the museum pink. Maybe he gets off on making people do his bidding." Her voice rose, and her words grew more agitated—but it was better than seeing her so pale and defeated-looking.

"I'm not saying you should burn the book, only that it was one option."

"I'm not going to burn the book. We need to find out who this person is and stop him—or her."

She was interrupted by a red car pulling to the curb in front of the house. Lacy got out and hurried up the walk, smiling widely. "Hey, Dwight," she said. "Still discussing security issues?" She laughed, then winked at Brenda.

Brenda's cheeks flushed a pretty pink. "You're certainly in a good mood," she said.

"I've been out at the ranch. The wedding planner needed me to take some measurements. It's such a gorgeous place for a wedding, and Travis's mom is as excited about it as I am." She sat in a chair near Brenda. "So what are you two really up to?" she asked.

"I've received a couple of disturbing letters," Brenda said. She glanced at Dwight. "Threatening ones."

"Oh no!" Lacy's smile vanished and her face paled. "I thought you were a little distracted this morning, but I assumed it was over the auction. I'm sorry for being so silly."

"It's all right," Brenda said. "The first note was taped to the door of the museum when I arrived this morning. We just found a second one here at the house."

"Threats?" Lacy shook her head. "Who would want to threaten you? And why?"

"The first note told me I should burn the rare book that's up for auction—or else," Brenda said.

"What did the second note say?" Lacy asked.

Brenda opened her mouth to speak, then pressed her lips together and shook her head. Lacy looked to Dwight. "You tell her," Brenda said.

"The second note contained a crime scene photo from Andy's murder, and said 'this could be you.'"

Lacy gasped, then leaned over and took Brenda's hand. "That's horrible. Who would do such a thing?"

"We're going to find that out," Dwight said.

"What are you going to do until then?" Lacy asked.

"Until this is resolved, I think you should move back in with your parents—or with Travis," Brenda said.

"You can't stay here by yourself," Lacy said.

Dwight was about to agree with her, but Brenda cut him off. "I'm not going to let this creep run me out of my own home," she declared. "I've been manipulated enough in my life—I'm not going to let it happen again."

Was she saying her husband had manipulated her? Dwight wondered. Certainly, Andy Stenson had kept her in the dark about his blackmailing activities and the real source of his income. "We'll put extra patrols on the house," Dwight said. If he had to, he'd park his own car on the curb and stay up all night watching over her.

"Thank you," Brenda said. "In the meantime, I'm going to contact the paper and let them know what's going on. I want whoever is doing this to see that I'm not afraid of him. Besides, if everybody knows what's going on, I'll feel safer. People complain about how nosy everyone is in small towns, but in a situation like this, that could work to my advantage."

"That's a good idea." He turned to look at the letter and envelope still lying on the table. "Let me take care of these, and I'm going to call in some crime scene folks to go over the scene and see if we missed anything. Come with me and we'll call the paper from there."

"All right," she said.

"I'll come with you, too," Lacy said. "Travis should be back from his class soon."

"Give me a minute," Dwight said. He walked out to his SUV to retrieve an evidence pouch. The women huddled on the porch together, talking softly. Brenda was calm now, but he could imagine how upsetting seeing that photograph had been for her. The person who had left that note wasn't only interested in persuading her to destroy the book. He could have done that with another death threat, or even a physical attack.

No, the person who had left that photo wanted to inflict psychological harm. The man—or woman—had a personal dislike for Brenda, or for women in general, or for something she represented. Or at least, that was Dwight's take, based on the psychology courses he'd taken as an undergraduate. He'd have to question her carefully to determine if there was anything in her background to inspire that kind of hate. With that photograph, the note-writer had gone from a possible annoying-but-harmless prankster to someone who could be a serious danger.

BRENDA RODE WITH Lacy to the sheriff's department, grateful for the distraction that talk about the upcoming wedding provided—anything to block out the horrible image of her dead husband on that note. The photo, more than the threat beneath it, had hit her like a hard punch to the stomach, the sickening pain of it still lingering. Dwight had been shocked, too, though, typical for him, he hadn't shown a lot of emotion. Somehow, his steadiness had helped her step back from the horror and try to think rationally.

Whoever had sent that note wanted to shock her—to terrify her and maybe, to make her reluctant to dig into the reason behind the threat. The letter writer mistook her for a weak woman who would do anything to make the pain go away.

She had been that person once. When Andy dismissed her questions about all the money he was spending on remodeling their home with an admonishment that she didn't need to worry about any of that, she had backed off and accepted his judgment. The idea made her cringe now, but she had been so young, and unwilling to do anything that might mar her happiness.

She wouldn't make that mistake again. Turning away from things that hurt or frightened her only made them more difficult to deal with later. Now she faced her problems head-on, and in doing so had discovered a strength she hadn't known she possessed.

Paige Riddell was waiting in the lobby of the sheriff's department, and confronted Dwight as soon as he walked in. "How dare you treat my brother the way you did this morning," she said before the door had even shut behind Dwight and the two women. "He was trying to help—to do something good—and you shut him down as if he were trying to rob the place. You wouldn't even give him a chance." Her voice shook on the last words—Paige, who to Brenda was the epitome of a tough woman. Paige, who had taken on Henry Hake's money and position and defeated his plans to build a luxury resort in an environmentally fragile location. Now she seemed on the verge of tears.

"Why don't we go into my office and talk about this?" Dwight gestured down the hallway.

"You didn't have any problem with confronting Parker in public, so we'll do this in public." Paige glanced at Lacy and Brenda. "I'm sure Dwight has already informed you that my brother has been arrested before. He's not trying to hide that. He made a mistake and he paid for it. He went through rehab and he's clean now, and trying to start over—if people like the deputy here will let him."

Dwight frowned, hands on his hips. "If Parker has a

problem with something I said, he should come to me and we'll talk about it," he said.

"Parker doesn't want to talk to you. He didn't want to talk to me, but I saw how down he was when he came back from the history museum this morning, so I pried the story out of him. He said you looked at him like you suspected him of planning to blow up the building or something."

Dwight's face reddened. Brenda sympathized with him—but she also related to Paige's desire to protect her brother. Dwight clearly hadn't liked the young man, and his dislike had shown in the encounter this morning. "Paige, does Parker know you're here?" she asked.

Paige turned to her. "No. And when he finds out, he'll be furious. But he's been furious with me before. He'll get over it."

"Why was Parker at the history museum this morning?" Dwight asked.

"Because he's interested in history. It's one of the things he's studying in college. I told him the museum was looking for volunteers and he should apply."

"That's kind of unusual, isn't it?" Dwight said. "A guy his age being so interested in the past."

"Tell that to all the history majors at his school," Paige said. "Parker is a very bright young man. He has a lot of interests, and history is one of them."

"Any particular type of history?" Dwight asked. "Is he, for instance, interested in the history of World War II? Or local history?"

Brenda held her breath, realizing where Dwight was headed with this line of questioning.

Paige shook her head. "I don't know that it's any particular kind of history. American history, certainly. Colorado and local history, probably. Why do you ask?"

"Does your brother have any history of violence? Of making threats?"

"What? No! What are you talking about?"

"I can check his record," Dwight said.

"Check it. You won't find anything." She turned to Brenda and Lacy. "Parker was convicted for possession of methamphetamine and for stealing to support his drug habit. He was never violent, and he's been clean for three months now. He's going to stay clean. He moved here to get away from all his old influences. He's enrolled in college and he has a part-time job at Peggy's Pizza."

Brenda wet her lips, her mouth dry. "Do you have any yellow stationery at your place?" she asked. "With dancing cartoon flowers across the bottom?"

Paige's brow knit. She looked at Dwight again. "What is going on? If you're accusing Parker of something, tell me."

"Brenda received a threatening note at the museum this morning," Dwight said. "It was written on distinctive stationery." Brenda noticed that he didn't mention the note at her home.

"The only stationery I use is made of recycled paper," Paige said. "It's plain and cream-colored. And Parker didn't write that note. He wouldn't threaten anyone—much less Brenda. He doesn't even know her."

"I'm not accusing him of anything," Dwight said.

"Right." Paige didn't roll her eyes, but she looked as if she wanted to. "I bet you're asking everyone in town about their stationery." She turned to Brenda again. "I know Parker would hate me if he knew I was asking this, but please give him a chance at the museum. He needs constructive things to fill his spare time, and he's a hard worker. And while he's not the biggest guy on the block, he knows how to take care of himself. He would be good protection in case the real person who's making these threats comes around."

Paige's concern for her brother touched Brenda. And she had always had a soft spot for people who needed a second chance. "Tell him to come around tomorrow and fill out a volunteer application. Most of my volunteers are older women—it will be nice to have a young man with a strong back."

"Thank you. You won't regret it, I promise." She squeezed Brenda's hand, then, with a last scornful look at Dwight, left.

Dwight crossed his arms over his chest. "I don't think it's a good idea for you to take on a new volunteer," he said. "Not until we know who's threatening you."

"I know you don't, but I trust Paige's judgment," Brenda said. "She's not a pushover."

"People often have blind spots for the people they love," he said.

She couldn't help but flinch at his words. She had certainly had a blind spot when it came to Andy. Her dismay must have showed, because Dwight hurried to apologize. "Brenda, I didn't mean…"

"I know what you meant," she said. "And I'll be careful, I promise."

The door opened again and Travis strolled in. The sheriff looked as polished and pressed—and handsome—as ever. If he was surprised to see them all standing in the reception area, he didn't show it on his face. "Hey, Brenda," he said. "What happened to the banner advertising the auction that was hung over Main Street at the entrance to town?"

"What do you mean?" she asked. "It was fine the last time I checked—just yesterday."

"It's not fine now," he said. "It's gone."

Chapter Four

"What do you mean, the banner is gone?" Lacy was the first to speak. "Did someone steal it?"

"I don't know," Travis said. "It was there when I left for my training this morning and it isn't there now."

"Maybe the wind blew it away," Lacy said.

"We haven't had any high winds," Brenda said. "And I watched the city crew hang that banner—it was tied down tight to the utility poles on either side of the street. It would take a hurricane to blow it away."

"Do you think this has anything to do with those nasty letters you received?" Lacy asked.

"What letters?" Travis was all business now.

"Let's take this into your office," Dwight said. "I'll fill you in."

They all filed down the hall to Travis's office. He hung his Stetson on the hat rack by the door and settled behind his desk. Lacy and Brenda took the two visitors' chairs in front of the desk, while Dwight leaned against the wall beside the door. "Tell me," Travis said.

So Brenda—with Dwight providing details—told the sheriff about the two threatening letters she had received: the cheerful yellow stationery, the black marker, the photocopy of the horrible crime scene photo and all about the book the letter writer wanted her to destroy.

Travis listened, then leaned back, his chair creaking, as he considered the situation. "What's your take on this, Dwight?" he asked.

Dwight straightened. "I think this guy has a real mean streak, but he isn't too smart."

Brenda turned in her chair to look at him. "Why do you think he isn't smart?" she asked.

"Because if he really wanted to get rid of the book, why not try to steal it? Get rid of it himself?"

"Maybe he knew I'd keep something so valuable locked up," Brenda said.

"Maybe. I still would have expected him to try to get to it before resorting to these threats. There's a lot of risk in writing a note like that—the risk of being seen delivering the notes or of someone recognizing that stationery."

"He—or she—I'm not going to rule out a woman," Travis said, "must think there's a good chance he won't be noticed. Maybe he thinks people wouldn't be surprised to see him around the museum or your house, or he's good at making himself inconspicuous."

"So someone who looks harmless," Lacy said. "That could be almost anyone."

"Where is this book now?" Travis asked.

"It's in my purse." Brenda opened her handbag and took out the small cloth-bound volume and handed it across the desk. "After we found that second letter, we never made it inside to put it in my safe."

Travis opened the book and flipped through it. "I think you're right that this guy isn't very smart," he said. "By demanding you destroy this book, he's focused all our attention on it."

"Or maybe he's really smart and he's trying to divert our attention from what's really important," Dwight said.

Travis closed the book. "I think it would be a good idea to keep this here at the sheriff's department until the auction," he said.

"Fine," Brenda said. "I'll sleep better knowing it isn't in my house."

"You can't go back to your house," Dwight said.

He was giving an order, not making a request, and that didn't sit well with her. "I won't let some nut run me out of my home," she said.

"Someone who would threaten you with that crime scene photo might be serious about hurting you," Travis said. "We can run extra patrols, but we can't protect you twenty-four hours a day. We don't have the manpower. You need to go somewhere that will make it harder for this guy to get to you."

"And where is that?" she asked. "A hotel isn't going to be any safer than my home."

"We can try to find a safe house," Travis said.

"Sheriff, I have a job that I need to do. I can't just leave town and hide out—if I do, then this jerk wins. I won't let that happen."

The two men exchanged a look that Brenda read as *Why do women have to be so difficult?* She turned to face Dwight. "If someone were threatening you like this, would you run away?" she demanded.

He shook his head. "No." He rubbed the back of his neck. "But what about a compromise—somewhere near town where you would be safer, but still be able to work at the museum?"

"Do you know of a place?" Lacy asked.

"I do."

"Not with you," Brenda said. "No offense, but if you want to really start wild rumors, just let people find out I've moved in with you."

Something flashed in his eyes—was he amused? But he quickly masked the expression. "I don't want to start any rumors," he said. "And I'm not talking about moving in with me. But my parents have plenty of room at the ranch, and I know they'd love to have you stay with them. There are fences and a locked gate, plus plenty of people around day and night. It would be a lot more difficult for anyone to get to you there." He let a hint of a smile tug at the corners of his mouth. "And my cabin isn't that far from the main house, so I can keep an eye on you, too."

Brenda recalled Bud and Sharon Prentice as a genial couple who had cheered on their son at every basketball game and helped out with fund-raisers and other school functions. They were the kind of people who worked hard in the background and didn't demand the spotlight.

Lacy leaned over and squeezed Brenda's arm. "You don't really want to go back to your house alone, do you?" she asked.

"Where are you going to be?" Brenda asked.

Lacy flushed. "I think I'll be staying with Travis until this is settled. I'm no hero."

Brenda didn't want to be a hero, either—especially a foolhardy one. "All right," she said. "I'll take you up on your offer. But only for a few days."

"Let's hope that's all it takes to find this guy," Dwight said.

DWIGHT RODE WITH Brenda to his family's ranch west of town. He wasn't going to risk her wrath by coming right out and saying he didn't want her alone on the road, so he made an excuse about having to get his personal pickup truck and bring it into town for an oil change. He wasn't sure if she bought the explanation, but she didn't object when he left his SUV parked in front of her house and slid into the passenger seat of her Subaru. She had packed up her laptop and a small suitcase of clothes—enough for a few days at the ranch. "Do you remember visiting the ranch when we were in high school?" he asked as she headed out of town and into the more open country at the foot of the mountains.

"I remember," she said. "Your parents threw a party for the senior class. I remember being in awe of the place—it seemed so big compared to my parents' little house in town."

"As ranches go, it's not that big," Dwight said. "To me, it's just home." The ranch had been the place for him and his brothers and sister to ride horses, swim in the pond, fish in the creek and work hard alongside their parents. For a kid who liked the outdoors and didn't enjoy sitting still for long, it was the perfect place to grow up. He had acres of territory to roam, and there was always something to do or see.

Brenda turned onto the gravel road that wound past his parents' property, the fields full of freshly mown hay drying in the sun. Other pastures were dotted with fat round bales, wrapped in plastic to protect them from the elements and looking like giant marshmallows scattered across the landscape. She turned in at the open gate, a wrought iron arch overhead identifying this as the Boot Heel Ranch.

"The house looks the same as I remember it," Brenda said. "I love that porch." The porch stretched all across the front of the two-story log home, honeysuckle vines twining up the posts, pots of red geraniums flanking the steps. Dwight's parents, Sharon and Bud, were waiting at the top of the steps to greet them. Smiling, his mother held out both hands to Brenda. "Dwight didn't give any details, just said you needed to stay with us a few days while he investigates someone who's been harassing you," Sharon said. "I'm sorry you're having to go through that, dear."

"Thank you for taking me in," Brenda said.

"I'm sure your mother would have done the same for Dwight, if the shoe had been on the other foot," Sharon said. "I remember her as the kind of woman who would go out of her way to help everyone."

Dwight remembered now that Brenda's mother had died of cancer while Brenda was in college. Her father had moved away—to Florida or Arizona or someplace like that.

"Thank you," Brenda said again. "Your place is so beautiful."

"I give Sharon all the credit for the house." Bud stepped forward and offered a hand. "I see to the cows and horses—though she has her say with them, too. Frankly, we'd probably all be lost without her."

Sharon beamed at this praise, though Dwight knew she had heard it before—not that it wasn't true. His mother was the epitome of the iron fist in the velvet glove—gently guiding them all, but not afraid to give them a kick in the rear if they needed it.

"Let me show you to your room," Sharon said.

"I can do that, Mom," Dwight said. He had retrieved Brenda's laptop bag and suitcase from the car and now led the way into the house and up the stairs to the guest suite on the north side of the house. The door to the room was open, and he saw that someone—probably his mother—had put fresh flowers in a cut-glass vase on the bureau opposite the bed. The bright pink and yellow and white blossoms reflected in the mirror over the bureau, and echoed the colors in the quilt on the cherry sleigh bed that had belonged to Dwight's great-grandmother.

"This is beautiful." Brenda did a full turn in the middle of the room, taking it all in.

"You should be comfortable up here." He set both her bags on the rug by the bed. "And you'll have plenty of privacy. My parents added a master suite downstairs after us kids moved out."

"Where do you live?" she asked.

"My cabin is on another part of the property. You can see it from the window over here." He motioned, and she went to the window. He moved in behind her and pointed to the modest cedar cabin he had taken as his bachelor quarters. "Years ago, we had a ranch foreman who lived there, but he moved to a bigger place on another part of the ranch, so I claimed it."

"Nice."

The subtle floral fragrance of her perfume tickled his nostrils. It was all he could do not to lean down and inhale the scent of her—a gesture that would no doubt make her think he was a freak.

"I hope you didn't take what I said wrong—about not wanting to move in with you," she said. "It's just—"

He touched her arm. "I know." She had been the center of so much town gossip over the years, first with her husband's murder, then with the revelations that he had been blackmailing prominent citizens, that she shied away from that sort of attention.

"I had the biggest crush on you when I was a kid," he said. "That party here at the ranch—I wanted to ask you to dance so badly, but I could never work up the nerve."

She searched his face. "Why were you afraid to ask?"

"You were so beautiful, and popular—you were a cheerleader—the prom queen."

"You were popular, too."

"I had friends, but not like you. Everyone liked you."

She turned to look out the window once more. "All that seems so long ago," she said.

He moved away. "I'll let you get settled. We usually eat dinner around six."

He was almost to the door when she called his name. "Dwight?"

"Yes?"

"You should have asked me to dance. I would have said yes."

SEEING THE ADULT Dwight with his parents at dinner that evening gave Brenda a new perspective on the solemn, thoughtful sheriff's deputy she thought she knew. With Bud and Sharon, Dwight was affectionate and teasing, laughing at the story Bud told about a ten-year-old Dwight getting cornered in a pasture by an ornery cow, offering a thoughtful opinion when Sharon asked if they should call in a new vet to look at a horse who was lame, and discussing plans to repair irrigation dikes before spring. Clearly, he still played an important role on the ranch despite his law enforcement duties.

Watching the interaction, Brenda missed her own parents—especially her mother. Her mother's cancer had been diagnosed the summer before Brenda's senior year of college. Her parents had insisted she continue her education, so Brenda saw the toll the disease took only on brief visits home.

She had met Andrew Stenson during that awful time, and he had been her strongest supporter and biggest help, a shoulder for her to cry on and someone for her to lean on in the aftermath of her mother's death. No matter his flaws, she knew Andy had loved her, though she could see now that he had assumed the role of caretaker in their relationship. By the time they married, she had grown used to depending on him and letting him make the decisions.

But she wasn't that grieving girl anymore. And she didn't want a man to take care of her. She wanted someone to stand beside her—a partner, not just a protector.

After dinner, she insisted on helping Sharon with the dishes. "That's my job, you know," Dwight said as he stacked plates while Brenda collected silverware.

"The two of you can see to cleanup," Sharon said. "I think I'll sit out on the porch with your father. It's such a nice evening."

"You don't have to work for your room and board," Dwight said as he led the way into the kitchen. "I could get this myself."

"I want to help," she said. "Besides, we need to talk. I never got around to notifying the paper this afternoon."

"You can do it in the morning," he said. "The deadline for the weekly issue is the day after tomorrow." He squirted dish soap into the sink and began filling it with hot water.

Brenda slid the silverware into the soapy water. "I've been racking my brain and I can't come up with anyone who would want to harm me or the museum."

"Maybe one of Andy's blackmail victims has decided to take his anger out on you," Dwight said as he began to wash dishes. "We don't know who besides Jan he might have extorted money from, though the records we were able to obtain from his old bank accounts seemed to indicate multiple regular payments from several people."

"Why focus on the book?" She picked up a towel and

began to dry. "Part of me still thinks this is just a sick prank—that we're getting all worked up for nothing."

"I hope that's all it is." He rinsed a plate, then handed it to her. "I want to dig into Parker Riddell's background a little more and see if I can trace his movements yesterday."

"Why would he care about me or a rare book?" Brenda asked. "He's a kid who made some mistakes, but I can't see how or why he'd be involved in this."

"I have to check him out," Dwight said.

"I know. I just wish there were more I could do. I hate waiting around like this." She hated being helpless.

"I know." He handed her another plate. They did the dishes in companionable silence for the next few minutes. The domestic chore, and the easy rhythm they established, soothed her frayed nerves.

Dwight's phone rang. He dried his hands and looked at the screen. "I'd better take this," he said. He moved into the other room. She continued to dry, catching snippets of the conversation.

"When did this happen?"

"Who called it in?"

"What's the extent of the damage?"

"I see. Yes. I'll tell her."

She set the plate she had been drying on the counter and turned to face him as he walked back into the room. His face confirmed her fears. "What's happened?" she asked.

"There was a fire at your house. A neighbor called it in, but apparently there's a lot of damage."

She gripped the counter, trying to absorb the impact of his words. "How did it start?" she asked.

"They think it's probably arson." He put a hand on

her shoulder. "We aren't dealing with a prankster here. Someone is out to hurt you, and I'm not going to let that happen."

Chapter Five

The smell of wet ashes stuck in the back of Dwight's throat, thick and acrid, as he stood with Travis and Assistant Fire Chief Tom Reynolds in front of what was left of Brenda Stenson's house the morning after the fire. The garage and apartment where Lacy lived were unscathed, but the main house only had two walls left upright, the siding streaked with black and the interior collapsed into a pile of blackened rubble. If Dwight let himself think about what might have happened if Brenda had been inside when the fire was lit, he broke out in a cold sweat.

So he pushed the thoughts away and focused on the job. "We found evidence of an accelerant—gasoline— at the back corner of the house," Tom said. "Probably splashed it all over the siding, maybe piled some papers or dry leaves around it and added a match—boom— these old houses tend to catch quickly."

"Do you think the arsonist chose that corner because it was out of view of the street and neighboring houses, or because he wanted to make sure the rooms in that part of the house were destroyed?" Dwight asked.

Tom shrugged. "Maybe both. The location was definitely out of view—someone in the garage apartment might have seen it, but he might have known Lacy wasn't in last night."

"Maybe they knew Brenda wasn't here last night, either," Travis said. He scanned the street in front of the house. "If they were watching the place."

"We'll canvass the neighbors," Dwight said. "See if they have any friends or relatives who have recently moved in, or if they've noticed anyone hanging around or anything unusual."

"What's located in this corner of the house?" Travis asked.

"I think it's where Andy's home office used to be," Dwight said. "I remember picking up some paperwork from him not too long after I started with the department." Brenda hadn't been home, which had disappointed Dwight at the time, though he had told himself it was just as well.

"That's probably where the safe was where Brenda wanted to stash that book," Travis said.

"Probably," Dwight said. "But safes are usually fireproof."

"Maybe whoever did this didn't know about the safe," Travis said.

"Or destroying the book wasn't even the point," Dwight said. "Frightening Brenda into getting rid of the book on her own would be enough for him."

"I guess I'd be frightened right now if I were her," Tom said.

"Brenda's not like that," Dwight said. "I'm not saying she's not afraid—but she's not going to destroy the book, either. This guy's threats are only making her dig her heels in more."

Travis checked his watch. "Thanks for meeting with us, Tom," he said. "I have to get back to the office."

"Yeah, I'd better get going, too," Tom said. "I'll get a copy of the report to you and to Brenda for her insurance company."

Dwight followed Travis to the curb, where both their SUVs were parked. "I'm supposed to meet with the DEA guy the Feds sent to deal with that underground lab we found out at Henry Hake's place," Travis said. "He's had an investigative team at the site and has a report for me."

"Mind if I sit in?" Dwight asked. "I've got a couple of questions for him."

"Sure. I asked Gage to be there, too."

Travis's brother, Deputy Gage Walker, met them at the sheriff's department. Two years younger and two inches taller than his brother, Gage's easygoing, aww-shucks manner concealed a sharp intellect and commitment to his job. "Adelaide told me you two were out at the Stenson place," Gage said as the three filed into the station's meeting room. "I drove by there on my way in this morning. The fire really did a number on the place."

"Tom says they're sure it was arson," Travis said.

"How's Brenda taking it?" Gage asked.

"She's stoic," Dwight said.

"She's been through a lot the past few years," Gage said.

Brenda had been through too much, Dwight thought. And most of it pretty much by herself. She had friends in town, but no one she could really lean on. He got the sense that Andy's betrayal had made her reluctant to depend on anyone. He wanted to tell her she didn't have to be so strong around him—but he didn't want her to take the sentiment wrong.

The bell on the front door sounded, and all conversation stopped as they listened to Adelaide greet a male visitor. Their voices grew louder as they approached the meeting room. "This is Special Agent Rob Allerton." Adelaide didn't exactly bat her eyes at the dark-haired agent, who bore a passing resemblance to Jake Gyllenhaal, but she came close. Gage grinned, no doubt intending to give the office manager a hard time about it later.

Allerton himself seemed oblivious to her adoration—or maybe he was used to it. He shook hands with the sheriff and each of the deputies as they introduced themselves. "Is this your first visit to our part of the state?" Travis asked as they settled in chairs around the conference table.

"My first, but not my last." Allerton settled his big frame into the metal chair. "You people are living in paradise. It's gorgeous out here."

"Don't spread the word," Gage said. "We don't want to be overrun."

"What can you tell us about your investigation of the underground lab?" Travis asked.

"Not much, I'm afraid," Allerton said. "So far our analysts haven't found any illegal drug residue, or really any signs that the lab has been used recently."

"What about World War II?" Dwight asked. "Could it have been used then?"

Allerton frowned. "Want to tell me how you came up with that time period?"

"The local history museum is having an auction to raise money," Travis said.

"Right, I saw the banner the first day I arrived in town," Allerton said.

The banner that had mysteriously disappeared—Dwight had almost forgotten about it in the flurry of activity since then. "One of the items up for auction—

probably the most valuable item—is a book detailing a World War II project to produce chemical and biological weapons," Travis said. "Supposedly, the work was done in underground labs in this part of the country."

"No kidding?" Allerton shook his head. "Well, the equipment we found wasn't old enough for that. In fact, some of it appears to have been stolen from your local high school, judging by the high school name stenciled on the glass. There are some indications—marks on the floor and walls—that other equipment or furnishings might have been in that space previously. There's no way of knowing when they were moved. It would be an interesting historical artifact if that were true, but I can't see anything illegal in it."

"Somebody is upset about the book getting out there," Dwight said. "They made threats against the museum director, and last night someone burned down her house."

"That's bad, but I don't see any connection to this lab."

"Seen anybody up there at the site while you were there?" Travis asked. "Any signs of recent activity?"

Allerton shook his head. "Nothing. I see why this guy, Hake, wanted to build a development up there—it's beautiful. But the ghost town he ended up with is a little creepy."

"Where do we go from here?" Travis asked.

"Me, I go back home to Denver," Allerton said. "If you have questions or need more help, give me a call. I'd love an excuse to get back out here."

He stood, and the four of them walked to the front again. Adelaide smiled up at them. Had she freshened her lipstick? Dwight forced himself not to react. "That didn't take long," she said.

"Short and sweet," Allerton said. "Though I know how to take my time when the job calls for it."

Adelaide blushed pink, and Dwight bit the inside of his cheek to keep from laughing. Allerton said goodbye and let himself out. When he was gone, Adelaide sat back in her chair, both hands over her heart. "Oh my! Did you see those eyes? He looked just like that movie star—what's his name? You know the one."

"Jake Gyllenhaal," Dwight said.

"That's him!" Adelaide crowed.

Travis and Gage stared at him. "You knew that?" Gage asked.

Dwight shrugged. "I like movies."

"He didn't find any signs of illegal activity in that underground lab on Henry Hake's property," Travis said. "That's all I care about."

"Mind if I go up there and take another look around?" Dwight asked. "I might take Brenda with me—she's a historian, or at least, that's her degree. I want to know if she sees anything that might link to the World War II labs that book talks about."

"Fine by me," Travis said. "Technically, it's still a crime scene, since that's where Gage and Maya and Casey were held after they were kidnapped, though I'm going to have to release it back to the owners soon."

"Who are the owners?" Gage asked. "Isn't Henry Hake's name still on the deed?"

"Apparently, the week before he went missing, he signed the whole thing over to a concern called CNG Development. I found out last week when I tried one of the numbers I had for Hake Development. I got a recording telling me the company had been absorbed by CNG, but when I tried to track down the number for them, I couldn't find anything. Then I checked with the courts and sure enough, the change was registered the day before Hake disappeared."

"Coincidence?" Gage asked.

"Maybe," Travis said. "But I'd sure like to talk to someone with CNG about it. The number listed on the court documents is answered by another recording, and the address is a mailbox service in Ogden, Utah."

"Be careful when you head up there," Gage said. "Allerton was right—that place is downright creepy."

TAMMY PATTERSON, the reporter for the *Eagle Mountain Examiner*, agreed to meet Brenda at the museum the morning after the fire. Dwight had tried to persuade Brenda to stay at the ranch and not go in to work that day, but she had refused. Dwight had gone with her the night before to see the house, when the firefighters were still putting out the blaze, but she had wanted to see it herself this morning, alone. She had driven in early and made herself stop at the house and stare at the ruins. Her first thought was that this couldn't really be her place—not the miner's cottage that she and Andy had worked so hard to remodel, the dream home she had lovingly decorated and planned to live in forever.

She had allowed herself to cry for five minutes or so, then dried her eyes, repaired her makeup and driven to the museum. She couldn't do anything about the fire right now, and crying certainly wouldn't bring her house back. Better to go to work and focus on something she could control.

"You don't know how glad I am you called," Tammy said when she burst into the museum, blond hair flying and a little out of breath. This was how Brenda always thought of her—a young woman who was always rushing. "Barry had me reading press releases, looking for story angles. Nobody else ever reads them, so we had this huge pile of them—most of them are about as exciting as last night's town council meeting minutes—which, by the way, I have to turn into a news story, too. So truly, you have saved me."

I'm hoping you can save me, Brenda thought, but she didn't say it—it sounded entirely too dramatic, and might have the wrong effect on Tammy's already-excitable personality. "Glad I could help," Brenda said.

Tammy plopped onto the wrought iron barstool in front of the museum's glass counter and pulled out a small notebook and a handheld recorder. "So what's this story you have for me?" she asked. "You said it was related to the auction, but not exactly? Something juicy, you said. Boy, could I use juicy. I mean, it's great that we live in such a peaceful town and all, but sometimes I worry our readers are going to die of boredom."

Brenda could recall plenty of non-boring news that had run in the paper—surrounding her husband's murder, the wrongful conviction of Lacy Milligan and her subsequent release from prison, revelations about Andy's blackmailing, Henry Hake's disappearance, etc., etc. But she supposed for a reporter like Tammy, that was all old news.

"So, did you find something scandalous in a donation someone made for the auction?" Tammy asked. "Or has some big donor come forward to shower money on you?"

"I wish!" Brenda pulled her own stool closer to the counter. "This has to do with that book we have up for auction—the rare one about the top-secret government plot to make biological and chemical weapons during World War II?"

"I remember." Tammy flipped back a few pages in

her notebook. "*The Secret History of Rayford County, Colorado*. Do you have a bidding war? Or you found out the whole thing's a brilliant fake? Or has the government come after you to silence you and keep from letting the secret out of the bag?"

At Brenda's stunned look, Tammy flushed. "Sorry. I read a lot of dystopian fiction. Sometimes I get carried away."

"You're not too far off," Brenda said. "Apparently, someone is trying to silence me."

Tammy's mouth formed a large O. "Your house! I heard about that and I meant to say first thing how sorry I am. But I just thought it was old wiring or something."

"No, the fire department is sure the fire was deliberately set."

Tammy switched on the recorder, then started scribbling in her notebook. "How is that connected to the book?" she asked.

"I don't know. But before the fire, I received two different threatening notes—one here and one at my home, telling me if I didn't destroy that book, I could end up dead."

"Whoa! Do the cops know about this?"

"I told the sheriff, yes." Brenda leaned toward Tammy. "I called you because I want you to make clear in your story that I'm not going to let some coward who writes anonymous notes and sets fire to my house bully me into destroying a valuable historical artifact. If he's so keen to destroy the book, then he can bid on it like everyone else."

"Ooh, good quote." Tammy made note of it. "Where is the book now? Or I guess you probably don't want to say."

"I don't have it," Brenda said. "It's in the safe at the

sheriff's office, where no one can access it until the day of the auction." That wasn't exactly true, but she didn't picture Travis or his deputies taking the book out to show around to just anyone.

"You're right—this is definitely more exciting than the town council meeting," Tammy said. She paused and looked up from her notebook. "I hope that didn't sound wrong. I really am sorry about your house, and those threatening letters would have totally freaked me out."

"They were upsetting," Brenda admitted. "But now that I'm over the first shock, they just make me angry."

"Another good quote." Tammy made a note.

The doorbells clamored and both women turned toward the young man who entered. Parker Riddell froze in the doorway. "Um, you said I should come by about the volunteer work."

"Of course." Brenda pulled a clipboard with the volunteer application out from under the counter. "Tammy, do you know Parker? He's Paige Riddell's brother. Parker, this is Tammy Patterson. She's a reporter for the local paper."

"Uh, hi." Parker hesitated, then stuck out his hand.

"Nice to meet you." Tammy shook hands, then turned back to Brenda. "I think I have enough here. I'll call you if I think of anything else."

"Thanks, Tammy."

When she was gone, Parker stood staring at the floor for a long moment, not saying anything. "I need you to fill out this application," Brenda said, offering the clipboard.

"Yeah, sure." He took the clipboard and looked around, then slid onto the stool Tammy had vacated. Brenda began straightening the shelves behind the counter, surreptitiously checking out the young man who labored over the forms.

Parker Riddell had the tall, too-thin look of a boy still growing into a man's body. His skin was so fair blue veins stood out on the back of his hands, while blue-lined tattoos of a skull, a scorpion and a crow—among those she could see—adorned his arms. He hunched over the clipboard, clutching the pen and bearing down on it as he wrote. He looked up and caught Brenda staring, his eyes such a dark brown the iris almost merged with the pupils. "Is something wrong?" he asked.

"You're the first person under the age of forty who's ever wanted to volunteer here," she said. "Well, except for Lacy, but she's my best friend. I'm curious as to why you did it. I'd think it would be boring for you."

He laid down the pen, still holding her gaze. "This whole town is boring for me," he said. "But I like history. I like old stuff." He shrugged. "It's weird, I know."

"It's not weird," Brenda said. "I always liked history, too." She moved to stand across from him. "Are you studying history in school?"

"Just one class this year—at the community college. But I'd like to take more." He signed the bottom of the form and turned the clipboard back to her. "You already know about my record, but it wasn't for a violent crime or anything. And you don't have to let me handle money or anything. I can file stuff or build stuff or, you know, whatever you need."

"Thanks." She smiled. Nothing about this young man seemed threatening. Of course, she had been fooled by people before, but she believed in second chances. "Why don't we start by having you help me pack up everything in our special exhibit room upstairs? I want to install a new exhibit on the war years in Eagle Mountain."

They worked the rest of the afternoon dismantling the installation on historic drugstores—including a mock-up of an old-time soda fountain. It took some time to take down and pack away, and Brenda was grateful for a young, strong and mostly silent helper.

"That was great," she said when she had taped and sealed the last box to go into storage in the basement. "When would you like to come again?"

"I have a class tomorrow, but maybe Thursday?"

"That would be great. Whatever you can manage."

He nodded. "Okay, I have to go to work now." He pulled out his car keys. "I deliver pizza for Peggy's."

"I'll remember that next time I need to place an order."

"Do you need me to carry these boxes down for you before I go?" He indicated the half dozen cartons piled around the exhibit space.

"No, that's okay. I need to decide where I'll put them first. They can stay in here until tomorrow or the next day." She followed him out of the room and pulled a velvet-covered rope across the doorway, then hung a sign that said New Display Coming Soon.

Downstairs, the bells on the door jangled. Brenda checked her watch. Ten minutes until five. She'd have to point out to whoever was down there that the museum would close soon and they would need to return tomorrow. But she took a step back when she recognized the man waiting in the reception area.

"Hello, Brenda." Eddie Carstairs smiled, showing the gap between his two front teeth. His straight black hair angled across his forehead and curled around his ears so that even when he had just had a haircut, he looked in need of another one. He wore a long-sleeved khaki shirt and pants—much like the sheriff's department uniform, sans any insignia. A utility belt equipped with flashlight, nightstick and holstered pistol added to his attempt to appear official. Or at least, that's how Brenda interpreted the look. Eddie had made no secret of his desire to be back in law enforcement since his discharge from the sheriff's department.

"What can I do for you, Eddie?" she asked.

Parker looked from Eddie to Brenda. "Do you want me to hang around a little bit?" he asked.

"No, she doesn't need you to hang around, punk," Eddie said before Brenda could answer. He rolled his shoulders back. "I'm here to protect her from people like you."

"It's all right, Parker, you can go," Brenda said. "And thank you again."

"Sure. See ya." He pushed out the door.

As it shut behind him, Brenda turned on Eddie. "What are you doing here?" she asked. "The museum is closed."

"Your boss, the mayor, decided after that fire at your house, he didn't want to take any chances on the museum, so he hired me as a security guard."

"No one told me anything about this."

He shrugged. "It was just decided. You can call the mayor and ask him, if you like." He leaned one hip against the counter, as if prepared to wait all day.

"I certainly will." She grabbed the phone and retreated into the workroom, shutting the door behind her. She punched in the number for the mayor's office and waited impatiently as it rang and rang.

"Town of Eagle Mountain," a pleasant female voice answered.

"Gail, this is Brenda Stenson. I need to speak with Larry." Mayor Larry Rowe had been elected after Jan

Selkirk had declined to run for reelection, running a well-funded campaign with promises of new jobs and opportunities for the town. He wasn't the friendliest person Brenda had ever met, but until now he had left her alone to do her job.

"I think he's still in, Brenda, let me check."

A few moments later Larry answered. "Brenda! What can I do for you?"

"Eddie Carstairs is over here at the museum saying you hired him as a security guard. Is that right?"

"Well, yes, but he wasn't supposed to start until tonight—after I had a chance to talk with you."

"I'm glad you thought it was a good idea to consult me on this."

Larry's voice hardened. "The city has a valuable investment in that museum, and since you seem to have attracted some unsavory attention, we find ourselves in the position of having to protect that investment."

"So this is all my fault?"

"The arson at your home seems to indicate the threats are targeted at you."

"There's no reason to think the museum is in any danger."

"There's no reason to think it isn't. Eddie came to us and offered his services, and we thought it prudent to take him up on the offer."

She hung up the phone and returned to the front room. "All good?" Eddie asked.

"Fine." She gathered up her purse. "You can follow me outside while I lock up."

"You can leave it unlocked and I'll hang out in here overnight," he said.

"You can follow me outside while I lock up and you can 'hang out' in your car overnight."

She could tell he wanted to argue, but thought better of it. He followed her onto the front porch and watched, frowning, as she locked the dead bolt. "You should be grateful to me for protecting your livelihood," he said.

"I may not have control over much in my life right now," she said, "but at least I get to decide for myself what and who I'm grateful for. Right now, you're not on my list."

The astonished expression on his face was almost worth the aggravation with the mayor. She stalked to her car, started it and had turned down the street toward her home when she remembered she didn't have a home to go to.

Part of her was tempted to keep driving—where, she had no idea. But she had never been one to run away from problems. So she turned around and headed out of town, to the ranch. Time to find out from Dwight how much longer she was going to be stuck in this limbo.

Chapter Six

Parker Riddell cruised slowly down Eagle Mountain's Main Street, careful to stay under the ridiculous twenty-five-mile-per-hour speed limit. He wasn't going to give the local cops any reason to hassle him—not to mention if Paige got a call from the sheriff's office about him, she would go ballistic. He didn't need another lecture about how she was doing him a favor and risking her own reputation and all she had worked for to look after him—yadda, yadda, yadda.

Nobody else was around after nine o'clock at night—talk about rolling up the sidewalks. This place was like a ghost town. The only cars were parked around Moe's Pub—it and Peggy's Pizza were the only businesses still open. There wasn't a movie theater or even a lousy bowling alley for a hundred miles. Paige always talked as if the lack of anything to do would help him stay out of trouble. Going to the movies and playing video games at the arcade weren't what had gotten him into trouble and she knew it.

But yeah, he was grateful for her—sort of—getting him away from his old hangouts. He'd worked hard in rehab and he didn't want to go back. But man, it wouldn't hurt to have a *little* excitement every once in a while, would it? He turned the corner and drove past the history museum. The pizza in the carrier on the passenger seat beside him was headed to one of Parker's regulars—a guy who worked second shift at the RV factory up in Junction. He ordered a couple times a week. Parker glanced over at the museum as he passed and was surprised to see two cars parked next to the old building. He slowed and craned his neck for a closer look. In the moonlight, he could make out that guy Eddie's pale face behind the wheel of a beat-up Jeep Wagoneer.

Eddie was talking to another man who had positioned his black SUV cop-style, so the drivers were door-to-door. What were they doing at the museum this time of night?

He made his delivery. His customer, Jason, tipped him a five, which was really decent of him. Parker slipped the five in his wallet and the rest of the money in the pouch for Peggy, then headed back toward the museum. He parked up the block and made his way in the darkness, sneaking up behind the two vehicles. He wasn't doing anything wrong, he reminded himself. Brenda clearly hadn't liked this Eddie fellow, and Parker owed it to her to make sure the guy wasn't ripping her off.

Parker hadn't thought much of the cop wannabe, either. It hadn't taken too many brains to figure out that Eddie was the guy Paige had talked about as the reserve deputy who had been fired and was trying to make trouble. And he'd looked at Parker like he was a dog he wanted to kick.

Parker heard Eddie and the other guy a long time before he got close enough to see them in the dark. Obviously, they weren't worried about being overheard.

But Parker couldn't make out everything they said, just phrases that drifted on the night breeze.

"I'm taking care of it," Eddie said.

A mumble from the other guy.

"You don't have to worry. I know how to handle this. That's why you hired me, right?"

The other guy said something and they both laughed. Parker needed to get closer, to hear the whole conversation. He moved carefully, keeping to the shadows from a row of bushes alongside the alley where the cars were parked.

He didn't see the pile of debris set out for trash pickup until it was too late. He stumbled right into it, sending boxes and cans tumbling down, making a racket that could probably be heard a block away.

"Hey!" Eddie shouted.

The other man started up his SUV and sped away. Parker lurched to his feet and tried to run, but Eddie was on him, shoving him back onto the ground, the barrel of his pistol pressed to the side of Parker's face. "What are you doing sneaking around here?" Eddie demanded.

"I saw the cars. I wanted to make sure everything was all right."

Eddie shoved Parker's face further into the gravel. "Were you trying to steal something? I'll bet that's what you were doing. You 'volunteered' so you could check the place out and come back later and help yourself."

"No!" Parker squirmed, trying to free himself.

"Shut up." Eddie shoved the gun harder into Parker's cheek. "Maybe I ought to shoot you now and do everyone here a favor."

"DO YOU THINK you could get away from the museum one day and go with me up to the Eagle Mountain Resort site?" Dwight asked as he and Brenda did dishes that evening. Dinner had been grilled steaks on the back patio, and Brenda had done her best to smile and join in the conversation, but he could tell she was distracted. No surprise—she was probably worried about her house, and about whoever had targeted her.

"Why do you want me to go up there with you?" she asked.

"When we rescued Gage and Maya and her little niece, Casey, from those kidnappers last month, they were being held in an underground chamber on the resort land," he said.

"Yes, I heard about that." She added a dried plate to the stack on the kitchen table.

"What you probably didn't hear is that next to the chamber where they were held was another underground space that looked as if it had been used as a laboratory. The DEA has been investigating it, and hasn't found any sign of illegal activity. Now I'm wondering if it could be related to the labs the government established in the area to work on biological and chemical weapons—like that book talked about."

She stuck out her lower lip, considering. "The book does talk about some of the laboratories being underground—in old mines or caves. What does the DEA say?"

"They don't think any of the equipment is old enough, but they're not historians. I thought if you had a look, you might interpret things differently."

"But Wade and Brock kidnapped Maya and Gage and Casey," Brenda said. "And they're dead—right?" Finding out that the two men who ran the town's successful outdoor store were behind the kidnappings, and responsible for the murders of Maya's sister and brother-in-law, had shocked the town.

"They're dead, but we suspect they were working for someone else."

"The same person who's been threatening me?"

"Maybe," he said. "But maybe not."

She fell silent, mechanically drying plates and glasses and silverware, but Dwight couldn't shake the feeling that something was wrong. When the last dish had been put away, he turned to her. "Something's bothering you," he said. "Is it the threats or your house, or something else on top of all that?"

"I think that's enough to bother anyone," she said.

"It is. But if it would help to talk about it—if you need someone to listen to you, I'd like to be that person."

She straightened the dish towel she had just hung on the handle of the oven. "It will probably sound silly, especially considering everything else that has happened."

"I've never thought of you as particularly silly," he said. "What's happened?"

"The mayor—without consulting me—decided to hire Eddie Carstairs as a security guard for the museum. At a time when our budget is so squeezed we don't know if we'll be able to keep the doors open, he decided to spend money on this. And when I objected, he insinuated this was all my fault—that I had somehow put the museum property in danger."

Anguish colored the flood of words. He waited until she fell silent once more and said, "I can see why you're upset. The mayor isn't always the most diplomatic person." Larry Rowe had spent a lot of money and effort on his campaign for the office, but once elected, he had developed a reputation as a no-nonsense administrator who did whatever it took to get what he wanted.

"To make things worse, Eddie showed up while Parker Riddell was still at the museum and treated him horribly. It was embarrassing."

"So Parker volunteered today?" Dwight kept his voice neutral, though he didn't like the idea of Brenda working closely with the troubled young man. Parker might be sincere in his desire to make a fresh start, but did Brenda have to be part of that?

"Yes, and he was wonderful. He's a very serious, quiet young man, and he's sincerely interested in history." Her shoulders sagged. "And I think he's lonely. There aren't a lot of people his age in this town for him to hang out with."

"It's great that you want to give him a chance," Dwight said. "Just…be careful."

"I will, I—"

His phone rang, interrupting her. "Sorry," he muttered, and took the call.

"Eddie Carstairs just hauled in Parker Riddell," Gage said when Dwight answered. "Eddie says he caught him trying to break into the history museum."

Dwight glanced at Brenda. "I heard that," she said.

"I'll be right down," Dwight said, and ended the call. He started toward the door, Brenda close behind him.

"I'm coming with you," she said.

"Brenda—"

"I'm in charge of the museum. And I agreed to take Parker on as a volunteer. If he was breaking in, then I need to address this, too."

He saw no point in trying to argue with her. "All right," he said. "Let's go see what this is all about."

BRENDA HAD NEVER been in this part of the sheriff's department—in the level below ground, and the single holding cell outside the booking area. Dwight had escorted her through a maze of locked doors without comment, until they stood outside the small cell where Parker sat, staring out from behind the bars. The young man looked angry, but behind the anger, she detected fear. Fear he was doing his best to hide, but she could see it.

"Brenda, I swear I didn't do the things he says," Parker said.

"Shut up, punk." Eddie, who had been talking with Gage at the far end of the booking area, turned to face them, frowning when he saw Brenda. "What are you doing here?" he demanded.

"I'm in charge of the museum," Brenda said.

"I'm going to check on a few things," Gage said to Dwight. "I'll leave you to look after things here."

Dwight nodded, then addressed Eddie. "What happened?"

"I caught him sneaking around in the alley, trying to pry open one of the windows," Eddie said.

"That's a lie!" Parker said.

"Quiet," Dwight ordered. "You'll have your turn in a minute."

"I did my job," Eddie said. "I cuffed him and brought him in."

"Why didn't you call nine-one-one?" Dwight asked.

"I didn't need backup to handle one punk."

Brenda balled her hands into fists. If Eddie used that word—*punk*—one more time, she might have to slap him.

"You aren't authorized to arrest anyone, much less bring them in and demand they be put in a cell," Dwight said.

Eddie folded his arms in front of his chest. "I made

a citizen's arrest," he said. "And apprehending a potential thief falls under my duties as security guard at the museum."

"He's lying," Parker said again, his voice less strident, more pleading.

"I'd like to hear Parker's side of the story," Brenda said.

Dwight turned to Parker. "All right, let's have it."

"I was driving home from delivering a pizza down the street from the museum. I saw this guy—" He pointed to Eddie. "He was sitting in a Jeep that was parked alongside the museum, in that alley. He was talking to another guy, in a black SUV."

Eddie leaned toward them, clearly about to object. Dwight held up a hand to stop him. "Let him continue."

"This afternoon, when I left the museum, I could tell Brenda was uncomfortable with this guy—Eddie—being there," Parker said. "I thought I should make sure he wasn't causing trouble."

Eddie laughed. "Oh, you'd know trouble, wouldn't you?"

Parker glared at him, then continued. "I wanted to hear what he and the guy in the SUV were talking about. I tried to get close enough to hear, but I tripped over some garbage and he heard me. The guy in the SUV took off and Eddie tackled me and held a gun to my head and demanded to know what I was doing there. He threatened to shoot me."

"Drama queen," Eddie said. "He's making that up. Wants you to feel sorry for him."

"Who was in the SUV?" Dwight asked Eddie.

"The mayor stopped by to see how things were going," Eddie said. "He knew Brenda was upset with me being there. We heard somebody rattling around in the alley and I ran back and caught Parker here trying to pry open a window. I figure he was going to steal some stuff to sell."

"No! I didn't try to break in," Parker said. "Go look for yourself. You won't find my fingerprints anywhere."

"You were probably wearing gloves," Eddie said.

"Then where are they now?" Parker asked.

Eddie shrugged. "You probably threw them away."

"Then they'd be in the alley, wouldn't they?"

"Eddie, did you threaten Parker with a gun?" Dwight asked.

"Of course not. I know better than that."

Brenda didn't believe him. Eddie wouldn't look Dwight in the eye—instead, his gaze kept darting to Parker.

"Look at my face." Parker pressed his cheek up against the bars. "You can see the bruises and cuts from where he pushed my face into the gravel." He turned to display the other cheek. "And there's a mark on this side where he held the gun barrel."

Brenda and Dwight leaned forward to view the faint round cut. "That could be from a pistol," Dwight said.

"The punk threatened me," Eddie protested. "I had a right to use force."

"You need to leave now, Eddie," Dwight said. "I'm going to take you upstairs and I'll deal with you later." He glanced at Brenda. "Will you be all right for a few minutes?"

"Of course."

Eddie opened his mouth, then closed it again. He followed Dwight to the first locked door, but before Dwight could unlock it, it opened, and another deputy escorted Paige Riddell inside.

"What is going on?" Paige demanded. Then she saw Parker in the cell and rushed over to him.

"Rich, take Eddie upstairs and see him out," Dwight said.

"I didn't do anything," Parker said. "I was trying to help."

"I believe you," Brenda said.

"I'm going to send someone over to the museum to check," Dwight said. "If we don't find anything, we'll let you go."

"Eddie Carstairs is a liar and a weasel," Paige said. "He always has been. And he's never liked me, ever since I turned him down when he asked me out."

"I swear, I thought he and that guy in the SUV were up to something," Parker said. "That's the only reason I stopped."

"Next time you see something suspicious, call us," Dwight said. "Don't investigate on your own."

Parker looked at the floor, saying nothing. Brenda imagined for someone in his position, only recently out of jail and rehab, calling the cops wasn't the first line of action that came to mind.

The door opened again and Gage stepped in. "I checked the museum," he said. "I can't find any sign of tampering with any of the windows."

"Any gloves lying around anywhere?" Dwight asked.

"No. But I did find where it looks like Eddie and Parker scuffled—and two sets of tire tracks."

"Did you get a good look at the man in the other car?" Dwight asked Parker. "Was it the mayor?"

"I couldn't see him very well," Parker said. "And I've never met the mayor, so I wouldn't know what he looks like."

"Clearly, Parker is telling the truth," Paige said. "You need to let him go."

"Brenda, do you want to press charges for trespassing?" Dwight asked.

"No." She shook her head.

"I think you should be charging Eddie with assault," Paige said.

"No, Paige," Parker said. "I just want to get out of here."

Dwight unlocked the cell, and Parker stepped out. He stopped in front of Brenda. "Thanks for believing me," he said.

"I do believe you." She lifted her chin. "I'm a good judge of character—not always, but most of the time. I think Eddie was the one lying, not you."

The four of them left together. "I'll take you home," Dwight said to Brenda.

She waited until they were in his SUV before she spoke again. "Why was Eddie lying?" she asked.

"I can't say for sure," Dwight said.

"But you have a theory. Tell me."

He sighed. "Eddie has always wanted to be the hero. I think, his first night on the job, he wanted to catch a burglar, prove it was a good idea for the town to hire him. But he always goes overboard. That's why Travis fired him."

"I think you're right," she said. "And I'm glad Travis fired him. He thinks wearing a gun makes him better than everyone else, and that's a dangerous attitude."

"Are you going to let Parker volunteer at the museum again?" Dwight asked.

"Yes. He did a great job for me today." She angled toward him, and studied the side of his face, illuminated by the dashboard lights. "Sometimes you have to go with your gut and trust people. And don't remind me I trusted Andy when he didn't deserve it."

"I wasn't going to say anything."

"I was younger then," she said. "And I was still grieving for my mother when we married. And later—later, I think I knew something wasn't right. It was why I kept questioning him about how we could afford all the work we had done on the house. But I was in love, and I wanted to believe him."

"I understand," Dwight said. "And I'm glad everything you've been through hasn't made you cynical."

"Not about everything," she said. "Though I don't trust as easily."

"That's all right. One thing being a cop teaches you is persistence."

She studied him, surprised by the word choice. "What is that supposed to mean?" she asked.

"It means I'm going to earn your trust. One of these days you're going to let down your guard with me and let yourself feel again."

She looked away. She didn't want to ask him what he thought she would feel. She could see it there, shining in his eyes. Dwight Prentice didn't think of her as just another crime victim who needed help. When he looked at her, he saw something more. He was letting her know that, but she wasn't sure what she was supposed to do about it. She wasn't ready to let down her guard with him or any other man. She wasn't ready to fall in love. The message Dwight had just sent her let her know he wasn't going to settle for less.

Chapter Seven

The next morning, Dwight met with Travis to review the previous night's events. "I spoke with the mayor," Dwight said. "Eddie's story about him stopping by last night checks out, though he says he doesn't know anything about Parker Riddell being there."

"What about the rest of Eddie's claim?" Travis asked. "Was Parker trying to break into the museum?"

"I don't think so," Dwight said. "I think the kid really was trying to sneak up on him and the mayor and Eddie overreacted—as usual."

"Gage didn't find any sign of an attempted break-in at the museum," Travis said.

"Brenda said she thought Eddie was lying, and I tend to agree with her," Dwight said. "He wouldn't look me in the eye."

"They could have chosen a better person for the job, but I don't think the town was wrong to hire a watchman for the museum," Travis said. "If the person who threatened Brenda thinks the book might be there, it's the next logical target."

"Brenda gave an interview to Tammy Patterson yesterday," Dwight said. "She said she told Tammy to make sure she stated in the article that the book was locked up at the sheriff's office."

"Good idea," Travis said. He leaned back in his chair, frowning. "Forensics didn't turn up anything on the notes. We did find the banner—ripped to pieces with a knife, probably a pocketknife—and stuffed into the Dumpster behind Moe's Pub. Nothing to go on there. The arson report on Brenda's house didn't turn up anything new, either."

"So we're back to wondering who wants that book destroyed and why," Dwight said.

"How's Brenda holding up?" Travis asked.

"Amazing. She's determined not to let this guy get to her. I thought later this morning I'd take her up to Eagle Mountain Resort and show her the lab—see if she spots any historical details the DEA missed."

"That's not going to prove a connection between what happened up there with Gage and Maya and what's going on with Brenda now," Travis said.

"No, but it might point us somewhere—to some collector and someone involved in the original project."

"When are you going?"

"She had some work to do at the museum this morning, then we're going to head up there," Dwight said. "Meanwhile, I want to take a look at that book."

"It's in the safe downstairs," Travis said. "Make sure you sign it back in when you're done."

"Yes, sir."

Dwight retrieved the combination to the safe, then got the book and sat down at his desk with it. After the first few pages, he struggled to keep going. The writer—S. Smith—had managed to take a potentially exciting subject and make it dry as sawdust. So he was relieved when the phone on his desk rang.

"There's a man here who wants to speak to you," Adelaide said. "A Professor Gibson."

Dwight closed the book and set it aside. "Send him in."

The professor was about eighty years old, thin and slightly stooped, with a full head of white hair and faded brown eyes peering from behind horn-rimmed spectacles. "The young woman at the newspaper suggested I talk to you," he said, peering into the office.

"Which young woman is that?" Dwight asked.

"Tammy? The reporter?" He stepped into the room and looked around.

"Why don't you sit down, Mr. Gibson." Dwight stood and closed the door behind the man.

"Val. Val Gibson." He lowered himself carefully into the chair across from Dwight's desk. "I'm a retired professor of history at Colorado State University."

Dwight returned to his seat. "Why did Tammy suggest you contact me?"

"She called me to get some information for a story she's working on—something to do with the government's activities in the state during World War II—Project Razor. She was researching the topic online and found an article I had written and realized I was a local. I retired to the area seven years ago."

"Project Razor?" This piqued Dwight's interest. "Do you mean the project to develop chemical weapons for use in the war?"

"Not just chemical weapons—biological ones, too."

"I'm not sure I'm clear on the difference," Dwight said.

"A chemical weapon uses a chemical agent to inflict harm," Gibson explained. "So, for example, mustard gas in World War I or sarin gas. A biological weapon uses a pathogen, such as smallpox or anthrax."

"Aren't those against the Geneva Convention or something?" Dwight asked.

"The Geneva Convention of 1925 did ban the use of biological and chemical weapons," Gibson said. "But by World War II almost every major power, including the United States and Great Britain, had development programs in place. We don't believe the biological agents were ever used, but it wasn't until 1972 that a UN treaty was formed that forbade production of biological weapons—and even then, not every country is a signatory."

"How effective are biological weapons?" Dwight asked. "I mean, they sound terrible, but can't people be vaccinated or something?"

"Are you vaccinated against Q fever and tularemia?" Gibson asked.

"I've never even heard of them."

"Many of the agents used in biological warfare are obscure. As weapons, they can be devastating, but their effect isn't immediate, delivery methods are awkward, and you can't account for individuals who might have a natural immunity. So they're not seen as very practical for large-scale warfare. Still, there is some concern that terrorists could use them as another way to wreak havoc—release a vial of botulism spores in the air-conditioning system of a large office building and you could kill a lot of people and create a panic."

Dwight held up the book. "Are you familiar with this?"

"I'm very familiar with it," he said. "I have reason to believe that copy you're holding belongs to me."

Gibson spoke calmly, his expression pleasant. "Why do you think that?" Dwight asked.

"That young man—a lawyer—asked to borrow it years ago. Andrew Stenson. I was reluctant to lend it, but he was very persuasive. By the time I tried to get it back, he was dead." Gibson shrugged. "I tried to contact the widow, but the person who answered the phone said she was too upset to talk to anyone. They promised to look for the book and return it to me. I never heard anything back. I probably should have pressed the issue more, but it seemed petty, under the circumstances."

Was he telling the truth? Dwight couldn't tell. On one hand, maybe he was—Andy must have gotten this obscure title from somewhere. On the other, maybe this was a less-violent ploy to get hold of the book.

"Why did Andy Stenson want this book?" Dwight asked.

"He said he needed it for research he was doing on a case. He didn't elaborate, and I didn't pry. It's been my experience that lawyers as a group are fairly tight-lipped. Which I suppose is as it should be."

"Why didn't you say anything to Brenda Stenson when you saw that the book was up for auction?" Dwight asked.

"I didn't know it was up for auction until Tammy told me about it yesterday afternoon," Gibson said. "I don't take the local paper."

Again, maybe true—maybe not.

"I'll admit I haven't read the book," Dwight said. "It's a little…dry."

Gibson chuckled. "I suspect the author had written one too many government reports. It reads much like one. But as far as I've been able to determine, the information in the book is factual."

"Is there anything in there that might lead someone to want the book destroyed?" Dwight asked. "Something that incriminates an individual or casts a bad light on someone?"

"Destroyed?" Gibson looked puzzled.

"Someone sent Mrs. Stenson threatening notes, ordering her to destroy the book—or else. What kind of stationery do you use, Professor?"

"I have never threatened Mrs. Stenson, Deputy. And I'm not the sort of person who would ever destroy a book, or ask someone else to—especially not a valuable collector's item, like that one." He straightened. "And I don't use stationery. Who does in these days of emails and text messaging? I may look like a dinosaur to you, but I'm not."

Dwight remained skeptical. "You said Tammy contacted you because of an article you wrote about the project?"

"Yes. I've thought of writing a book about the history of biological and chemical warfare. The research has been a hobby of mine for some time now."

"Do you know where in Rayford County Project Razor took place?"

"I haven't been able to discover that, no." He nodded toward the book on Dwight's desk. "All that says is that abandoned mines were used for the laboratories, but considering how many of those are in the area, that isn't much of a clue."

"Do you know of anyone alive today who was involved in this research?" Dwight asked.

"No. From what I can gather, the scientists involved were in their thirties and forties at the time. That would make even the youngest over a hundred years old."

"Then it's not one of them threatening Mrs. Stenson. Maybe a child or grandchild?"

Gibson shook his head. "There's nothing in the book to implicate anyone. As I recall the author, Mr. Smith— which I suspect is a nom de plume—didn't use any real names in his book. There's a disclaimer in the front that says so."

Dwight nodded. He had skipped over the book's front matter, but he had a vague recollection of an author's note. He'd go back and read it later. "Maybe this book isn't even the point," he said. "It could be a distraction to keep us from looking at the real reason for the threats."

"Why did Mrs. Stenson decide to auction the book?" Gibson asked.

"The museum she directs is in financial trouble. When she found the book in her late husband's belongings, she researched it online and saw how valuable it was, so she decided to sell it and use the money for the museum. She's been collecting donated items from others to auction, as well."

Gibson nodded. "I suppose I would rather see the book used for something like that than for personal gain."

"You could always bid on the book yourself."

He smiled. "My days of having that kind of money to spend on a hobby are gone. I lucked on to the book at a secondhand shop in Denver a good twenty years ago. I think I paid seven dollars for it at the time."

"Are you going to ask Mrs. Stenson to return the book to you?"

"I don't think so. I wasn't savvy enough to ask her husband for a receipt or any other proof of the loan. That was my own foolishness." He stood. "Now that you've told me what Mrs. Stenson intends to do with the book, I'm happy to see it used for those purposes." He gave a wry smile. "As you observed, it's not exactly light reading material—and I never was one for owning things I wouldn't use or enjoy. Though I hope the threats toward Mrs. Stenson don't continue."

"We're watching the situation closely." Dwight walked with the professor toward the front of the station.

He was surprised to find Brenda waiting in the reception area. She stood as he approached. "I'm ready to leave when you are," she said.

"Brenda Stenson, this is Professor Val Gibson," Dwight said. "He—"

"I have some expertise in the history of biological and chemical weapons development in the US," Gibson said. "I wanted to offer my services to law enforcement in regard to the book that I understand has been the subject of threats to you."

"You know something about the threats?" Brenda asked.

"No, only about the book and its subject matter," Gibson said. "I'm afraid I wasn't much help." He nodded to her, then turned to Dwight. "Feel free to contact me if you have any questions."

As soon as the professor had left, Brenda moved closer to Dwight. "What was that about?" she asked.

"I'll tell you on the drive up to the resort. Come on." He led the way out the back of the building to his cruiser.

She waited until they were belted in and he had started the engine before she spoke again. "Why did the professor really come to see you?" she asked.

"You don't believe what he told you?" Dwight asked.

"You were about to say something about him when he interrupted." She sat back in the seat. "Don't ever play poker, Dwight. Your face is full of tells."

"You should have been the attorney in the family," he said. "You'd be good at interrogating witnesses. But before I answer your question, tell me if you've ever heard of Professor Val Gibson before."

"No. Who is he?"

"He's the man who owned that book before Andy. He said Andy wanted to borrow it to do some research for a case he was working on. The professor never saw the book again and had put it out of his mind until Tammy called him up yesterday to interview him for the article about the threats being made against you."

"Whoa, back up a little. Andy stole the book from the professor?" In addition to being a blackmailer, was her late husband a thief, also?

"I don't think he intended to steal it—I think he borrowed it and was murdered before he could return it. Then it just kind of fell through the cracks."

She nodded. "Does he want the book back? Is that why he came to you?"

"That may have been his intention originally, but after he learned about the auction to raise money for the museum, he seemed okay with that. And he admitted he didn't have any proof that it ever belonged to him."

"Maybe learning someone is threatening me because of the book made him think twice about wanting to own it," she said.

"That may have had something to do with it, too," Dwight said.

"I still don't understand how he ended up talking to you," she said. "Why not contact me directly?"

"Apparently, Tammy called him for some information for the article she's writing about the book and the threats to you," Dwight said. "She found him through an article he wrote about the top-secret government labs in Colorado during World War II and learned he was in the area. He told me he retired here seven years ago. When she learned he knew all about the book, she suggested he get in touch with me."

"But he wasn't able to help you?"

"He seemed to know a lot about what was in the book, and about the government's activities in general, but neither of us could think of any reason someone would want the book destroyed. He told me the author used pseudonyms for all the people who were involved in the project, and it's doubtful any of them are alive anymore, anyway."

"So he really wasn't much help."

"No. He doesn't know where the work was done, although he did say the weapons they developed were never used."

"I suppose that's comforting—sort of," she said.

"Everything okay at work this morning?" he asked.

"Eddie wasn't there and nothing was missing. No new threatening letters. So I'd call it good."

"Have you heard from Parker?"

"No, but I don't expect to. He said he had classes today." She shifted toward him. "I know you aren't crazy about Parker, but I really like him. I think at heart, he's a good kid."

"There's such a thing as being too trusting," he said.

"And there's such a thing as being too cynical," she shot back.

To her surprise, he grinned. "Guilty as charged. It's part of the job."

He looked so comfortable in his uniform, here in this cruiser, surrounded by the tools of his trade. "When we were growing up, I never would have pegged you as a future cop," she said.

"What did you think I would do?" he asked.

"I don't know—ranching, I guess. Or maybe business." He had always made decent grades, and been the serious, thoughtful type.

"I thought about both of those," he said. "But I have an uncle who is a small-town police officer in Wisconsin, and I always admired that. And I didn't want to sit behind a desk at a job where I'd be bored."

"I can't think law enforcement in Eagle Mountain is that exciting—at least most of the time."

"Some days are more of an adrenaline rush than others—for me, the pace is about right. And my ranching background comes in handy when we have to put cows or horses back in pastures."

She laughed. It was a local joke that the weekly sheriff's department activity reports printed in the local paper always contained a number of calls to put livestock back in pastures.

"It's good to hear you laugh, in spite of everything that's happened," he said.

"I'm still alive. I still have a job and friends, and I'm going to get through this." Saying the words made her feel stronger—and they were true. The threats were frightening, and she had lost things in the fire she would miss forever, but she still had so much.

"Yes, you are," he said. They fell silent as the cruiser headed out of town. Soon houses gave way to a solid wall of evergreens on either side of the road, and beyond that the red-and-gray cliffs of the mountains. "Have you ever been up here, to Eagle Mountain Resort?" Dwight asked.

"Once—they had some kind of ribbon-cutting or ground-breaking and I attended with Andy. That seems like a lifetime ago." It had been four years—she had definitely been a different person, then.

"What did you think?" he asked.

"That it was a shame to build fancy houses that would stay empty half the year in such a beautiful spot. I kept that opinion to myself. It didn't seem wise to criticize the man who was pretty much paying for the roof over my head and the food on my plate."

"You haven't been up here since?"

"No. Though I've heard it's a ghost town now. Paige and her group think it's an eyesore. Before Henry Hake went missing, they were lobbying him to restore the property to its natural state.

"I guess everything is in limbo until Hake is found."

"Hmm."

It was the kind of non-comment that made Brenda suspect Dwight knew more about Hake's disappearance—or about the future of the resort—than he was willing to say. That was probably part of being a cop, too—knowing things you couldn't talk about. But she didn't care. She had never been particularly fond of Henry Hake, and though she missed his regular donations to the museum, she couldn't pretend to grieve for him now that he was probably dead. As for his proposed resort, it would either be developed or not, and there were plenty of other people in town—like Paige Riddell and her environmental group—to worry about it. Brenda had other things to focus on—the upcoming auction, securing funding to keep the museum open, and finding a new place to live.

Dwight pulled the cruiser into a paved drive and parked in front of a pair of massive black iron gates. The gates stood partially open, remnants of yellow-and-black crime scene tape flapping from the crossbars. "Those gates aren't supposed to be open," Dwight said. He put the cruiser in Park and got out to examine the gates. A moment later, he was back. "Someone cut the lock," he said.

"Didn't you say the DEA had been up here, investigating?"

"I don't think they would have been so sloppy as to leave a broken lock hanging on the gate." He eased the vehicle through the opening and up the drive. Brenda studied the boarded-up buildings, crumbling foundations and dying landscaping that was all that remained of the proposed luxury development. Dwight steered around a waterfall of rock that spilled down an embankment and she knew without asking that this was where Wade Tomlinson and Brock Ryan had died, after they had left Gage and Maya and little Casey for dead.

Dwight stopped in front of a Quonset hut partially built into the hillside. "The lab is in here," he said.

She followed him out of the vehicle and walked to the entrance. The door—a massive metal rectangle with no window—leaned against the side of the hill. "Travis had that removed," Dwight said. "He didn't want anyone to end up locked inside—accidentally or on purpose."

Brenda repressed a shudder. "I'm glad he did. I'm not sure I'd want to go in if it was on there."

"Come on. I'll show you the lab." Dwight switched on his flashlight and led the way inside. The first room was a large, bare space, the dirt floor packed down and clean, save for a handful of dry leaves that skittered across the space, stirred by their entrance. A second door stood open at the far end of the room, and as they drew closer, Brenda realized it had been removed from its hinges also.

Dwight played the beam of the flashlight into the next room and swore under his breath. "What's wrong?" she asked, and moved up beside him to look inside.

"The place is cleared out," he said. "There was a workbench and tables and lab equipment in here before."

The space—with a floor of concrete, not dirt, and chains hanging from the ceiling that might have once held light fixtures—had been swept clean, not so much as a speck of dirt on the floors or walls, which were completely bare, except for a fly that crawled up one wall. "Maybe the DEA took everything away," she said.

"They didn't bother to mention it to us." He pulled out his phone and took several pictures.

Brenda's gaze shifted to the opening at the far end of the room. "Is that where Gage and Maya were held?" she asked.

"Yes." Dwight led the way across to it. Brenda hung back. "It's all right," he said. "There's nothing in here. It's pretty much like that first room—empty."

He was right, of course. It wasn't as if she were sight-seeing in a torture chamber. Still, she had to make herself cross the room to stand beside him. "Why are these rooms even here?" she asked.

"I don't know," he said. "Storage, maybe." He shone the light through the opening, and they both leaned in to examine the space. The beam of light illuminated a dirt floor, concrete walls—and something suspended from the ceiling—a suit of old clothes or a dummy or—

"Don't look." Dwight shoved Brenda back as the realization of what she was looking at hit her.

"Is that a body?" she asked.

He put his arm around her and hurried her toward the door. "We need to get down and call for help," he said. "I think we might have found Henry Hake."

Chapter Eight

Dwight stood beside his cruiser as the EMTs loaded the body into the back of the ambulance. Brenda sat inside, pale but silent, staring through the windshield toward the emergency vehicle's strobing lights. She hadn't said much of anything since they'd driven away from the resort to call for help, then headed back to wait for the sheriff and others to arrive. Dwight had tried to think of something to say to comfort her, but he hadn't been able to come up with anything. She was shaken but not hysterical, which pretty much described his own feelings.

When the EMTs had closed the doors behind them and driven away, Travis came over. "What made you think it was Henry Hake?" he asked.

"The suit," Dwight said. "Henry always wore those brown suits—I don't know. Something about it just struck me as him. I probably should have verified before I blurted it out like that."

"The coroner will verify, but it's probably Hake," Travis said. "There was a wallet in the back pocket, with Hake's driver's license. A money clip with the initials *HH*, but no money."

"Where's he been all this time?" Dwight asked. "It's been weeks."

"The body looked sort of—mummified," Travis said.

"I didn't do a really thorough examination, but there wasn't any obvious sign of trauma. We'll have to wait for the medical examiner's report."

"When we got here, the lock on the gate had been cut and it was open," Dwight said. "And everything's been cleaned out of the lab."

"I saw that. I'll contact Allerton, but I don't think the DEA did that."

"Yeah. I'm guessing whoever left Hake's body cleaned out the lab, too. They must have known we'd find him."

"They've had plenty of time to cover their tracks," Travis said. "They could have left the area—even the country—by now." The ambulance drove past and he signaled the crime scene techs to move in. "There goes my theory that Wade and Brock killed Hake."

"You thought that?" Dwight asked.

"Why not? They killed Maya's sister and brother-in-law and would have killed Gage and Maya if they'd had the chance."

"But why?" Dwight asked. "What was in it for them?"

"I haven't come up with an answer to that yet." He glanced toward Dwight's SUV. "Why the threats to Brenda? Why burn down her house?"

"Do you think what's going on with her is connected in some way to Hake's disappearance and what happened with Maya and Gage?" Dwight asked.

Travis rubbed the back of his neck. "I don't know, but it feels that way. This is a small county—historically very low crime, and nothing very serious. And now we have a crime wave. Everything else has been related to this property, starting with Andy Stenson's murder three and a half years ago."

"Andy is the one who first got hold of that book the guy who's targeted Brenda wanted destroyed," Dwight said. "He told Professor Gibson he needed it to research a case. I'm wondering if the case had something to do with Hake—and if Andy was killed because he found out something he shouldn't have."

"Ian Barnes never said why he killed Andy," Travis said. "But he told Lacy he needed to kill her because she knew too much—something she didn't even realize the significance of. She has no idea what he was talking about."

"We've always assumed Maya's sister and brother-in-law were killed because they saw Wade and Brock with Henry Hake," Dwight said.

Travis nodded. "But what if they saw something else?" He glanced over his shoulder toward the Quonset hut. "Something to do with that lab, maybe."

"Every time we pull at one thread in this case, everything gets more knotted up," Dwight said.

"But we're going to keep pulling until we find the solution to the puzzle," Travis said. "I'll finish up here. You take care of Brenda."

Dwight returned to the SUV. "What now?" Brenda asked.

"If you feel up to it, you'll need to make a statement. We just need to get down your account of what happened for the case file."

She nodded. "I can do that."

"It's better to do it now, while it's fresh in your mind."

"Fine. I'll do it now."

"After that I can take you home. To my home, I mean."

"All right."

He started the cruiser and headed back toward town. Beside him, Brenda was still as a statue, not making a sound. She was too calm. Finding Henry Hake's body that way must have shaken her—it would have shaken anyone. It had shaken *him*. Yet she showed no emotion at all. Not reacting was probably a defense mechanism, especially considering how much tragedy she had faced recently. But walling off emotions never worked for long, and the fallout could be worse than giving in to tears now.

BRENDA DICTATED HER statement to Dwight, getting through the ordeal by pretending the events of that morning had happened to someone else. Every time she closed her eyes, she could see the shapeless figure in the baggy suit hanging there, twisting slowly in the breeze… Then she would snap open her eyes, take a deep breath, and focus on something else—the crooked diploma on the wall behind Dwight's desk, the chipped paint near the doorway of his office, the dust on the toes of her own shoes.

When she had signed the printed statement, he ushered her back to his car and drove out to his parents' ranch. She appreciated that he didn't try to talk to her. She didn't have anything to say. She felt empty—hollowed out and fragile, less woman than paper doll.

It wasn't until they passed the turnoff to his parents' house that she stirred. "Where are we going?" she asked.

"I'm taking you to my place," he said. "I thought you might appreciate the peace and quiet there. My mom means well, but she tends to hover."

"Thanks." She had to speak around the lump in her throat. His thoughtfulness touched her. She cleared her throat. "I'm sure you have work to do," she said. "I shouldn't be keeping you from it."

"I don't have anything urgent right now." He glanced at her. "I want to make sure you're all right."

"I'm fine." She spoke the automatic lie she had been using for years now. The assurance kept people from prodding too deeply. She was keeping it together so they didn't have to worry.

Dwight said nothing, merely pulled up to his cabin and parked. The square cedar-sided cabin featured a porch across the front, and a gray tabby cat asleep in a rocking chair beside the door. The cat stood and stretched at their approach. "This is Otis," Dwight said, pausing to scratch behind the cat's ears before he opened the front door.

Otis purred like an engine humming along and followed them into the cabin, long tail twitching. "Oh, this is nice," Brenda said, stopping three steps into the front room. She wasn't sure what she had expected—something utilitarian and maybe a little worn, filled with hand-me-down furniture and the clutter of a bachelor life. Instead, the open, high-ceilinged room had the comfortable Western vibe upscale design magazines strived for, with a layer of authenticity that welcomed a visitor to sit down and kick off her shoes.

A Persian carpet in shades of red, black and blue covered the worn wooden floor, and a cast-iron-and-soapstone woodstove dominated one wall, flanked on either side by big windows that offered a view of golden hayfields and the mountains beyond, the peaks dusted with the autumn's first snow. A caramel-colored sofa and two matching armchairs were arranged around a table made from a slab of wood worn smooth by years of use. A flat-screen TV on an oak sideboard was the chief reminder that this was a modern home and not some backcountry retreat.

"Make yourself at home," Dwight said, motioning toward the sofa. "I'll fix us something to drink."

Not waiting for a reply, he headed toward the kitchen, which was separated from the living area by a massive island. Brenda moved to the sofa and sat, looking around at the shelves of books between the windows and the artwork on the walls—pen-and-ink drawings of elk, moose and other wildlife interspersed with paintings of rodeo cowboys. She leaned closer to peer at one of the paintings, of a young man in jeans and chaps carrying a saddle, a number pinned to the back of his leather vest. "Is that you?" she asked, when Dwight rejoined her in the living room.

"Me a long time ago," he said. "The artist is a family friend." He handed her a short, squat glass filled with ice and a dark liquor, and sat on the sofa beside her— close, but not touching.

She studied the drink. "What is this?"

"A brandy old-fashioned."

"Dwight, it's only one in the afternoon."

"Drink it. You need it after what you experienced this morning. I know I do." He took a long swallow of his own drink.

She took a tentative sip. It was sweet—and had a definite heat as it went down. She set the glass on the edge of the table and continued to look around the room.

"We should talk about what happened," Dwight said.

She turned to him. "I gave you my statement."

He frowned. "I don't mean the events that occurred— I mean, what's going through your head right now."

"Nothing's going through my head right now."

"And you don't think that's a problem?"

"I don't know what you mean."

He scooted forward to the edge of his seat and set his drink beside hers on the table. "Then I'll be frank. I'm worried about you. You've been through more awful things in the past few days—much less the past four years—than most people have to suffer through in a lifetime. Yet you go on as if nothing has happened. That's not normal."

She stiffened. "I'm not the hysterical type," she said. "And I did break down after Andy died." For months she had barely been able to function. She didn't want to go back to those helpless, out-of-control days.

He moved closer. "I'm not saying you have to get hysterical," he said. "But it's okay to let yourself feel. To acknowledge that some awful things have happened. And that it's not fair."

She nodded. She'd heard this advice before—read it in the books she turned to after Andy's death, told it to herself even. But taking the advice and letting go wasn't so easy. "Life isn't fair," she said. "I know that. And I don't see any point in dwelling on it."

Dwight took her hand. "I know you're tough. I admire that about you. But if you keep trying to bear the weight of all this by yourself, I'm afraid you're going to crumble."

His fingers twined with hers, so warm and strong. She held on in spite of herself, wanting to draw courage from him. "I don't know what you want from me," she whispered.

"I want you to trust me enough to believe that you don't have to put up walls between us," he said. "You've been hurt and it's okay to acknowledge that."

She stared down at her lap, her vision blurring. "I'm afraid," she said.

"Afraid of what?"

"Afraid if I let myself think about how awful things are right now, I'll start crying and never be able to stop."

"I'm no expert," he said. "But I think sometimes, if you let the hurt out, it makes room for good things to fill up that space."

"What good things?" The words came out harsh and full of bitterness she hadn't wanted to acknowledge. "I don't have a home. I may not have a job soon. Some maniac is threatening to kill me." Her voice broke. "I've never been so afraid or felt so alone."

He drew her to him, his arms a firm barrier to keep away harm. She buried her face against his shoulder, her tears flowing unchecked. She hated breaking down like this, yet it was such a wonderful release to do so. As the first wave of emotion subsided, she became aware of him stroking her back and gently kissing the top of her head. A different sort of emotion welled within her—a fierce awareness of Dwight as a man. New tears flowed, but these were tears of relief that after all she had been through, she could still feel the things a woman should feel—she was still alive and capable of desire and passion.

She tilted her face up to his and found his lips, pressing her body more firmly against his. He responded with an urgency that matched her own, pulling her onto his lap, one hand caressing her hip while the other cradled her cheek. She wrapped both arms around him, her breasts flattened against his chest, her mouth open, tongue eagerly exploring his mouth, reveling in thrilling, too-long-forgotten sensations shooting through her.

She rocked her hips and smiled as he let out a low groan, his erection hard and hot between them. He pressed his lips against her throat and spoke in a voice ragged with lust. "We'd better stop now unless you want it to go further," he said.

"Oh, I want it to go further." She trailed one hand along his cheek, the prickle of five-o'clock shadow along his jaw sending a fresh wave of heat through her. "I want you. I think I have for a while now, I just wasn't ready to admit it."

He grinned in answer and shoved to his feet, carrying her with him. She laughed, and he gripped her tightly and kissed her until she was dizzy and breathless. "Put me down," she pleaded, laughing.

"Oh, I'm not putting you down," he said. "Not until neither one of us is capable of standing."

He stalked toward the bedroom, her legs wrapped around his waist, his fingers digging into her buttocks. He didn't release her until they both collapsed onto the bed, and then only to begin stripping off her clothes as she tore at his shirt and pants.

Only when they were both naked, cuddling together side by side, did their fury give way to tenderness—still urgent, but more deliberate, each intent on savoring the moments. She trailed her fingers across the taut skin of his shoulders, tracing the contour of muscle and bone, memorizing the shape and sensation of him. He did the same, brushing kisses along her jaw and down the column of her throat, his tongue following the swell of her breasts and dipping into the valley between them, then sliding along to suck at first one breast and then the other, until she was quivering and all but whimpering with need.

She reached between them and grasped him, satin-smooth and hot, all but pulsing in her hand. "Do you have any protection?" she asked.

In answer, he gently pried her fingers from him and

slid over to the side of the bed and took a condom from the drawer of the nightstand. He ripped open the package and rolled on the rubber, the movement leaving her dry-mouthed and ready to pounce on him.

Instead, he lay back and pulled her on top of him. "Ready to go for a ride?" he asked.

"Oh, yeah." She lowered herself over him, closing her eyes against the exquisite pleasure of him filling her. When she opened them again, she found him smiling up at her, his eyes full of such wanting and tenderness that it all but undid her. She began to rock, gently at first, then with more movement, drawing out their pleasure, holding back as the need built between them. He grasped her hips, encouraging her, and they began to move together, thrust and withdrawal, advance and retreat, until she shuddered, her climax overpowered her, filling and overflowing. "Dwight!"

His name still echoed around them as he found his own release. He pulled her close to him and kissed her hard, then rolled with her onto his side, where they lay, still connected, his eyes reflecting all the wonder she felt. "Feel better now?" he asked.

She laughed. "I do." She kissed the end of his nose. "Thank you."

"No thanks needed," he said. "I'm just glad you're here."

"Me, too." She hadn't felt all that glad to be anywhere in a long time, and though he wouldn't let her thank him for it, she was more than grateful that he had given her back this part of herself—this ability to feel so alive and whole.

Chapter Nine

Dwight never got around to taking Brenda up to the main house that night. His parents could see his cruiser parked at his cabin from their house, and he suspected they would draw their own conclusions about Brenda's whereabouts. He was happy to have her stay with him, and he wasn't about to put a damper on the new closeness they shared by suggesting she leave. Whatever barriers she had erected before had melted away somewhere between her flood of tears and the passion they had finally given in to.

She slept in his arms that night and woke early to make love again, a satisfying, leisurely coupling that left him so ridiculously happy he was afraid the grin he wore was permanently etched on his face.

He made breakfast while she showered, and when she joined him in the kitchen, smelling of his soap, damp tendrils of hair curling around her face, he had to focus to get his breathing under control. "Did you find everything you needed?" he asked, deliberately playing it cool.

"Oh, I think so." She moved to the coffeemaker and filled a cup.

Dwight turned back to the frying pan. "How do you like your eggs?" he asked.

"However you want to cook them. I'm not picky."

He scrambled eggs and made toast, aware of her eyes on him. Conversation, which had before now been easy with her, was apparently choked off by the lust that hovered like a cloud around him. How was it that at thirty, he could be reduced to the incoherence of adolescence?

She smiled when he set the plate down in front of her. "I could get used to this," she said.

"So could I."

She said nothing, but polished off the breakfast as if she were famished—which she probably was, considering they had never gotten around to eating last night. When she finally pushed her plate away, she sighed. "That was delicious."

"Thanks," he said. "I'm no gourmet, but I manage to feed myself."

She put her chin in her hand and studied him, her silent scrutiny making him nervous. "What is it?" he asked. "Why are you looking at me that way?"

"I'm just wondering why it is you're still single."

That definitely wasn't a question he had expected. "Last I heard, being single isn't a crime," he said.

"Of course it isn't. But you're an attractive man with a good personality, a nice home, a good job. There are plenty of unattached women in this county who would love to go out with you. But I can't remember you ever being in a relationship with any of them. Why?"

"You worried I'm gay?"

The pink flush that spread across her cheeks made her look even sexier. "Um, no."

"I've dated," he said. "I'm just discreet about it."

"Then you definitely have a talent for subterfuge. It's not easy keeping a secret like that in this town."

"I like to keep my private life private."

"So do I," she said. "But I haven't had much luck with that, so far. The *Examiner* might be broke by now if it weren't for me and those I'm close to supplying them with juicy headlines."

"You're not responsible for the things Andy did," he said gently.

"No, but I'm part of them. I can't get away from that. And as you might imagine, it hasn't made me eager to trust another man."

"You can trust me."

"Can I?" The expression in her eyes had hardened. "Haven't we already established that you're good at deception?"

"I don't deceive people I care about."

"I'm sorry. I didn't mean to suggest that." She looked away. "It's not you who's messed up, it's me."

"Don't say that." He leaned across the table toward her. "There's nothing wrong with you. You're perfect."

A choked laugh escaped her. "Oh, no I'm not."

"You're perfect for me. I've always thought that." He straightened. "Maybe you're the reason I'm not married. I was waiting for you."

"Dwight." She shoved out of her chair and stood, backing away from him. "Last night—what happened between us was amazing. But that doesn't mean I'm ready for more, I—"

"I know." He resisted the urge to move toward her, forcing himself to remain still, to rely on his words to reach her. "I'm not asking for anything. But you asked me an honest question—I figured I owed you an honest answer."

She considered this for a moment, then nodded. "All right. But what happens now?"

"Now I think I should take you to work." He stood,

the movement slow and easy, as if she were an easily frightened animal. "Your car is still there, right?"

"Right. I'll get my things." She started to turn away, then stopped. "Thank you for being so understanding."

Oh yeah. He was understanding all right. Understanding that when it came to Brenda Stenson, he was pretty much at her mercy. Not a position he liked to be in.

BRENDA PRIDED HERSELF on keeping her emotions in check, but Dwight's declaration that he had been waiting for her had left her reeling. While last night had been an incredibly pleasurable and yes, healing, experience, she hadn't been prepared for what amounted to a declaration of love from a man she had always considered as taciturn and frankly, hard to read.

And now she had to sit here beside him in his cruiser and pretend that her emotions weren't all over the place. Wouldn't it be nice if she could have even a single day that wasn't full of drama? She'd almost forgotten what that was like.

Her morning didn't get any better when Dwight drove her to the museum and she spotted Eddie Carstairs seated on the bench beside the front door. "What is he doing here?" she asked as Dwight pulled his cruiser to the curb.

"Let's find out," Dwight said.

Her first instinct was to tell him that she could take care of Eddie herself, but maybe it wasn't a bad idea to have a witness to back her up if things got heated. For whatever reason, Eddie seemed to have the mayor on his side, and since the town council was Brenda's employer, she ought to tread carefully.

"Hello, Eddie," she said as she climbed the steps to the front porch of the museum. "Did you need something?"

"Just keeping an eye on things," he said.

"I thought you were a night watchman," she said.

He ignored her, turning instead to Dwight. "I heard there was some excitement yesterday afternoon, up at Eagle Mountain Resort," he said.

"I imagine the news is all over town by now," Dwight said. But he didn't elaborate on what that news might be.

Eddie shifted from foot to foot. "Pretty funny to find Henry Hake up there after all this time, don't you think?" he said.

"I don't know of anyone who found it amusing," Dwight said.

Brenda opened her mouth to tell Eddie to get lost when he turned to her. "You were there, weren't you?" he asked.

"Yes." She crossed her arms over her chest. "But I don't have anything to say to you about it."

"I heard the body was practically mummified," Eddie said. "I figure his killer stashed him up there in one of those caves up on the cliffs. The Indians used to do that and the cool, dry air just desiccates the body. Sort of like beef jerky."

"I wouldn't know about that," Brenda said.

Eddie turned to Dwight again. "You must know how he died," he said.

"If I did, I wouldn't share it with you," Dwight said.

"You ought to think twice about that," Eddie said. "I know a lot of people in this town, see a lot of stuff. I might have information that could help you."

"If you have information, tell me what it is," Dwight said. "But the exchange doesn't work both ways."

The two men glared at each other like two roosters

about to face off. Brenda was grateful when a new arrival interrupted.

"Hi, Brenda," Parker Riddell said as he headed up the walkway. "You said you might need help with that new display today."

"Yes, Parker." She offered him her warmest smile. "I'm glad to see you."

The two slightly older men studied the younger one as he mounted the steps to stand by Brenda. "Hello, Deputy, Eddie," Parker said.

Dwight greeted Parker, but Eddie only nodded, his lip curled in a sneer. Neither man gave any indication of budging. "Eddie, Dwight, you need to take this conversation elsewhere," Brenda said. "Parker and I have work to do."

Dwight's eyes met hers. She remained firm, but gave a slight nod, to show she wasn't holding anything against him. "Come on, Eddie," Dwight said. "Let's get out of Brenda's hair."

"This is public property," Eddie said. "I have a right to be here."

"Yeah, but if you waste the whole day standing around here, people are going to get the wrong idea," Dwight said.

"What do you mean?" Eddie asked.

"They're going to figure you don't have anything better to do. That you're too washed up to get a job."

"I have a job," Eddie said. "I'm establishing my own private security company."

"Right. Then go find some more clients. Don't stand around here harassing Brenda."

"I'm not harassing her. I—"

"Eddie!" Brenda snapped the word, more than tired of

this conversation. "Get out of here or I'll call the mayor and tell him you're interfering with museum business."

She could tell he wanted to argue with her, but he set his jaw and stalked down the steps and across the yard to his Jeep.

"I'll be going, too," Dwight said, keys in hand.

"I'll see you later." Then, without another look back, she walked into the museum. For now, at least, this was her domain—the kingdom she ruled without a consort. Yes, it was lonely, but there was a kind of security in that loneliness, a way to keep her heart safe even if her head argued she was being stupid.

Parker followed Brenda inside, where she greeted Emma Waide, who had been volunteering at the museum since it first opened. "We're going to be working on the new exhibit if you need anything," she said.

"How is school going?" she asked Parker as they climbed the stairs to the second floor.

"It's okay. My history class is pretty interesting. Just basic American history, but still, the professor is good."

"The classes will get more interesting if you pursue the degree," she said. "You can home in on areas of particular interest."

"I like the World War II era. There was so much happening all over the world back then."

The exhibit in progress was just as she had left it the day before yesterday, with most of the material they would display still in boxes. Brenda consulted the plans she had drawn up. "I hope you're ready to work," she said. "I need you to move some shelves and tables around for me. Some of them are pretty heavy."

"No problem."

For the next two hours, they worked arranging the space. Parker proved both strong and fast, and able to work well without supervision—in other words, a dream volunteer. "I'd never get this done so quickly without your help," she said as she surveyed the newly arranged furnishings. "Now all we have to do is set out the items on display. Later today I'll work on printing out all the labels and signs."

"This is the fun part," Parker said as he opened a carton and lifted out a World War II-era uniform. "Like opening Christmas presents."

"It is sort of like that," Brenda agreed. "I've seen all this stuff before, but it's been packed away for a while. And some of it has never been on display. People give us things all the time that we have to save for the appropriate exhibit." She set a canteen and mess kit side by side on a shelf.

"What do we do with the clothes?" Parker asked, as he laid out a navy uniform next to the army gear.

"We have mannequins we'll need to dress," she said. "We'll save them for last."

After another hour, they had everything unpacked and arranged. Brenda might move some items later, after she had time to consider the flow of the exhibit. The idea was to display things in a logical order that led visitors from one area of the room to the next. They retrieved the mannequins from her workroom and arranged them in the center of the room, the navy man clutching a pair of binoculars, his army counterpart holding a field radio.

"It looks pretty good," Parker said as he and Brenda stood in the doorway, surveying their work.

"It will look even better when the signs and labels are up. And I may add a few things in. Sometimes after a new exhibit goes up, someone will come in and donate something that fits the theme."

"What about that book you're auctioning?" he asked. "The one about the secret labs that were here in the county in World War II?"

She shook her head. "It's far too valuable—and apparently, controversial—to display."

"Do you think I could see it some time?" he asked.

"Why do you want to see it?" she asked.

He shrugged. "To try to figure out what all the fuss is about, I guess."

"The sheriff has the book and it's going to stay with him until the auction."

"Yeah, I guess that probably is best. Have you had any more threatening letters?"

"No. I hope the article in the paper will scare off whoever wrote the letters. I tried to make it clear that I was immune to threats."

"I hope you're right and you scare him off," Parker said. "And don't just make him angry and want to try harder."

His words sent a shiver through her. She watched him out of the corner of her eye as they moved empty boxes back into storage and swept up the room. Maybe he was only curious about the book and concerned about her—but what if he had other motives?

She said goodbye to him and the afternoon volunteer and prepared to lock up the building and leave herself. She hated feeling this way—untrusting and suspicious. Was Dwight's cynicism rubbing off on her? If that was the case, she wouldn't thank him for it.

Chapter Ten

"We have the coroner's report on Henry Hake." Travis distributed copies around the conference table, two days after Dwight and Brenda discovered the body. "There was a fair amount of deterioration, but he's ruled out physical violence as the cause of death. He found no sign of gunshots, knife wounds or asphyxiation."

Dwight skimmed the paperwork, flipping over to the end of the report. Next to "Cause of Death" was a single word: *Inconclusive*.

"Does that mean it's possible Hake wasn't murdered?" Gage asked.

"We can't rule out murder," Travis said. "Especially considering how the body was found. But the coroner did say the body was strung up after death—and that it hadn't been hanging where we found it long."

"We knew that already," Gage said. "The Feds only left the place three days ago."

"Maybe Hake was poisoned," Dwight said. "One of those poisons that leaves the body in a relatively short time."

"Did the coroner say how long Hake had been dead?" Gage asked.

"Approximately seven weeks—maybe a little more," Travis said.

"So he died not too long after he disappeared," Dwight said.

"The coroner did find evidence of heart disease," Travis said. "It's possible Hake was kidnapped and the stress brought on a heart attack. The kidnappers panicked, ditched the car and hid the body."

"Then why not keep the body hidden?" Dwight asked.

"Maybe because now we don't have a way of linking Hake to the killer?" Gage asked. "They think they're in the clear."

"Hake's car was found near the resort, and his body was found on the resort," Travis said. "The Hoods died because they saw something at the resort they shouldn't have. Wade and Brock kidnapped Gage and Maya and Casey and imprisoned them at the resort."

"So the resort is key to solving all of this," Dwight said. "What is going on up there that someone is willing to kill to protect?"

"We need to know that," Travis said. "And we need to know who." He consulted his notes. "Gage, you saw a black SUV at the resort when you were fired on. Casey reported seeing a similar SUV—and two men in dark suits—when she went for help. Wade and Brock were talking to those men before they were killed."

"So the suits were running the show." Gage nodded. "Two strangers in suits are going to stand out around here, where pretty much everybody wears casual clothing unless they're going to a wedding or a funeral. Even the bankers and lawyers seldom put on a jacket and tie."

"So why haven't we been able to find them?" Dwight asked. "And why haven't we been able to find whoever is threatening Brenda?" Their canvass of the neighborhood had turned up not a single clue to help them find the arsonist who had burned down her house.

"The only link we can find between Brenda and the resort is the fact that her late husband was the lawyer who represented the development company," Travis said.

"And he was killed because of something he saw or said or did that didn't please his murderer's boss," Gage said.

"Ian Barnes was Henry Hake's bodyguard," Travis said. "But in talking with him before he died, I got the impression that there was someone above Hake who was calling the shots. My feeling is that that mysterious someone ordered Andy Stenson's murder."

"Why did Hake need a bodyguard?" Gage asked.

"Because he was afraid of the people over him?" Dwight asked. "He thought they were dangerous?"

"Or because those people had enemies who were dangerous," Travis said.

"Henry Hake had enemies of his own," Gage said. "Paige Riddell's environmental group didn't make any secret of their loathing for him and his development. And let's not forget his own lawyer, Andy Stenson, who was probably blackmailing him."

"So maybe Hake did order the hit on Andy," Dwight said. "But then who kidnapped Hake?"

"If he was kidnapped," Travis said, "we don't have any proof of that."

"When a guy disappears and his car ends up in a ravine—but his dead body is found hanging in an underground chamber a month later—that didn't all happen of his own free will," Gage said.

"And the coroner said no physical trauma," Dwight

said. "So it's not as if Hake somehow managed to escape his car, only to die of his injuries later."

"And what—someone found the body and decided to hang it up as some kind of sick joke?" Gage asked.

Dwight shrugged. "Stranger things have happened."

"Right now all we have are a lot of questions and no answers," Travis said. "But maybe I'll get some answers this afternoon. I have a meeting with the new owners of the Eagle Mountain Resort property."

Dwight and Gage exchanged looks. "What was that company's name again?" Dwight asked.

"An investment group called CNG Development," Travis said. "I'm meeting with their representative on the property at two."

"Who is CNG Development?" Dwight asked.

"That's what I'm hoping to find out," Travis said. "As far as I can determine, at least some of the principals were silent partners in the original development. Before Hake disappeared, they signed an agreement with him to take over control of the property."

"How come nobody else knew about this?" Gage asked. "I mean, the way gossip spreads in this town, I would have thought someone would have said something."

"I think they kept it deliberately low-key," Travis said.

"Do they plan to go ahead with developing the property?" Dwight asked.

"That's one of the questions I'm going to ask them." Travis consulted his notes again. "What else do we have going on right now?"

"I'm working the high school basketball tournament this evening," Gage said. "Maya says the girls' team has a good chance of winning."

Gage's fiancée, Maya Renfro, had snagged a position teaching English at the high school when another teacher's husband was transferred. A former avowed city girl, she had thrown herself into small-town life and signed on as assistant coach of the girls' basketball team.

"Dwight, what are you working on?" Travis asked.

"I'm going to take another look at that book of Brenda's, see if I can figure out what Andy might have been looking for when he borrowed it from the professor. And I'm going to touch base with Brenda and see who has made a bid on the book so far."

"I thought the auction wasn't until next Saturday," Travis said.

"It isn't, but she said bidders had the option of mailing in a bid ahead of time. I want to know if anything has come in that might raise a red flag."

"There's a reception next Friday night where people can view all of the items up for auction, including the book," Travis said. "I want as many of us as possible there, keeping our eyes open for anyone suspicious."

Everyone was beginning to look suspicious to Dwight—not a feeling he especially liked.

"We still have our regular patrols," Travis said. He read off their assignments for the day and they dispersed.

Dwight resisted the urge to drive by the museum first thing. Brenda had been polite but decidedly cool toward him since he'd made the mistake of revealing his true feelings to her yesterday morning. So much for the honesty women said they wanted.

But maybe that wasn't a fair judgment, either, he admitted. Brenda had made it clear she wasn't ready for a relationship, and he could see how his comment might make her think he was trying to rush things.

Instead of saying he had remained single because he was waiting for her, he should have shared another bit of truth: staying single was a lot easier than navigating the land mines inherent in any relationship.

WITH THE AUCTION fast approaching, Brenda spent the next few days working long hours at the museum, proofing the final copy of the auction catalog and updating listings on the website she had established as new items continued to come in. The work needed to be done, but when she was being honest with herself, she admitted that staying late at the office gave her an excuse to avoid Dwight. She couldn't think clearly when she was with him, what with her body demanding to be back in his bed and her mind focused on the benefits of sticking close to a man with a gun and a desire to protect her. She could shut up her mind with a reminder that she had received no more threatening letters. Her body, awakened from long dormancy, wasn't so easily reasoned with. Better to avoid the object of her lust until she had gained a little perspective.

Work was one thing that allowed her to focus. The interest and support from the people of Eagle Mountain and the surrounding county touched her. Surveying the growing collection of items in her workroom, it seemed as if half the residents of the area had raided basements and attics for great-granddaddy's miner's lamp or great-grandmother's Victrola to contribute to the museum's fund-raising efforts.

But their generosity wasn't going to be enough. The money the auction would bring would keep things going for a few more months, at most, but an ongoing donor was needed to insure continued operation—and Brenda's continued employment. In addition to getting ready for the auction, she continued to send letters to potential sponsors, both corporate and private.

She was composing such a letter, long after the museum had closed, on the Tuesday before the auction when a pounding on the door broke her concentration. A glance out the window showed a distinguished-looking man in a dark suit standing on the porch. Annoyed but curious, she opened the door. "The museum is closed," she said. "You're welcome to come back tomorrow morning after nine." She tried to see past him, into the parking lot. Wasn't Eddie supposed to be around somewhere, doing his security guard duties? She hadn't seen any sign of him all evening.

"I'm here to see Mrs. Brenda Stenson." He offered a smile that transformed his expression from businesslike to breathtaking. Of average height and build and in his forties, he had the thick dark hair and piercing gray eyes of a matinee idol. "Would that be you?"

"Yes." She maintained her composure under the force of his movie-star smile. "What can I do for you, Mr…?"

"Brownley. Robert Brownley. Could we go inside to talk? It's awkward, standing here on the doorstep."

If she admitted she was alone in the building, would that make her more vulnerable? She had certainly been alone in the museum with strangers many times, given that she operated with a skeleton staff. But always before, that was during regular business hours, when another person could have walked in any time. She should tell Mr. Brownley to come back tomorrow.

"I have a financial proposal to make," he said. "I would have come earlier, but my business demands my attention during working hours. I saw your car out front and decided to take a chance that you were here."

He certainly looked like a man who had money to give away—his deftly tailored suit, gleaming leather shoes and even his haircut advertised wealth—and the black SUV parked beside her Subaru was a brand she was sure retailed for close to $100,000. That didn't mean he wasn't a serial killer, but could she really afford to pass up the chance that he was going to offer up a much-needed donation to the museum? She stepped back, holding the door open wider. "Come in."

He strode past her, the spicy fragrance of his cologne trailing in his wake. He admired the photographs on the walls and the books displayed on the shelves. Brenda perched on the high stool next to the cash register, keeping the glass display case that served as the front counter between them. "What can I do for you, Mr. Brownley?" she asked.

"I'm interested in one of the items you have listed for auction," he said.

"Oh." She tried not to show her disappointment. "You're welcome to make an early bid online, or attend the live auction Saturday night," she said.

"I'm prepared to make a preemptive bid now," he said. "I'll beat any subsequent bid you might obtain."

"What's the item you want to bid on?"

"It's a book. *The Secret History of Rayford County, Colorado.* An esoteric item, I admit, but I'm a collector, and you know how collectors are obsessive about completing our collections."

The hair on the back of her neck stood at attention at the mention of the book, but she remained cool. "We've had quite a bit of interest in that item," she said. "As I'm sure you're aware, it's quite rare."

"Yes." Did she imagine that his smile held less warmth? He looked around the room, scanning the titles on the shelves, as if he expected to find the book there. "And as I explained, I am prepared to meet or beat any other bid you receive, provided the volume meets with my expectations. I'd like to see it and assess its condition."

"The book is in a secure location. Off-site," she added. "All the auction items will be on display at the reception Friday evening, which you're welcome to attend. And of course, you can see everything the morning of the auction."

No smile now. Without it, his expression was forbidding. "I'm prepared to offer a substantial sum to acquire this volume," he said. "I don't think it's too much to ask for a private showing ahead of time."

"That isn't possible," she said. "The book isn't here. It isn't anywhere I can get to it."

"That's a very poor way to do business," he said.

"That may be your opinion, but it's how we've chosen to handle it." She pulled her cell phone from her pocket. "I think you'd better go."

He scowled at the phone, then turned and stalked out. When the door had slammed behind him, she laid the phone aside and slumped on the stool. She hated confrontation. But even worse, she hated people who tried to push her around.

Five minutes later, the jangle of the doorbells had her grabbing up the phone again, heart pounding. Dwight stepped into the room, and the sight of his lanky figure in the familiar khaki uniform left her weak with relief. "Everything okay here?" he asked.

She laid down the phone and smoothed her damp

palms on her skirt. "Fine. I'm just working late on auction stuff."

"Who was that in the black Land Rover that just went tearing out of here?" he asked.

"A man who wanted to place an auction bid. I explained he could go to the website or attend the live auction Saturday."

Dwight's alert posture didn't relax, and his gaze remained fixed on her. "What did he want to bid on?"

She opened her mouth to tell him, but what came out was, "Oh, it doesn't matter." She began shutting down her laptop. "I'm about ready to call it a night."

He quickly crossed the room and placed his hand over hers. "I thought you were going to trust me."

Yes. She wanted to trust him. But the encounter with Robert Brownley had shaken her, reminding her of how vulnerable trusting made her.

But this was Dwight, not an angry stranger. Dwight, who had loved her so fiercely and held her so tenderly and stayed by her side even when she pushed him away. "He said he wanted to bid on the book. He said he was a collector and he was anxious to complete his collection. He promised to outbid anyone else."

"Did he give you a name?" Dwight asked.

"Robert Brownley."

"I'll try to verify that. So you told him he'd have to bid online or at the auction Saturday?"

"Yes. But he asked to see the book. I told him it was being kept at a secure location—not here. He didn't like that."

"Did he threaten you?" The words were almost a growl.

"No." She smiled weakly, recalling Brownley's reaction. "He said that was no way to run a business, or something to that effect—as if that would make me give in to his demands. It was ridiculous, really."

"And then he left?" Dwight asked.

"Then I picked up my phone and told him to leave. I would have dialed nine-one-one if he hadn't headed for the door. I'm sure he knew that."

"He lit out of here fast enough," Dwight said. "I would have stopped him for speeding if I hadn't been concerned about you."

"You didn't have to worry about me." Though she had been relieved to see him when he walked in. "I think he was just a rich businessman who's used to always getting his way. When I dared tell him no, he stormed off in a fit of temper. If he wants the book as badly as he said he did, I'm sure he'll come back Saturday."

"If you see him before then, let me know," Dwight said. "In the meantime, I'll see what I can find out about him."

"I invited him to the auction reception Friday evening," she said. "I hope he shows up. If he's as wealthy as he appeared to be, and a collector, maybe he'll see a few more items he can't live without."

She closed her laptop and slipped it into her bag. "I'm leaving now. What about you?"

"I'm headed home, too. I'll follow you out to the ranch."

"I really need to find somewhere else to stay," she said as she walked with him out of the museum. "I can't keep imposing on your parents, and it's going to be months before my house can be lived in again."

"My parents are happy to have you." Dwight waited while she locked the door.

"I need my own place."

"Fair enough. But where? Eagle Mountain doesn't have much in the way of affordable rentals. That's why Lacy ended up in your garage apartment, and one reason Maya and Casey are living with Gage."

Brenda thought he would suggest she move in with him and was grateful when he didn't. "It may take me a while to find something," she said. "So I should start looking now."

"Then let me help," he said. "I'll put the word out and let you know if anything comes up. We can put Adelaide to work on it, too. She knows everyone and everything—at least to hear her tell it."

"All right. I'd appreciate that."

Dwight walked her to her car. "Where's your security guard tonight?" he asked.

"I don't know." She looked around, half expecting to see Eddie lurking in the shadows. "I don't know what kind of schedule he and the mayor worked out. They haven't bothered to inform me."

Dwight switched on his flashlight and played the beam over the darkened lot. He stopped with the light shining down the alley. "Isn't that Eddie's Jeep?" he asked. He shifted the light and Brenda gasped at the sight of a figure slumped over the steering wheel.

"Call an ambulance," Dwight said, and took off running for the Jeep.

Chapter Eleven

Dread filled Dwight as he raced toward the Jeep, but when he reached the open driver's-side window he realized Eddie wasn't dead. The figure slumped over the steering wheel snored softly and mumbled when Dwight shook his shoulder. Dwight leaned in closer and spotted a half-eaten pizza on the passenger seat. He sniffed, but didn't smell alcohol—only sausage and pepperoni. He shook the security guard again. "Come on, Eddie, wake up."

But Eddie only leaned sideways, mouth open, snoring away.

"The ambulance is on its way." Brenda joined him and stared in at Eddie. "Is he drunk?" she asked.

"I don't think so," Dwight said. "I think he's drugged."

"Drugged? By who?"

"I don't know. But he was eating a pizza."

Brenda frowned at the pizza, in its cardboard box with Peggy's Pizza on the front. "Do you think someone put something in his pizza?"

"I think we'd better have it tested, just in case."

"Has anyone else been to the museum—or in the parking lot—in the last half hour or so?" he asked.

"No one's been inside except Mr. Brownley," she

said. "When I answered his knock, his was the only vehicle I saw. But why half an hour? Couldn't someone have done this earlier?"

"I'm just guessing, but the pizza is still warm." He frowned at Eddie's slumped figure. "I'll find out from the mayor what time Eddie was supposed to start his shift."

A wailing siren announced the arrival of the ambulance. The paramedics parked and jogged up to the Jeep. "What have we got?" Merrily Rayford, one of the squad's senior paramedics, asked.

Dwight nodded to Eddie. "I think he's been drugged. No idea with what."

She and her partner donned gloves and opened the door of the Jeep. While they examined Eddie, Dwight retrieved an evidence bag from his cruiser and bagged the pizza, box and all. Brenda moved in beside him. "You don't think Parker had anything to do with this, do you?" she asked.

"I don't know what to think," Dwight said. They watched as the paramedics shifted Eddie onto a stretcher.

"His vitals are good," Merrily said. "I don't think he's in any danger, but we'll take him in for a closer look."

"I'll want to question him about what happened," Dwight said.

"From the looks of him, it might be a while," Merrily said. "Maybe in the morning."

"I'll check with the hospital later." He held up the evidence bag. "Meanwhile, I'll get this to the lab."

Brenda waited by her car, arms hugging her stomach, as the ambulance left the lot. "I need to take this in and file a report," Dwight said. "I probably won't be in until late."

She nodded. "Eddie isn't my favorite person, but I hope he's all right."

"I'll let you know." He wanted to kiss her, but settled for squeezing her shoulder. "Go home and try to get some rest. Try not to worry about this."

"It's been so long since I didn't have anything to worry about, I've forgotten what that's like," she said.

THE NEXT MORNING, Dwight and Gage faced a sullen Parker Riddell in the sheriff's department interview room. Gage had picked up the young man at his sister's house, where he and Paige were eating breakfast. Paige had argued against him going to the sheriff's department and had wanted to call a lawyer, but Gage had persuaded her that wasn't necessary. All they wanted was for Parker to answer a few questions. The young man had agreed, as much, Dwight suspected, to get his sister off his back as to placate the cops. He sat now, clothes rumpled and the dark shadow of a beard across his jaw, tattooed forearms crossed over a faded black T-shirt advertising a metal band that had been old when Dwight was a teen.

"I didn't deliver a pizza to Eddie," Parker said in answer to Dwight's first question.

"You were working last night," Dwight said. He had verified this with Peggy at her home earlier this morning.

"Yeah. But I didn't deliver a pizza to that jerk. If he says I did, he's lying."

Eddie wasn't saying anything yet—he was still out of it at the hospital in Montrose. When Dwight had called to check on him, the nurse on duty had reported that he was sleeping well and not in danger, but they didn't expect him to wake before midmorning.

"He had a pizza from Peggy's on the seat beside him when we found him last night," Dwight said. "He was unconscious."

Parker only looked more sullen. "I don't know anything about that. He must have picked up the pizza at the store."

"Peggy says Eddie didn't pick up a pizza, and he didn't order one delivered, either."

"Then I don't know what to tell you," Parker said.

"Maybe you made up this pizza special and delivered it between your regular orders," Gage said.

"Why would I do that?" Parker's voice rose. "The guy hates me. I wouldn't want to give him a free pizza."

"Maybe you told him it was a peace offering," Dwight suggested. "You were trying to get him to see you aren't a bad guy."

"I don't have any reason to want to impress him."

"What do you know about zolpidem?" Dwight asked.

"It's a sleeping pill, right?"

"So you have heard of it."

He shrugged. "I've heard of lots of things. I mean, I read books, and I watch movies."

"Do you have any zolpidem?" Gage asked. The lab report had come in that morning, showing that the pizza was loaded with the stuff—probably in the form of ground pills sprinkled on top. "Know where to get any?"

"No!" Parker uncrossed his arms and sat up straighter. "I don't have anything to do with drugs anymore. Even when I did, I didn't use downers."

"But they might be a good way to get back at somebody," Gage said. "Load a pizza up with them, put them out of commission for a while."

"Is that what happened to Eddie? I didn't do it. Why would I?"

"Revenge?" Dwight asked. "Or maybe you wanted to break into the museum and didn't want him around."

"I don't want to rob the museum. And it would have been stupid to pull that kind of thing last night—Brenda was working late at the museum."

"How do you know that?" Dwight leaned over him. Was this kid stalking Brenda?

Parker shifted in his chair. "I drove by there on the way to one of my deliveries and saw her car."

Dwight sat back. "I'll bet that disappointed you," he said. "Here you'd gone to all the trouble to make that special pizza for Eddie, and Brenda was foiling your plans."

"No! I told you, I didn't have anything to do with that pizza. Ask Peggy. She would know if I made a pizza."

"She said she left the kitchen to use the bathroom for a few minutes," Dwight said. "You could have slipped in and thrown one together then."

"And she would have noticed if the ingredients were missing. Not to mention it takes more than a few minutes to put together a pizza."

Dwight tried another tack. "When you drove by the museum and saw Brenda's car, did you see Eddie or his truck?"

"No."

"Anyone else?" Gage asked.

"No one else was there—just Brenda's Subaru."

"What time was this?" Dwight asked.

Parker paused, as if considering the question. "I was

delivering a Mountain Man special to Mr. Wilbur over on Sixth Street. So that was about seven. A little after."

When Dwight and Brenda found Eddie, it was after nine.

Parker held Dwight's gaze, defiant. "Are you going to charge me with something, or can I go? I have class this morning."

"You're not being charged with anything." Dwight stood. "We appreciate you coming in for questioning."

Parker said nothing, but left in a hurry. Dwight and Gage returned to Gage's office. "Peggy was pretty insistent that Parker didn't make an extra pizza," Dwight said.

"Her place is pretty small," Gage said. "Even from the bathroom, I think she'd have heard someone messing around in her kitchen."

"She's also positive Eddie didn't order or pick up a pizza," Dwight said.

"Maybe someone else ordered it, added the sleeping pills and took it to Eddie," Gage said. "It's not hard to imagine he's made other enemies."

Dwight grunted in assent. He reviewed their conversation with Parker, searching for any inconsistencies and finding none. "What's a Mountain Man special?" he asked.

"Pork carnitas, green chili and onions," Gage said. "A personal favorite."

Dwight let this pass. "Parker is the most obvious suspect," he said. "But maybe that's just what someone wants us to think."

"Yeah," Gage agreed. "The kid strikes me as smarter than that."

"Drugs can make even smart people do dumb

things," Dwight said. "But I think you're right. So, who else had it in for Eddie?"

"Or for Parker," Gage said. "Whoever did this wasn't trying to kill Eddie—just put him out of commission for a while and make it look as if Parker did it."

"So—somebody who wanted to get into the museum?" Dwight shook his head. "Brenda was there until the two of us found Eddie."

"Nobody else was there with her?"

Dwight sat up straight. He'd almost forgotten about Robert Brownley. "A man stopped by to ask about bidding on that book she has up for auction," he said. "He was just leaving when I showed up—in a black Land Rover. Said his name was Robert Brownley. He wasn't too happy when she told him he couldn't see the book."

"So—before he goes in to see Brenda, he delivers a doctored pizza to Eddie?" Gage shook his head. "Why?"

"To get him out of the way? Maybe he planned to try to take the book if Brenda wouldn't sell it to him."

"I'm definitely going to do a little more checking into Brownley."

"We should be able to interview Eddie in a few hours," Gage said. "Maybe he can solve this whole puzzle."

"Or he'll just throw in another piece that doesn't fit," Dwight said. Every new development only made this case more frustrating.

BRENDA HAD INTENDED to work through lunch the day after her encounter with Robert Brownley and all the excitement with Eddie, but Lacy showed up and insisted she take a break. "You have to eat," Lacy said. Fresh from the hair salon, she looked young and happy—looking at her, Brenda felt old and exhausted.

"I have so much to do," Brenda said, indicating her full desk. "I don't think I can spare the time."

"The work will be here when you get back," Lacy said. "Besides, we need to catch up. We don't see each other as much, now that I'm not living next door."

Brenda did miss her friend. "All right," she said. "You've convinced me."

They walked to Kate's Kitchen on the town's main street. A brisk breeze made a jacket necessary, but the sun shone brightly, and the aspens in people's yards and on the mountainsides above town glowed gold.

"How do you like living at the ranch?" Lacy asked when they were settled into a booth at the café.

"It's very comfortable, but…" Brenda didn't finish the sentence, pretending to study the menu.

"But it's not your place," Lacy said. "You're a guest."

Brenda should have known her friend would understand. "I need to find a place of my own," she said.

"What's the word on your house? Are you going to rebuild?"

"I don't know," she said. "I have a meeting with someone from my insurance company this afternoon. I hope that will give me an idea of how much money I have to work with. I'll probably rebuild, though something different." Something that would be just hers—not the grand house Andy had convinced her she wanted. "Whatever I do, I'll need someplace to live for the foreseeable future. But you know how scarce housing is around here."

"I wasn't thrilled about moving back in with Mom and Dad, but it's only until the wedding," Lacy said.

"I wondered if you would move in with Travis."

"I considered it, but I guess I'm a little old-fashioned. I want to wait until we're married to live together."

The waitress arrived to take their orders. Brenda

opted for the chicken salad, while Lacy chose a burger. As soon as they were alone again, Lacy resumed the conversation.

"Another reason I'm waiting to move in with Travis is that once we're husband and wife, I'll have free rein to redecorate his bachelor pad," she said. She made a face. "It definitely needs some changes."

Brenda thought of Dwight's cabin. There wasn't much about it she would change.

"Dwight has a cabin out at the ranch, doesn't he?" Lacy asked as though reading Brenda's mind. "Have you seen it? What's it like?"

Brenda cursed the blush that heated her face, but she tried to play it cool. "It's really nice," she said. "Comfortable. He has better taste than I expected."

"I'd say he has excellent taste."

Brenda ignored the knowing look in her friend's eyes, and was saved from having to answer by the arrival of their iced teas.

"I'm dying to know the scoop on what happened with Eddie Carstairs," Lacy said. "Travis mentioned he was in the hospital after someone tried to poison him or something. He said you and Dwight found him."

"We found him as we were leaving the museum last night." Brenda added a packet of sweetener to her tea and stirred. "He was slumped over the steering wheel of his Jeep. I thought he was dead."

"That must have given you a turn," Lacy said. "Especially after what happened with Henry Hake."

Brenda shuddered. "Yes. Thankfully, Eddie was just drugged."

"What, did someone shoot a poison dart into him or something?" Lacy asked.

The waitress arrived with their food, her expression not giving any indication that she had heard this alarming question. Brenda crunched a potato chip, then said, "There was a half-eaten pizza on the seat beside him. Dwight sent it to the lab to see if the drugs were in there."

"Ooh, that makes it interesting." She bit into her burger and chewed.

Both women ate silently for a few minutes, then Brenda said, "I think Dwight suspects Parker Riddell." Saying the words out loud made her realize how upset she was by the possibility that Parker—a young man she had grown to like—might be responsible for something so horrible.

"He works at the pizza place, right?" Lacy asked. "Did he and Eddie have some kind of run-in?"

"You know Eddie," Brenda said. "He likes to throw his weight around."

"And I guess Parker had some trouble with the law before." At Brenda's startled look, Lacy held up her hands. "I'm not gossiping—Paige told me."

"Yes, but he's trying to put that behind him," Brenda said. "He's going to school and working at Peggy's Pizza and volunteering at the museum. I think he's a good guy—and I don't think he hurt Eddie, even though Eddie gave him a really hard time. Parker is trying to make a fresh start." Something she also wanted desperately to do. Not that any of the trouble she had been through was her fault, but she longed to take her life in a different, calmer direction.

"Okay, so why don't you think Parker did it?" Lacy asked.

"He's too smart to do something so obvious," Brenda said. "I mean, putting the drugs in a pizza points the finger right at him."

"So you think someone set it up to look like Parker was the guilty party," Lacy said. "But who? And why?"

"I don't know," Brenda said. She stabbed at her salad. "I'm just hoping that for once, it doesn't have anything to do with me or the museum."

"Or maybe whoever doctored the pizza *is* the same person who's been threatening you," Lacy said. "Dwight can arrest him and then you wouldn't have to worry about him anymore."

"Right." She could go back to worrying about her job and where she was going to live. Those were the kinds of problems most people had to solve at one time or another. It had been a while since she had had anything that resembled a "normal" life. She thought she'd welcome the change.

"What you need is a real break," Lacy said. "Why don't we call Paige and Maya and the four of us go out tomorrow night? Dress up, dinner, drinks—just fun. No men, no worries allowed."

"I don't know," Brenda said. "I've got so much to do with the auction and the reception Friday night."

"If I know you, you've already got everything done. If you sit at home tomorrow you'll just fret over all the details you've already gone over a dozen times."

Brenda had to smile at this. "You do know me, don't you?"

"Come on—how about it? We can call it my pre-bachelorette party. Or, I know—we'll say it's an early party for your birthday."

"I don't know," Brenda said. "I'm not much on big celebrations."

"It'll just be four of us. And you need to do something to mark your thirtieth."

Brenda nodded. "All right." She had had her nose

pretty firmly to the grindstone the last few weeks. Maybe a night out was exactly what she needed.

No GROWN MAN could avoid looking ridiculous in a hospital gown, Dwight decided, as he and Gage entered Eddie Carstairs's hospital room. Eddie, paler than usual, with dark circles under his eyes, pulled the sheet up farther on his chest when he recognized them. "I hope you two have come to get me out of here," he said.

"You'll have to talk to your doctor about that," Gage said. "We're just here to interview you about what happened at the museum last night."

"The doctor was supposed to stop by here an hour ago to sign my discharge papers," Eddie said. "But he's disappeared."

"Then you've got time to talk to us." Dwight stopped beside the bed, while Gage took up position on the opposite side.

Eddie looked from one to the other of them. "The nurse told me someone tried to kill me with poisoned pizza."

Of course Eddie would go for the most dramatic story first, Dwight thought. "Someone added ground-up sleeping pills to the pizza," he said. "But there wasn't enough there to kill you. It looks like whoever did it wanted to put you out of commission for a while. Who would want to do that, Eddie?"

Eddie looked away. "How should I know?"

"Where did you get the pizza?" Gage asked.

"It was the Tuesday special from Peggy's," he said. "Pepperoni and sausage."

"Peggy says you didn't order a pizza from her last night," Dwight said.

Eddie said nothing.

"Did someone deliver the pizza to you?" Gage asked. "A friend who knew you were working last night?"

Eddie pressed his lips together, as if holding back words. Then he burst out, "That punk Parker Riddell probably put drugs in the pizza to get back at me," he said.

"Did Parker deliver the pizza to you?" Dwight asked.

Again, Eddie didn't answer right away.

"Do you want us to find who did this or not, Eddie?" Gage asked. "Because we have other things we could be spending our time on than finding out who wanted you to take a long nap."

"Parker didn't deliver the pizza," Eddie said. "But he works at Peggy's. He probably knew it was for me and messed with it."

"Who delivered the pizza?" Dwight asked again, struggling to keep his temper. Gage was right—they had plenty to do without wasting time like this.

"A friend," Eddie said. "But he wouldn't do something like that."

"What is the friend's name?" Dwight asked.

"I don't have to tell you that."

Dwight stared at the man in the bed. "If you know he's innocent, why not give us his name?"

"Because I don't want to."

Dressed in that faded hospital gown, his hair uncombed, mouth set in a stubborn line, Eddie reminded Dwight of an obstinate little kid. He stepped away from the bed. "Call us if you change your mind," he said.

"I'd be careful accepting any more gifts from your friend," Gage said. "Next time, he might decide instead of putting you to sleep, he'll finish you off."

It was possible Eddie went a shade paler beneath the day's growth of beard, but he said nothing as Dwight and Gage left him. They were in Dwight's cruiser before Gage spoke. "Do we know who Eddie's friends are?"

"No. But I'll be asking around." He put the cruiser in gear. "Let's start with the mayor."

"The mayor?"

"He stopped by to talk to Eddie the night Eddie arrested Parker," Dwight said. "Maybe he was there last night, too."

"With a pizza?" Gage asked.

"That's what we're going to find out."

Chapter Twelve

Mayor Larry Rowe's office was so small it scarcely had room for his desk, a filing cabinet and a credenza so covered with piles of paper its surface wasn't visible. When Gage and Dwight entered, he looked up from the screen of a laptop computer, scowling. "What's wrong now?" he barked.

"We just have a few questions for you." Dwight pulled out a chair and sat, while Gage remained standing by the door.

"I don't have time for questions," Larry said, turning his attention back to the computer.

"When was the last time you saw Eddie Carstairs?" Dwight asked.

"I don't know. A few days ago."

"You didn't see him last night?" Dwight asked.

"I went to dinner in Junction with my brother."

"Who's your brother?" Gage asked. "Does he live here?"

"He lives outside of Boston. He's an actor—Garrett Rowe."

Dwight and Gage exchanged glances—neither one of them had ever heard of the mayor's brother. "What time was your dinner?" Dwight asked.

"We left here at five, drove to Junction, had cocktails, then dinner, and lingered, catching up. I don't get to see him that often. I probably got back to my place about midnight."

He swiveled his chair toward them. "Why are you asking these questions?"

"Eddie Carstairs is in the hospital," Dwight said. "Someone fed him pizza laced with sleeping pills."

Larry made a snorting sound that might have been a laugh. "Eddie never did turn down a meal."

"Do you have any idea who might have given him the pizza?" Gage asked.

"None. Eddie Carstairs is a city employee, not a personal friend."

"Is your brother still in town?" Dwight asked. "We'd like to confirm your story with him."

Larry stiffened. "Are you saying you don't believe me?"

"It's just standard procedure."

"I can give you his number. He's gone back to Boston."

Dwight took the number, and he and Gage left. "What do you think?" Gage asked.

"We'll check with the brother. Not that I think the mayor is really involved, but I don't like to leave loose ends."

As BRENDA PULLED into the drive at her house, her phone pinged with a text from the insurance appraiser, telling her he was running a few minutes late. She sat for a moment, phone still in hand, studying the charred ruins of what had once been her dream home. The stones that had trimmed the foundation stuck up like blackened teeth arranged around a jumble of fallen timbers and empty window frames. She had avoided looking at any of this since the fire, but she was going to have to deal with it sooner rather than later. If nothing else, her neighbors were probably already tired of looking at this eyesore.

She stuffed the phone in her pocket and got out of the car and walked up the stone path to what had been the front door. Everything in the house was a total loss. She still had her laptop and the few clothes she had packed to take to Dwight's parents' home. It didn't matter, she tried to reassure herself. It was all just stuff.

But it was all stuff that she had, for the most part, personally chosen over the years—things it pleased her to look at and to use—the transferware teapot decorated with kittens, the dishes with a pattern of morning glories, the ginger jar bedside lamp with the pale green silk shade. She would miss these little items more than she would grieve the loss of the bedroom furniture and wedding china.

She spotted something glinting in the sunlight and stepped over the threshold and bent down to fish a silver teaspoon from the rubble, blackened, but intact. She found two more nearby, along with the silver top to a teapot and a silver salt cellar—though the walnut buffet that had held them all was a heap of charred wood nearby.

She picked her way across the rooms to the back corner that had been Andy's home office. The fire had started here, and everything in the room had been destroyed, all the little things she kept of her husband's reduced to ash—his desk and chair, a few law books, his university and law school diplomas, his law license. It didn't feel as awful as she would have imagined to lose those things. She supposed she would have eventually put those items away somewhere. They didn't have any children to save them for.

Brakes squealed as a car slowed, and she turned to watch a silver Toyota pull into the driveway and a tall, thin man in khakis and a blue polo unfold himself from the front seat, a folder tucked under one arm. She walked out to meet him. "Alan Treat." He introduced himself and handed her a card, then turned to survey the house. "I understand it was arson," he said.

"That's what the fire department investigator determined, yes."

Treat fixed her with a watery blue eye. "Have they determined who set the fire?" he asked.

"No. Someone has been making anonymous threats. They assume the arsonist was the same person."

His eyebrows were so bushy they looked fake, pasted on like a stage costume. One rose in question and she had a hard time not staring, to see if she could spot the glue. "What has a woman like you done to receive threats?" he asked.

She resented the implication that she had done anything to bring this on herself. "I don't see what any of that has to do with you," she said. "I only want to know what the settlement will be on the house, so that I can make plans."

"We don't pay claims where homeowners burn down their own homes," he said.

"I didn't burn down my own house!" She had raised her voice and glared at him. "I sent a copy of the fire investigator's report to your office. Did you even read it?"

"Most home arson fires are set by the homeowner," he said, his expression bland.

"Well, mine wasn't. And if that's all you came to say to me today you can leave, and I will be contacting my attorney."

"Now, now, there's no reason to fly off the handle."

As far as she was concerned, she had every reason to be upset with him, including but not limited to the fact that she absolutely hated being placated with phrases such as "now, now."

"Mr. Treat," she said through clenched teeth, "are you going to discuss the insurance settlement I am entitled to, or not?"

He sighed and opened the folder. He handed her a single sheet of paper. She scanned it until she came to the number at the bottom. She blinked and read it again. "The house was worth far more than this," she said.

"Your settlement is not based on the market value of your home," he said. "It is based on the amount you chose to insure the home for, less your deductible, less the cost of things that weren't destroyed in the fire."

"Everything was destroyed in the fire," she said.

"Not your foundation and the portion of the house below ground level."

She stared at the paper again, trying to make the numbers add up in her head. "I was expecting more," she said.

"Your policy had not been updated in several years," he said. "We do recommend an annual policy review and increased coverage to reflect current market conditions. You are, of course, welcome to appeal, but these things seldom come out in the homeowner's favor."

She looked at the ruins of the home again. "I understand there wasn't a mortgage on the home," Treat continued. "So you will receive a check made out to you, to do with as you wish, though you will, of course, have to pay for cleanup of this lot. I'm sure there is a city ordinance to that effect."

Yes, she would have to pay for cleanup. And then what? She had already considered building a less elaborate home, but would the amount the insurance company was offering be enough?

"If I could have your signature here, we can get the check in the mail to you in a few days." Treat pointed to a blank line at the bottom of the page.

"I don't want to sign anything right now," she said.

Treat closed the folder. "Call us when you're ready." Then he turned, got back in his car and drove away.

When Brenda was sure he was out of sight, she swore and kicked at the front stoop. But that only made her swear more, her toe throbbing. She felt like screaming and throwing things, but had no inclination to provide a free show for neighbors or passing motorists.

A familiar SUV pulled to the curb and Dwight got out. "Are you following me?" she demanded as he walked toward her, his slightly bowlegged gait so distinctive.

He stopped. "No," he said. "I saw you were here and stopped to talk. Do you want me to leave?"

"No. I'm sorry." She held up the paper, as if in explanation. "The insurance appraiser was here. Mr. Treat. And he wasn't."

"He wasn't a treat?" Dwight started forward again and came to stand beside her.

"No. He was a jerk. He accused me of burning down my own home. And then he offered me this paltry settlement and as much as said it was all my fault for not updating my policy."

Dwight glanced at the paper in her hand, but didn't ask to see it. "Is it enough money to rebuild?" he asked.

"I don't know. I don't think so." She shoved the paper at him. "And he's right—I didn't update the policy. Andy always did those things and I assumed he had purchased replacement coverage. The premium certainly went up every year. I'm mad at Andy all over again for not taking out enough insurance, and angry at myself for not thinking to review the policy once the house was in my name alone. And I'm furious with whoever put me in this position." She glared at the burned-out house. If the arsonist had come along and confessed at that moment, she thought she could have strangled him with her bare hands.

"You've had a rough morning," Dwight said.

"Yes, and you came along at just the wrong time."

"I can take it."

"I don't suppose you're any closer to knowing who did this?" She gestured toward the house.

"I'm sorry, no."

She started back toward her car, and he walked with her. "What are you up to this afternoon?" she asked, making an effort to be more cordial than she felt.

"I'm meeting Gage in a few minutes to head up to Eagle Mountain Resort. We're supposed to meet a representative of the new owners."

"New owners—already? I mean, Hake's body was only just found." A small shudder went through her at the memory.

"Apparently, these people officially took over only a few days before he disappeared."

"Who are they?"

"Another real estate development company, out of Utah, I think."

"I wonder what they plan to do with the property."

"That's one of the things we're hoping to find out." He held open the car door and returned the settlement statement to her. "What are you doing this afternoon?"

"I'm putting the finishing touches on preparations for the reception tomorrow night and the auction Saturday. Everything is almost in place. Then, tonight, I'm going out with Lacy and Paige and Maya."

"That's a good idea. You've been working hard—it will be good for you to relax a little." His eyes met hers, so serious and at the same time, tender. "I'm on duty. But call me if you need anything."

"What would I need?" She tried for a flirtatious tone, but wasn't sure she succeeded. "Are you expecting trouble?"

"I didn't mean it that way," he said. "Just that I'm here for you. Whenever."

She waited for the automatic resistance she expected at such a statement, but it didn't come. Instead she felt warmed—comforted by his words. "That's nice to know," she said. "So if I drunk-dial you at two a.m. you won't hang up on me?"

He laughed. "I promise I won't. Though I can't imagine you doing something like that."

"You never know," she said. "I'm beginning to think it's time to try a lot of new things in my life." Maybe even trusting this kind, patient man who was coming to mean so much to her.

DWIGHT TRIED TO put Brenda's troubles out of his mind and focus on work as he and Gage headed out of town toward the Eagle Mountain Resort property. "I talked to the mayor's brother, Garrett, this morning," Dwight said.

"Oh?"

"Yeah. I looked him up online. He actually has quite a few acting credits—dinner theaters, some commercials, some walk-ons in movies. So Larry was telling the truth about that."

"What about their dinner?" Gage asked.

"He confirmed that he met Larry in Junction about six and they were together until after eleven. So the mayor is off the hook."

"Yeah, well, he wasn't at the top of our list anyway," Gage said. "My money is on the guy who was with Brenda—Brownley."

"I haven't been able to find out much about him," Dwight said. "But I'm still looking."

"I ran some more background on these folks we're meeting," Gage said. "Came up with nothing. The company itself—CNG Development—is a subsidiary of a subsidiary of a holding company, and part of a consortium of capital improvement corporations, etc. etc. etc." He waved his hand. "One of these big corporate tangles even the IRS can't figure out, which I guess is the whole point."

"What about the men we're meeting today?" Dwight asked.

"Pierpoint and Reed," Gage said. "Sounds like a law firm. Nothing on them, either. Low-level corporate drones."

Dwight nodded. That was all he'd been able to come up with, as well. "I don't expect to get much out of them," he said. "They'll tell us about as much as a press release, but at least we'll be able to size them up."

"Size them up, and let them know we'll be keeping an eye on them," Gage said.

Marcus Pierpoint and Bryce Reed met the two deputies at the entrance to the property. Dressed in gray business suits and white shirts with no ties, they were cut from the same mold—middle-aged and serious, with firm handshakes and big smiles. Pierpoint was the taller of the two and did most of the talking. Reed tended to echo whatever his colleague said.

"Thanks for meeting with us this afternoon, officers," Pierpoint said after the introductions, as if the meeting had been his idea and not the sheriff's. "We're always interested in establishing good relations with local law enforcement."

"Always good to have the police on our side," Reed agreed.

"What do you know about the activities that have gone on here the past few months?" Dwight asked.

The two businessmen exchanged looks. "You're referring to illegal activities?"

Dwight and Gage said nothing.

"We're aware that wholly unauthorized persons have used the property for illegal activities," Pierpoint said.

"Wholly unauthorized," Reed echoed.

"Did you know any of these persons?" Dwight asked. "Wade Tomlinson or Brock Ryan?"

"No," Pierpoint said, while Reed shook his head.

"What about Henry Hake?" Gage asked.

"What about him?" Pierpoint asked.

"When was the last time you saw him?" Gage asked.

"We never met Mr. Hake," Pierpoint said.

"Do you know anything about his disappearance and subsequent death?" Dwight asked.

"No." Pierpoint shook his head emphatically. "We had nothing to do with any of that." He looked around the property, at the bare limbs of the aspen trees, and the piles of golden leaves among the concrete foundations of buildings that had never been completed. "We were, of course, horrified to learn of the goings-on up here. I assure you both that we intend to put a stop to anything like that."

"Oh?" Dwight waited for Pierpoint to fill in the silence that followed. He struck Dwight as a man who liked to talk.

"We will be installing new gates and locks to keep out trespassers," Pierpoint said. "And we're going to be hiring a security service to patrol the area. We want to make sure everyone knows that this is private property and trespassing will not be tolerated."

"What about the public trail?" Gage asked.

Again the look between the two. "What public trail?" Pierpoint asked.

"The one on the west side of the property," Gage said. "A court case last year established that it is a public right of way and can't be blocked."

"We contest that assertion and will be appealing," Pierpoint said.

Did the man always talk like he was presenting a case in court? Dwight wondered. "Until the court order is overturned, any gates or locks you install blocking the trail will be removed," Dwight said.

Pierpoint's expression made it clear he didn't like this, but wisely didn't argue.

"What are your plans for the property?" Gage asked.

"We will be building a private research facility on-site," Pierpoint said.

"What kind of research?" Dwight asked.

"We're not at liberty to say, but the remote location and high altitude could prove beneficial," Pierpoint said.

"Was the laboratory we found here on the property, in the underground bunker, yours?" Dwight asked.

"No," Pierpoint said. "That has nothing to do with us. We'll be building a completely modern, state-of-the-art facility."

"You'll be applying for all the proper permits from the county," Gage said.

"Of course." Reed apparently decided it was time for him to get another word in.

"Is there anything else we can do for you?" Pierpoint asked. He pulled a set of car keys from his pocket. "We have another meeting we need to get to."

"That's all for now," Dwight said.

He and Gage returned to Dwight's SUV. Pierpoint and Reed followed and Reed shut and locked the gate behind them. Dwight waited until he was on the road again before he spoke. "What do you think?" he asked Gage.

"Hard to say if they were telling the truth or not," Gage said. "I can't think of any good reason they would be linked to Henry Hake's disappearance and death—the transfer of the property was completed before he died. And it doesn't make sense they would have a connection to Wade and Brock." He shrugged. "But stranger things have happened."

"Interesting that they're going to use the place for a research facility," Dwight said.

"I don't know," Gage said. "I think high-altitude research is kind of a thing these days. There are a couple of facilities around Denver—and one in Crested Butte—studying climate and who knows what else."

Dwight nodded. "I guess so. Just seems like a remote place to do research."

"Maybe the remote location is an advantage," Gage said. He shifted in his seat. "The environmental folks might like that idea better than a big resort."

"Maybe. And the place is an eyesore in the condition it's in now."

"Do you really think they had no idea what was going on up there?" Gage asked. "I mean, that underground lab, what happened with me and Maya—and don't forget someone shot at me and at Travis on different occasions. It was like they were using that place as a headquarters for something."

"These guys are based in Utah," Dwight said. "I can see how they might not know if someone was up to something on the place. And I can see how it would attract the wrong element—all those empty buildings and the remote location. I'm glad they're going to be looking after the place now."

"That public trail is going to be a sticking point. If they try to close it, Paige and her group will fight them on it."

"Let's hope we don't have to get involved," Dwight said. "I'd be happy if I never had to go up to Eagle Mountain Resort again."

Chapter Thirteen

It didn't take long for the four women to agree that a proper night out on the town meant a town other than Eagle Mountain. "There's only one bar there, there's no place to dance, the only fancy places to eat are full of tourists, and everyone we know will see us and gossip about every move we make." Paige ticked off all the reasons the quartet had to leave town if they were really going to cut loose.

"Just how wild do you plan on this evening being?" Maya asked. A recent transplant from Denver, the high school teacher with dip-dyed blue hair probably had more party girl experience than any of them.

"I don't know," Lacy said. "Do you think we can get enough drinks in Brenda that she'll dance on a table?"

"It will never happen," Brenda said. "You know I don't drink that much. And someone has to stay sober enough to drive."

"I've already taken care of that," Lacy said. "No worries about any of us getting behind the wheel with too much to drink."

"What do you mean?" Paige asked, clearly skeptical.

"We have a driver." She gestured to the window and the street outside her parents' house. A young man dressed in jeans, a navy blazer, and a chauffeur's cap saw them all peering at him and tipped his hat.

"Parker!" Paige exclaimed.

"He had the night off, he doesn't drink as a condition of his parole, and he's a good driver," Lacy said. "I figure it would be the perfect solution."

"I'm not sure how I feel about going out with my kid brother," Paige said as the women gathered their purses and wraps and headed for the door.

"He's not going to go into the restaurant or club with us," Lacy said. "And I've already told him that if he tries to take any photographs of any of us in compromising positions, I'll take his phone and step on it." She extended one foot to display a wicked-looking stiletto heel. "I think he believed me."

Parker drove them to Junction, a college town about an hour away, in the dark blue Toyota sedan he usually used for pizza delivery. Paige had made the dinner reservations, selecting a Japanese grill where they sat on cushions around a low table while a chef made their meals to order—and flirted outrageously. They took turns daring one another to eat unfamiliar foods—they all tried the octopus, but Paige was the only one who would brave eating eel.

By her second glass of wine, Brenda realized she had laughed more in the last hour than she probably had in the last year. While a waitress cleared away their dinner plates, she excused herself to use the ladies' room.

"I'll go, too," Lacy said, and hurried after her.

"Thank you for pulling this together," Brenda said when the two friends found themselves alone in the ladies' room. "You were right—this is exactly what I needed."

"It's what I needed, too," Lacy said. "I've been working so hard at school and on plans for the wedding—it feels great to relax with friends. As much as I love Travis, being with him isn't the same as being with female friends, you know?"

Brenda nodded, too choked up to speak. In the months following Andy's death, she had too often cut herself off from others. Only recently had friends like Lacy reminded her how important other people were in her life.

A few moments later, they emerged from the restroom into the hallway that divided the restaurant into two halves—their table was in a large space full of low tables, colorful cushions, shoji screens and traditional Japanese décor. The other side of the restaurant had a more Western vibe, with dark booths and small tables.

Brenda glanced into this space and stopped short.

"What is it?" Lacy asked.

Brenda took a step back, behind a large potted firm. "That booth on the far side of the room—the second one from the left." She kept her voice low, just above a whisper. "Is that Eddie Carstairs?"

Lacy peered around the firm. "It is him! But who is he with?"

The two women stared between the fronds of the fern at Eddie, who was dressed in a dark suit a little too big for his slight frame, and at the man across from him. This man also wore a dark suit, though better tailored and obviously more expensive than Eddie's. His upper face was in shadow, only his chin visible. "I can't tell who that is," Brenda said.

"Eddie looks upset about something," Lacy said. At that moment, Eddie leaned forward, jaw set, and stabbed his finger at the man opposite. The man didn't even flinch, merely waited for Eddie to finish whatever he was saying.

Brenda tugged on Lacy's arm. "It doesn't matter. Let's get out of here before he sees us." Having to deal with Eddie would definitely put a damper on the night.

"What do you think Eddie is doing here?" Lacy asked.

Brenda shook her head. "I don't know. Maybe his brother is in town. Or a friend from college or a cousin. Or maybe it's a business meeting." The more she thought about the scene at the table, the more it struck her that way—very businesslike. Or maybe it was just that the other man seemed like a businessman to her— the tailored suit, the stoic demeanor.

"I told them to go ahead and bring our checks," Paige said when Brenda and Lacy returned to the table.

"What's next on the agenda?" Brenda asked as she fished her wallet out of her purse.

"We're going to a great club a friend told me about," Maya said. "They have a fantastic DJ and a big dance floor. Plenty of room for the four of us to get out there and show our stuff." She laughed at what must have been the expression on Brenda's face. "It's okay to dance without men, you know," she said. "Women do it all the time at places like this."

"Sure," Brenda said. "It sounds like fun." Though she couldn't help feeling a little pang of nostalgia for the times she and Andy had danced arm in arm. For all his faults, he had been a great dancer.

They paid their bills, then gathered their belongings and filed out of the dining room. Brenda and Lacy waited while Maya and Paige went to the ladies' room. They were standing in the foyer when two men emerged from the other side of the restaurant and almost collided with them. "What are you doing here?" Eddie demanded. He glared at Brenda, face flushed.

"We're having dinner," Brenda said. "The same as you." She glanced behind him, toward his companion, but the other man was already gone. She'd been so focused on Eddie, she had never gotten a good look at him.

"You must be feeling better," Lacy said. "Have they caught whoever it was who tried to poison you?"

"It wasn't poison," Eddie said. He glared at the two women. "I have to go." Then he turned and hurried out the door.

"Was that Eddie Carstairs?" Paige joined them, Maya close behind.

"Yes," Lacy said. "He apparently decided to have dinner here, too."

"I guess he won't want pizza for a long time." Maya covered her mouth and giggled. "I'm sorry, that was probably mean."

"He wasn't happy to see us, that's for sure," Brenda said. The women trooped out to the parking lot, where Parker met them at the car. He had opted to go across the street to a popular burger place for dinner.

"How was your dinner?" Brenda asked as he unlocked the car for them.

"Good. I met a couple of cute girls." He grinned. "One of them gave me her number."

"Since when are you such a flirt?" Paige asked.

"You should try it sometime, sis," he said. "It's fun."

"Oh no!"

At the cry from the rear of the car, the others turned to find Maya staring down at the rear wheel. She looked up at them, dismayed. "We've got a flat."

"Let me see." Parker moved to her side and knelt to check the tire, which was, indeed, deflated.

"You have a spare, right?" Paige asked.

Parker stood and walked around the rear of the car to the other side. "I have one spare," he said. "But both rear tires are flat."

"Did we run over nails or something?" Lacy looked around, as if expecting to find the cause of the tire damage nearby.

"Or something." Parker turned to Paige. "Maybe you'd better call the cops."

"Why?" she asked, even as she pulled out her phone.

"We didn't run over anything," Parker said. "Both tires have been slashed."

"EDDIE'S THE OBVIOUS suspect for slashing the tires, but he denies everything," Dwight said when he saw Brenda the next night before the museum reception. Whereas when she had called last night to tell him about the incident in the restaurant parking lot she had been clearly upset, tonight she was the picture of calm, in an ankle-length midnight-blue dress that bared her shoulders and clung to her curves, subtle silver threads shimmering with every movement. She wore her blond hair piled on top of her head, delicate tendrils framing her face. The overall effect was elegant and incredibly sexy.

He had traded in his uniform for a dark gray Western-cut suit and polished python boots, though he was technically on the job, his service weapon in a holster beneath the jacket. Travis and Gage were in attendance as well, to beef up the security provided by Eddie. They would keep an eye on the valuable auction items, but Dwight's main focus was on protecting Brenda.

"I don't think Eddie did it," she said. "I don't see

how he would have had time. We were talking to him in the lobby of the restaurant right up until we walked out to the car."

"What about his friend?" Dwight asked. "The man he was having dinner with. You said he left the restaurant ahead of Eddie."

"Maybe." She frowned. "But why? Neither Lacy nor I recognized him. We really didn't get a good look at him. His face was in shadow in the restaurant."

"I wish you had seen him. I'd love to know who he is."

"Do you think he's the same person who brought Eddie the doctored pizza?" she asked.

"Maybe." Dwight had already considered this—whoever had dosed that pizza with sleeping pills had been someone Eddie either wanted to protect, or didn't want to admit to knowing. "But then, why would Eddie go out to dinner with him a few nights later?"

"Maybe Eddie set up the meeting to confront the guy about the pizza. He wanted to do it away from Eagle Mountain, where someone might see them together. That would explain why he was so upset to run into us."

"Maybe." He looked around the crowd. At least eighty people were in attendance, drifting through the rooms of the museum, sipping cocktails and nibbling canapés, admiring the items on display and checking out the auction items arrayed on tables in the front rooms. Attire ranged from business suits and cocktail dresses to jeans and T-shirts. He didn't recognize a dozen or more of the guests, though he spotted the mayor across the room, in conversation with the woman who headed up the local beautification committee. "Is Robert Brownley here?" he asked.

"I haven't seen him. Why?"

"I tried to find out some background information on him, but I couldn't come up with anything."

"I did an online search, too," she admitted. "But nothing I came up with sounded like him. But if he's as wealthy as he seemed, maybe he purposely keeps a low profile."

"Maybe." There were too many maybes involved in this case.

"Oh look, there's Professor Gibson." She touched Dwight's arm. "Excuse me, I want to speak to him."

"Of course." Dwight watched her cross the room and greet the professor. She smiled at the older man, and Dwight felt a now-familiar catch in his chest. He would never get tired of looking at that smile, of watching the play of emotions on her face. He could imagine himself looking at her this way when they were both twenty or forty or sixty years older. The problem was—how could he persuade her to see that kind of future? She had been hurt so much in the past, he had the sense that she was afraid to look too far ahead.

Patience, he told himself. That was the key to dealing with Brenda—and the key to investigating any case. He went to join Travis by the auction display. The sheriff wore a black Western jacket, black jeans and a black Stetson, with a white shirt and string tie. Lacy, in a sleeveless red cocktail dress trimmed with fringe, stood beside him. They made a striking couple.

"Hello, Lacy." Dwight touched the brim of his hat and nodded to her.

"Don't you look handsome." She turned to Travis. "All of you clean up so well."

Travis's answer was a grunt. Lacy laughed. "You'd rather be in uniform, wouldn't you?" She kissed his cheek. "Dwight has a look in his eye like he wants to talk shop, so I'm going to visit with Paige." She smiled at Dwight and left them.

"Anyone particularly interested in the book?" Dwight asked.

"Nope." Travis glanced toward where the book sat on a raised platform in the very center of the table to their left. "A couple of people have looked at it, but no one has lingered." He shifted toward his deputy. "How's Brenda doing?"

"She seems calm. I think the whole episode with the tire annoyed her more than it frightened her."

Travis nodded. "She doesn't frighten easily."

"She said Robert Brownley hasn't shown up."

"Anybody else here who shouldn't be?"

"Brenda didn't mention anyone." Laughter rose from a knot of people near the door to the hallway and he turned to look toward them. "There are quite a few people from out of town."

"Let's hope they bid high and the museum makes some money," Travis said. He looked toward the auction items again. "Lacy has her heart set on that quilt. I put in a bid on it—thought it might make a good wedding present."

"I imagine it would." This brought to mind the question of what *he* should give the happy couple as a gift—something that hadn't occurred to him until this moment.

Fortunately, he didn't have to wrestle with this question for long. The arrival of Eddie Carstairs interrupted him. Unlike the dressed-up sheriff and deputies, he wore khaki pants and shirt that looked very much like the Rayford County Sheriff's Department uniforms, though in place of the sheriff's department patch, his shirt had a dark blue star with the word *Security* embroidered in gold lettering across it. "What are you two doing hovering around the auction items?" Eddie asked.

"Just keeping an eye on them," Travis said.

"That's my job." Eddie rested his hand at his hip, very near the holster for a pistol. He had a permit for the weapon, and his sheriff's department training would have ensured he knew how to use it safely, but the sight of it still made Dwight uncomfortable. Maybe that was behind Dwight's decision to make Eddie uncomfortable in turn.

"Who were you having dinner with last night?" Dwight asked.

Eddie's cheeks flushed. "We already went over all that," he said. "It's none of your business."

"It's my business if he slashed the tires on the car Brenda and her friends were in." Dwight could feel Travis's steady gaze on him. Was the sheriff going to reprimand him for interrogating a witness in a public place like this? Or was Travis merely waiting to see what Eddie would say?

"Maybe Parker slashed the tires himself to make me look bad," Eddie said. "Did you ever think of that?"

Dwight looked over Eddie's shoulder to where Parker Riddell, in black pants and a white long-sleeved shirt that hid his many tattoos, offered a group of silver-haired women a tray of bacon-wrapped shrimp. He had considered the idea that Parker had slashed the tires, either to frighten the women or to call attention to himself for some reason. But everything he had learned from the people who knew and worked with him confirmed that Parker was staying on the straight and narrow. Brenda certainly thought so, and her opinion carried more and more weight with Dwight.

"What is he doing here, anyway?" Eddie asked. "He

doesn't have any business being around all these valuable items. If anything disappears, he's my number one suspect."

Travis and Dwight both ignored the comment. Dwight could almost hear Eddie's teeth grinding in frustration at his failure to elicit a response.

"Who is that man Brenda is talking to?" Eddie asked.

Dwight followed Eddie's gaze to where Brenda stood with Professor Gibson, their heads inclined toward each other, deep in conversation. He was tempted to tell Eddie the man's identity was none of his business, but Travis answered, "That's Professor Gibson. He owned that book—*The Secret History of Rayford County*—before Andy Stenson got hold of it."

Eddie studied the couple. "He and Brenda certainly look cozy," he said. He turned to Dwight. "You might have some competition, Prentice."

Dwight glared at him. He could either deny anything was going on between him and Brenda—which would be a lie—or remain silent and confirm Eddie's suspicions. The man was a worse gossip than Adelaide, and in Eddie's case, Dwight always had the sense Eddie was searching for any scrap of information he could use to his own advantage. He decided to play it cool. "I wasn't aware we were running a race. Excuse me. I see someone I'd like to speak with." The mayor had just entered the room, and as long as he was here, Dwight wanted to find out where Brenda's boss—and Eddie's, for that matter—had been when Brenda's tires were being slashed.

"Professor, I'd like you to meet Parker Riddell. He's one of my best volunteers—and he's studying history at the community college." Brenda had waylaid the young man as he hurried past with yet another tray or hors d'oeuvres.

"Always good to meet a young person who's interested in history." Professor Gibson offered his hand. "Is there a particular period you'd like to focus on?"

Parker shifted the serving tray and shook the professor's hand. "I'm not sure, sir. American history. The West. And I'm really interested in World War II."

Gibson nodded and asked a few more questions about the classes Parker was currently enrolled in, and made some recommendations of books he should read. "History isn't the most lucrative field these days," he said. "But it can be a very rewarding one."

"I hope so, sir." Parker shifted the tray again. "I'd better go pass these out before they get cold. It was nice to meet you."

"Nice to meet you, too, young man."

When Parker had left them, the professor turned back to Brenda. "You've done a wonderful job with this place," he said. "It's a real gem."

"We think so," Brenda said. Now seemed as good a time as any to bring up what was, after all, an awkward subject. "I want to thank you for being so understanding about *The Secret History of Rayford County, Colorado*. I truly had no idea my late husband had borrowed it from you when I listed it for auction."

"If I thought you had, I might not have been so understanding," Gibson said. "As it is, proving my claim would have been difficult, and I'm pleased to have the sale go to support a worthy cause. I'm curious, though—did you read the book?"

"I did. More than once. And I made quite a few notes."

He nodded. "At one time I tried very hard to determine where the secret lab might have been located. My theory is the government destroyed it once the project ended. Otherwise someone would have found it by now."

"The sheriff's department found what looked like a laboratory up at Eagle Mountain Resort, but it apparently wasn't nearly old enough to have been used during the war."

"Government documents are being declassified all the time," Gibson said. "I imagine before too many more years, someone will find out the location. In the meantime, that book attracts attention from everyone from conspiracy theorists to serious collectors. I hope it brings a high price to help support the museum."

She looked around, past the well-dressed guests to the photos and displays on the walls. To many people, the items in these rooms were just old junk, relics of a time long past. But to Brenda and other history lovers, they were links to the past—a look at how the people who had settled this part of the country had once lived. She believed those people still had lessons to teach. "I love this place," she said. "And I'm determined to do everything I can to keep it going."

"I have some ideas about that I'd love to talk to you about," the professor said. "I know—"

But a terrified scream cut off his words and silenced the conversations of those around them. A man Brenda didn't know, face blanched paper-white, staggered into the room. "Upstairs…a body…hanging," he gasped.

Chapter Fourteen

Dwight pushed through the crowd toward the stairs, Travis close behind him. "Police! Let us through!" he shouted, over the panicked voices of those rushing down the narrow staircase. Men and women turned sideways to let him pass, their frightened faces a blur as he mounted the steps two at a time. At the top, he paused and looked around.

"In there!" A man motioned toward a room to the left. Travis moved up beside Dwight, his gun drawn. "You take right. I'll go in on the left."

Dwight nodded. They had no reason to believe anyone dangerous was inside the room, but best to be prepared. Heart hammering, he moved to the right side of the door. Travis positioned himself across from him. At his nod, they went in, guns drawn.

Dwight's breath caught as he came face-to-face with a man in white—then he felt foolish, and a little shaky, as he realized the figure was actually a mannequin in a World War II sailor's uniform. He scanned the rest of the room, which was filled with old military paraphernalia, from helmets and maps to a Vietnam-era field radio and navy semaphore flags.

The body hung from the ceiling in the corner, positioned so that someone had to enter the room to see it.

In the dimmer light in that part of the room, it did indeed look human—but closer inspection revealed that this, too, was a mannequin, dressed in the olive drab of a World War II-era sergeant.

Travis holstered his weapon. "Someone's idea of a sick joke," he said.

"What is it? Someone said there was a body?"

Eddie, red-faced and out of breath, appeared behind them, his gun drawn.

"Put that weapon away," Travis barked. "And go back downstairs."

Eddie holstered the gun, but made no move to leave. "I'm the security guard for the museum," he said. "I need to know what's going on."

"Nothing's going on," Dwight said. He gestured to the hanging mannequin. "Some joker decided to play a prank."

Eddie started to approach the mannequin, but Travis waved him back. "Stay out of the crime scene," he ordered.

Eddie laughed. "Crime scene? It's a mannequin."

"Someone wanted to frighten the people here tonight," Travis said. "I want to know who."

Brenda appeared behind Eddie in the doorway to the room, looking pale but determined. "What is going on?" she asked.

"Someone hung one of your mannequins from a ceiling beam," Travis said. "Then someone looked in, thought it was a body in the dim light and panicked."

Brenda moved into the room and looked toward the mannequin in the corner. She shuddered. "It certainly does look like a body from here. Who would do such a thing?"

"Where have you been, Eddie?" Dwight asked.

"Are you accusing me of doing something like this? I've been working, protecting the visitors to the museum and the museum's valuable property."

Dwight didn't let his disdain show on his face. Eddie acted as if he had personally been guarding every exhibit.

"The auction items!" Brenda's eyes widened and she started to turn away.

"Gage is guarding them," Travis said.

Dwight nodded. "You thought this might be a distraction—get us all up here and the thief could help himself to whatever he liked downstairs."

"It was a possibility." Travis looked up at the dangling mannequin. "Let's close off this room until we can get a crime scene team in to take a look. And we'll need to talk to whoever was up here when it was discovered."

"Some people have already left," Brenda said. "I think we can safely say this has put a damper on the evening." She turned around to look toward the hallway. "There have been dozens of people in and out of these rooms all night. How could someone do this without being seen?"

Dwight studied the layout of the room. "You can't see this corner from the hallway," he said. "If our prankster had the rope handy, he could wait until he was alone in here and loop it around the mannequin's neck. Throw the rope over the beam, hoist up the mannequin, secure the rope and stroll out. It might take less than a minute."

"You can ask if anyone saw anything," Brenda said. "Maybe you'll get lucky."

"Maybe." Travis didn't sound convinced.

"Do you have a guest list or anything with the names of everyone who attended tonight?" Dwight asked.

"There's a guest book—but whether or not people signed it was up to them."

"Let's go get it."

He descended the stairs right behind her, and a crowd of people surrounded them, firing questions—most versions of "What happened?"

"False alarm," he said, one hand at Brenda's back. He leaned closer to whisper in her ear, the floral scent of her perfume momentarily distracting him, but he forced his attention back to the task at hand. "You'd better make an announcement and send them home."

She nodded and climbed back up a few steps until she was above the crowd. Everyone fell silent. "Thank you all so much for coming tonight," she said. "I hope we see all of you at the auction tomorrow morning. You'll be able to get another look at all the items available tomorrow starting at nine a.m. See you then."

Eddie had appeared on the stairs behind Brenda as she spoke. As he came down after her, Dwight snagged his arm. "Help herd everyone out the door," he said.

Eddie opened his mouth as if to argue, but apparently thought better of it. He nodded and moved on, murmuring, "Good night," and, "Thank you for coming," as he urged people toward the open front doors.

"I want to check with Gage that the auction items are all right," Brenda said to Dwight.

"Good idea." They fought their way against the flow of the crowd to the next room, where Gage stood between the tables of auction items. "Any problems?" Dwight asked.

"Everything is still here, and I didn't notice anyone paying particular attention to me or the merchandise," Gage said. "What happened up there?"

"Someone hung a mannequin from a ceiling beam,"

Dwight said, keeping his voice low, though only a few people remained, waiting for their turn to exit.

"Sick joke," Gage said.

"Maybe," Dwight said.

"Eddie is supposed to be on duty all night," Brenda said. "But I'd feel better if one of you would take the book back to the station and lock it in the safe until morning." She picked up *The Secret History of Rayford County, Colorado.* "It's by far our most valuable item."

"I'll make sure it's safe." Dwight took the book from her. Gone was the sparkling, happy woman of earlier in the evening. She looked exhausted, weighed down by worry. "We don't know that the hung mannequin had anything to do with the book," he said.

"No, but too many unsettling things have been happening." She looked around the room. "I need to get you that guest book."

He followed her back to the entry hall, where they found Lacy with Travis. "Do you need me to stay and help with anything?" Lacy asked.

"No, thank you," Brenda said. "I'm going to go in a few minutes myself."

"We'll be here a little while longer," Travis said. "We'll lock up when we leave, and we'll be back in the morning for the auction."

"So will I." Lacy squeezed Brenda's shoulder. "Are you okay?"

Brenda nodded. "I'm fine."

Lacy frowned, but didn't say anything else. "I'll walk you to your car," Travis said, and they headed out the door.

"The guest book is over here," Brenda said, walking to a small desk to the right of the door. The guest book, bound in blue leather, lay open on the top, a brass can filled with pens next to it. Signatures half filled the open page. Brenda picked up the book and flipped through it. "I don't see Robert Brownley's name here," she said. "And I didn't see him among the guests. Maybe he changed his mind about bidding for the book."

"Or maybe, since he plans to outbid everyone else, he'll be here tomorrow." Dwight slid the book from her hand, closed it and tucked it under his arm. He stroked her cheek. "Are you okay?"

She sighed. "I'm ready for all this to be over." She shook her head. "I don't know why that stupid mannequin upset me so much. It's just a sick joke, like Gage said. But it took me back to when we found Henry Hake…"

Her voice trailed away. Dwight set the book on the desk once more and pulled her to him. She rested her head on his shoulder, and he held her tightly for a long moment, saying nothing. He closed his eyes and let himself revel in the sweet scent and soft feel of her. When all this was over, he'd ask her to go away with him somewhere—a beach where they could lie side by side on the sand and sip fruity drinks. He smiled, picturing Brenda in a bikini.

"What are you smiling about?" She pushed away from him.

"How did you know I was smiling?" he asked, his expression solemn once more.

"I felt it." She rested a hand on his chest.

"I'll tell you later," he said. "Now, go home and get some rest. I'll take care of everything here."

She looked past him, at the crime scene techs filing up the stairs. "I feel like I should stay."

"There's nothing you can do. Go home and rest."

"All right. Let me get my purse." He waited while

she retrieved her purse from her office, then walked with her to her car.

"We'll talk in the morning," he said. "Try not to worry."

She nodded. "I'm not going to let a stupid prank get the best of me." She rose on tiptoe to kiss his cheek. "I was thinking…instead of going to the ranch house, I might wait for you at your cabin."

The words sent a current of heat through him. "I'd like that." He fished his key from his pocket and pressed it into her palm. "You'll need this."

"Try not to be too late."

No, he'd be wrapping up his business here as quickly as possible. One lifeless mannequin couldn't compete with the very live woman he would have waiting for him.

AT LEAST HER bold suggestion to Dwight had provided a welcome distraction from the terrible way the evening had ended, Brenda thought as she drove through town. When he had pulled her to him and held her—just held her, without offering empty words or advice—she had felt so comforted and *supported*. He wasn't hovering or trying to control her or dismiss her or any of the things she had experienced at the hands of other men. Dwight was simply there for her, letting her find her own strength by lending her some of his. His calm, practical nature was exactly what she needed.

But Dwight was more than a calming presence or a strong friend. He was a man she wanted to be with more and more. Time to stop denying that and admit what was happening. In spite of all her efforts to resist— all the *logical* reasons this shouldn't be happening—

Brenda had fallen in love with Dwight. The realization made her a little light-headed.

Maybe, when things had calmed down—after the auction at least—she would find a way to tell him.

That is, if she could get through the auction with no more disasters. At least it hadn't been a real body hanging in the display room, but who would do something like that? Was someone trying to frighten her?

Everyone in Eagle Mountain—and anyone who read the local newspaper—would have known that she and Dwight had found Henry Hake hanging in that underground laboratory at Eagle Mountain Resort. Was that mannequin supposed to be a sick reminder of that event—or some kind of warning?

She rubbed her temple, trying to ward off the headache that was building there. It didn't make sense, but then, nothing that had happened really did. She went over all the events in her mind—the two threatening notes on cheery yellow stationery, the crime scene photo from Andy's murder, the stolen banner announcing the auction, the fire that had destroyed her house, the slashed tires on the car that had been transporting her and her friends—and now this hanging mannequin. It was such a crazy combination of shocking violence and almost juvenile pranks. Everything seemed to have been aimed at either her or the museum, but why?

She turned onto the county road that led from town up to the Prentices' ranch. She couldn't keep from going over the events in her mind. It was like trying to find a missing piece in a jigsaw puzzle—find that piece, that link, and everything would make sense. She would have a clear picture where there had been only chaos before.

Glaring lights filled the car, reflecting off the rearview mirror and into her eyes as a vehicle with its brights on came up behind her. Brenda put up a hand to shield her eyes from the glare and stepped on the brakes. She pulled the Subaru toward the shoulder, hoping the rude person behind her would pass. The car—or probably a truck, judging by the height of the headlights—was approaching very fast, obviously in a hurry to get somewhere. She would have pulled off the road altogether, but there wasn't room. The Eagle River followed the road here, the waters spilling over rocks some ten feet below.

She shifted her gaze to her side mirror and realized the other driver wasn't slowing down. He was traveling much too fast for this narrow, winding road. She took her foot off the brake and sped up, thinking she should drive until there was a safe place to pull over. But she had no time to gain much speed before the other vehicle was on her. Horrified, she realized the other driver wasn't going to stop. He hit her full-on, throwing her forward, her airbag exploding with painful violence, the car skidding off the pavement, rocketing down the bank of the river and into the icy water.

Chapter Fifteen

Pain throbbed in Brenda's head, and her chest hurt. She moaned and tried to shift into a more comfortable position, held upright by her seat belt. Confused, she opened her eyes and stared through the spiderwebbed windshield into a tangle of broken tree limbs and underbrush illuminated by one headlight. The lights on the dash bathed the interior of the car in a faint blue glow. The airbags had deflated, though their powdery residue lay like a dusting of sugar over everything. As her still-painful head began to clear, Brenda realized the car was still running. She felt around on the steering column and found the key, and turned it to cut the motor.

She had expected silence, but instead heard a car door slam and someone approaching, clumsy footsteps slipping and sliding on the steep embankment down from the road. The memory of the bright headlights rushing toward her sent panic through her, and she grappled to unfasten the seat belt. If her attacker was coming after her, she would have to run, to hide—

She was still fumbling with the seat belt when her door was wrenched open. A tall, dark figure, face covered by a black ski mask, grabbed her arm and shook her. "Give it to me!" he demanded, in a gruff, unfamiliar voice.

"G-give you what?" Brenda stared up at him, fighting for calm. She had to think, but her head hurt so much—the pain made her nauseous.

"Give me the book!"

The book. She wished she had never laid eyes on that cursed book. "I don't have it," she said.

"It's not at the museum. Where is it?"

"The sheriff has it."

Her attacker let loose a stream of invective that had her shrinking back. But even as she did so, she put her right hand down by her side, on the button to release the seat belt. As soon as she saw her chance, she would leap from the car and run. Better to risk the dangers of the mountainside than this madman.

"You're lying!" He punctuated this statement by thrusting a pistol in her face. Brenda had seen plenty of firearms in her life. Her father had collected guns. The museum owned several antique pistols and rifles. But she had never been eye to eye with a weapon that was pointed directly at her. She was both terrified and icily calm.

"I'm not lying," she said, shocked by how even her voice sounded. It was almost as if some other person— a cooler, more courageous person—had taken over her body. "The sheriff has the book."

"Give me your purse." He thrust the gun toward her.

"It's in the passenger seat," she said. "You're welcome to it."

He reached past her and grabbed the purse, as well as the tote bag that contained auction paperwork she had planned to look over before she returned to work in the morning. He riffled through these items, then tossed them onto the ground at his feet. She bit her tongue to keep from pointing out that she had already told him she didn't have the book. Why wouldn't he believe her?

"Where were you going tonight?" he asked, the end of the barrel of the gun only a few inches from her forehead.

"I was going home," she said.

"You don't live out this way," he said.

I didn't until you burned down my house, she thought. But then, maybe this man hadn't burned her house. She had no way of knowing. "I'm staying with friends," she said.

"Friends? Or one particular friend?" He reached over and unsnapped the seat belt, then dragged her from the car. "You're staying with that cop, aren't you? The tall, dark-haired one."

Brenda said nothing.

"He lives on a ranch, doesn't he?" the man asked. When she didn't answer, he yanked on her arm—hard.

She cried out and tried to pull away, but he only held on tighter and dragged her after him. "Come on," he said.

"Where are you taking me?" she asked.

"To wait for your boyfriend."

WRAPPING THINGS UP at the museum took longer than Dwight had wanted. Usually, he appreciated how methodical and thorough Travis could be, but tonight the routine had chafed. Brenda was waiting, and Dwight didn't want to lose the chance to be with her—not just to make love, though he certainly hoped they would do that, but to talk to her about something besides the case. About their future.

Finally, he had gotten away, with a reminder from Travis that he would need a report on his desk in the morning. Dwight had suppressed a groan and nodded, then hurried away, leaving Travis and Gage to lock up the museum. He pushed the SUV on the drive to the ranch, though the narrow, curvy road limited how fast he could safely travel. He watched the sides of the road for deer or elk that might decide to leap out in front of him. He had attended more than one wreck caused by wildlife. Most of the people involved escaped with only minor damage, but he still remembered one young woman who had been killed when her truck rolled down the embankment, crushing her, after she swerved to avoid a deer.

His headlights glanced off a vehicle parked ahead, half on the shoulder, half in his lane, and he braked. The car appeared empty, not running. Had someone abandoned it like this? He prepared to pull in behind it. He might have to call a tow truck to retrieve the big SUV—another delay, but necessary. Parked as it was, the vehicle was a real hazard.

But as he pulled in behind the SUV, two figures emerged ahead of the vehicle, climbing up from the stream bank. The larger figure—a man—appeared to be dragging the smaller one—a woman—behind him. Dwight hit his brights and recognized Brenda's battered face even as his windshield was shattered and the sound of a gunshot echoed around them.

Dwight threw himself to the floorboard, drawing his pistol as he wedged himself beneath the steering column. "You can come out now, Deputy," a man's voice shouted. "Come out with your hands up and I promise I won't shoot you. But try anything and I'll kill your girlfriend here."

Dwight didn't answer. He glanced at the radio, wondering if he could reach it and call for help. But a woman's scream, sharp and filled with pain, froze him. "Come out now!" the voice demanded. "Unless you want me to kill her now."

"I'm coming out!" Dwight answered, and raised his hands, though the rest of him remained shielded by the cruiser's door.

"Throw out your weapon."

Dwight tossed the gun onto the ground.

"Now come out with your hands up."

Everything within him resisted the idea of stepping out and exposing himself to the shooter, but the idea that Brenda could die if he hesitated propelled him to open the door and step into the open. A stocky man with a black knit ski mask pulled over his face held Brenda by one arm, a long-barreled pistol pressed to the side of her head. Brenda locked her eyes to Dwight's, determination shining through the fear. She trusted him to get them out of this, and that knowledge made him stronger.

"What do you want?" Dwight asked.

"I want the book," the man said.

"The Secret History of Rayford County?" Dwight wished he had urged Brenda to burn the book when she received the first threatening note.

"Yes. I want it."

"I don't have it."

The man drove the barrel of the gun into Brenda's cheek so that she cried out. "Don't lie to me!"

"The book is at the sheriff's department," Dwight said. "In the safe."

"Then we're going to go get it," the man said. He adjusted his grip on Brenda's arm. "But we don't need her to get it."

Instinct overwhelmed reason as Dwight realized what the man intended to do. With a roar, he launched himself at the other man, even as the pistol flashed in the darkness and the explosion of gunfire rang in the night stillness. Brenda's scream merged with his own cry of rage as he and the shooter grappled on the ground. Dwight clawed and kicked at the other man, who was shorter but heavier than him. And he knew how to fight.

He slammed his fist into the side of Dwight's head as Dwight grabbed hold of the pistol and tried to wrench it away. Dwight drove his elbow into the man's stomach, then thrust up his head, striking his assailant's chin and forcing his head back. The man roared in either pain or anger, and punched Dwight in the nose. Pain exploded behind his eyes and his vision went black, but he kept hold of the gun and struggled onto his knees, battling for equilibrium.

When the other man tried to kick him, Dwight scrambled out of the way, keeping hold of the gun and forcing the man's hand back at an awkward angle. The man cried out in pain, and Dwight shoved harder, putting all his weight behind the move. The man's fingers loosened, and Dwight seized the gun and trained it on the man.

But the other man shoved up to his feet and ran, the black of his clothing blending into the darkness. Dwight fired, but the shot went wide. Seconds later, the man was in the big SUV. Dwight steadied the gun with both hands and fired again, but only succeeded in taking out one taillight as the vehicle sped away.

Dazed and vaguely aware of blood streaming down his face, Dwight clutched the gun and tried to steady his breathing and think past the pain. A low moan cleared some of the fog engulfing him. "Brenda!" He looked around and heard the moan again, to his right. He unhooked his MagLite from his belt and played the beam along the shoulder of the road until he saw her. She lay back in the gravel and leaf litter, blood bathing her torso, her face ghostly white, her eyes closed.

"Brenda!" He shouted her name, but she didn't stir. He shoved to his feet and ran to her, dropping to his knees beside her. "Brenda!" He took her hand, staring at the blood covering the front of her shirt.

She moaned again, and her eyes fluttered open. "Dwight." She struggled, as if trying to sit.

"Don't move." He put one hand on her shoulder to keep her from rising. "Where are you hurt?"

"My shoulder."

He trained the light on her left shoulder and surveyed the round hole that was seeping blood. The blood loss was a concern, but at least she hadn't been shot in the chest or stomach or head. "Lie still," he said. "I'm going to call for help and get the first aid kit from my cruiser."

"All right."

He ran to the cruiser, ignoring the pain from his nose, which was probably broken. Once there, he grabbed the radio, identified himself, asked for an ambulance for a gunshot victim and gave his location. "The shooter is a man about five ten, a hundred and eighty pounds, driving a black Land Rover, license Alfa, Foxtrot, Sierra, two, two, eight."

He retrieved the first aid kit and returned to Brenda. "I'm going to put some gauze on this wound and apply pressure to try to stop the bleeding," he said. "It might hurt, and I'm sorry about that."

"It's okay." She blinked at him, clearly dazed. "What happened to your face?"

He reached up and touched his nose, and winced as

a fresh jolt of pain made him catch his breath. "I think the guy who shot you broke it."

"He ran me off the road," she said. "My car is down by the creek somewhere. My head hurts." She closed her eyes.

Did she have a concussion, too? Other injuries he didn't know about? "Talk to me," he said. "Try to stay awake. Do you know the guy? Did you recognize him from anywhere?"

"No. He wore a mask. Why did he shoot me?"

"I don't know." He made a thick pad from the gauze and pressed down hard on the wound. Brenda cried out and tried to roll away, but he held her firm. "We need to stop the bleeding," he said. "The ambulance will be here soon." Or he hoped it would be. If the ambulance crew were out on another call, it could take a while before they reached them. Meanwhile, he would do everything he could to help. "Do you think the man was Robert Brownley?" he asked.

She furrowed her brown. "Robert Browning? The poet?"

"Robert Brownley. The man who came to see you at the museum and wanted to bid on the book."

"I… I don't know." She looked at him, eyes full of questions behind the pain. "Why do you think that?"

"I recognized the SUV he was driving." In which case, Robert Brownley probably wasn't the man's real name, but Dwight had alerted his fellow law enforcement officers about the license plate of the Land Rover and the fact that it only had one taillight. He hoped someone would stop Brownley before he had time to ditch the vehicle and switch to another.

"I don't know," Brenda said. "I can't think very clearly right now."

"Don't worry about it now. Do you hurt anywhere else—besides your head and your shoulder?"

Before she could answer the question, headlight beams illuminated them, and tires crunched on gravel as a red Jeep Wagoneer pulled in in front of Dwight's cruiser. Still pressing down on the gauze pad, Dwight squinted over his shoulder at the vehicle and the man who climbed out of the driver's seat.

"What happened?" Eddie Carstairs asked, hurrying toward them.

"Brenda's been shot," Dwight said. "An ambulance is on its way. Maybe you can walk down the road a little ways and watch for it and flag it down."

"Sure." Eddie took a few steps closer. "Is she okay?"

"I'm going to be fine," Brenda said before Dwight could answer. The strength in her voice encouraged him. He reached out to stroke the side of her face.

"Yes, you're going to be fine," he said. "I think the bleeding has almost stopped."

"What happened?" Eddie asked again.

"Some guy ran her off the road and shot her," Dwight said. "He wanted that book—the one about the World War II laboratories. I got his plate number and every cop in the state will be looking for him soon."

"Looks like he almost got the better of you," Eddie said, leaning down to peer at Dwight's face.

"Eddie, what are you doing here?" Brenda asked. "You're supposed to be at the museum."

"I came to find you. You and Dwight." He reached behind him and drew his gun. "I need you to take me to the book."

Chapter Sixteen

Dwight reached for his weapon, but Eddie lashed out, kicking him viciously. Brenda's scream echoed around them as Dwight fell back. When he sat up, Eddie had the gun trained on Brenda. "You need to cooperate with me or I'll shoot her." His voice shook a little, but his hand remained steady. "Don't think I won't do it."

"Eddie, why?" Brenda asked.

"Nothing personal against you," Eddie said. "But I'm sworn to do my duty." He motioned to Dwight. "Stand up. We need to get going."

Dwight stood, and Brenda struggled to prop herself up on one elbow. "What do you mean, your duty?" she asked.

"I don't have time to explain now." He took Dwight's elbow. "We have to go."

Where is that ambulance? Dwight thought. "I'm not leaving Brenda," he said.

"Of course not," Eddie said. "Do you think I'm stupid enough to leave her to tell the paramedics where we are and what we're doing? She's coming with us."

"She's injured," Dwight protested. "She needs medical care."

"Then I'll just have to finish her off." Eddie shifted the gun toward her.

"No!" Brenda struggled to sit, one hand keeping the gauze pad in place over her wound. "I'll go with you. You just have to help me up." This last she directed at Dwight. He wanted to argue that she should lie still, but he didn't trust Eddie not to carry out his threat to kill her. The security guard looked desperate and a little unhinged.

"It's going to be all right," Dwight whispered in Brenda's ear as he helped her to stand. "Just hang in there." Eddie thought they were at his mercy, but at the first opportunity, Dwight would prove he was wrong.

BRENDA FOUGHT WAVES of nausea and dizziness as Dwight half carried her to Eddie's Jeep. Her shoulder throbbed with pain, and she took shallow breaths, trying to avoid moving it. But that didn't help much, as every step over the rough ground jarred the wound. Dwight pressed the gauze tightly against her, adding to the agony, though she knew it was necessary to keep her from bleeding to death. She fought back panic. She wasn't going to die. Not over some stupid book.

Not when she had finally found Dwight.

Eddie stood beside them while Dwight helped her climb into the Jeep. She loathed the idea of sitting next to Eddie, but he wasn't giving her any choice. When Dwight had buckled her seat belt, Eddie prodded him with the gun. "Now let's take care of your cruiser."

"What about my cruiser?" Dwight asked.

"You don't think I'm stupid enough to let you leave it here, where anyone coming along might see it and call in a report about an abandoned cop vehicle?" He jabbed Dwight in the shoulder with the gun. "Come on."

Dwight looked at Brenda. Maybe if she'd been in better shape, she could have used this opportunity to run for help, but it was taking every ounce of strength she could muster to remain upright in the truck. "I'll be right back," Dwight said.

She nodded.

As soon as he had left her, she closed her eyes, but opened them again as that seemed to make the dizziness worse. She studied the contents of Eddie's Jeep—fast-food wrappers and discarded cups stained with coffee littered the floormats, while gas receipts, maps and other papers almost obscured the dashboard. She saw nothing in the debris that gave her a clue as to why he was doing this. Were he and the man who had shot her working together—or were they rivals, both wanting *The Secret History of Rayford County, Colorado* for some reason?

Maybe all this had something to do with money, she thought. Eddie struck her as a man who was very motivated by money. He was always talking about how hard up he was since he had been let go from the sheriff's department—even though as a reserve officer, he had worked only part time and made very little. But it was probably easier to blame Travis for his woes than admit that his own actions had led to his downfall.

An engine raced, startling her. She raised her eyes to the rearview mirror and gasped as Dwight's SUV rolled toward the drop-off on the opposite side of the road. The front wheels left the pavement and the vehicle lurched forward, then tumbled over the edge, the sound of it hitting and bouncing off the rocks echoing in the still night air.

The two men returned to the Jeep. Dwight's hands were cuffed behind his back—Brenda assumed with his own handcuffs. Eddie waited until he had slid into the passenger seat beside Brenda, then he shut the door and walked around to the driver's side. "What are we going to do?" Brenda whispered.

"Wait for an opportunity," Dwight said.

Eddie slammed the door behind him and put the Jeep into gear. He held the gun in his right hand, his left on the steering wheel. "Just remember, Dwight. If you try anything, I'll shoot Brenda. I know you don't want that."

Dwight said nothing, though Brenda felt his tension, the muscles of his forearm taut beside her. "Where are we going?" she asked as Eddie turned the truck back toward town.

"We're going to get that book out of the safe."

"Why do you want the book?" she asked.

But he didn't answer as the flashing lights of an ambulance approached, the siren wailing. Eddie slowed and edged to the shoulder, turning his face away as the ambulance passed, bathing the interior of the Jeep in red light. When it was past, Eddie pulled onto the highway again.

Maybe someone will be at the sheriff's department when we arrive, Brenda thought. But as soon as they pulled into the dark, empty lot, she knew that was a false hope. The force was so small they often had only one or two officers on duty overnight, and they spent most of their time in the field, patrolling. No one else was out at this late hour, either, the streets empty of cars or pedestrians. A quarter moon rose over Dakota Ridge, stars like sequins on a cocktail dress shining around it. Under other circumstances, she would have admired the view. A new pain shot through her as she wondered if this would be the last night she ever saw these stars.

Eddie drove around the back of the sheriff's department and parked in the shadow of the building. Security lights bathed the area around the back door in a silvery-white glow, but inside Eddie's truck was pitch-black. "Where are your keys?" he asked Dwight.

"My front pocket."

Eddie nudged Brenda with the gun. "Get them," he ordered.

She looked to Dwight. He nodded and lifted his hip to make it easier for her to reach into his pocket and retrieve the keys. She handed them to Eddie. "All right," he said. "We're going to all go in, and you're going to get the book out of the safe. And remember—you try anything and Brenda is dead."

The words sent a chill through her, but she fought back the fear. She had to stay calm and alert for any chance to help get them out of this. They climbed out of the Jeep. She had to hold on to Dwight's shoulder to stand, she felt so shaky and weak. "Come on," Eddie said, one leg bouncing with agitation. "We don't have all night."

They made their way toward the door. Before they reached it, Eddie shot out the security camera focused over it. Brenda stifled a scream as the report of the gun rang in her ears. A second shot took out the light. Maybe someone would hear the shots and come to investigate, she thought. If only they would come in time.

The security keypad beside the door glowed with a red light. "What's your code?" Eddie asked.

Dwight said nothing.

"Give me the code." Eddie grabbed Brenda's arm— the wounded one—and jerked her toward him. Pain blinded her and she screamed, her knees giving way.

"One six three four," Dwight said. He bent over Brenda. "Are you all right?"

It was a moment before she could speak. She struggled to control her breathing and managed to nod, then, realizing he might not be able to see her in the dark, said, "Yes."

"Get up," Eddie said, then he turned and punched in the code.

Hands bound behind his back, Dwight couldn't help her, but he braced himself so that she could pull herself up against him. She leaned on him for a moment, still breathing hard, while Eddie opened the door. Then he motioned them inside.

He led the way down a flight of stairs to a small room at the back of the building, and used a second key to unlock it. When he flipped on the light, Brenda saw shelves full of guns and ammunition. Eddie moved aside a cardboard box labeled "SWAT" to reveal a small safe. "What's the combination?" he asked.

"It's in the sheriff's office," Dwight said.

Eddie looked at Brenda.

"I'm telling the truth!" Dwight said. "Why would I have the combination to the safe?"

"You put the book in the safe after you took it from the museum tonight, didn't you?" Eddie asked.

"It was open. The book was the only thing in the safe, so when we removed the book, we left it open. All I did when I put it back in there was close the door."

"Then come on." They trooped back down the hall and up the stairs to Travis's office. The door was closed, but not locked. "Where does he keep the combination?" Eddie asked.

"There's a shelf that pulls out on the right-hand side," Dwight said.

Eddie found the shelf and pulled it out. A piece of paper was taped to it. From her position by the door, Brenda could see what looked like a list of phone numbers, but apparently, the combination to the safe was there, too.

"I really need to sit down," she said, and sank into the chair across from Travis's desk.

Eddie scowled at her. "Get up."

"I can't," she said, her voice so weak she could hardly hear it. She closed her eyes. She didn't really care what happened to her now. She was beginning to think she was going to die, anyway.

"Leave her alone," Dwight said. "You've got your combination. Go get the book."

Eddie glared at them, as if about to argue, then jerked his head up. "Is that a siren?" he asked.

Brenda heard nothing, but Dwight said, "Someone must have heard those shots you fired."

Eddie sprinted out of the office and down the hall. Dwight bent over Brenda. "Hang on just a little longer," he said.

She opened her eyes and focused on his hands, the wrists bound with the silver cuffs. "Do you think someone is really coming?" she asked.

"I didn't hear anything," he said. "I think Eddie might be cracking up, but we'll take advantage of that. Can you get the key out of my pocket and unlock these cuffs?" He turned so that his other side faced her.

Energized by the prospect of freeing him, she found the key. He turned his back and held out his hands to her. She fumbled with the lock at first, but after a moment, he was free.

He rubbed his wrists, then put his hand on her uninjured shoulder. "Come with me to my office and hide there," he said.

He helped her up and together they made their way as quietly as possible across the hall to the office Dwight shared with Gage. She sat in his chair while he slid open the bottom drawer of the desk and took out a pistol. He checked to make sure it was loaded, then bent and kissed her cheek. "Wait here," he said, then slipped quietly out of the room.

Brenda clutched her wounded shoulder and rested her head on the desk. She prayed this nightmare would be over soon—and that Dwight would come out the winner. Eddie definitely seemed unbalanced, but that just made him more dangerous.

DWIGHT MOVED AS quickly and as soundlessly as possible toward the door of the armory. Eddie probably had the safe open by now. What would he do when he had the book? Would he simply leave? The supposed siren had seemingly spurred him to grab the book and make his escape, but maybe he would come back to finish off the witnesses to his crime.

Dwight stopped outside the door to the room. Eddie had turned on the overhead light and he stood beside the safe, the book in his hand. He was tearing pages from the book, a few at a time, and dropping them into a metal trash can. As Dwight stared, he took a cigarette lighter from his pocket and touched the flame to the edge of one of the pages. The paper flared, and Eddie dropped it into the trash can with the rest.

Dwight braced himself and aimed the gun. "Eddie Carstairs, you're under arrest," he said.

Eddie turned, openmouthed, and started to raise his gun. Dwight fired, and Eddie lurched away, so that the bullet caught him in the shoulder—almost exactly the spot where Brenda had been shot.

Eddie dropped the gun and sank to his knees beside the trash can, the contents of which were burning brightly, filling the small room with smoke. Dwight scowled at the blaze, then kicked Eddie's gun out of the way. He grabbed him by the arm and hauled him up. "Get up!" he ordered. "Or do you want to give me an excuse to shoot you again?"

Eddie said nothing, but stood and let Dwight push him down the hall to the holding cell. He cuffed him by one hand to the metal grating of the cell and locked the door behind him. About that time the smoke alarm started blaring. Dwight grabbed a fire extinguisher and ran to douse the trash can in the armory, then pulled out his phone and called for an ambulance as he jogged down the hall to Brenda.

He stopped in the doorway of his office. She had her head down on the desk, and she was so still he went ice cold. "Brenda?" he asked.

No reaction. Heart in his throat, he crossed the room and knelt beside her. When he laid his hand on her back, she stirred and raised her head. "What happened?" she asked.

"It's over," Dwight said. "Eddie's locked in a cell." He didn't tell her that he had shot him. She'd find that out soon enough. "Are you okay?"

She tried to smile, though succeeded only in lifting the corners of her mouth a scant half inch. "I've been better."

"Hang on," he said. "The ambulance is on its way."

"I'm not going anywhere." She rested her cheek against his hand and closed her eyes. "Not when I've finally found you."

He wanted to ask her what she meant by that, but had no time, as someone was pounding on the door, demanding to be let in. He stood and went to answer it, light-headed and a little unsteady on his feet, but how much of that was the adrenaline that had flooded him earlier draining away and how much was sheer love for this woman who had endured so much, he couldn't say.

Chapter Seventeen

Dwight sipped the tepid hospital coffee and tried to will away the fog of sleeplessness that dulled his senses. The early-morning hours had passed in a blur of dealing with the ambulance and the sheriff, who arrived as the paramedics were wheeling Brenda out of the sheriff's department. A second ambulance arrived a few minutes later to transport Eddie to the hospital. Travis agreed to go with Eddie, while Dwight followed Brenda.

They had agreed to team up this morning to question Eddie, as soon as doctors gave the go-ahead for them to do so. Dwight stared into the dregs of the coffee and decided he had had enough. He tossed it in the trash can and turned toward the door of the surgery floor waiting room just as Travis walked in. Despite having been awake as many hours as Dwight, Travis managed to look as sharp as ever. Dwight narrowed his eyes at his boss. "How is it you look ready to lead a parade and I feel like death warmed over?" he asked.

"I went home and showered and shaved," Travis said. "Gage is keeping an eye on Eddie, though I don't think he's in any shape to go anywhere."

"The bullet shattered his collarbone." Dwight grimaced. "If he hadn't jerked away, it would have been a heart shot."

Travis put a hand on Dwight's shoulder. "If you hadn't shot him, he would have killed you. Say what you will about the job Eddie did as a reserve officer, but he was always one of the top qualifiers at the range."

"I'd forgotten about that." Not that it would have made any difference in how he had reacted last night—his life had been in danger and his training had kicked in to protect him.

"His doctor says we can have a few minutes with him," Travis said. "He's on pain medication, but lucid."

"Let's hope the meds loosen his tongue enough for him to tell us what's going on," Dwight said. Though even then, a good lawyer might argue that Eddie had revealed information under the influence of narcotics. They had enough other evidence against Eddie that it was a chance Travis felt they could take.

"How is Brenda?" Travis asked.

"She's going to be fine." Saying the words out loud made him feel a little lighter. "The surgeon was able to remove the bullet, and he said there's no permanent damage. I looked in on her a little while ago, but she was still sleeping."

"I'm glad to hear it," Travis said. "Are you ready to talk to Eddie?"

"I am." He had a lot of things he would like to say to the man who had harassed and almost killed Brenda, but most of them he would have to keep to himself. Knowing Eddie was going to prison for a very long time to pay for what he had done would have to be enough.

Eddie's room was at the opposite end of the corridor from Brenda's. Since he was technically in the custody of the Rayford County Sheriff's Department, he rated a private room, and a guard on duty outside his door

24-7. Gage rose from a chair he'd placed against the wall opposite that door as Travis and Dwight approached.

"He's awake," Gage said after the three men exchanged greetings. "I looked in on him a few minutes ago and he wanted to tell me about how none of this was his fault, but I told him to save it for you two."

"Not his fault?" Dwight shook his head. "This should be interesting."

Gage checked his phone. "I need to get going if I'm going to make the auction."

"The auction?" Dwight asked. With everything that had happened in the last few hours, he had forgotten all about the museum's auction.

"Lacy and Paige decided that they needed to go ahead with it, since some of the bidders are here from out of town," Travis said. "They wanted to do it for Brenda."

"I'm sure she'll appreciate it," Dwight said. "Of course, the most valuable item is gone. All that's left of *The Secret History of Rayford Country, Colorado* is a bucket of wet ashes."

"They still want to get what they can," Gage said. "I'm going to run security, along with one of the reserve officers."

"You'd better go, then," Travis said. "We can handle things on this end." He pushed open the door to Eddie's room.

A muted television, and a bank of monitors provided the only illumination in the room. Eddie lay on his back in the bed, the head elevated forty-five degrees, a mass of white bandages around his left shoulder. His right hand was cuffed to the railing of the bed, an IV tube trailing from it. He turned his head toward them, his skin pale against a day's growth of dark beard and

the cuts and bruises from his struggles with Dwight.
"Hello, Sheriff," he said, his voice surprisingly clear.

"Hello, Eddie." Travis stopped beside the bed. "We
need to ask you some questions about what happened
yesterday."

"I know. And I can explain everything. I—"

Travis held up one hand. "Before you say anything, I
need to tell you that you have the right to remain silent.
Anything you say could be held against you in a court
of law. You have the right to have an attorney present.
If you cannot afford an attorney, one will be appointed
by the courts."

"I know my rights," Eddie said. "I read them off to
other people enough. I don't need a lawyer for what I
have to say to you."

Dwight moved in on the other side of the bed. Eddie
turned his head to look at him. "How is Brenda doing?"
he asked.

"Why are you even asking?" Dwight said, unable to
hold in his anger.

"If she'd just cooperated like I asked her to, none of
this would have happened," he said, his voice a plain-
tive whine.

"Were you the one who sent those threatening notes
to Brenda?" Travis asked.

"I didn't do it for myself," Eddie said. "It was a matter of national security. All she had to do was get rid
of that book."

Travis's and Dwight's eyes met across the bed. *National security?* "Why was that book so important?"
Travis asked.

"The man who hired me told me I had to make sure it
was destroyed so that it didn't fall into the wrong hands."

"Who was this man?" Travis asked.

"I don't know his real name," Dwight said. "He told me to call him B."

"Bee?" Dwight asked.

"The letter B. He called me E. They were, like, code names. He worked for a top-secret government agency."

"Did he show you credentials?" Travis asked.

"Of course he did." Eddie looked indignant. "I'm not stupid."

"And his credentials said his name was B?" Dwight asked.

"Yes." Eddie glared at them.

"What branch of the government was he from?" Travis asked.

Eddie frowned. "Something top secret. I mean, his credentials said Department of Homeland Security, but the more we talked, the more I got the impression that he was really CIA or something like that."

"What did he promise you in exchange for your help?" Travis asked.

"He told me he could get me a job with the Secret Service."

"Is that all?" Travis asked.

"He paid me a lot of money. Ten thousand dollars. Don't look at me that way! Since you fired me from the sheriff's department, my bills have been piling up. I needed that money."

Travis leaned over the bed railing. "Eddie, why would the Feds ask you to threaten Brenda Stenson?"

"I wasn't threatening her. I was just, you know, intimidating her so that she'd get rid of that book. B said it was a security risk and we couldn't let it fall into the wrong hands."

"Did he say why?" Travis asked.

"No."

"Did you ask?" Dwight asked.

Eddie looked even more sullen. "No."

"Did you burn down Brenda's house?" Dwight asked.

Eddie shifted in the bed. "I think I need to speak to my lawyer."

"You're in this so deep no lawyer is going to be able to get you out," Dwight said. "Your only chance is to help us get to the truth."

"B was putting a lot of pressure on me. He said I was failing my country. I figured if I destroyed her house, I'd destroy the book and the problem would be solved. I figured she had insurance, and I knew she wasn't home. I mean, I'd never hurt her, even if she does treat me like something she scraped off the bottom of her shoe."

"Where did you get that crime scene photo of Andy Stenson?" Dwight asked.

Eddie flushed and looked away. "I don't see why that matters."

"Did you take it from the case file when you were with the department?" Travis asked.

"You'll never prove it," Eddie said.

"What do you know about Henry Hake's death?" Travis asked.

"Nothing! I didn't have anything to do with that. All I did was try to get Brenda to get rid of that book, like B asked. You find him and he'll tell you."

"How do we get in touch with him?" Travis asked.

"I don't know. He always got in touch with me. But he must be staying nearby. Maybe you could just call the Department of Homeland Security and ask."

"We will," Travis said. Though Dwight had his doubts they would find out anything.

"What was in the book that was so important?" Travis asked. "Did he give you any indication?"

"I already told you, I don't know. He said I didn't need to know."

No one would know now, Dwight thought, since the book had been destroyed.

"I know you think what I did was wrong," Eddie said. "But I didn't have a choice. B threatened to kill me if I didn't get the job done—the sleeping-pill-laced pizza was supposed to prove how easily he could get to me."

"Was B the man you were meeting with at the restaurant that night Brenda and Lacy and the others saw you?" Dwight asked. "Did he slash the tires on Parker's car?"

"I don't know anything about that. And I'm not going to say anything else." He sagged back against the pillow, his face pale. "I'm exhausted and in pain. You can't badger me this way."

Travis looked at Dwight and jerked his head toward the door. Dwight followed him out. "Do you buy his story, about all this being his patriotic duty?" Dwight asked.

"I think the money and the promise of the Secret Service job and the idea of being a hero would appeal to him," Travis said. "I'll talk to Lacy and get her description of the man who was with Eddie that night at the restaurant."

"I remember Brenda saying they didn't get a good look at the man—his face was in shadow."

"We'll get what we can."

"I'm wondering if B was Robert Brownley," Dwight said. "If he's the one who gave Eddie the doctored pizza, we know he was at the museum that evening."

"Good thinking," Travis said. "Get Brownley's description from Brenda and we'll compare notes."

"I'm going down to check on her now," Dwight said. "If she's awake, I'll ask her."

BRENDA HAD BEEN awake for some time that morning. There was nothing like a near-death experience to make a person take stock of her life. She had made some bad decisions, and had had more than her share of bad breaks, but instead of focusing on the past, she needed to come up with a plan for the future.

A light tapping attracted her attention to the door. Dwight leaned in. "Feel like some company?" he asked.

"Definitely." She found the controls for the bed and elevated the head so that she could get a better look at him.

"Why are you frowning at me?" he asked, coming to stand beside her.

"You look worn out," she said. Two black eyes from his broken nose and the dark shadow of beard along his jaw made him look dangerous—and utterly weary. "Have you been home at all since last night?"

"I'll go in a little bit. I wanted to make sure you were all right."

She reached up and took his hand. He squeezed it, and the tenderness in his touch made her feel a little choked up. She cleared her throat. If she started crying, he would think something was wrong. "I'm going to be fine," she said. "The surgeon said so. I can probably go home this afternoon."

"You'll come back to my place," he said.

She might have argued, but why bother? With him was where she wanted to be. "That sounds good. But it's going to be a while, so you should try to get a few hours' sleep. I can get Lacy to take me to you if you aren't back when the doctor signs the discharge papers."

"Lacy is going to be busy for a while," he said.

"Oh? What? Did she and Travis decide to elope or something?"

He smiled, a little more life coming into his eyes. "Nothing like that. But she and Paige are handling the auction at the museum."

"The auction?" She tried to sit up, and regretted it as pain shot through her bandaged shoulder. With a groan, she settled back against the pillows. "I've been lying here, trying to convince myself that it didn't matter that we had to cancel the auction. But they're going through with it?"

"With some of the bidders here from out of town, they figured they had better."

"That's so sweet of them. Though the most valuable item we had is gone now."

"You still had a lot of items left. You'll bring in a good chunk of change."

Not enough, she thought. But no sense dwelling on that. "How is Eddie?" she asked. "I know they rushed him into surgery before me."

"His recovery is going to take a little longer, but he'll live." Dwight certainly wasn't smiling now. "He admitted he sent you those threatening letters—and he burned down your house."

"But why?" She had scarcely said a dozen words to Eddie Carstairs in all the years they had both lived in Eagle Mountain.

"Apparently, someone posing as a federal agent offered him a lot of money to make sure the book was destroyed."

"What was so important about that book?" she asked.

"I read through it more than once and I couldn't see anything significant there."

"I don't know. And Eddie says he doesn't know, either."

"Then why would he agree to do it—to harass me and commit arson—even threaten to kill the two of us? Surely he isn't that hard up and greedy."

"You know Eddie always wanted to be a hero. This man—who I don't for a minute believe was really with the government—convinced Eddie that he had to destroy the book to keep it out of enemy hands—that it was a matter of national security. When Eddie failed the first couple of tries, this mysterious agent delivered that doctored pizza—supposedly to prove how easily he could kill Eddie if he wanted to. That made him desperate to fulfill his 'mission.'"

Brenda tried to take this all in. "That's incredible. Do you think this mysterious secret agent is the one who ran me off the road and shot me?"

"Maybe."

"Did Eddie tell you how to find this supposed agent?" she asked.

"He says he doesn't know. The only name he has is B. But I'm wondering if it was Robert Brownley— or rather, the man who came to you posing as Robert Brownley. I don't think that's his real name."

"He was very insistent on getting his hands on the book that night. And I'll admit he seemed rather menacing." She shivered, remembering being alone with the man.

"Do you think the man who attacked you and the man who posed as Robert Brownley were the same person?" Dwight asked.

"I don't know. It was dark and he wore that mask." She shook her head. "Maybe."

"I need you to give me your description of him again," Dwight said. "We're going to use every resource we can to find him."

She closed her eyes, trying to remember. "So much has happened since then," she said. "I don't know if I can give you enough information."

"Take your time. Describe him to me—what he looked like, as well as your impressions."

"He was in his forties, I think. Average height and build. Dark hair. His eyes were light—gray, I think, and really intense. I guess my biggest impression of him was that he was the kind of man who was used to getting what he wanted. Powerful—but personality-wise, not so much physically. He was well-dressed. His suit looked expensive, not off-the-rack. And he drove that black Land Rover—not a cheap car." Her eyes met Dwight's. "He looked like what he said he was—a rich businessman."

"I may ask you to look at some photographs later and see if you recognize him."

"I'll do whatever I can to help."

"We may be too late," Dwight said. "My guess is that now that he got what he wanted and the book is gone, he'll leave the county, maybe even the country."

"Give Travis my description and then promise me you'll go home and get some sleep," she said. "You're not going to be good to anyone if you fall asleep at the wheel of your cruiser."

"I could get used to you nagging me that way." He leaned over and kissed her on the lips. When he started to pull away, she grabbed his collar and prolonged the embrace. When at last she released him, he looked decidedly less weary. Later, they would talk, and she would tell him some things she had decided.

In the meantime, she liked giving him something to think about.

Chapter Eighteen

Dwight gave Travis Brenda's description of Brownley, then did as he had promised and went home, where he slept for four hours before a phone call awakened him. Groggily, he groped for the cell phone and answered it.

"You need to get back to the hospital," Travis said. "The judge is on her way over to conduct the arraignment for Eddie."

Dwight checked the clock at his bedside—it was almost one in the afternoon. "That was quick."

"Frank Rizzo is Eddie's attorney. He pulled some strings to rush the arraignment."

"Frank Rizzo? How did Eddie afford him?" Rizzo had represented a number of high-profile, very wealthy defendants.

"Eddie was as surprised to see Rizzo as I was," Travis said. "He said obviously the government had come through to support him. He's practically giddy, and I don't think it's all from the painkillers his doctor prescribed. He's convinced he's going to be exonerated as a national hero."

"I'm going to shower and change, and I'll be right over," Dwight said.

By the time Dwight arrived at the hospital, the lot was crowded with news vans and broadcast trucks from every major television and radio network. Dwight's uniform attracted their attention, and he found himself pushing through a crowd of reporters with microphones who demanded to know what his role was in the case. He ignored them and made his way inside.

Fortunately, the hospital's corridors were closed to reporters. Travis met Dwight outside Eddie's room. "Did Rizzo alert the media?" Dwight asked.

"Probably," Travis said. "That's his style."

The man himself stepped out of Eddie's room and closed the door behind him. Clean-shaven and bald, dressed in a gray wool suit and wearing old-school horn-rimmed glasses, Frank Rizzo was well-known to television viewers and readers of the most popular gossip mags. From professional athletes to B-list celebrities to corporate moguls, his client list was a who's who of misbehaving millionaires. His eyes narrowed when he saw Dwight. "Deputy Prentice?" he asked.

Dwight nodded.

"You're the man who shot my client," Rizzo said.

"Your client was shooting at me at the time."

"So you say. My client has a different story."

Dwight kept quiet. Rizzo liked to goad his opponents into saying things he could use against them in court. Dwight wouldn't play his game.

"The judge is here," Travis said. The three men turned to see an older woman with silver-blond hair, dressed in a red business suit, striding down the hallway, followed by a young man who was carrying a court stenographer's machine and a second man who was probably the clerk of the court. Several feet behind them came a very tall man in a blue suit—District Attorney Scott Percy.

The woman stopped in front of them. "Judge Miranda Geisel." She shook hands with each of them in turn. "Let's get this proceeding started."

Travis entered the room first, followed by the judge and her attendants, the DA and Frank Rizzo, with Dwight bringing up the rear. He stationed himself by the door, while the others crowded around the bed, jostling for position in the small space.

The man who had harassed Brenda, destroyed her home and her car, and threatened to kill her, managed to look frail and vulnerable in the hospital bed, his shoulder bandaged and his unshaven face white with pain.

Judge Geisel looked around and, apparently satisfied that all was as it should be, nodded. "Let's begin, gentlemen."

The clerk read off the date, time and nature of the proceedings for the record, then listed the charges against Eddie. Though Dwight was aware of all of them, read together they formed an impressive list—everything from harassment to arson to theft to attempted murder. It would be a very long time before Eddie was a free man again.

"How does your client plead?" Judge Geisel asked.

"Not guilty, Your Honor," said Rizzo.

No surprise there, despite the fact that Eddie had been caught red-handed in the commission of the most serious charge, and had admitted to most of the others. Rizzo would no doubt be contesting those previous confessions. Dwight was almost looking forward to hearing the defense's case, especially if Rizzo could produce the mysterious B.

"I request that my client be released on his own recognizance," Rizzo said.

"The nature of these crimes are such that we request Mr. Carstairs be held without bail," Percy countered.

Eddie watched this exchange, wide-eyed, his gaze shifting from one side of the bed to the other.

"These are very serious charges," the judge said.

"Your Honor, my client has absolutely no record of previous violence," Rizzo said. "He isn't a flight risk. The man is seriously injured and will be recovering for some time."

"My understanding is that Mr. Carstairs could be released from the hospital as early as this afternoon," the judge said.

"If you will authorize his release, I will be personally transporting him to a rehab facility," Rizzo said. "You don't have to worry about him getting into trouble there."

"Your Honor, Mr. Carstairs tried to kill a woman and a police officer," Percy said. "He has been relentless in his pursuit of Mrs. Stenson and remains a threat to her still."

"As Mr. Rizzo has pointed out, Mr. Carstairs's injuries are such that he can't drive a car or go much of anywhere," the judge said. "I think that mitigates the threat. And I am cognizant of the burden on the county if he must remain in protective custody while undergoing rehabilitation and continued medical treatment." She turned to Rizzo. "I'm setting bail at $500,000."

"Your Honor, Mr. Carstairs is unemployed," Rizzo said. "He can't possibly afford such a sum."

"Yet he can somehow afford your fees," the judge said. "Or are you doing pro bono work these days, Mr. Rizzo?"

Rizzo compressed his lips into a thin line and said nothing.

"Bail is set at $500,000," she repeated. "This arraignment is adjourned."

No one said anything while the court reporter packed up his recording equipment. Travis and Dwight left Rizzo to confer with his client and followed the court personnel and the DA into the hall. Percy waited until the judge and her staff had left before he spoke. "No surprise on the bail," he said. "And she's right—in his condition, I don't think he's a flight risk."

"I'm not so sure about that," Dwight said. "He's got someone behind the scenes pulling strings."

"I figured someone else was paying Rizzo's fees," Percy said. "Any idea who?"

"We're still digging," Travis said.

"All that stuff in the report you sent me about secret government agents—do you believe any of that?" Percy asked.

"No," Travis said.

The door opened and Rizzo stepped out. "I'm going to make arrangements for Eddie's release," he said. "I'll see you gentlemen in court."

They watched him walk down the hall and enter the elevator. "Want to bet he stops off downstairs to talk to the media?" Percy asked.

"No bets," Travis said.

"This is going to be an interesting one," Percy said. They said goodbye and he left them. "I'll take over guarding Eddie," Dwight said. "I know you have things to do."

"I think it's best if you limit your contact with him," Travis said. "Just in case Rizzo follows through with any countersuit. Besides, I know you want to be with Brenda."

"She's supposed to be discharged this afternoon," Dwight said. "I'd like to take her home."

"Go." Travis clamped him on the back. "I'll take care of things here."

Dwight found Brenda in a wheelchair beside her bed, wearing a pink hospital gown and fuzzy pink socks. She could have been wrapped up in old sacking for all Dwight cared. The fact that she was upright and smiling made her the most beautiful person he would ever see.

"You look much better," she said, tilting her cheek up for him to kiss. "Did you get some sleep?"

"A little." He rubbed his smooth chin. "A shower and a shave helped, too."

"I just talked to Lacy. She said the auction made over $20,000. A lot more than I expected, since we no longer had the book."

"That will keep you going another few months at least," Dwight said. "It will give you more time to find a new benefactor."

"Professor Gibson may have come through for us there. He said he was so impressed with the museum, he's recommended us to the Falmont Foundation."

Dwight sat on the end of the bed, so that they were more or less at eye level. "What is the Falmont Foundation?" he asked.

"You know the Falmont family—Falmont semiconductors?"

He shook his head. "Never heard of them."

"It doesn't matter. They have a charitable trust that gives money to worthy causes. Apparently, Julius Falmont was a great history buff. And Professor Gibson used to be on the board of the trust. He's recommended us for underwriting. This could be exactly what we've been hoping for." Her eyes shone, and Dwight couldn't remember when she had looked so happy.

"That's great," he said. "It's good to know all the

hard work you've put into the museum is getting the recognition it deserves."

"I don't know about that—I'm just glad we don't have to close the doors and I don't have to start looking for another job."

He stood. "Are you ready to go home?"

"I'm ready, but we're still waiting on the doctor to sign the paperwork. A nurse is trying to locate him now."

Dwight sat back down. "We just had Eddie's arraignment," he said.

"Already?" she asked.

"The judge came here. It's not unusual when someone being charged with a crime is hospitalized. He's being released on bail. Somehow, he has Frank Rizzo as his attorney."

"He's being released?" Much of the elation went out of her face.

"To a rehab center." He took her hand. "He's not in any shape to harm you anymore—and I'll be keeping an eye out for you."

She nodded. "I guess I'm just surprised he would be released."

"He doesn't have a criminal history, and he's not considered a threat at the moment," Dwight said. "Plus, I'm sure having Rizzo as an attorney helped. He has a reputation for making life miserable for judges who don't do what he wants. He has lots of friends in the media."

"How did Eddie afford someone like Frank Rizzo?" she asked.

"I don't know, but that's one thing we'll try to find out." He squeezed her hand. "I don't want you to worry. I'm going to keep you safe—even though I know you don't like relying on others."

Her eyes met his, a new softness in her face. "I've been doing a lot of thinking, and I've come to some decisions," she said.

He tensed. Was this when she told him "thanks, but no thanks" to any prospect of a relationship? "I don't know that now is the best time to be making decisions," he said.

"Hush, and let me talk." She tempered the words with a smile. "I realized as I was lying in that bed, reviewing everything that has happened to me over the last couple of years, that I've been going about things the wrong way. I've been reacting to whatever happened by becoming defensive. Andy was killed and I kept to myself, upset and ashamed and really, not coping very well. Then I found out he was blackmailing people in town and using the money to renovate our house and I reacted again, this time by deciding not to trust other people—not to trust other men. Not to trust you."

He waited, afraid of saying the wrong thing if he interrupted her.

"But just reacting to what other people did was the wrong approach, I think. Instead, I needed to step back and focus on what *I* want to happen. Where *I* want to go in life." She took a deep breath and let it out slowly. "It's time to follow my feelings instead of my fears. I love you, Dwight, and I think you love me."

"I do love you," he said. "I have for years."

She smiled again, and he felt like shouting for joy. But all he did was remain very still, holding her hand and waiting to hear what she had to say next. "Life is too short for us to be apart anymore," she said.

"Yes." Then he did what he had wanted to do for weeks now—maybe even years. He dropped to his knees in front of the wheelchair. "Brenda Stenson, will you marry me?" he asked.

"Yes," she whispered, tears glinting in her eyes.

He leaned forward and kissed her, a long, passionate kiss to seal their pledge. And that was how the doctor found them when he and a nurse walked in.

"Well, it looks like you're feeling much better," he said as Brenda and Dwight moved apart and Dwight stood. The doctor scribbled his signature on the papers on a clipboard the nurse handed him. "Follow the instructions the nurse will give you and I'll see you in my office next week."

The doctor left and the nurse took charge of the wheelchair. Dwight gathered up Brenda's things and followed her into the hallway. They stopped short at the turn to the elevator when they saw Eddie, also in a wheelchair, with Frank Rizzo at his side. "Stop," Brenda ordered.

They stopped and waited for Eddie and his attorney to pass. Neither man looked their way. When the elevator doors closed behind them, Brenda sagged against the chair. "Eddie looked bad," she said. "I'm still not happy about him getting bail, but he really doesn't look like a threat." She looked up at the nurse. "Okay, we can go now."

They arrived downstairs to a scene of chaos. People filled the front lobby, many of them members of the press with cameras and microphones. "I should have thought of this," Dwight said. "We need to go out the back entrance."

But they had already been spotted. A trio of reporters and cameramen surged toward them, shouting questions. Brenda covered her face. "No comment," Dwight shouted. He took control of the wheelchair and pushed toward the doors.

But their progress was blocked again by Frank Rizzo, who stood in the portico, holding forth to an audience of media and bystanders. More cameras flashed as he proclaimed his client's innocence. Eddie slumped in his wheelchair beside Rizzo, the picture of the aggrieved victim of injustice.

Dwight was searching for the best escape route when Rizzo concluded his comments, just as a black sedan pulled into the portico. Rizzo wheeled his client toward the waiting car, then someone screamed. At almost the same moment, the *pock!* of a silenced weapon sounded, and Eddie sagged further down in his chair.

"Get her inside!" Dwight shoved the wheelchair toward a man in scrubs, then sprinted toward Eddie. A bloom of red spread across Eddie's chest. Around them, people screamed, some dropping to the ground, others fleeing either back into the building or across the parking lot.

Another man, also wearing scrubs, reached Eddie at the same time as Dwight and felt for a pulse. He shook his head. "He's gone," he said.

Dwight looked around. Frank Rizzo and the black sedan were both gone also, though Dwight was sure the shots had come from farther away—possibly the parking garage across from the main hospital building.

Two uniformed police officers ran up to him. "Did anyone see the shooter?" the older of the two, a muscular black man, asked.

"No. But I think he might have been firing from the parking garage," Dwight said.

The officer studied the parking structure. "Long shot," he said.

"Not too long for a professional," Dwight said. He had no doubt Eddie's murder had been carefully orchestrated. Someone—B?—didn't want him to tell whatever he knew.

DWIGHT SPENT THE rest of the day running down leads that went nowhere. He and local police searched the parking garage and the area around the hospital and came up with nothing—no video, no eyewitnesses, no bullet casings, no foot impressions—nothing. One more indication that whoever had killed Eddie was a professional.

Lacy showed up with Travis and offered to drive Brenda to Dwight's cabin—an offer she gratefully accepted. "If you need anything, call Mom," he told her as he helped her into Lacy's car. "I'll be there as soon as I can."

"Don't worry about me. Go do your job. I plan to take a nap and be there when you do get in."

"If you're tired, go ahead and go to bed," he said. "I'll just have a bunch of paperwork to deal with." This case had generated more than its fair share of forms and reports.

"Then I'll pour coffee and offer moral support," she said, before waving goodbye and settling back against the seat.

She had the right attitude to be a law enforcement officer's wife, he decided, then went to confer with Travis, who was on the phone with Frank Rizzo. He motioned Dwight to lean in, and together they listened to Rizzo's defense of his sudden departure from the hospital. "Clearly there was nothing I could do for Eddie and there was no sense staying around when there was a shooter on the loose."

"Who hired you to represent Eddie?" Travis asked.

"That information is confidential," Rizzo said.

"I can get a subpoena for not just that information, but anything having to do with Eddie Carstairs," Travis said. "If I have to do that, I promise to take up as much of your and your staff's time as possible. Or you could just answer my question now."

Rizzo's sigh was audible on the phone. "He said he was a friend of the family who wished to remain anonymous. He contacted me by phone—I never saw him, and the number was blocked."

"How did he pay you?"

"With a bank draft made out to my firm, delivered by a private courier within the hour."

"That didn't strike you as odd?" Travis asked.

"No. I deal with any number of very rich and sometimes very eccentric people. I don't question their methods as long as the payment is prompt and in full."

"Has he contacted you about a refund, since your client is dead and won't be needing your services?" Travis asked.

"My fees are nonrefundable."

"Has this man or anyone else contacted you about this?"

"No."

"Let us know if they do," Travis said.

"I don't see how this relates to Mr. Carstairs's death," Rizzo said.

"You don't? You demanded and got bail for Eddie, which put him in a position where the killer could get to him."

Rizzo was silent for a long moment. "I hope you're wrong," he said. "And I have to go now."

The call ended. Travis put away his phone. "Want to bet we'll never hear from him again?" Dwight asked.

"I doubt B or whoever set this up will contact him," Travis said. "They knew when they paid him this case wasn't going to go to trial. They only needed Rizzo to get Eddie released on bail so that they could get a shot at him."

"It had to be a professional hit," Dwight said. "A military sniper couldn't have made a better shot, and the killer didn't leave a shred of evidence."

"Maybe it was a military sniper," Travis said.

"What do you mean?"

Travis shook his head. "I don't know. I'm not ruling anything out right now."

"What's next?" Dwight asked.

"Let's go through Eddie's apartment and try to figure out what he was involved in. So far, B has been very careful. I don't think we're going to find much."

The first item of interest in Eddie's apartment was a box of yellow stationery, a row of cartoon flowers dancing across the bottom of each sheet. "We already knew he sent those threats to Brenda, but it's good to have confirmation," Dwight said.

Dwight flipped through the rest of the contents of the desk in Eddie's bedroom. He pulled a folder from the bottom drawer and looked inside. "Check this out," he said, and handed the folder to Travis.

The sheriff scanned the half dozen photocopies in the folder—all crime scene photos from sheriff's department case files. "Now we know where the photo on that note Eddie sent to Brenda came from," he said.

"That's sick," Dwight said. "It's a good thing you fired him when you did."

The rest of the apartment was full of used furniture,

take-out cartons and dirty clothes. Dwight was grateful to leave it and head to his own comfortable home—and the woman waiting for him there.

Brenda smiled up at him when he entered. She was settled on the sofa, her injured arm propped on a pile of pillows. She had dressed and combed her hair and though she was still pale, the tension had faded from her face. Dwight sat beside her. "How are you feeling?" he asked.

"Better," she said. "Much better now." She turned his face toward hers and kissed him, long and hard. Not breaking contact, he slid one arm under her thighs and scooped her onto his lap, being careful not to jostle her injured shoulder.

When they did finally come up for breath, her eyes sparkled. "Tomorrow is my birthday," she said.

"I hadn't forgotten." He tucked a lock of hair behind her ear. "Not a very fun way to spend it."

"I don't know about that. I'm alive. I'm with you. It's funny—before all this happened, I was a little depressed about turning thirty. I felt as if I had reached a milestone in my life and I had nothing to show for it. I don't feel that way anymore."

"Do you think it's because you faced down death and lived?"

"Partly. But I also think it's because I had reached a point where I had lost everything—I was a widow, my job was in jeopardy, my house had burned down, and then my car was wrecked. I had nothing, but instead of all that making me feel defeated, it was incredibly freeing. I had nothing left to lose. I could do anything. I could be with whoever I wanted to be with." She stroked his cheek. "I don't have anywhere to go from here but up."

"As long as you go there with me."

"I've been thinking about my house," she said.

"What about it?"

"I want to rebuild it."

"Sure. We can live wherever you want to live." He would miss the ranch, but there were probably advantages to living in town. And he wanted her to be happy—she deserved that so much.

"I want to stay on the ranch, here with you," she said. "It's beautiful and peaceful here. I love it."

He hoped the relief he felt didn't show on his face. "Then what will you do with the house—rent it out?"

"Something like that. I don't want to build just one house. I want to build a triplex or a fourplex, and make it affordable housing—something Eagle Mountain really needs."

"That sounds like a great idea."

"I'm full of great ideas. I have all kinds of things I want to do at the museum with the money from the Falmont Foundation, and of course, we have a wedding to plan."

"I like the sound of that one. What other ideas do you have?"

"This one." She kissed him again. "And this one." She began unbuttoning his shirt.

"Hey." He wrapped his hand around hers. "You're supposed to be taking it easy. You're recovering from surgery."

"Oh, we can take it easy." She leaned forward and nipped at his jaw. "Slow and easy. Doesn't that sound good?" She leaned back, grinning at him. "Or if you'd rather, you can get a head start on all that paperwork."

"What paperwork?" He hugged her more firmly against him, then leaned over and switched off the lamp, so that the room was lit only by the glow of moonlight through the front windows. Then he pulled her close in a kiss once more. Paperwork could wait—but he didn't have to wait for Brenda anymore.

* * * * *

THE
NEGOTIATION

TYLER ANNE SNELL

This book is for Dianne. Not only are you the
best mama-in-law I could ask for, you're also insane.
In the best way possible. Thank you for all of your help
with this series. And for creating my favorite human.
May all your days be blessed with pineapples.

Prologue

Dane heard the call the same time Rachel did.

Both were sitting in the belly of the sheriff's department. They were two of several who heard what the men had to say.

"These men are sinners," the man shouted, voice slightly distorted over the speakerphone. "Plain and true! Just like this town. Just like this county. Just like this state. Sinners, all sinners!"

Dane's fists had already been balled. Now his fingers were eating into his palms. It wasn't until Rachel silently covered one hand with her own that he loosened the tension. Her wedding band was cold against his skin.

"Then why take them? They were on their way to the prison," Sheriff Rockwell said. "You're the one who kept them from facing justice."

The man on the other end of the phone call was fast to answer, like he'd rehearsed the whole thing beforehand.

"They represent corruption. A corruption that has taken over," he said, voice still high and filled with unmistakable self-reverence. "And we, the Saviors of the South, represent the consequence to that corruption! The answer! We will show this town that this corruption will no longer be tolerated. These sinners will be the first of many demonstrations on how we will cleanse this place!"

Rachel's hand tightened over Dane's while he shared a look with the sheriff. Rockwell was a solid man who Dane had felt privileged to work alongside as his chief deputy for the past few years. He was fair, to the point and levelheaded. He was also a mean shot, and that didn't count for nothing.

"But you didn't just take prisoners," the sheriff pointed out, "you also took two guards. Two good men through and through. What's your plan with them?"

Dane held his breath. He knew Rachel was doing the same. One of those men was David Roberts. And he was one of the best of them.

That's why Rachel had married him.

That's why Dane was his best friend.

That's why both were willing to do whatever it took to get him back.

"The men who protect sinners are no better than the sinners themselves," the man answered.

Anger swelled in Dane's chest but he kept his mouth closed. Popping off at an obviously unstable man wasn't going to save David or the other guard. It wasn't going to save the inmates they had been transporting, either. Good or bad, they'd undergone trials and received a sentence by their peers. Neither Dane, the sheriff nor the Saviors of the South had any room to change those sentences. Certainly not to make the decision of whether they should live or die.

And that's really what the man on the phone was saying without saying it.

They aimed to kill the seven men they'd kidnapped that morning.

Dane knew it. The sheriff knew it. Even Rachel knew it.

She'd rushed to the department the moment she'd heard the transport van had been hit, ready to help in any way she could.

"I have money," she'd told him. "Not a lot, but maybe we can exchange it."

That had been before the call had come in. Before they'd realized the men didn't want money at all. They wanted to be heard. They wanted attention. They wanted fame.

"I can't just let you do what you want with them, no matter who they are," Sheriff Rockwell said, stern. "So let's find us a way to work this out where no one gets hurt."

The man, who would later be known as Marcus the Martyr by his followers who found themselves in prison, laughed. Without realizing it, Dane locked that sound in his memory for life. It was cold and callous. It didn't care about corruption, no matter how falsely perceived, and it didn't care about justice. It, like the man, only cared about being louder than everyone else.

Marcus wanted violence.

Dane knew it the moment he heard the man laugh and then hang up the phone.

He'd later realize it was in that moment that he knew his best friend might not make it to see the next day, but at the time all he could feel was the deep need to do something.

So when the sheriff was done cursing at the dial tone, Dane straightened and felt his world settle on his shoulders.

"I have a plan."

Chapter One

Seven years later Rachel Roberts surveyed the black-top ahead of her with a pang of annoyance. It was an early Saturday morning and the Darby Middle School building was absolutely teasing her in the background. Between her and it stood the two reasons why she was sweating in her jeans instead of lounging in her pajamas, catching up on the backlog of television shows burning a hole in her DVR.

"Now, I know none of us want to be here, but we are and that's that," she started, making sure she split her narrowed stare between both boys equally. "I guess the two of you are at that age where you don't know how ridiculous it is to call each other names in the school hallways or during class presentations, so instead of making you write long essays about compassion and being polite…"

Rachel motioned to the two buckets of chalk she'd found in the closet filled with art supplies in her classroom and the rectangle outlined in painter's tape in the middle of the blacktop. The one she'd made right before spilling her coffee onto the grass next to it. The one she'd said a few harsh words over in the silence of the school's empty front lawn.

Lonnie Hughes was the first to voice his concern. His scowl had only deepened since he'd hopped off his bike.

Lonnie was a thin twelve-year-old with tightly coiled black hair, dark, always-questioning eyes and a mouth more than ready to voice one of his many opinions. The latter was one of several reasons he was at the bottom of the school's popularity totem pole. He talked too much, listened too little and had almost no filter. This, plus an ingrained aversion to authority figures, had earned him dismissive attitudes from most of the teachers. Rachel wasn't one of them, though most of the staff had assured her that if she had more than one art class with the boy she'd think differently.

The boy standing next to him, however, was completely opposite in that respect. Teachers and students alike seemed to love Jude Carrington. Even for a seventh-grader, he had charm and was clever enough to know when to speak, what to say and how to hide all the devious things most kids that age did. His hair was a shock of red, his skin was covered in freckles, and he wore thick-framed glasses. Yet, according to Mrs. Fletcher, who had him in her homeroom, he seemed to be the leader of the seventh-grade class. Instead of being the stereotypical outcast from an '80s movie, he was Mr. Popular. With a side of bully when it came to Lonnie.

Which was why Rachel wasn't shocked to see the two of them there, though she was surprised their guardians had opted for Saturday detention instead of after school. Darby Middle rarely implemented what she called the Breakfast Club punishment. Yet here they all were.

"You want us to draw for detention?"

What I want to do is to find out what's going on with

Jon Snow from Game of Thrones, she wanted to say. Instead she decided to go with a more stern response.

"Unless you really do want to write a five-page essay about why you're so sorry about what you did, I suggest you show a little enthusiasm. It wasn't exactly easy to convince Principal Martin that doing art projects was punishments for you two."

"It is when it's on a Saturday," Jude interjected.

Rachel nodded and grabbed one of the buckets.

"That's what I told him." She took out a thick piece of white chalk and sat in the middle of the empty rectangle. The blacktop was warm but nowhere near as hot as it would be by midday. If they didn't get it going now, the heat would force them inside and she'd be the one coming back in the morning to finish it alone. Rachel loved her job, but she wanted at least one day off before having to go back to it.

"This is our fall-themed mural, but I was thinking we could make it more Halloween-y. Do a bigger collage of doodles like we did in class last week to help make this slab look a bit more fun. Then, after we're done here, we're going to go inside and cut out a few hundred leaves, pumpkins and maybe some bats from construction paper. Then we're going to go hang them."

Despite his constant need to charm the adults, Jude actually groaned. Lonnie kept scowling. Rachel adopted a look caught between the two.

"Unless you want me to go inside and tell Principal Martin that you actually want to write an essay explaining why you two said what you did and how you two are going to work together in the future?" She shrugged. "I could always do this later."

For a second Rachel was afraid they would decide to go for the essays. It was fall, but in South Alabama that didn't mean much. They'd all be sweating after a few minutes. The air-conditioning inside might be enough of a draw to sway the boys from the manual labor of arts and crafts to tackling papers. Though she hoped that wasn't the case. Gaven, the principal, had mostly agreed to her suggested punishment activities because they were projects she had volunteered to do out of the goodness of her heart.

No sooner had she thought that than Rachel acknowledged it was a lie.

It hadn't just been something she'd felt she needed to do to better the school or to help raise the spirits of those who attended it. No. She had needed a distraction.

One that would keep her mind away from the one place it had been traveling recently. A place she didn't like to visit often.

"Whatever," Lonnie finally said. Rachel breathed an internal sigh of relief as he took a seat on the bottom line of the taped-off empty mural. Jude followed suit but as far away from Lonnie as was possible while staying near the chalk.

Rachel tried to clear her head as it started to fill with sorrow. She smirked. "Glad to see we're on the same page."

Despite Rachel's not wanting to be at school on a Saturday, the next half hour that went by did so with little fuss. The boys drew white, orange and red bats and spiders and skeletons with surprising skill. Rachel had seen both of their drawings before in class, but there was more precision and focus in their actions today. After Lonnie made a jab at Jude and then Jude returned that jab before Rachel could step in, she realized their new passion to do a good job on the mural was probably because they were trying to outdo each other. Meanwhile she filled the center of the blacktop with a giant spider web. It was oddly soothing.

"Why don't we see what Principal Martin thinks about it before we start on the inside work?" Rachel said, stretching out her long limbs when they were done.

Lonnie rolled his eyes.

Jude perked up. "Can I go get him?" He was already turning in the direction of the school's front doors. "Is he in his office?"

Rachel nodded but held up her index finger.

"Go straight there," she warned. Jude gave her a wide smile and was off. Lonnie looked after him, scowl back in full force.

Now it was time to try to distract someone other than herself. "I think the mural looks really good, don't you?" She pulled out her cell phone. "I'm going to take a picture. Maybe I can post it on the school's website the week of Halloween."

"Whatever," Lonnie muttered. He turned on his heel. Goodness forbid he act interested. Rachel pulled up the camera app and was readying to take the picture when he spoke up again. His tone had changed. It was like night and day. Immediately she knew something was wrong.

"Who are they?"

Rachel heard the car doors shut before she turned to see a van at the front of the parking lot a few hundred yards from them. A tall, broad-shouldered man met her stare with a smile. Sandy hair, cut short, and broad, broad shoulders. She didn't recognize him. Nor the man who had gotten out of the vehicle behind him. He wore a full set of overalls. He didn't meet her eyes.

A cold feeling of worry began to swish around in Rachel's stomach. It should have been the warning that sent her inside. However she held her spot, only instinctively taking a step forward so Lonnie was just behind her elbow. Whoever was driving the van didn't get out or cut its engine. She couldn't see the driver's face through the tint from this distance.

"Hi there," she called out to the man in front when it was clear he only had eyes for them. "Can I help you?"

The man, who she guessed was a few years older than her thirty-one, didn't lessen his stride over the curb and onto the grass. He was coming straight for them, his friend at his back.

"Yes, ma'am, you can," he answered, voice carrying through the air with ease. "I'm looking for someone." His eyes moved to Lonnie for the briefest of moments. "Maybe you two can help me out."

That cold in Rachel's stomach began to expand to the rest of her. She tightened her grip on the phone. Her gut with it.

"Maybe you'd like to talk to the people inside," she responded. Her voice had climbed to an octave that would let anyone who knew her well enough realize something was off. She was trying to tamp down the growing sense of vulnerability, even around her lie. "They'd probably know better than anyone who's around. We've been outside all morning."

The only people inside the school were Gaven and Jude, but at the moment, all Rachel wanted to do was to curb the men's attention. Darby Middle was nestled between one of the small town's main roads, a wide stretch of trees that hid an outlet of houses and an open field for sale that had once been used for farming. This being Saturday morning or not, there were rarely people out and about who could see the front lawn of the school. The two men continuing, unperturbed, was a reminder of just how quiet the world around them was.

Who were the men?

Why were they at a middle school on a Saturday morning?

Was she overreacting?

Sandy Hair's smile twisted into a grin. Like she'd just told a joke that only he knew the punch line to. He kept an even pace but was getting close enough to make her stomach knot.

Something isn't right.

The thought pulsed through her mind so quickly that it physically moved her another step over. This time cutting Lonnie off from the men's view altogether.

"Nah," Sandy Hair answered. "I think you will do just fine."

In that moment Rachel knew two things.

One, something was about to happen and it wasn't going to be good. She wasn't a pro at reading people, but there were some nuances that were easy to pick up. The way the man in the overalls looked between her and Lonnie and then back to the building behind them. The way he tilted his body ever so slightly forward as if he was getting ready to move. The way his partner's eyes narrowed and his nostrils flared. The men were about to do something.

Which was how, two, she knew her gut had been right to worry. She should have listened sooner. While there was an unwritten law of Southern hospitality her parents had taught her from the moment she could walk and talk, Rachel wasn't about to give the men the benefit of the doubt. Not any longer. She'd learned the hard way that there were bad people in the world who did bad things.

They'd taken David from her.

She wasn't going to let another set of them take her or the child at her side.

And with a shock of adrenaline, Rachel realized that was what they were about to try to do.

There was about to be running.

There was about to be chasing.

So Rachel decided she wanted her and Lonnie to have the head start. Holding on to her cell phone like the lifeline it might become, Rachel spun on her heel and grabbed Lonnie's hand. "Run!"

Chapter Two

Dane Jones, for once, wasn't in the office. Instead he was at the park, sitting on a bench with Chance Montgomery, trying to convince the man that there wasn't a conspiracy about to swallow Riker County whole.

"It's been a helluva year—I'll be the first to admit that," Dane said. "But it sure does feel like you're looking for trouble that's not there. And we surely don't need any more trouble here."

Chance, formerly a private investigator from around Huntsville, Alabama, was what Dane liked to call a pot-stirrer, among other things. He was a good man and had been a good friend over the years, but he had the nasty habit of not just getting antsy when he was bored but turning into somewhat of a lone ranger detective when the mood struck him. It occasionally reminded Dane how different he was from the man.

Dane was contemplative. The kind of man who worked well in the quiet. Chance was brash. He spoke up, out, and didn't think twice about the feathers he ruffled, especially when he was between jobs as he was now.

"I'm telling you, Dane, something isn't adding up around here," he implored. "Last week three warehouses were unloaded in Birmingham. All weird stuff, too.

Radio equipment, dog crates and enough bubble wrap to wrap an eighteen-wheeler were stolen at the same time."

"I'm not saying that isn't strange," Dane admitted. "I just don't see why you've come to me with the information. We're several hours away from Birmingham. I can't see how I could help from here. Or why it would fall into my purview at all."

Chance took off his cowboy hat and put it on his knee. He came from a long line of Alabama cowboys. They didn't just wear the hats or have the accents, they had the attitude of an old Western movie lead. Dane wouldn't even be surprised if Chance practiced drawing his pistols back at his family farmland outside the county. The same land Chance retreated to when he had nothing else to do. Or, again, got bored. Like he must have been now if he was looking into thefts of mass amounts of bubble wrap.

"I'm telling you because one of the vans spotted loading up the crates had a plate that traced back to a deceased Bates Hill resident."

That caught Dane's attention. Bates Hill was the smallest town in Riker County, which put it square in the sheriff's department jurisdiction. It also made Chance's insistence that they meet make more sense. Still, he wasn't about to jump to any conclusions.

"Who did it trace back to?"

Chance dug into his jeans' pocket and pulled out a piece of paper. He handed it over but read the name out loud.

"Tracy Markinson," he said. "Ring a bell?"

Dane felt like he'd jammed both feet in a bucket of ice water. His mind skidded to a halt and instead of staying in the present where it was needed, it did one hell of a job throwing itself backward.

"Rings a loud one." Dane looked at the paper but only saw the face of a man he'd never forget. "Tracy Markinson's been dead for almost a decade," he said. "Definitely not stealing bubble wrap in Birmingham."

Chance slid his finger around the brim of his hat and then thumped it once. "Which is why I thought I needed to take a drive out to see you." He cast Dane a knowing look. "And why I thought talking in private might be the best move. I didn't want to waltz into the department and just throw this at you. Thought doing it here, in the fresh air, might be better. Plus, you know how much I hate offices."

Dane didn't speak for a moment. He was seeing ghosts. Ghosts of his past. Ghosts he'd created. And where there were ghosts, there was her.

He didn't say it, but Dane was glad Chance had told him outside the department. He prided himself on being surefooted when it came to his job. Right now? Right now he felt like he was treading air.

"How exactly did it trace back to him?" he finally asked. Even to his ears his voice had gone low, nearing a whisper. "You said license plate?"

"Yes, sir. It was attached to a burgundy van that left the warehouse with the dog crates. Tracy was the last person who legally owned it, but past that, I'm not sure on any more details. Once I saw the name, I thought I'd come talk to you first."

Dane's gears were still moving slow. Like a cup of molasses had been poured over them. He'd worked a lot of cases since Tracy was killed. Ones that had made his blood boil. Ones that had kept him up at night. Ones that had shaken the entire sheriff's department and county to their cores. Yet what had happened to Tracy? That was a case that had changed Dane's entire life in the blink of an eye.

An eye that might be looking at him now.

"After Tracy died, his things were given to the family he had left and then the rest were donated, if I'm not mistaken. Birmingham might be far for some, but it's definitely within driving distance. Not hard to get his van up there. It could be just a coincidence that it happened to be his old one," Dane pointed out.

Chance picked his cowboy hat off his leg and put it on. He looked out at the small park and the autumn leaves that had started to fall. The scene contrasted with the heat that hadn't yet left South Alabama.

"It could be," he admitted. "Coincidence, maybe. Bad luck, maybe that, too. But my gut says it's not, and I aim to find out why it's telling me that." Chance stood. "I'll be at the hotel on Cherry for a few days, looking into some things. You've got my number. Don't hesitate to call it. I'll do the same if I find anything. Unless you want me to keep this one out of your hair?"

Dane shook his head.

"If there is a loop, keep me in it if you don't mind," Dane said. "And, Chance? Thanks for reaching out."

The cowboy gave a small nod and walked over the fallen leaves to his truck in the parking lot. Dane watched as he drove away. Riker County was nothing short of surprising, no matter the season. It might only house one large city, but the trouble that found its way into its borders never ceased to amaze Dane. If it wasn't a new criminal organization trying to take over, it was kidnapped children, manhunts and enough gunshots traded between the bad guys and their department to last him a few lifetimes.

Dane left the bench in an attempt to exit his current road of thought.

Even before the recent uptick in chaos around his home, there had been only one night that had burned its way into his soul.

The night he'd made a decision.

The wrong one.

Dane hopped into his truck and pointed it toward the department in the heart of Carpenter, Alabama. He had too much on his plate to fight with his past again. Now wasn't the time.

He turned the volume up on the radio, let a crooning song croon, and was about to write off Chance's gut when his phone vibrated in his pocket.

"I need a vacation," he told the cab of his truck, fishing out the ringing phone. "One where I just don't answer this blasted phone." Hell, he'd needed one for years now. No time like the present, right?

Dane didn't recognize the number but unlocked his phone all the same. As the captain of the Investigative Bureau at the Riker County's Sheriff's Department, he had to be always ready for the unknown. Not to ignore it just because it was easy. Life wasn't easy. There was no reason to suspect work would be, either.

He turned down the radio and cleared his throat. "Captain Jones, here."

"Dane!" The sound of a bad connection was almost as loud as the woman's scream. On reflex he held the phone away from his ear for a moment. "Dane! There are men at the school trying to take us!"

All at once Dane's body and mind synced. No sighing. No thoughts of vacations. No molasses on the gears.

That wasn't just any woman.

It was the widow he'd helped make seven years ago.

"Rachel?"

"There are three of them! One in a van and two—two are chasing us!"

A shout sounded in the background. Dane tightened his hold on the steering wheel, knuckles going white. The rustling noise wasn't a bad connection. It was movement. It was running.

"Rachel, where are you?"

There was more rustling and the sound of something slamming shut before she answered.

"We're in—we're inside Darby Middle," she said, out of breath. "Only four of us here when they—when they showed up."

Dane cut the wheel hard, turning in the opposite direction. Another shout sounded in the background.

This time the shout was closer.

"We gotta hide," came a small voice, much closer to the phone. A student at school on a Saturday? Rachel didn't get a chance to respond before someone else was yelling.

"Rach—" Dane started. She cut him off.

"Dane, there're children here," she stressed. Something made a scrapping noise.

The fear in her voice was unmistakably true and poignant. It stirred something inside Dane's chest he didn't have time to investigate.

"Dane, please hurry!"

Dane pressed his gas pedal to the floor. Any more force and it felt like it would have gone through the floorboard.

"I'm coming," he promised, voice rising to show he meant it. "Just stay on the—"

A series of crashes cut him off again. There was another wave of rustling. This time it sounded violent.

On cue Rachel cried out.

"Rachel," Dane yelled into the receiver.

"Ms. Roberts!"

"Run, Lonnie," she yelled in response. But it wasn't to him. Instead Dane felt like he was under water, unable to break the surface to get to her.

"Run!"

Dane heard a new voice. It belonged to a man. An angry one at that.

"Oh no, you don't," he yelled.

Dane held the phone away from his ear again as a loud crash reverberated out of it. "Rachel!"

But it was too late. The call dropped.

And then Dane was left alone with nothing but silence.

THE FINGERS THAT threaded into her long hair were angry. They wasted little time in pulling her backward in one violent motion. The change in Rachel's momentum was jarring. She yelled out as she fell into the man in overalls, feet coming out from under her.

There was a moment of pause when her terrified mind let her know that she could give up right then. It would be easier to let the men take her, especially since one had her by the hair. Like trying to hold your breath under water as long as you could but having to surface and breathe in air when you couldn't stay down any longer.

"Rachel!"

Dane's voice coming through her dropped phone was small compared to that of the man at her back, but it heralded in her good sense. She wasn't going to let terror seize her body; she wasn't going to let the men, either. With both hands, she did something David had once showed her. Cupping both hands, she threw them up and behind her with all the force she could muster at this awkward angle. Her head burned where he was pulling her hair, but her hands slapped over the man's ears with surprising precision.

He howled in response. The pain at her roots lessened as he let go.

However he wasn't the only man in the room. No sooner had she scrambled to her feet than the sandy-haired man lunged at her. Rachel didn't have time to ready to fend him off. Luckily she didn't have to. A large-bristled broom swung so close to her head she felt the wind off it seconds before it connected with her attacker's face. Instead of swinging it around again, the broom's wielder used it like a batting ram, charging forward enough that it sent the surprised man on his backside.

Lonnie let get of the handle when she was clear. Rachel didn't have time to thank the boy for saving her. The men behind her were a tangle of limbs but neither was hurt enough to be down for too long. She and Lonnie had to get away.

She grabbed his hand again and ran toward the second doorway leading out of the classroom. While she was seeking safety, Rachel had run in the opposite direction of the front office. She didn't know where Jude was and didn't want to chance having him walk out in the middle of the men.

"You bitch," one of the men yelled from the other room. The sound of desks overturning followed. Rachel tightened her grip on Lonnie's arm and skidded around the hallway corner. They'd been lucky that the study hall room had been open. The rest of the classrooms were not. If she'd needed any open for decorating, she was supposed to go to Gaven to unlock them.

Now?

Now she was doing the fastest recall she'd ever attempted, trying to remember which doors might be open while adrenaline had her heart thumping a mile a minute, trying to drill itself out of her chest.

Heavy footsteps echoed down the hallway they'd just left.

Rachel didn't want to admit it, but they were running out of time and out of distance.

She just hoped they weren't also running out of luck.

Chapter Three

The heat from outside did nothing to break through the chill that had fallen in the cab of his truck. It moved into Dane's bones and stayed there even when he screeched to a stop in front of Darby Middle and jumped out onto the lawn.

In the time it had taken to book it over to the school, he'd called everyone on the horn that could help. Local PD had a cruiser on the way. Billy was sending deputies and flooring it over, too, and their dispatcher, Cassie, had even managed to contact the principal. Gaven Martin had been given orders to protect himself and one of the children who had been at the school. He'd also confirmed that the only other people at Darby Middle were Rachel and another student named Lonnie.

It was nice to have so much communication and movement on the ground. However the time it took to get from point A to B had stretched too long. Dane's gut dropped to his feet when he saw the parking lot was empty. No driver. No van.

Which meant the mystery men, or at least one of them, had left the premises.

Dane only hoped Rachel and the boy hadn't been along for the ride.

He pulled his gun out and didn't stop long enough

to even think about waiting for backup. Instead he hurried to the front double doors like the devil himself was nipping at his heels.

Dane didn't have any kids, and the ones he did occasionally babysit for friends didn't live in Darby. Point of fact, he'd never been inside the middle school before. A wave of cool air mixed with the faint smell of cleaning supplies pressed against his face as he moved from the outside concrete to the beige tile inside. The door shutting behind him was the only sound that reverberated across the hall in front of him. For once, the quiet didn't sit right with him.

He held his gun higher and went to the glass door closest to him marked Main Office. It was locked. Another closed door could be seen at the end of the room with the principal's nameplate across it. Gaven and the other student were hiding on the other side.

Dane moved his attention back to the hallway in front of him. It cut to the right and was empty. Closed doors lined each side along with small lockers around the bottom half of the walls. Dane stayed alert as he hurried to the first set of doors. Both were locked. He went to the next two. They were also locked. He kept on until there was a room with a door wide open. His heart hammered in his chest. Some of the desks inside had been toppled over, a broomstick was broken in two and, in the middle of it all, there was a discarded cell phone.

Dane didn't bother picking it up. He knew it belonged to Rachel.

This was where she must have fought the men.

Her cry echoed in Dane's mind.

He hadn't liked hearing it over the phone.

He didn't like remembering, either.

Moving as quietly as he could, Dane exited the room

through its second door. If Rachel had run in through the main school entrance and then into the classroom, he'd bet she would have gone deeper into the school rather than back outside. That was *if* she had broken away from the men and wasn't in their custody now.

Dane shook his head.

He wasn't going to think about that just yet.

The adjoining hallway led to another that formed three sides of a box that made up the school. Most of the doors were shut and locked. Dane checked the bathrooms quickly and wordlessly. Nothing seemed out of the ordinary. No one made a sound. If Rachel and Lonnie had run this way, their options to hide had been limited. By the time he made it to the end of another hallway, he worried that they might not have had the chance to even make it that far.

But then he saw it. An open door at the end of the hall.

Dane hurried over. The door led into a small gym. Bleachers were pulled out, a few soft mats were pushed into the corner and light from outside streamed in through the tall windows on either side of the room. Two doors that must have led to the locker rooms were located on the far wall, another was in the corner and had a set of locked chains around the handles. A soccer field, surrounded by trees, at the end of the property could be seen through the glass on the top half of each door.

Or at least where the glass had been.

One window was completely busted out.

Dane cursed beneath his breath as he got closer. There was blood on the broken glass. Someone had busted it in an attempt to escape. Dane cursed again as he shook the handle of one of the doors. The chains clinked their objections. If Rachel had broken out of the school, she must have been desperate.

Dane lowered his gun and kicked the door hard.

He should have been there sooner.

He should have—

Movement out of the corner of his eye made him spin on his heel. His gun came up high and ready.

"Dane?"

Rachel peeked out from under the closest set of bleachers. A boy was at her side.

Dane could have sung in relief.

While it had been years since he'd seen the woman in person, he realized right then and there he hadn't forgotten the details of what made Rachel Rachel.

Her hair might be shorter, but it was still dark, smooth and straight. It framed a long, thin face with high cheekbones and a faint dimple in her chin. Her complexion was tanned, though, if memory served him correctly, Dane would bet it was a farmer's tan. Rachel had always liked to go outside but wasn't a fan of sunbathing. He'd often teased her when she wore shorts and her ankles and feet were different shades.

But of all the details Dane remembered, it was her eyes that made him feel like they were suddenly in the past.

Denim blue. Like a favorite pair of worn blue jeans.

They fastened to him now, a mix of emotions he didn't have time to separate and examine. "Are you two okay?"

He lowered his gun but didn't holster it. Just because he hadn't seen the mystery men didn't mean he was letting down his guard.

"Yeah, we're—" Rachel started but the boy, Lonnie, interrupted.

"She cut herself good when she broke the window," he said, voice stronger than Dane would expect in the situation. He motioned to her arm. It was pressed against her chest, her other hand cradling her wrist.

"It's not that bad. Just a little blood. I'm fine." She must have read the question in his expression. "I thought if it looked like we made it outside, *they* would go outside and we could hide and wait it out here."

Dane couldn't deny that plan was impressive, if not risky. "The van you said was out front is gone. And, as far as I could tell, the rest of the school is empty. Except for Gaven and the other student."

Rachel had opened her mouth, worry already in her eyes, when he hurried to add, "Who are both fine and locked in the office."

Rachel let out a sigh of relief, but her body didn't start to relax until a welcomed sound started in the distance.

Sirens.

Dane flashed the boy a small smile. "Backup has arrived."

THE EMT HAD cleaned and bandaged the cut along the top of her wrist but hadn't gotten to scolding her until he'd looked at the swollen parts of her knuckle.

"You're lucky the glass was already compromised," he had said. "Or else you might have *broken* your hand instead. It's going to hurt for a few days, regardless."

Rachel had kept her mouth shut on the EMT's commentary. While he had only been trying to help, he hadn't been the one running through the school trying to keep away from men hell-bent on grabbing her and the kid in her care. She had broken the window because she *was* going to try to get Lonnie and herself through.

They'd already used up their luck by losing the two men for a minute or two, giving them enough time to get into the gym. But the moment after she'd cleared the glass away, Rachel had made a split-second decision to keep hiding.

Guilt and worry and fear wound around her stomach, even though she was now safe. It was just dumb luck that the men had seen the broken window and believed what she had wanted them to. That she had run to the woods with Lonnie at her side. Once they'd seen the empty window, they'd run in the opposite direction, both swearing.

It could easily have gone the other way.

Now Rachel was sitting in the Riker County Sheriff's Department, staring at a nameplate that read Captain Dane Jones and struggling to shake loose the added sorrow trying to creep in. Even without the morning she'd just had, being in the building was enough to turn her mood. Down the hall, years ago, she'd listened to Dane and his colleagues attempt to do their best to save her husband.

She'd seen the way their bodies had been as tense as hers as they'd gone through each scenario with vigor. The way their determination had kept their brows furrowed and their lips thinned. The way they'd tried to assure her everything would be okay.

However, perhaps the singular thing she remembered most from that day was just after the storm had broken outside and Dane had walked in. She'd been waiting for news, but the department had gone radio silent. Though, she realized later, the silence was for her. They were just waiting for Dane to come back. Waiting for him to tell her.

And there he had been, walking through the hallway with rain clinging to his clothes and sliding off his hair. He wasn't walking with purpose. He'd been walking on reflex.

Rachel fisted her hand in her lap.

She had known the moment their eyes had met that David was gone.

That day had put a hole in her heart, one that had only grown as the year went on.

Now?

She looked down at the bandage on her arm and felt the dull ache of her swollen hand.

Now, after more time had passed, it was less of a hole and more like a window. She could see the memories in the distance and occasionally, if she opened the window, she could feel their joy and sorrow they often brought.

Rachel smiled to herself with no real mirth.

She'd been a widow for years and yet always around the anniversary of David's death she found herself revisiting the day when the word was still so foreign. After the day she'd had, though, she supposed she shouldn't be too harsh on herself.

The door behind her opened and Dane pushed through. He didn't look at her as he put a file on his desk, along with his phone, and then settled into his chair. This had been par for the course between them after she gave her statement. He'd been avoiding her.

Just as he'd been doing for years.

An old anger started to weave itself around her chest again, making her hot.

She cleared her voice.

"Any luck finding the men?" she started, hopeful.

Dane was already shaking his head before she finished.

"No one has been able to pin down the men or their

vehicle, but there's an all-points bulletin out." He met her gaze. His eyes were hard, dark. "We're running your and Lonnie's descriptions of the men through our database, seeing if anyone matches. Hopefully we'll get a hit so we can make some moves."

"And if they aren't in the database?"

Dane's expression softened, if only a little. "Don't worry, we'll find them. It's not a matter of if, just a matter of when." On cue, a knock sounded against the doorway. A man with a detective's shield around his neck gave her a curt nod.

"Rachel, this is one of our newest detectives, Caleb Foster. You might remember Detective Matt Walker, but currently he's enjoying his honeymoon." Dane's tone changed, if only briefly, to humor. "But it pains me to admit this, Foster here is more than capable of getting to the bottom of this."

This time the detective chuckled. He extended his hand, which Rachel took with a smile.

"If Dane has faith in you, you must have deserved it," she responded truthfully. The detective nodded and then all humor was gone.

"The chief is here and wants to talk to us ASAP. I tried to tell him you were busy, but—"

"But the anxious chief of Darby PD waits for no woman or man when he's ready to get some answers," Dane finished.

The detective nodded.

"All right, tell him I'm coming."

Caleb said a quick goodbye to her and was gone as fast as it took Dane to get out of his chair. His brow was furrowed. He was already miles away from her.

And that brought the anger back.

"I'm going home," she said before he could disappear

on her again. "Unless there's something else I need to do? Or there's something else you need to say?"

Dane paused midstep. For a moment Rachel thought he was going to actually talk to her about something, but he did what the Dane from the past few years had done perfectly.

He took the easy way out and avoided her.

"No, that's all," he said. "We'll call you if we have any more questions or need to follow up."

"And how do I get back to my car?" she pressed.

"I'll send someone in to take you back."

Rachel knew her expression had hardened. She felt the anger tensing her up. Dane started to say something more but hesitated. She remembered a time when they'd had no problem talking.

But now everything was different.

"I'm glad you're okay," he finally said, though his eyes were already on the door.

Rachel waited until he was gone to respond. "Thanks for picking up the phone."

Chapter Four

Dane was a jackass, plain and true. He thought it the moment he left his office and he thought it through his meeting with Darby's chief of police, Detective Foster, and Riker County's sheriff, Billy Reed. A meeting that had gone over their limited facts and debated who would handle the case, seeing as it had happened outside the sheriff's department's jurisdiction.

However, unlike Dane, Billy was a charmer. The people of Riker County loved their sheriff, and that included the chiefs of police from the towns and city that they encompassed. When Billy took office, he had worked hard to keep relations between all local law enforcement friendly, so when the time arose where they wanted to cash in some favors, it wasn't frowned upon. At least, not for long.

Dane grabbed a water from the break room afterwards and sat down at one of the tables, relieved the chief had agreed to let them take lead. He wondered if he would have been able to talk the man into it had he followed through and become sheriff when he'd had the opportunity. He had a familiar pang of regret at the question. He remembered his younger self, eyes wide and mind set on leading the sheriff's department when Sheriff Rockwell had been around.

But things had changed.

Now he was just the jackass who had gotten their off-duty dispatcher to take Rachel back to the school instead of doing it himself.

After all she had been through, there he was, still trying to put distance between them.

Guilt, old and new, created tension in his shoulders. Dane rolled them back. It didn't help.

"So there I was, coming out of my doctor's appointment, when I run into a very peculiar scene." Dane turned to see the sheriff's right-hand woman, Chief Deputy Suzy Simmons-Callahan, in the doorway of the break room, brow raised and hand on her pregnant belly. Even with a rounded stomach, Suzy was not to be taken lightly. "Chance Montgomery and that black cowboy hat of his asking the vet next door about dog crates and bubble wrap. Know anything about that? Because I can't imagine that man being in town and not dropping by to see you."

Dane nodded. "We met this morning. He's following a case in Birmingham involving a series of thefts."

"Dog crates and bubble wrap?"

"And radio equipment."

Suzy sat down at his table, curiosity clear in her eyes. "And why is he here? We might occasionally work with other counties, but usually that county is next to us, not hours away."

Dane sighed. He had planned on keeping what Chance had told him under his hat, but he wasn't about to lie to Suzy. She was one of the few friends he'd kept throughout the past few years. He'd like to keep it that way for many more.

"A vehicle at one of the crime scenes was registered

to Tracy Markinson." Suzy looked down at her hands, brow pulling in.

He gave her a second to remember. Then it was written all over her face.

"It definitely wasn't Markinson driving, if that's what Chance was after," she said.

Dane nodded. "That's why he's in Riker County. He's following the vehicle's trail."

"And asking local vets about dog crates and bubble wrap," she added with a grin.

"I never claimed to know his methods." He mimicked the grin. "He told me he'd keep me in the loop if he did find anything, but I'm sure I'll see him sooner rather than later, especially after what happened earlier."

They both sobered.

"I'm glad Rachel and the boy were okay," she said. "But I'll tell you what I told Billy, it sure doesn't make sense what happened. Though I guess a lot of the things we deal with don't make sense to us. Some people just do what they want, and sometimes what they want makes my blood boil."

"You've got that right."

He didn't need to ask Suzy to clarify her viewpoint. It *didn't* make sense that Rachel and Lonnie had been targeted. Even if it had been a crime of opportunity, abducting two people in broad daylight in a public place was brave.

And stupid.

The worst kind of combination when it came to the criminal mind.

"And how are you doing?" she asked. It was Dane's turn to raise his eyebrow. She clarified. "Not one but two reminders of the past all within one morning? That has to be *interesting* for you."

"It definitely wasn't how I thought today would go," he admitted, hedging on a concrete answer. "But I guess part of living in and around small towns means that eventually we all run into our pasts. One way or the other."

Suzy surprised him with a laugh. "If I was Deputy Ward I'd tell you that you sound like a fortune cookie." She got up and patted her stomach with another laugh.

"Good thing you aren't Deputy Ward," he deadpanned.

Suzy waved him off. "You did good today, Captain. Just make sure you don't stay here all night. Like your cowboy friend said, we'll keep you in the loop if anything happens. Until then let's trust our women and men out in the field."

"Sure thing, Suzy."

Dane watched her disappear into the hallway and finished off his water. She *was* right. It had been years since the Saviors of the South had terrorized the department. In the time after, he'd managed to limit how much exposure he had to reminders of that fateful day. Even when it had been hard.

His thoughts went back to a pair of blue eyes.

Angry blue eyes.

Dane pulled out his phone. He went to Recent Calls.

Who were the men who had gone after Rachel?

And why?

HER NEIGHBOR MARNIE GABLE was front and center the moment Rachel drove up to her house later that night. No sooner had her door opened than she was enveloped in a tight, teary embrace. Marnie's wild hair of curls even seemed to be trying to pull her in.

"You could have died," she squalled.

Rachel rubbed her back and smiled. "But I didn't."

Marnie pulled back so Rachel could see the shine in her eyes but didn't let go. "But—"

"But I didn't," Rachel interrupted. "I'm here and okay."

Marnie was a ball of energy at any given time, but as Rachel gently pulled away from her, she saw that the girl was barely holding it together. She had really been scared.

Rachel felt a tug at her heartstrings.

Marnie wasn't just a neighbor, she was the daughter of her neighbor. Rachel had somewhat adopted the young woman, just twenty-one now, as a friend when she was a teen. Her parents often traveled for work and Rachel had been the ideal babysitter, if only for location. Both of their houses were out in the most rural part of Darby. It was a fair drive from town no matter where you were coming from. There was even a good distance between their two houses. Marnie used to ride her bike over. Now she drove her beat-up green Beetle.

Marnie didn't seem to believe her claims of being okay. She detached herself and moved to the side so the security light could help her see Rachel better. Her eyes widened when they took in her bandaged wrist and bruised knuckles.

Rachel beat her to addressing them.

"Just some minor aches and pains," she hurried to explain. "Nothing too bad." Rachel tried on a reassuring smile and walked around the woman to the front porch. She pulled out her keys.

"I just don't get it," Marnie said, following. "Who were those creeps? What were they doing?"

A burst of cool air pushed against them as they moved into the house. Rachel felt tension she didn't realize she'd been holding start to seep out. From the back of the house a string of meows started.

"That's the mystery of it all," Rachel responded. She made a beeline for the kitchen at the side of the house. The sliding-glass door that lined one wall showed the soft glow of the garden lights she'd set up along the side deck. It was comforting in a way. "It's still an open investigation."

June the Cat's meows got louder. Rachel pulled her dry food from the pantry and headed for her bowl. She paused before pouring. "Wait, how did you hear about what happened?"

Marnie managed to look sheepish. "I heard about it on the radio, or at least, they said something had happened at the school. After that I kind of went into snooping mode. Called a few people until I found someone who knew something."

Rachel gave her a stern glance. "What have I told you about looking into the gossip mill?"

Marnie huffed but answered.

"That the answers aren't worth the trouble," she said. "And just looking for those answers usually only makes more gossip for others."

Rachel nodded. June the Cat looked up at her with mild interest.

"Well, I was worried," Marnie grumbled. "So sue me." She went to the breakfast bar and plopped down. Rachel took advantage of the silence to reheat some leftover lasagna. She cut an extra piece and slid it to her guest. It was enough to get the young woman talking again.

"I just can't believe it happened is all," she said around a bite. "And they haven't even caught the men? I mean, what if they didn't just try to grab you because you were out in the open? What if it's *you* they wanted to begin with?"

Rachel was already gearing up to combat Marnie's worries but came up short. Not because what Marnie had said made sense—she'd already entertained the thought, though she'd pushed it away just as quickly—but because light moved across the deck.

Headlights.

"Your mom wasn't coming over tonight, was she?" Rachel asked, hopeful.

Marnie put her fork down. She shook her head.

"She's in Tennessee for the week." Rachel pulled out her phone.

"Great," she muttered. It was dead. The battery rarely lasted an entire day without needing a charge. She'd been meaning to get a new one for months.

Marnie peeked over her shoulder. "Are *you* expecting anyone?"

"No, but I also wasn't expecting you." Rachel gave her a quick smile but it didn't stay long. She left her plate and hurried into the bedroom and straight to her closet. She bent in front of the safe David had insisted they have and typed in the combo. When Rachel turned around holding a handgun, Marnie was there to gasp.

"Stay here," Rachel warned.

Marnie's eyes were the size of quarters but she listened.

Rachel went into the hallway, slowly moving across the hardwood to the front of the house. Her earlier insistence that she was okay started to fade away. The weight of the gun in her bandaged hand helped remind her that things could have turned out a lot differently this morning. And they still could. Every step she took toward the front door ate up her calm.

Was she overreacting?

Had she just been in the wrong place at the wrong time at the school?

Or were the men coming for *her*?

She tightened her grip on the gun. Her nerves shook her hand. The muscles in her legs readied to run. It didn't help matters when a booming knock sounded against the front door.

She paused, a few feet from it.

There were no windows to show her who it was, so she walked softly to the peephole. Holding her breath, heart in her throat, Rachel looked through it.

"Holy buckets." She breathed out and lowered the gun to her side. She opened the door in time to catch Dane's fist in midair. He was quick to take in her expression and the weapon.

"Before you use that on me, know that, in my defense, I called you. Three times, in fact."

It wasn't lost on Rachel how much seeing the man made her feel better. Just as seeing him standing in the gym, cursing at the chained doors, had this morning. Capable, sturdy, a force to be reckoned with. Handsome, too. Though that wasn't anything new.

"I just realized my phone died," she said, trying to get her heartbeat back on its normal path.

Dane motioned to the gun. "Well, I'm glad to see that you're more cautious than not. It makes my—the department's—job easier in making sure you stay safe." His eyes strayed over her shoulder as footsteps echoed up the hallway.

"Everything okay?" Marnie called out.

Rachel turned to find the woman holding something in her hands. It surprised a laugh out of her. "Yeah, Marnie. Everything is fine, but is that my bedside lamp?"

Marnie shrugged.

"I wanted to help," she said defensively. She raised her chin a fraction, proud.

"Well, you can help by putting that back. Please."

Marnie rolled her eyes but went back into the bedroom.

Dane grinned.

"I guess it's a good thing I didn't just barge in," he said. "If a bullet didn't do me in, the lamp just might have."

A look she couldn't place passed over Dane's expression. He took a small step backward and jutted his thumb over his shoulder. His truck was parked at the mouth of the drive, since there was no true curb around the property unless you drove back to the two-lane that connected to the town. "Everyone's still looking for the men, but until we have more information, I thought I might hang out here for a while, just as a precaution."

Rachel couldn't stop her surprise from surfacing.

"Deputy Ward is keeping an eye out on Lonnie, too," he added.

She recovered. "Oh, yeah. Well, that's good. Especially after everything Lonnie went through today. Better safe than sorry."

Rachel omitted that she felt another surge of relief having someone so close. It was only after he started to turn away that she wondered if that feeling was because her someone just happened to be Dane.

"Okay, well, charge your cell and give me a heads-up if anyone else is coming over," he said, already moving down the steps. "I'll see you in the morning."

"Hey, Dane."

The words left Rachel's mouth before her mind could

catch them. Dane turned, but his expression was blank. He was shutting down.

Again.

Still, Rachel was riding the high of feeling relief and, after the day she'd had, she didn't want it to stop.

"You could stay inside," she said. "In the spare room or on the couch. It isn't like you haven't slept on either before."

She tried to smile. She really did. She tried to remember the man who had been her husband's best friend. The man who had been *her* friend. The one who had smiled and joked and never turned down an invitation from them to come over.

But time had a funny way of making memories hurt, even when they were good ones.

And maybe that showed.

Dane shook his head and averted his gaze. "I can't."

He went back to his truck without another word.

Then, all at once, Rachel felt her anger returning.

This time it was aimed at a man named Marcus. Not only had he taken her husband from her, he'd all but taken her friend, too.

Chapter Five

Rachel took her coffee out onto the back patio the next morning. It was her second cup and not strong enough to combat her nearly sleepless night. Every time she seemed to close her eyes, there was the sandy-haired man smiling at her. Then there was Overalls grabbing her hair. Both images together and separate had gotten her out of bed and roaming the house. Or, really, going to the front windows and peeking out to see if Dane's truck was still there.

It had been.

Every single time.

Now she was trying not to think too much and just hoping the caffeine would kick in and make her feel less sluggish. And more normal.

The sun shone through the tops of the pine trees and warmed the wooden rail she was leaning against. The side patio would always be her favorite spot in the world, she was sure. Worn, in need of a new coat of stain, and filled with past moments when she'd spent countless hours across its surface, it was Rachel's idea of peaceful.

She looked out toward the creek in the distance. It wound around the two acres of her land in a half circle before going through the next two properties. She remembered how much she'd disliked having water near the house when she'd moved into David's family home right after they married, perpetually afraid of flooding that never came. Now it was her favorite feature. She supposed there was some comfort in the fact that no matter how unexpected the turns her life took, she could look out at that creek and watch it keep going the same way it had been going for years.

It didn't stop for tragedy.

It didn't stop for sorrow.

It didn't stop just because there were bad men with bad intentions out there.

It just kept going.

Rachel sighed into her coffee.

Clearing her head wasn't as easy as she'd hoped.

Her thoughts turned to Lonnie. If she was having a hard time coping with what had happened, then she had to believe Lonnie might be struggling, too. Playing it tough in the schoolyard or in the hallways was one thing. He might have held it together at the school and in the department before his uncle had picked him up, but now that it had had time to settle?

Rachel tightened her grip around the coffee cup. She kept her gaze on the creek. There it was, apathetic to how rapidly her thoughts jumped from fear to worry and then to anger.

Yesterday had felt like one long dance between her and Dane, both trying to move around each other without getting too close. She knew why she'd done it. Anger and frustration. But him? He'd pawned her off on a stranger once she needed to leave the department. The old Dane? Her friend? He wouldn't have left her.

But he had.

Yet, even after years of no contact, when danger had

found its way to her, Rachel's first instinct had been to call him.

Because you still trust him.

"Hush it," she responded into her coffee.

The coffee complied.

Something moved against her hip, earning a knee-jerk reaction of nearly jumping out of her skin. Her coffee sloshed over the edge of the mug. "Sweet crickets!"

Even with the coffee and the soothing creek in the distance, she couldn't deny that she was still on edge.

Rachel finagled the vibrating phone from her pocket and shook some of the coffee off her other hand. The Caller ID showed Dane again.

"To be fair, I called to try and not scare you."

Rachel looked from the phone to the patio stairs. On the path that led from around the house to the front porch stood Dane. Trying to look apologetic.

Rachel put her hand to her chest and took a deep breath.

"I guess I'm a little jumpy this morning," she admitted. Dane nodded but kept to the bottom of the stairs. He was still wearing his button-down and jeans, but now there were bags beneath his eyes, too. He hadn't slept. "Is everything okay?"

"Detective Foster thinks he found a potential lead. He and Billy are looking into it."

"Good." The faster the men were caught, the better.

Dane ran a hand across his jaw and nodded. "No suspicious activity was reported at Lonnie's by Deputy Ward and no one other than your friend came or went last night."

"Also good."

He nodded again. It was off. Like the motion was on reflex. Like he wasn't actually listening to himself.

Rachel tilted her head slightly to the side, trying to figure out his thoughts. But, while she'd been good friends with the man years ago, it felt like a lifetime had passed between them. She could no sooner tell what he was thinking than she could tell what he was feeling.

"We'll keep someone on both today, but I need to go relieve Henry from Lonnie's until another deputy can step in," he continued. "His kid has the flu and his wife woke up with it, so he needs to hustle home."

Rachel felt herself perk up. "So you're going to Lonnie's right now?"

She already was turning with her coffee cup in hand.

"Yeah, just long enough until someone comes and relieves me."

"Can I come with you?" Rachel was positive it was exactly what she needed to feel better. She could either sit around worrying about the boy, or check on him herself. Maybe even talk to his uncle and learn a little bit more about his home life, too. Maybe set some of the rumors straight when it came to the teachers at Darby Middle. "I mean, I can take my own car if you'd like," she added. "I just— I'd like to see how Lonnie's doing."

Dane surprised her with a small smile.

"If you don't mind me stopping by somewhere that has coffee, I'm fine with you riding along."

It was Rachel's turn to smile. "I can do you one better."

THEY SET OUT from the house a few minutes later with two cups of homemade coffee, a Tupperware container filled with cookies, and too many things left unsaid between them. Dane had already known that Rachel asking to come along was a possibility, but until she'd asked, he hadn't known what he was going to say in response. He'd planned his day around sticking close to her while working the case from a stationary spot—which he'd gotten good at over his career as captain—so if she wanted to leave, coming along with him definitely made things easier.

Or, at least, the work side of things.

Their personal issues weren't as easy to work around.

So Dane decided not to address them at all. He was going to treat Rachel like just another civilian. There was a bigger picture. One he'd hopefully see when the men were caught.

He didn't need to, nor had the time to, get lost in the past.

"I'm surprised that Marnie girl didn't stay the night," he said once they were on the county road. "She seemed ready to fight by your side. Never seen a lady brandish a lamp before."

He kept his eyes on the road but heard the smile in her voice when she answered.

"You've seen a man brandish a lamp?"

Dane felt his smile pull up the corner of his lips. "Actually, I have."

And so Dane ate up the time between the outskirts of Darby to the other side of town by relaying the story about Marty Wallace, drunk as a skunk, coming into a restaurant to confront his cheating girlfriend. Who'd just happened to be on a date one table over. Dane had barely saved the new beau from receiving a whack upside the head by a fancy lamp when he restrained the cursing-like-a-sailor Marty.

"Want to know the kicker? After he got out of jail, he went back to the restaurant and picked a fight with the owner."

Rachel let out a small gasp. "Why did he do that?"

"The lamp that he broke cost five hundred dollars. Marty didn't want to pay it."

"Five hundred dollars?" She whistled. "I don't blame him. I might have started a fight with the owner, too. Did he end up paying it or did he get arrested again?"

"Billy ended up feeling so bad for him that he talked the owner out of pressing charges." Dane couldn't help chuckling. "Then Billy managed to convince the man that the lamp was too ugly to be worth that much, so the owner went out and got a new one anyways."

Rachel laughed a good laugh. Dane hadn't realized how much he had missed the sound.

"That's our sheriff for you," he added. "A fearless leader with a bleeding heart when it comes to overpaying for lamps. I don't know what Riker County would do without him."

This time Rachel didn't laugh. He glanced over. Denim blue. Staring straight ahead.

"You know, I always thought you'd run for sheriff." Her voice sounded different. Off. Distant. "Wasn't that a part of your five-year plan?"

There it was.

One of those unsaid things. Dane fought the urge to tense up.

"I decided I wanted something different," he answered. "Now I can't imagine anyone other than Billy running the county. He's a good man and good at what he does. Plus, I like my job. I may not be hitting the streets as much, but I still get done what needs to get done."

It was all honest enough. His plans had changed and he was sure as sure could be that Billy had found his true calling. Dane, on the other hand, felt like he had found his in being captain. He might be a desk jockey most of the time, but he made it work. The only lie? It had taken a while for him to accept it.

"So what you're saying is that you stepping out of your office to do guard duty isn't on your normal roster of daily activities?"

Dane had to look over again. If only because of the humor he heard in her response. She was no longer distant. Dane was surprised. He thought talking about their pasts at any length would bring out the flash of anger he'd already seen several times in the past twenty-four hours.

"No, it's not something I typically do," he admitted. "I guess I just needed to hit my abnormal quota before the year ran out."

Rachel snorted.

Silence followed. It settled in the cab of the truck like pollen to the ground on a summer day. Dane kept his gaze forward as he navigated an older neighborhood. Darby wasn't the smallest town in the county, but it wasn't the largest, either. This was one of the three neighborhood clusters within the town limits. It was also the oldest. All the strings of houses they passed revealed their age. Almost all of them showed disrepair, while some showed signs of renovation. It was also typically a neighborhood that housed a mostly older generation of residents. Not a popular children's or young family's neighborhood, if Dane wasn't mistaken.

"Does Lonnie live with his grandparents?" Dane asked. "I wasn't there when he was picked up and can't remember if I ever knew what his relation was to his guardian other than that his parents are gone."

"I don't know much about their family life, but I know he lives with his uncle, Tucker. His parents passed away when he was a toddler." Rachel's voice held a whopping dose of concern as she continued. "If you believe the gossip at school, his uncle views him more as an obligation than family."

He could tell Rachel didn't like what she was saying. Dane didn't, either.

He kept quiet, though, and turned onto Amber Street. Henry's car was parked curbside in front of the house. Dane pulled up behind it and cut the engine. He didn't get out right away.

"I probably should have mentioned this before, but Henry's wife, Cassie, the one with the flu?" he started. "She's the one who took you back to the school yesterday."

Rachel sighed.

"That's just what I need on top of everything else," she muttered. "The flu."

Dane tried on another apologetic look and went out to talk to Henry. Deputy Ward was one of the newest additions to the department but, Dane had to admit, one of his favorite people to work with. Not only did he make Cassie, a friend and coworker happy, but he was a nice guy with a good sense of humor. Especially when it came to being a husband and a father.

"Sorry again, Dane," he said through his rolled-down window. "Cassie's sister is out of town…with my brother." He gave Dane an exasperated look. "The first time they decide to go on some romantic getaway together and my house breaks out with, as my lovely wife put it, 'exorcist-style vomiting.'" He ran a hand down his face. "If there was anyone else to help out, I'd call them in, but—"

Dane cut the man off with a wave. "Don't worry about it. Deputy Medina said she was more than happy to switch." Henry's eyebrow rose. Dane cracked a grin.

"She got tricked into helping with courtroom duty, and we both know how much she hates being in there. For her this is an ideal way to spend the day."

"Glad I'm not putting her out, then." Henry motioned to the house. "As for why I'm here, no one has showed up or left the house since I followed them here last night. In fact, you're the only movement I've seen all night and morning. Anything interesting happen at your place?"

"No, just the same."

Henry's phone buzzed in his cup holder. Dane spied his wife's name on the Caller ID. He laughed and tapped the top of the car twice.

"Go ahead and get out of here," he said. "We can handle it."

Henry nodded and was gone by the time Dane walked back to his truck. Rachel was standing next to it, a smile on her face and a container of cookies in her hand. When she looked at him, Dane felt like he was putting his feet back into that ice-cold water.

This time, though, it was different.

Soft blue eyes that had a life of their own met his.

For a moment they tricked him into believing that nothing had changed between them. That they were still close friends. That he hadn't dropped out of her life on purpose for years. That he hadn't been the reason her husband had been killed.

That, even if he tried to deny it, there wasn't something inside him that seemed to open up when around her.

But just like that, Dane remembered everything.

He remembered finding his best friend's body.

He remembered feeling Rachel quake in anguish against him after he'd told her the news.

He remembered the guilt that took root in his soul and had only grown through the years.

And most of all, Dane remembered Rachel wearing a yellow sundress, trying to change a tire a year after the funeral.

She hadn't seen him, but he'd seen her.

That was when he'd known he needed to keep the distance between them.

No matter what.

"Ready?"

Dane nodded and, despite his resolve, he followed.

Chapter Six

The two-story house was a mixture of dark and faded wood with a missing porch step and a patch of shingles in disrepair. The whole building seemed to be sagging, pulled downward and tired, but that might just have been an illusion from the way the entire lot sloped toward the road.

Rachel held the container of cookies to her stomach. She felt oddly nervous.

Traumas had a way of changing people.

She hoped Lonnie was okay.

"You might want to take the lead," Dane said, falling back by her elbow. "After what happened, Tucker Hughes might be more inclined to open the door to a friendly face."

Rachel shored up her shoulders and knocked. She wondered, belatedly, if Lonnie and his uncle had slept in—it was barely nine in the morning—but then she heard movement in the house.

"Someone just peeked through the blinds," Dane said after a moment. "I'm guessing Lonnie, since it was toward the bottom."

A few seconds later the sound of locks turning came through. The door opened slowly but only an inch.

"Ms. Roberts? What you doing here?"

Lonnie's nose peeked through the crack in the door, followed by a suspicious stare.

Rachel shook the container in her hand.

"I was wondering if you had a sweet tooth like me," she hedged. Coming right out and admitting she was worried about the boy might make him defensive. She didn't want him to shut the door in her face. "It's the least I could do for helping me yesterday."

Lonnie eyed the cookies a moment before slowly opening the door the rest of the way. Rachel immediately knew two things.

One, the boy hadn't slept. Or, at least, hadn't slept well. His eyes, like the house, sagged. Second, she wasn't leaving until she talked to his uncle. For whatever reason she wanted—no, needed—to make sure he was okay. With an ache in her heart, Rachel realized it was the closest thing she'd ever felt to maternal.

"What kind of cookies?"

Rachel forced a smile. "Chocolate chip and oatmeal raisin. Both from scratch. My great-grandma's secret recipe, too."

Dane leaned in. "And let me tell you, they're awesome."

Lonnie looked between them. He seemed sold. Dane stepped forward enough to bring Lonnie's attention back to him.

"How about you go get your uncle?" he asked. "Then Ms. Roberts here can wow you with some of the best cookies I've ever had."

Lonnie shrugged. "He's not here."

Out of her periphery Rachel saw Dane tense. She probably didn't fare much better. When he spoke she could tell he was holding back.

"He brought you home last night, though, didn't he?"

Lonnie looked bored, but he nodded. "Yeah, but then he said he had to leave and took off."

Rachel took great pains to hide her surprise. "Did he have to go to work?" Her voice was not as calm as she wanted it to be. She felt Dane's hand press lightly on her back. "Did he say when he was coming back?"

"Nah. He said he was going out of town and that was it."

Lonnie didn't seem to notice that both adults in front of him had gone from worried to angry in the drop of a hat. At least, that was what Rachel was feeling. Anger mixed with a hefty amount of confusion.

"Hey, Lonnie, why don't you take those cookies inside and we'll come in in a minute to have some, too?" Dane said. "If that's okay with you?"

Lonnie shrugged again. "Whatever."

Rachel handed the container over and then let Dane steer her off the front porch and onto the lawn. He didn't speak until the front door closed behind them.

"I'm going to hunt that man down and ask him why the hell he isn't here." He was fuming, his voice low. He pulled out his phone. "We still have his number on file."

"How did he get past Deputy Ward? Didn't he follow them home from the department last night?"

Dane ran a hand through his hair while the other scrolled through his contacts. "Yeah, Henry followed them here." He hit a number and gave her a severe look. "Henry has a keen eye and doesn't slack off." He pointed over her shoulder to the side of the house. An old truck was parked next to it. "And if I'm not mistaken, Henry told me last night that that was Tucker's truck. So if both of those things are true—"

"Then Tucker must have snuck off last night," she finished. "But why?"

Dane had straight steel in his voice when he answered. "I don't know, but I'm sure about to find out."

RACHEL TRIED TO keep an open mind as she went inside while Dane did whatever he was doing. Surely if Tucker had left Lonnie alone, there had to be a good reason. Maybe it was work-related. There had been many times when her mom had had to leave her for work when she was young, even when her mother hadn't wanted to. It came with the territory of being a single, working parent. Not every boss was understanding and not every parent or guardian could cross a boss who didn't understand.

But then Rachel was in the house and her open mind started to close.

It was a nice house. Sparse. Run-down but clean. She went through the foyer and the living space, and then into the kitchen, where she found Lonnie. Even before she saw him eating a cookie, she felt like something was off. It wasn't until she took a cookie in her own hand that she realized what felt wrong.

The house felt empty.

Sure, it had furniture, but that was the end of it. There were few to no pictures in the foyer and living room and just as many knickknacks. All the small details that made a house feel like a well-lived-in home weren't there. It just felt empty. Certainly not a place where a child lived.

A shell of what should be a home.

"I'm not dumb, you know," Lonnie said around a bite of oatmeal raisin. Rachel immediately feigned innocence. Was her worry and anger that apparent?

"I know you're here to check up on me."

Rachel quirked an eyebrow but didn't deny it.

"You didn't have to. I'm fine. Just like I said I was yesterday a billion times." He took another large bite of his cookie as if to prove his point.

Rachel leaned against the counter opposite him. She tried to look nonchalant.

"Maybe I just wanted to hang out with someone who knows how I'm feeling," she tried. "I mean, you said you're fine, but maybe I'm not. Yesterday was definitely scary."

Lonnie's eyes narrowed but he didn't take the bait. "I think you just came with that cop because he had to switch with that other one that was outside all night."

Rachel motioned to the cookies, surprised the boy had been so observant.

"Or maybe I couldn't sleep last night, so I made some cookies and thought you might like some," she countered.

The idea seemed laughable to him that someone might have thought about him unprovoked. That was clear in the look of disbelief he gave her. It pulled at her heartstrings. She decided to tell him the truth.

"You deserve more than a box of cookies," she continued. "Even though I never want you to put yourself in danger like that again, yesterday you showed a whole lot of courage when you attacked that man when he had a hold of me. Not everyone would try to help in the same situation, especially if it meant they had to put themselves in harm's way. It was selfless and brave. And I wanted to sincerely thank you for it."

Lonnie looked like he wanted to say something sarcastic. However he seemed to change his mind. He didn't acknowledge what he'd done, but he didn't lash out, either.

"Does your arm still hurt?" He eyed the bandage at her wrist. He seemed genuinely curious. "Is it still bleeding?"

"I don't know, actually. Want to find out?"

Like with most little boys, Lonnie's intrigue tripled. He closed the gap between them to watch her unwrap the bandage. It wasn't bleeding, but it still seemed to impress him.

"That was cool what you did with the window," he said after they inspected the healing cut. "I thought you were crazy when you punched it."

Rachel laughed.

"You weren't the only one." They both turned. Dane was standing in the doorway. He had a smile on his face but it wasn't right, just like the house. It was empty. Off. "Lonnie, could I use your bathroom?"

He shrugged, keeping his eyes on her cut. "I don't care," he answered. Rachel lowered her arm so he could get a better view. It gave Dane the perfect opportunity to mouth a message at her.

Keep him in here.

DANE WENT PAST the bathroom and up the stairs as quickly and quietly as he could. Then he was in the master bedroom and trying his best not to curse too loudly. Tucker Hughes had been a mystery to him before because he'd had no reason to know the man.

Now?

Now he wished he had done his homework on Tucker.

Unlike the rest of the house, his room was chaotic. Like someone had ripped through it looking for something.

Dane stepped over discarded clothes and went to the closet. It was partially open and mostly empty. With a sinking feeling he did a cursory sweep of the rest of the room. He came up empty. Nothing pointed him to any answers as to why Tucker Hughes had up and left his nephew the way he had. Nor why he had seemingly packed most of his belongings. There was no empty luggage or bags that Dane could find.

He left the bedroom and went to the one across the hall. It was Lonnie's bedroom and while it was a little messy, it didn't look like Tucker had started or even attempted to pack up the boy.

It would have made more sense to leave with Lonnie than to leave him behind.

Though, again, neither course of action made sense.

Dane's cell phone went off in his hand. He hurried out of the room and back down the stairs. He nodded to Rachel as he passed the kitchen. Lonnie didn't stop talking.

"Captain Jones," he answered on reflex, closing the front door behind him.

"Cowboy Montgomery," Chance replied with a grin in his voice. Dane rolled his eyes.

"I'm not in the mood," he warned. It worked to snap the man out of any follow-up jokes or sarcasm.

"Why? What's going on?"

Dane paced himself right off the porch. Last time he'd talked to Chance was yesterday after Suzy had left him alone in the break room. He had wanted to tell Chance what had happened at the school. It was too much of a coincidence to have two pieces from the past surface, just as Suzy had said. Not that Dane believed it wasn't just coincidence one hundred percent. But, just in case, he'd told the man. They hadn't talked since.

"Just more things not adding up," Dane replied, skirting clarification. "Why? What's up with you?"

"Remember that guy I was waiting to call me back

about the radio equipment that was stolen? Just got off the phone with him. Apparently what was stolen is specific only to someone who's trying to broadcast."

"You mean like air their own show?"

"Yep. They already have the means. Now all they need is the know-how. Then they can get on their own frequency, depending on how much they actually know. They can say whatever they want."

Dane didn't like that.

Why would thieves need to broadcast? "And you still have no idea where these guys are?"

"No. According to my contact in Birmingham local PD, the only lead they have is the van and Tracy Markinson. You know, the same van that could have been at the school yesterday."

Dane gritted his teeth.

"Just because two crimes happen around the same time doesn't mean they're connected," Dane reminded him.

"And just because two crimes don't make sense doesn't mean they *aren't* connected," Chance countered.

They were both right.

"Speaking of not making sense, I'd like to hire you as a consultant on something," Dane announced. "You interested?"

"Is it connected to what happened yesterday?"

"I don't know, to be honest, but it's definitely a mystery we need to solve ASAP." Dane could hear movement on the other side of the phone.

"Okay, got a pen and paper. Hit me."

Even though Dane was outside, he kept his voice low and walked farther down the sidewalk that led to the curb. As if Lonnie could hear him. He just didn't want to spook the boy. He'd already been through enough.

"I want you to find someone for me. Tucker Hughes. H-u-g-h-e-s." He waited a beat for Chance to write it down. "He's Lonnie's uncle. The boy from yesterday."

"And now he's missing?"

Dane balled his fist.

"More like he left." Dane relayed what he'd found and didn't find. "I already tried his cell. It's off. Can you tell me why he snuck out of his own house with packed bags but not the kid?"

"Sounds like running away to me," Chance answered.

"It sounds like Tucker Hughes knows something," Dane said. "And I'd like to ask him what that something is."

"All right, Captain, then let me work some of my magic and see if I can't pull this rabbit out of a hat."

Once their call ended, Dane took a second to let a breath out. He could feel a tension headache rising behind his eyes. Too many questions. Too many isolated events *or* too many connected ones that made no sense.

Yet.

Dane rubbed the back of his neck and looked at the houses around them. A car was parked in the driveway across the street. Maybe they had seen something or knew something. Dane pulled up Rachel's number and called her.

"I'm going to ask the neighbors some questions," he said by way of greeting when she answered. "I'll just be across the street."

"Sure thing, Mom."

Dane felt his brow rise.

"You're trying not to freak the kid out, aren't you?" he ventured.

"Yes, ma'am," she answered. "Anything else?"

Dane started toward the road. "Yeah, go ahead and

lock the door. There's something weird going on here. Stay on your toes."

"Sounds good," she said, voice chipper.

"I'll be back in a few minutes."

Dane was a second away from ending the call when Rachel responded.

"Love you, too. 'Bye."

The call ended. The surprise at Rachel's words and how they resonated with something he couldn't deny was pleasant within him, didn't.

Chapter Seven

Rachel talked Lonnie into showing her his art portfolio while Dane went to talk to the neighbors. It wasn't due until the end of the year, but she was surprised to see he had been vigilantly filling it. Lonnie was sitting on his bed trying to look like he didn't care, but Rachel called his bluff.

"These are really good, Lonnie. You must have worked really hard on them." She paused at a collection of doodles. They were in the style of a comic. She wasn't lying. They were really good. "This looks cool."

She held out the page.

For the first time since she'd known the boy, Lonnie's eyes lit up.

"It's not finished," he said. "I'm working on the other pages still. Then it'll be an entire comic book."

Rachel didn't have to check the smile that sprang to her lips. Any child expressing genuine passion for art made her happy. Add in the fact that that child had been written off by most as just an angry, unhappy boy? Well, that made it doubly wonderful to see him so enthused.

She delicately placed the picture back in the portfolio. "And what does your uncle think of all your art? Surely he has to be as impressed as I am."

Lonnie shrugged. "He's not into art."

Rachel was careful to put the portfolio back in the space between the bed and the wall.

"Just because someone's not into art doesn't mean they can't appreciate a good job," she pointed out.

He shrugged again. This time he didn't meet her eyes. "It's just not his thing."

"You know, I don't know much about your uncle," she started. "Why don't you tell me a little about him? Like what do you two do for fun?"

Rachel once again tried to get that open mind back, but she saw her answer in his eyes when he finally met her stare. Tucker was rarely home and they didn't do anything for fun. Still, she let him say it.

"He works a lot," he said. "And when he comes home he's tired. But it's okay. I don't mind. I like being alone."

A vise went around Rachel's heart and squeezed.

She didn't know what she wanted to say but knew she wanted to say *something*. Yet movement out of the corner of her eye turned her attention to the window.

A black Lincoln pulled into the driveway.

It wasn't a van, but the anxiety was immediate.

"Does Tucker have a second vehicle?" she asked.

Lonnie followed her gaze. "No."

"Recognize that car?"

He shook his head. "No."

Rachel looked across the street to the house Dane had walked to. She couldn't see him or any neighbors outside it. She pulled out her phone as the back door of the Lincoln opened. Tucker Hughes stepped out—or rather, he spilled out. Even from the second-story window, Rachel could see the blood caked across his face. He limped as he started toward the house.

"He's hurt," Lonnie whispered.

The front two doors of the car didn't open, but Rachel knew better. Just because no one got out of the front, didn't mean they weren't threats.

"And he's not alone," she said.

It was a moment of pure déjà vu.

Rachel went straight for Dane's number.

THERE WAS NO doubt that Tucker Hughes was in pain. Dane stood in the shadows of the house across the street and watched as the man wobbled to his front door. Whoever'd driven him stayed in the car. Dane took a picture of the vehicle and its tag.

Tucker knocked against the door.

Dane's phone rang. It was Rachel.

"Hide," he greeted. "Something's not right. I'm coming over."

"Okay," she whispered. "We're upstairs."

Her voice was so soft. Vulnerable. It moved Dane to action.

He called Billy. Sliding his free hand down to his holster, he crouched low and hurried across the street to the back of his truck. He'd had to park farther back, since Henry's car had been in the way. Maybe Tucker and the men in the car thought Dane's vehicle belonged to the neighbor. Either way, he didn't give it or Dane a second glance as he pulled his keys out and worked on the front door.

"Reed here," Billy answered. Once again, Dane didn't bother with pleasantries. Tucker went inside. Whoever was in the car didn't try to follow. Dane couldn't see past the window tint to get a description.

"Tucker just showed up, bloody, from a black Lincoln," he said, copying Rachel's whisper. "At least two people are still inside the car. Rachel and Lonnie are in the house. I told her to hide, but I'm going in."

"Be there as fast as we can."

Dane ended the call and slipped the phone into his pocket. If the passengers in the car were looking toward the other side of the house, there was no way he was going to be able to stay unseen while he made a dash through the side yard. But that was a chance he was going to take. Dane still didn't know what was going on. He could have been jumping to conclusions, but then again, his gut was firm in its assessment that something was *not* right.

Keeping his hand on the butt of his gun, Dane took a deep breath and ran.

No one shot or yelled or tried to get his attention when he got to the side of the house. He didn't pause to celebrate. Keeping low to avoid being seen through the first-floor windows, he looped around the back of the house to the porch. It wasn't missing any steps like the front was, but it wheezed something awful under his weight. Dane cringed, trying to make it to the door. The floor went from a wheeze to a wicked creak.

He wasn't surprised when the doorknob turned.

Instead he was ready.

Tucker's expression went from confused to afraid in the blink of his swollen eye. The gun pointing at him probably wasn't helping matters.

"Don't make a sound," Dane warned. "I don't want your friends coming in before we can talk. Got it?"

Dane didn't know much about Tucker, he'd be the first to admit that, but at least he knew the man wasn't wholly stupid. He nodded and retreated backward into the house, both hands in the air. Dane kept the gun trained on him. If he really was blowing this whole thing out of proportion, he was going to get a lot of grief over how he was acting.

But he wasn't going to apologize for it.

Not when Rachel and Lonnie were still in the area.

Dane eased the door shut behind him. Tucker watched, eyes as wide as they could go considering how swollen and bloodied he was.

"I'm Captain Dane Jones with the Riker County Sheriff's Department." Dane introduced himself. He didn't whisper, but his voice was low. "I have some questions." He started to lower his gun. "Okay?"

Tucker nodded. He kept his eyes on Dane. "Where's Lonnie?" he asked.

"Who are the men outside?" Dane countered. Tucker lowered his hands to his sides.

"Where's Lonnie?" Tucker repeated.

"Don't worry. He's okay. But judging by your face, you're not. *Who* are the men outside?"

Tucker shifted his weight. He threaded his fingers together. His gaze bounced from Dane to his gun and back again. He was uncomfortable and not just because he was hurt. Something else was bothering him.

"I need to know where Lonnie is," he said. "Now."

"You mean the kid that you left in the middle of the night?"

Tucker's lips thinned.

"I came back," he muttered.

"*You still left.* Why?"

Dane was mindful of his service weapon's weight in his hand and the space between him and Tucker. Was the man stupid enough to try to disable Dane?

And if so, why?

What the hell was going on?

A car door shut in the distance. With that, Tucker's weird behavior took another turn. This time it was straight to fear.

"They can't know you're here," he rasped. "No one but Lonnie is supposed to be here."

"That's not how it works," Dane said, eyeing the front door. "I'm not leaving until you tell me what's going on."

Tucker followed his gaze. It was like he was seeing a ghost.

"They'll kill me," he said simply. "They'll kill me if they think I called in the cops."

There was no more fear. No. It was worse than that. The man was terrified.

It made up Dane's mind. "You do *anything* and I'll take you both down."

Tucker jerked his head up to nod. Dane raised his gun to prove he meant what he said. He fell back to the doorway that led from the main hall into the kitchen. If anyone wanted to get to the stairs, they'd have to get past him first. Until then he was going to listen. He needed to know what was going on.

The front door opened without a knock. Whoever it was, even their movements into the house sounded aggressive.

"You're not thinking about running again, are you, Tuck?" The voice belonged to a man. It was deep, but Dane couldn't place it. It also clearly held no love for Tucker Hughes. "Levi might have given you a second chance, but I'm here to tell you there won't be a third." His footsteps slowed. Dane tightened his grip on the gun. If Tucker decided to give up his location, he'd have to fight sooner rather than later.

"I'm not running," Tucker declared. There was more backbone in his voice than Dane expected of the man he'd just seen drowning in fear. The other man must have heard it, too.

"You're damn right you're not running." The other man spat. "Fool me once, Tuck."

"I'm not fooling anyone," Tucker snapped back. "I was just looking for Lonnie, is all."

"What do you mean you're looking for him? You're saying he's *not* here?"

"I didn't say that, I—" Tucker stopped. Dane hoped he didn't look toward the kitchen.

"I—I what?" Heavy footsteps barreled down the hallway. Dane held his breath, muscles tensing. "You know when Levi told me your part in all this, I laughed. Do you wanna know why, ol' Tuck? Because I couldn't believe the entire plan came back to you of all people." The other man snickered. "You buckle under even the slightest pressure. Hell, I remember how you quaked at every football game and you weren't even off the bench. Ready to cry if the coach even thought about putting you in. And now?"

Dane heard a soft thud and Tucker's intake of breath. The man must have hit him.

"Now I'm the only one who isn't surprised that you royally screwed this."

Dane imagined Tucker cowering on the other side of the wall. However, he was wrong. Tucker bit back.

"At least I'm not the one who got outmatched by a woman and a kid."

They could have heard a pin drop in the silence that followed. Dane's own anger cascaded over him, coiling his muscles even tighter. His gut continued to grumble. Tucker wasn't just a neglectful uncle, he was a suspect.

"You listen here, Tuck," began the other man. His words had turned toxic, slithering around in a barely contained rage. Dane recognized the sound. Years ago he'd heard the same in his own voice. "For whatever reason, the boss thought he needed you to keep the boy safe. The operative word? *Thought*. The moment we caught you trying to get the heck out of Dodge was the moment you became even more useless than you already were. We don't need *you*. Not anymore."

Another sharp intake of breath let Dane know the man was getting physical again. Tucker whimpered. "What you *are* going to do for me is tell me where that boy is or else I'm going to kill you. Plain and simple. So make your choice. *Now*."

In Dane's head he was already turning the corner, gun ready, to keep Tucker from making a choice and to keep the mystery man from dishing out the consequence of whatever that choice might be. Planning ahead hadn't always been Dane's strong suit, but now, after what had happened to David, he tried his damnedest to keep two steps ahead of the game. Yet not even the most skilled of strategists could account for every piece on the game board. A lesson Dane was reminded of when something happened that neither he, Tucker nor their mystery man had planned.

A thump shook the ceiling.

The mystery man laughed. "Looks like I might not need you at all. Sounds like the boy is upstairs. Safe and sound."

Dane swung around the corner. "Don't move or I'll shoot!"

The mystery man didn't have a gun, but he did have a knife. It was an angry-looking thing with a blade that stretched at least six inches. It drew a stark contrast to the skin of Tucker's neck. All the man had to do was change his gaze to Dane and he was still in a position of power.

And he knew it.

After the surprise shook free, a smirk drew up one side of his lips.

"I figured Tuck would pull something," he said, all humor. "Other than trying to run away. And who might you be?"

Without declaring his intentions verbally, the man only had to press the knife to Tucker's skin. It held Dane and him both captive without the man having to utter any threats.

"I'm with the Riker County Sheriff's Department and you need to drop your weapon. Now."

The man was tall and lean and had a farmer's tan peeking out from beneath his plain T-shirt. His jeans weren't faded like Dane's but dark and new, like they'd just been bought, and his shoes were shiny enough that the reflection of the fluorescents in the hallway bounced off them. It was like he was a man caught between two worlds. Like he was still in the process of getting ready for a party or in the process of winding down from one. Even his blond hair was slicked back, yet he had a chin covered in stubble.

He also didn't seem nonplussed that a man of the law had a gun trained on him. He pressed the knife forward. Even in his profile, Dane saw Tucker cringe.

"I'm warning you," Dane said, pulling out his lowest baritone. Still the man didn't move a muscle or show any signs of fear. "Backup is on the way," Dane added. "And I'm here to tell you, you're leaving this house in either cuffs or a body bag. Those are your choices."

Dane took the smallest of steps forward.

It only made the man's grin widen.

Dane heard the creak behind him two seconds too late.

"There's always a third choice," said a new voice from behind him. Dane's blood froze. "Always."

Chapter Eight

Rachel kept one arm wrapped around Lonnie's body, fastening his back to her chest and his arms to his sides. She had the other over his mouth, trying her best to keep him quiet. She didn't like to get physical, but she also didn't like what they'd heard downstairs.

She definitely didn't like it when Lonnie had tried to run down the stairs toward the men who seemed to want him.

Telling Lonnie to hide in his own home when Tucker approached the house wasn't something he'd taken too well. He hadn't understood why they'd needed to hide. Rachel had still been struggling to convince him to hide in his room when Dane started talking to Tucker. Lonnie had, thankfully, quieted by then. Like Rachel, he'd wanted to listen to what his uncle had to say. So that was why they had been in the small hallway connecting all the rooms on the second floor when the third man came in.

Then Rachel had seen the same fear she felt reflected in Lonnie's eyes when that man had spoken.

It was the same sandy-haired man who had shown up at the school.

Rachel didn't dare move as three of the men spoke, but she heard every word.

So did Lonnie.

If Rachel wasn't so afraid that they would hear her move, she would have gone the few feet between her and Lonnie and pulled him back to his room. Instead the two of them stood in silence, letting the conversation below float up the stairs. Apparently their run-in with the man at the school hadn't been a stroke of bad luck on their part. They had wanted Lonnie. But why?

And how did Tucker play into it all?

Rachel had waited to see what happened next with bated breath until the man had laid it on the table. The bottom line.

Tucker was to bring him Lonnie or he would kill Tucker.

Rachel had shared a look with the boy after the violent directive.

Then she'd had to act fast.

Lonnie was going to give himself up.

Rachel had less than a second to meet the boy in the middle, throw one arm around him and cover his mouth with her hand. It was a plan that wasn't without mistakes. The awkward height difference between them pulled Rachel off balance. They hit the floor hard.

The men downstairs quieted.

Lonnie squirmed, but Rachel kept both grips tight.

The mystery man started to talk again, but Rachel couldn't concentrate on it.

"You're not going down there," she whispered in Lonnie's ear.

She needed to get them out of the open. If either Tucker or the man walked up the stairs, there wasn't a hope in the world that they wouldn't see them.

But then Dane joined the fray, sounding like the lawman he was. Together Rachel and Lonnie stopped fighting each other to listen.

Rachel's stomach went straight to the floor when another voice entered the conversation. The man in overalls.

"We're going to go hide," Rachel directed, careful to keep her voice as low as possible. "Okay?"

Lonnie nodded. Rachel wasn't about to roll the dice, though. She lowered her hand but kept her arm around him. Together they stood slowly and crept backward. She didn't realize she was still holding on to him until they were in his room.

"They're going to kill him if I don't go down there," Lonnie whispered. Rachel spun with her finger to her lips. "But—"

"You listen to me, Lonnie Hughes," she hissed. "*I* would die before letting those men get their hands on you, so you better—"

A yell from downstairs was swiftly followed by the sounds of a heated scuffle. Then a gunshot rattled the inside of the house. Rachel's heart squeezed with worry over Dane, but she knew he could handle himself better than Lonnie could if three men came upstairs after him.

Rachel shut the bedroom door and threw the lock. She turned around, surveying the room with new attention. The closet door was already open, but it was small. The window over his bed overlooked a small roof overhang, but with nowhere to go *and* if anyone was left in the Lincoln, they would have an unobstructed view of whoever went out there. The only place left was the bed. It would have to do.

"I want you to get under that bed," she said, bending to make sure he could fit. "And I don't want you to make a sound, okay? *No matter what.*"

More yelling from downstairs seemed to convince Lonnie to listen to her. He dropped to the floor and wiggled underneath the bed. Rachel grabbed the blanket and stuffed it under, too, running it along his legs.

"Here, put this in your pocket." Rachel pulled out her phone and slid it to him. "If we get separated for whatever reason, you call 9-1-1 when you're alone."

Rachel pushed the blanket the rest of the way under. She grabbed the sheet and pulled it half off, draping some of it over the edge of the frame. She hoped it looked like a kid's messy bed and that said kid was not hiding beneath it.

Another gunshot went off, followed swiftly by footsteps thundering up the stairs. Rachel whirled around, heart in her throat and adrenaline flooding her system. She had nothing to protect herself and nothing to protect Lonnie, either. If someone who wasn't Dane came through the door, she didn't like the odds.

So she made another split-second decision as she had the day before.

She jumped on top of the bed and fumbled with the window latch. Maybe she could recreate what she had done in the gym. Redirect their attention to stall for Dane and the backup she only assumed he had called. Though she knew she couldn't hide inside the room, the roof outside the window was flat enough that she could walk across it without falling.

At least, she hoped.

The doorknob started to rattle behind her.

"Hey, kid, open up!"

If her stomach wasn't already on the floor, it would have dropped to it. The voice wasn't Dane's. It wasn't Tucker's, either. Her fingers slipped, but she managed to unlock the window. The door behind her shook violently.

"Don't make a sound," Rachel said, hoping Lonnie could hear her. The dull ache in her hand became more pronounced as she placed both palms on the pane of glass and pushed up. Thankfully, the window slid up easily enough.

However, before she could use that in any way, a loud crack made her turn. She watched the old door split in two like it was made out of nothing but cardboard. Dark eyes met hers. They widened in surprise. The sandy-haired man hadn't expected to see her—that was for sure.

"You," he breathed. He huffed as he moved some of the splintered wood out of his way. He had blood on one of his hands. Too much of it.

Rachel didn't need to see any more.

She turned and scrambled out the window like it was an Olympic sport and she *really* wanted a medal. The man yelled out at her, but she wasn't about to stop and listen. She crawled far enough away that he couldn't grab her unless he came out onto the overhang with her. If there was someone in the car and they were armed, all they had to do was get out and shoot her. Like fish in a barrel. Rachel didn't care. She just needed to distract the man. She needed him to follow her.

And follow her he did.

He just also changed her plan, or at least the gun he held up did. "I will shoot you in the head if you take even one more step."

Rachel held her hands up but stayed on her knees.

"Don't shoot," she pleaded. "I'm unarmed."

The man didn't flinch.

"Where's the kid?" he seethed, no smiles like he had worn the day before. He was hurting. Rachel hoped the blood on his hand was his.

"At the sheriff's department," she lied. "A deputy took him there a few minutes ago."

The man's nostrils flared. He was starting to fume. "You're lying."

"No, I'm not," she countered, rallying what she hoped was a sincere expression. She stuck as close to the truth as she could to make it easier to bluff. "We came to check on him and realized his uncle left him in the middle of the night. So we sent him off to the department until we could figure out where Tucker went and why. I was just closing up the house when you all showed up, so I hid."

Rachel had taken an acting class in college as an elective. It had been torture once she'd realized how bad at it she truly was. The unending scowl from her professor still haunted some of her stress dreams to this day. He'd always complained that her performances felt fabricated, like she was reading straight from a script. One time, much to her horror, he'd even told her in front of the entire class that watching her perform was like watching her recite a grocery list. One that didn't even have anything exciting written on it.

She'd once told David about that class, still experiencing mild embarrassment when a random memory sprang up from it. He'd laughed quite a bit before backing down enough to realize her feelings were hurt. Then he'd done what David had always done best and made light of the situation.

"It's because you don't like to lie," he had said. "So much so that I bet *that's* why you get all stiff when you're trying to be someone you're not or when you're trying to say something you don't mean. It's nothing to be ashamed of. In fact, I'll tell you what. I'm pretty proud of you for being terrible at it."

Rachel knew that what he said wasn't true—there were plenty of good people in the world who acted and didn't like lying—but it had made her feel better. She'd even started to be proud of the fact that she couldn't act her way out of a paper bag if she had tried. However, *now* she hoped beyond all hope that David's assessment didn't hold. Not today. Not when the man in front of her was so close to Lonnie's hiding place.

"If you don't believe me, call the department and ask," she added. "Tell them you're Tucker."

Rachel felt like she sounded confident. She just hoped he heard it, too. He was gritting his teeth hard. She could see the muscles in his jaw moving. A car honked in the distance. Dogs were barking a street or two over. What must have been only seconds stretched into what felt like minutes.

Within that time Rachel knew no matter what the man decided—to believe her or not to believe her—the outcome wouldn't be a good one. If she couldn't give him Lonnie, she was useless. If she could give him Lonnie, she would become useless right after he had the boy.

Either way, she realized there was a good chance she would die out on Tucker Hughes's roof. The thought should have scared her. Heck, it should have terrified her. Yet the fear that she felt around her heart wasn't for her.

It was for the kid who was hard to like but loved drawing comics.

It was for the captain who had answered her call without hesitation.

The man finally opened his mouth. Words filled with venom poured out. "We would have had him already if it wasn't for you."

Thinking he had been the cool one between him and

the man with overalls the day before, Rachel changed her mind. He looked like a powder keg in the process of igniting. One who had pinpointed her as someone who needed to explode along with him. "This was supposed to be *easy*," he said with the shake of his gun. Rachel flinched. He didn't miss it. A smile broke through his anger. It sent a chill up her spine.

"You know, he might have been the endgame, but grabbing you was supposed to be a bonus if we could swing it. I think I'm going to go ahead and make an executive decision for the group." He readjusted his aim a few inches upward. Directly at Rachel's head. "This time we just couldn't swing it."

Rachel turned her head away. She squeezed her eyes shut. *I hope you're okay, Dane.*

A gunshot tore through the morning air.

Rachel waited for the impact, the burn. The end to a life that was filled with the good, the bad, triumphs and regrets. A life ended by something that made no sense out on Tucker Hughes's roof.

All she felt was something warm against her cheek and then a small thud that vibrated through the knees of her jeans.

She opened her eyes.

Then she was looking at Dane.

Chapter Nine

"Rachel, I need you to keep looking at me." Dane holstered his gun as best he could while hunched over. "Don't look at him. Just look at me."

The "him" he was referring to was lying dead between them. Dane knew that without checking his pulse because he'd shot him in the head. It didn't matter if he could have helped them know more about what was going on. Hell, it wouldn't have mattered what he'd known, because the moment he'd aimed at *Rachel's* head was the moment Dane knew he wasn't taking any chances.

Not again.

Not with her.

Rachel listened. At least, only partially. She got to her feet but glanced at the man. Her face paled.

"Rachel Mary Roberts, you look at me and nothing else," he barked. It was a little too harsh, but it did the trick. Her blue eyes swung to him and him only. He reached out toward her through the window. "Just move a little to the right and then you're with me."

Rachel nodded and followed direction. Her hands were warm as they slid into his. Dane took it slow as he pulled her inside. Her eyes were wide. There was blood across her cheek. Dane knew it wasn't hers.

"Where's the other man?" she managed to ask. It came out with a waver. "Where's Tucker?"

"Tucker is downstairs. He's hurt but alive." Dane didn't like the next words he had to say. "The other man got a lead on me and ran off. I would have chased but…" He let his sentence trail off. He didn't have to spell it out. "Where's Lonnie?"

It was like someone had put ice down the back of her shirt. Rachel's spine zipped straight and she turned toward the bed. "Lonnie, you okay?"

The sheet hanging over the side shifted and then a blanket came out with it. Rachel knelt to help him wiggle his way out.

"Are *you* okay?" he asked, focusing on Rachel. "You're bloody."

Rachel started to touch her face, but Dane grabbed her wrist. "She's not hurt," he said. "But why don't we go to the bathroom and help her out?"

They both looked confused but let him lead the way. Fear was a powerful thing. Even if you didn't know what to fear, it had a way of making you move to avoid more of it. However, Rachel wasn't about to let Lonnie see the body whose image was no doubt burned into her mind. Dane watched as she kept at Lonnie's back. The last line of defense between him potentially losing a piece of his innocence.

Lonnie took a seat on the lip of the tub while Dane guided Rachel to the sink. She started to turn toward the mirror. Once again Dane stopped her. Their eyes met. She was close enough that he could see the few freckles across her nose. He'd never noticed them before.

She cleared her throat. "I'm assuming backup is on the way?"

Dane took the hand towel off the wall. He turned the

faucet on and dipped it underneath. "Yeah, I called in the cavalry when Tucker showed up. I'm surprised we aren't hearing sirens yet."

Lonnie stood. Dane held his hand out in a stop motion.

"You need to stay up here for now," he warned.

The boy's expression hardened. "You said my uncle was hurt downstairs!"

"He is, but help is coming. What you need to do now is stay in here with Ms. Roberts and make sure *she's* all right."

Dane hoped Rachel was reading him. He didn't want Lonnie downstairs. He didn't want him to see Tucker. The blood on her cheek was nothing compared to what had gone down on the first floor.

"I sure would like the company, Lonnie," she said after a moment.

Lonnie didn't say anything but he sat back down. Dane turned to Rachel. She was searching his face. He tried to smile. He really did. But the contrast of the man's blood against her skin wouldn't let him. He almost hadn't made it in time to save her.

Dane took the towel and brushed it across her cheek. She didn't look at him. He didn't meet her eyes. Silence settled in the room. Dane continued to run the towel over her skin. Then, when he was almost done, their eyes met. He was so close he could almost feel the coolness from them. Two pools of the most crystal-blue water you ever did see.

The same water he'd known for years and yet not.

They were different.

The freckles were different.

And that was when Dane realized that something *felt* different. Past the adrenaline, past the excitement of trying to survive an attack, there was something that had happened within him. Getting a phone call from Rachel in trouble had been one thing, but seeing her on her knees, hands up in the air, ready to take a madman's bullet?

There it was again. Burrowed into Dane's chest.

Something had shifted.

Something had changed.

It prompted a truth from him. One that was more than just about that day.

"I'm sorry I didn't show up sooner."

It was simple and honest. The way Dane tried to live his life. He should have reached out to Rachel years ago. Hell, he should never have left in the first place. Being out of touch had caused a rift between them.

Dane had never noticed her freckles before.

And that bothered him now.

"You saved me," she said. She glanced at Lonnie. "You saved us. That's not for nothing." A small smile tugged at her lips. Dane tried to return it.

What was he doing?

What was he hoping for?

They were in an active crime scene, Tucker was hurt downstairs, one of their attackers was on the loose, Dane's phone had been smashed in the tussle and was of no use to them, and backup still wasn't there. And yet there he was, thinking about Rachel Roberts's freckles.

Dane cleared his throat.

"There we go," he said, tossing the towel in the sink. "You still might want to wash your face, but the bad part is gone."

"Well, what about *your* blood?" Lonnie chipped in. He pointed to Dane's right side. Dane didn't bother looking.

"You're bleeding?" Rachel asked, worry lacing through each syllable.

"It's fine," he assured her.

"I can see it," Lonnie continued. "Your shirt has a cut in it."

Rachel reached out but Dane was quicker. He put distance between them by stepping out the door.

"It's nothing," he repeated. "Just a little thing."

"But—"

Dane shook his head. "I'm going to go back downstairs to be with Tucker. You two stay here until I come back. Okay?" He gave Rachel another one of those looks he hoped said more than he could out loud. "Okay, Rachel?"

There were those eyes searching him again.

"Okay. Be careful."

If Dane had had Sheriff Reed's cowboy hat on, he would have tipped it to her. "Yes, ma'am."

"Son of a—"

Dane took in a deep breath.

"Don't be such a baby, Captain." The nurse gave the man a scowl that would put hardened criminals he'd seen to shame. "I just disinfected the thing. Not performed some kind of surgery. I didn't even put you in a room."

"I think you're lying, Nurse Bean," he said. "But I guess I'll let it slide. You are on your break, after all."

Nurse Bean rolled her eyes. As best friend to Detective Walker's wife and friend of the department's as a whole, the nurse had seen her fair share of them in her emergency room. Which meant she was more than comfortable giving any of them flack when they deserved it. Dane didn't think he did, but he wasn't about to backtalk a woman who might change her mind about him needing stitches.

Nurse Bean finished cleaning the cut and bandaged it, all while standing in the hallway outside the ER. She'd only seen him because the nurses on duty had had their hands full with a car accident, a cardiac event and Tucker Hughes. The latter was still in surgery. The first mystery man had done a job on him with the knife. The second mystery man?

He'd taken a bullet before getting around Dane and bolting out the back door.

It was still burning Dane's chest.

"And I think we're all done here. Now let me go get some butterfly bandages."

Dane brought his attention to the forefront. He turned just enough to get a look at the bare skin on the side of his lower back. It was a nasty cut, no doubt. Would have been nastier had Dane not been able to retrieve his gun. If the first mystery man had still been downstairs, Dane wouldn't have been so lucky. All he would have had to do was to use his gun on him.

Dane fisted his hand into the shirt he was holding.

Being in the nick of time wasn't a badge of honor in his book. It just meant that he'd only been able to get there during the last possible second.

And it didn't sit right with him.

"I'm guessing you still aren't a fan of getting doctored."

Two blue eyes with a smile hanging beneath them met Dane's gaze when he looked up. Dane tried to play off his anger. It made him compensate too much. He answered with sarcasm. "I just like hanging around shirtless in hospitals. Drives the ladies crazy."

He wanted to put his foot in his mouth as soon as he

said it but was surprised when Rachel glanced down at his chest. He wasn't a man keen on bragging about his appearance, but he wasn't above himself to know his weekly gym visits paid off.

"So *this* is where you pick up dates," Rachel responded with a snort. "And here I guess I've been doing it wrong these past few years."

She matched his sarcasm with her own. Dane hadn't expected it or her talking about dating. Even if he'd been the one to bring it up and it had been a joke. Still, the idea of her dating someone put a sour taste in Dane's mouth.

"How's Lonnie doing?" he asked, changing gears. "I haven't gotten a chance to really talk to him since we got here."

Rachel sobered immediately. She shrugged.

"Honestly, I feel like he's doing better than I am," she admitted. "He's been talking to me like all this is normal. Even with all this confusion, he's somehow managing to keep his feet on solid ground."

"Unless he's just internalizing it all," Dane had to point out. She nodded.

"There *is* that," she conceded. "I just— Well, I just want to help him but don't know how. I guess I just wish we knew more about everything that's happened." She lowered her voice and took a small step forward. There were those freckles again. Up close and personal for him to see. "Why do they want *him* and why am *I* a bonus?"

It had been an hour since the local PD and Billy had showed up to the house. In that time nothing had been made clearer about the mystery men or their interests in Lonnie and Rachel. The only new leads they had seemed to have a pitfall.

They had the first mystery man, but he was deceased.

They had the vehicle that seemingly belonged to the mystery men, but so far it was empty.

They'd finally found Tucker, but he was now in surgery, fighting for his life.

And even if he did pull through and manage to talk to them, that didn't mean Dane was ready to trust the man. He had made it clear he not only knew about the men but had known of their interest in his nephew. Who, on an even more infuriating point, he'd left high and dry for an entire night before returning with trouble on his heels. Not to mention one of the men had said they'd caught him trying to leave town.

That surely didn't sound like Tucker had originally planned to come back home.

"I wish I knew," Dane finally said. "But we'll figure it out. Whatever is going on."

Rachel searched his expression, just as she had earlier in the bathroom at Tucker's house. She'd done it again when they first all bused together to the hospital, too.

What was she hoping to see?

And did he even want her to see whatever it was?

Chapter Ten

Dane wished Nurse Bean would hurry back so he could put on his shirt. He felt silly trying to keep a serious conversation going in the hallway. It wasn't a busy intersection, but he'd already gotten a few looks from the occasional wandering patient or nurse.

"So, what happens in the meantime?" Rachel asked. Her eyes stayed up to his now. "What happens with Lonnie? Surely he can't stay here. What if…what if Tucker… Well, you know."

"That's actually something I was coming to talk to the two of you about."

Sheriff Billy Reed looked more world-weary than he had in a while. A case always weighed heavier on him when kids were involved. It weighed heavier on all of them. Billy took his hat from his head and ran a hand through his hair. Dane knew the look, pulling the man's shoulders tense. They weren't going to like what he had to say.

"I just spoke to the doctor. Tucker Hughes is out of surgery and they're optimistic that he'll survive the night, but given the limited knowledge we have about the situation, I agree that Lonnie shouldn't stay here." Billy cut his gaze between them. "So I'll be looking after him until we figure out what's what."

"Why can't he just stay with me?" Rachel asked. "It's no trouble. I've got a big house with plenty of room for him. I wouldn't mind."

Dane was surprised or, maybe not, that she was so gung-ho to stay with Lonnie. They *had* been through a lot in such a short amount of time. Not to mention, as far as Dane knew, Lonnie didn't have any other family than Tucker.

Billy looked apologetic. "As much as I appreciate your offer, I don't think it's a good idea. If these men are after Lonnie *and* see you, Rachel, as a potential target, then having the two of you together might make another attempt at taking you both too tempting. So I'm taking Lonnie to an undisclosed location where I know he'll be safe. I won't leave his side. Neither will Deputies Medina and Grayson. Two *very* good people who are *very* good at their jobs."

The last part was for Rachel's benefit. Dane already knew and liked Medina and Grayson. They'd been personally vetted and hired by Billy.

"Lonnie will be out of harm's way. We'll make sure he stays that way."

"Well, then what about me?" Rachel asked. She was frustrated. That much was clear in the set of her furrowed brow and tone. It caught Dane off guard.

"Are you going to ship me off to some undisclosed location too?"

"No, I can't force you into protective custody or hiding," Billy said, not skipping a beat. "Though I *do* think it would be a good idea to find someplace unexpected to lie low at for a little while. Someplace our mystery men might not be able to find you if they kept looking. You could even, if you felt so inclined, bunk at the department. We have a second-floor room that's been converted to act as a place to sleep when needed. It's not the most comfortable place, but it gets the job done."

Rachel didn't like that idea. Dane could see that plain as day.

"She could stay at my place." The words were out of his mouth before he could think to stop them. "Again, it's not like many people even know where I live to begin with *and* Deputy Mills is down the road." Dane turned to Rachel. He was surprised to see her nod.

"If it'll keep me off those men's radar, I'm all for it."

Billy gave Dane a look that said more than he did out loud. "I wouldn't be doing my job if I didn't point out you need some rest. I know you didn't sleep last night." He motioned to Dane's side. "And now you're hurt on top of that."

Dane waved him off. "Nothing you haven't done yourself before."

The men shared a knowing look. It wasn't too far back that Billy had put everything on the line to protect his then-ex, now-wife and their daughter. In fact, Dane could name a few more in the department who had gone over and above the call to action to make sure those they cared about were safe.

And he did care about Rachel.

True as true.

Billy sucked on his teeth. Then, slowly, he nodded.

"I'll let Deputy Mills know to keep an eye out," he conceded. With that he slipped his hat back on and nodded over their shoulders. Nurse Bean nodded back. "I'll keep in touch, Captain."

The sheriff left Nurse Bean to put the bandages on and inspect the cut one more time. Rachel stood silently next to them, watching. Even though she was within touching distance, Dane saw that her mind was a million miles away.

Lonnie wasn't excited about leaving the hospital with Sheriff Reed. He even told the lawman that straight to his face. Thankfully, Billy was a patient man. He took no offense while Dane and Rachel made a makeshift huddle to the side of the lobby, trying to convince him. It took a few minutes, but finally Lonnie agreed not to put up a fight. The twelve-year-old acted as if he had another viable choice. Even if his options were limited. But Dane liked Lonnie. He was confident and tough when it counted.

Though it was that toughness that made Dane angry. Kids his age shouldn't have to be *that* tough. That was for their parents. For their loved ones. Both Lonnie was lacking for one reason or the other.

"You have that look going again."

Dane glanced over at his driver. The city of Darby was streaming by the window. Sunny, humid and turning into country. They weren't heading for Rachel's house on the outskirts. They were going to the town of Carpenter, following behind Deputy Mills.

"That look?" he repeated. "What look?"

Rachel kept her eyes on the road, but he could still see the furrow of her brow and the crease in her forehead.

"The look you get when you're trying to dissect whatever is bothering you. Like if you think about it long enough, if you focus *only* on that, then you can figure out how to handle it." She pressed a finger between her eyes for emphasis. "It's not good for you to use it all the time."

"I didn't realize I had a look." He smirked. "I also didn't realize I *dissected* things."

Rachel snorted. Dane didn't want to admit it, but she looked good behind the wheel of his truck. She'd said it was a non-starter that he do the driving when he was still in fresh pain. He'd told her he wasn't but then had tried to angle down into the seat. He'd been unable to hide how he flinched at the movement. The cut might not have needed stitches, but it stung enough to remind him exactly where it was and how awkward driving with it would be.

"Do you remember when you got your wisdom teeth taken out when we were younger?" she asked.

Dane groaned. "You mean when I ate steak on Day Two because I thought I was invincible? Then I got dry socket and had to take that godawful medicine." To this day the taste of it made Dane cringe.

Rachel chuckled and nodded. "That girlfriend of yours was *supposed* to pick you up from the appointment, but she bailed last second. What was her name?"

Dane groaned again. "Jennifer Hartley."

Rachel snapped her fingers over the steering wheel. "Yeah, that's her! She said she had a work emergency but—"

"But we found out later she was really meeting up with Tom McNolty," Dane supplied. "An investment banker in Kipsy with an awful goatee."

Rachel nodded. "I didn't really know you that well at the time. I think we'd only hung out once or twice. But—"

To the rest of the world, Rachel carried on with the next statement just as she had with the one before. To Dane, however, he heard the way her words softened ever so slightly. Treading near a memory. Being careful.

In turn it made Dane stiffen. Not out of fear or worry, but out of anticipation. They hadn't talked about David in any context in a really long time.

"...then David called me," she continued. "He'd seen Jennifer in the city and knew you were trying to go it alone. And he wasn't about to have that. So he asked me to pick you up."

A whisper of a smile danced across the profile of her lips. They were a dark pink. Like peaches. Dane averted his eyes out the windshield. How could he be admiring her now, of all times?

"I still remember seeing you there. Sitting in the waiting room, basically stoned as you came off anesthesia, with gauze all in your mouth and still trying to talk to everyone. Do you remember what you said to me when I tried to get you into the car?"

Dane kept his gaze forward, but that didn't mean he was any less curious. He didn't remember what he'd said. In fact, everything from that day had been and still was fuzzy.

"I don't," he admitted.

Rachel sat straighter and pointed with purpose at him, her brow furrowed again. "I had just opened the door and was trying to get you inside when you turned to me and you said, and I directly quote, 'Thank you for saving my ass.'"

That earned a surprised laugh from Dane. "I don't remember that."

She joined in with the mirth.

"I figured you didn't." She laughed. "At least, you never brought it up again if you did."

Like a switch that had been flipped, her mood shifted again. This time Dane couldn't track where.

"Do you remember that you also didn't know who

I was when I first came in to get you?" she said. "I had to get David on the phone to convince the nurse I wasn't just some strange woman off the street, trying to take you."

"I don't remember that, either," he said, honestly.

Rachel waved her hand at him dismissively. "Don't worry, my feelings weren't hurt. You were just having a hard time fighting through the haze of medication. Again, it's not like we knew each other that well to start off with. I think that's the first time I actually found out your last name. Still, once David did his sweet-talking to the nurse, I was worried you wouldn't come with me. I mean, you were a lawman, you thought you didn't know me, and your head wasn't in the best place. Yet…"

The truck slowed, coming to a four-way that was only a few minutes from the town limits. Rachel took the pause to look his way. She wasn't smiling, but she wasn't frowning, either. Dane tried to read her, to try and understand what she was getting at and why, but was coming up short.

"Then you gave me the same look you gave me in Darby Middle's gym yesterday. The same one you just had when you were thinking about, I'm assuming, the case. The very same look you're giving me now." Rachel let out a soft sigh. "You were trying to figure something out then. Trying to make sense of what you knew and fill in the blanks of what you didn't. You were trying to puzzle out if you could trust me." She shrugged. "And for whatever reason, back then that's exactly what you did. You got into my car, let me drive you home and then babbled nonsense to me once I had you tucked into bed."

She turned back to the road and kept on following Deputy Mills. "To be honest, I count that as the beginning of our friendship. Even if you were still hopped up on medication."

"I'm sorry I don't remember it," Dane finally responded. "I don't remember most of that day."

Rachel surprised him once again. She extended her hand and placed it on top of his. Every part of his body wanted to lean into the movement, into the warmth of her hand. It only made everything he was already feeling worse.

"The *point* of this walk down memory lane isn't really about Jennifer Hartley or a younger Dane Jones spouting hilarious nonsense. I just… I just wanted to let you know that everything can't be so easily figured out. Not everything has a straightforward answer and not everyone makes sense. And when you run into a situation like that or come across those people, you can't beat yourself black and blue trying to solve *everything*. Especially on your own." She squeezed his hand but then let go. Her demeanor didn't change again, but her tone did. It was harder. Stern. "Years ago a younger Dane Jones decided within the span of a walk from an oral surgeon's office to the parking lot that he was going to trust me. So now I'm asking that same man, do you trust me?"

Dane didn't hesitate. "I do."

"Good." She nodded. "Then trust me when I say, with this case, don't do what you always do. Don't get lost in your own head and then beat yourself up when it's hard to find a way out. I'm here, you know. I want to help, especially for Lonnie's sake. So please, Dane, don't shut me out. Not again."

There it was.

Dane had finally run out of the distance between them that kept their past firmly in the past. If he'd only seen her at the school gym, he might have had a chance to keep avoiding it all. But now?

Now their paths were being forced together and here he was, trying to pretend he didn't like the closeness. That he hadn't missed her.

Maybe it was time to finally tell her the whole truth. The *whole* reason he had stayed away.

But could he?

"Rachel," he started, bolstering the courage even if he wasn't sure of what he was going to say. "Listen, I—"

The lights on Deputy Mills's cruiser came on, distracting their attention. He flashed his blinker and then drove off onto the dirt of the shoulder.

"Follow him," Dane said.

They were on an older county road, one of many that wove through the county. The particular one they had been on rarely had much day traffic. No one was in front or behind them and hadn't been for a few minutes. Dane instinctively went for his phone but remembered two seconds too late that it was as busted as busted could be thanks to his earlier brawl.

Whatever Deputy Mills had to tell him, it must have been pretty urgent. He jumped out of his cruiser and waved for Dane to roll down his window like his life depended on it.

"Turn your radio to channel 93.7," Mills insisted. "Now!"

Rachel put the truck in Park while Dane pushed the seek button on his dash. Each channel that scrolled by on the radio's small digital screen felt like a stab in his gut. A few of the pieces to the past forty-eight hours were starting to come together.

"What is it?" Rachel asked. "What's going on?"

Before Deputy Mills could answer, Dane remembered what Chance had said earlier that day.

"It's a broadcast," he proclaimed, guessing. "One I don't think we're going to like."

Sure enough, the first thing the three of them heard froze Dane's blood in place.

"—is finally here," a man's voice boomed through the truck's speaker. "It's time to pay the consequences, Riker County. Once and for all."

Chapter Eleven

"For those of you fine lawmen and women just now tuning in, I want to say a good ol' 'how do you do?' The sun is shining, the heat is cooling, and just because we have a bone to pick with you doesn't mean we can't be civil. So, let's remember that going forward."

Rachel stared at the radio like it could show her who was behind the broadcast if she looked hard enough. It was the third time the recording had played, fashioned on a loop. They'd been quiet while listening to the first one, but Dane and Deputy Mills had gone into action by the second. Now, on the third, Rachel was alone in the truck while the two talked together outside with Mills's cell phone on speaker between them.

"The time is finally here," the man continued. Like he was preaching gospel. "It's time to pay the consequences, Riker County. Once and for all. But what does that mean? What does that mean for all of you who have been singled out? Well, I'm here to tell you. Today a man, a good man, was killed in cold blood. His name? His alleged crime? None of that matters. But what does matter is the reason behind why the man pulled the trigger."

He paused. Rachel had already heard it before, but still she leaned forward in her seat.

"Power."

The skin of her arms erupted in goose bumps. Whoever the man was, he knew how to speak well.

"This power came with a badge and ended with a bullet in a good man, and I'm here to tell you that we're fed up with it. And we're fed up with those who stand behind that man and that badge. This isn't the first time this has happened, but it will be the last."

Now to the part that tightened Rachel's stomach.

"At least, it'll be the last for Riker County's very own Captain Dane Jones."

The broadcast extended long enough to hear the man's laughter erupt and then end. Shortly after, the loop started from the beginning.

Rachel looked out through the windshield at the man of the hour. Dane had his hands resting on his hips, attention on the phone between him and the deputy. His eyes had a hawk-eye intensity to them. He was focused, no doubt, and the look she'd just talked about was back in full force.

This time, she didn't blame him.

This time, Rachel couldn't help copying that same look.

She was no stranger to knowing how to feel when people she cared about were in danger. It made you reevaluate what you felt. Put things in perspective. Rachel turned the volume down on the radio and really looked at Dane.

Back around the time when Rachel had wrangled Dane into the car at the oral surgeon's office, they had been several years younger. Dane had been a new deputy then and on the wrong side of cautious. He listened to his gut before he listened to the rules and was more prone to jump into the fray than to stand back and make a plan. It was a series of traits that could have been career-killers or -makers, depending on how they were used.

Dane? He decided to turn his potential weaknesses into strengths.

He'd risen through the ranks until the idea of running for sheriff hadn't been so far out of reach.

By that time Rachel had easily called him a close friend.

But then everything had changed. One day Rachel had looked around and not only was David gone, but Dane was, too.

There had been many sleepless nights, unasked and unanswered questions, and feelings of abandonment on her part between then and now. Rachel wasn't stupid and she wasn't completely unsympathetic. David and the hostages had been executed during Dane's plan to storm the gate, so to speak, and try to save them. It had been his plan, his decision, and it hadn't worked.

But never once had Rachel blamed him for it. Never once had resentment or anger colored her thoughts of the man or the department that had backed him up.

The only person she had ever blamed for her husband's death was the man who had shot her husband in the head.

Rachel balled her fist.

She'd told that to Dane every time she saw another part of him draw away from her. She'd told them all that her sorrow wasn't their fault. A lot of them had felt it, too. But that hadn't been enough for Dane.

So Rachel decided one day to be patient. To let him distance himself until he could face her without feeling the undeserved guilt he obviously was drowning in.

Yet once he was gone, he never came back.

That is, until Rachel had called him in trouble. There had been no hesitation to try to help her. Though she couldn't say it was the same Dane she remembered. He was older now, and with that age had come experience. He had become captain instead of sheriff. He spent his days mostly behind a desk, only going into the field when needed. She would bet his gut still spoke to him, but he was more wary when it came to listening. And she'd be remiss if she didn't note the physical transformation was just as different. He'd definitely taken a shine to the gym. Even through his button-down she could see the cut of his biceps and the firmness of his chest. When he'd helped her off Tucker Hughes's roof and guided her to the bathroom, she'd even felt the strength in his hands. The steadiness.

It made her wonder how the rest of him felt, too.

The thought sprang up so fast that Rachel had to take a few seconds to process it. Had she really just thought of Dane's body? Dane's body against hers?

Heat traveled up her neck and pooled in her cheeks.

Rachel shook her head.

The man's voice on broadcast continued to ramble on.

Now wasn't the time to puzzle over her past *or* her future with Dane Jones.

All at once, Rachel made up her mind. She opened the truck door and walked over to the captain and deputy. They were ending their current call. It was easy to see that both men were a mile past concerned. Which only strengthened Rachel's new resolve.

Dane raised his eyebrow as she approached.

Rachel didn't let it sway her. Mirroring his stance, she placed both hands on her hips and hardened her jaw.

"So," she started, "what's the plan?"

"I DON'T LIKE this plan."

Dane was one of many in the briefing room at the sheriff's department. After the broadcast, they'd changed course. Since Dane was being singled out, there was a good chance going to his house was what their unknown broadcaster might want. Sure, he believed his house was safe, but that was before he had become a target. Now? He wasn't about to roll the dice.

However that didn't mean he was okay with the new plan Billy had come up with.

The sheriff gave him a knowing look. "Everyone in this room has, at one point during their careers, not liked a plan," he pointed out. "Especially when it involves them taking a step back."

A chorus of agreements swept through the room. Dane knew for a fact that some of them had complained about the same thing when their personal lives had been threatened. But that didn't mean he had to like it.

They wanted to not only bench him but hide him in a safe house. Or, really, hide them. Rachel sat next to him, back ramrod-straight. It wasn't exactly protocol to have her there, but sometimes the department had gotten flexible when loved ones were thrown into the mix.

Dane didn't even have the patience to think on the fact that he'd automatically lumped Rachel into the category of his "loved ones."

Billy held up his hand to stop any more guff.

"Let's refocus here," he said. "We need to put all our cards on the table and try to figure out who is holding what."

Dane nodded. He was right.

Billy leaned forward on the podium at the head of

the room. He motioned to the whiteboard. Dane was already up and moving toward it.

"It's almost like we have three cases running parallel to each other. Let's do facts only first and then we'll do theories." Dane picked up a marker and drew two lines next to each other. He started working on the first one. "Three men in a van show up at Darby Middle yesterday morning. They approach Rachel and Lonnie before chasing them into the school. Rachel gets creative, makes the men think they're gone, and the men leave. As a precaution I watch Rachel's house and Henry watches Lonnie's, following him and Tucker from here straight there." He paused to finish writing everything he'd just said. Everyone remained silent, waiting.

"The next morning—God, I guess *today*—" it felt like a lifetime away "—Rachel and I go to Lonnie's to relieve Henry and wait for Deputy Medina. That's when we find out that Tucker Hughes isn't home. In fact, he's packed up his things and snuck out in the middle of the night, leaving Lonnie alone."

This time there were grumbles from behind them. Half of the people in the room were parents. They were saying without doing so out loud that they would never have left their kids.

"While I go across the street to talk to a neighbor, a black Lincoln pulls into the driveway and out comes Tucker, beaten black and blue," Dane continued. "He tells me he wants to know where Lonnie is before we're interrupted by Knife Guy."

They still hadn't found out the now-deceased man's identity. Rachel had said she called him Sandy Hair because of his hair color, but Dane wasn't about to refer to the man as that.

"He doesn't like Tucker and is pissed Tucker tried to leave town. He says a man named Levi had given Tucker a second chance and that he couldn't believe Tucker was in charge of keeping Lonnie safe. Then he gives Tucker a choice—tell him where Lonnie is or Knife Guy kills him. That's when I enter, but so does a second, unknown man."

"Overalls."

Dane turned around.

Rachel cleared her throat. "He was wearing overalls when he tried to grab us. So I call him Overalls."

Dane would have given her a smile under normal circumstances—the name *was* cute—but the thought of the man trying his best to take her left a sour taste in his mouth. Still, he wrote "Overalls" on the whiteboard.

"Knife Guy doesn't waste any time in going at Tucker while I fight with Overalls." Dane decided to purposefully omit the close call of Knife Guy nearly gutting him or Overalls nearly shooting him with his own gun that had been knocked out of Dane's grip. "I manage to get a shot in on Overalls's shoulder as he flees. Then I run upstairs to neutralize Knife Guy." Dane didn't miss how his knuckles turned white as he gripped the marker. "Before that he tells Rachel that Lonnie was their endgame and she was just a bonus."

More grumbles went through the room behind him as he made another note. This time it wasn't just the parents. "Tucker is then hospitalized and, while he's out of the woods, he's still not conscious, so he can't tell us anything. Though, to be honest, I wouldn't be inclined to believe what he said anyways."

Dane was at the end of the first line on the board. He switched to the second and wrote his name next to it.

"A few hours after we leave Tucker's house, Dispatch gets a call saying to turn to channel 93.7 and then hangs up. It's a lovely broadcast that talks about a man with a badge killing a good man and then point-blank calls me out." He paused and turned to look at Detective Foster. He had his notepad out. "And the call was traced to…?"

"The only damn pay phone still in service in downtown Darby," Caleb answered. "Detective Ansler is there now canvassing the area for any possible witnesses or working security cameras that might have gotten a good look at the caller."

Dane nodded and added the pay phone to the board. He hadn't asked about the call earlier because he'd already known that whoever had put the broadcast on the air probably wasn't stupid enough to call from a personal cell phone and keep it on them.

He would only be so lucky.

"We also are still working on finding the location of the broadcast," Caleb added. "Our friends at the local FBI office are spearheading that."

Dane drew a third line. He put four notes along it before capping the marker and turning to explain.

"Consultant Chance Montgomery approached me yesterday morning, before the incident at the school, and told me he was following a case about a series of thefts that occurred at the same time in Birmingham. Three warehouses reported missing shipments of dog crates, bubble wrap and radio equipment. Radio equipment *capable of broadcasting*. Chance followed it to Riker County because the van used to steal the bubble wrap had a plate that belonged to a deceased resident." He stepped aside to make sure everyone could see the name he'd written. "Tracy Markinson."

Rachel's eyes widened, but she didn't stop him to ask any questions.

"Last time I talked to Chance, he was still trying to figure out where that van went after Tracy passed." He looked to Billy. "He's also retracing Tucker's steps as best he can from where he fled last night."

Billy nodded.

Dane put the marker back in the whiteboard holder.

He didn't have to look at the notes. They'd already been blaring through his head since the broadcast. "*Those* are the facts as we know them, folks. I don't think it's a stretch to say that all cases are connected. We just need to know how. So, now it's time to start asking questions." He smirked. "And I can't believe I'm saying this, jumping to conclusions."

Suzy kicked the group off.

"It sounds like Levi is pulling the strings," she said. "He's not just after kids. He's after Lonnie specifically. Considering Tucker, as far as we know, isn't the richest guy and Lonnie's only family to boot, I think we can rule out ransom. Since Levi also mentioned Tucker's job was to keep the boy safe, that could also mean we rule out any obscure revenge-type plans. And this certainly doesn't seem random. To be honest, it sounds like this Levi guy might be sentimental about the kid."

"You killed Knife Guy and then the broadcast happens a few hours later," Caleb interjected, picking up the conversational thread. "But if Chance is right, then they were planning to broadcast way before you even knew about him. Even before they showed up at the school. He either anticipated someone was going to take one of his guys out or you doing it made him change his message."

"Why need a message at all?" Billy asked. "A question that leads us right back to why Levi wants Lonnie in the first place."

"And why Rachel was a bonus," Suzy added. "Did they mean because she just happened to be with Lonnie both times? Or was she on the list with him, just not the 'endgame' as Knife Guy said?"

Dane wished he could answer *any* of the questions. Instead he looked to Rachel. She hadn't stopped staring at the whiteboard. Her expression was blank. A fresh wave of guilt went through him. She'd almost been killed less than a few hours ago and now there they were, talking about the unknown men, their intentions and their targets like it was just another day.

Which, sometimes for the Riker County's Sheriff Department, it was.

Still, he shouldn't have agreed to her coming into the briefing room. He should have let her take a break in his office. Dane was about to offer that spot in his office when she beat him to getting up.

"Can I write on the board?" she asked, hesitating for only the briefest of moments.

He nodded and stepped aside. "Yeah, sure."

Everyone quieted as she approached the board.

She took the marker and moved to the corner. She wrote quickly. Dane couldn't see it as she turned around on the spot.

"The gospel," she started simply, addressing the room as a whole. "The man on the broadcast gave his message like it was the gospel." Then she was looking just at him. Blue eyes almost too perfect to be real. "Dane, who else have we heard that sounded like that?"

Rachel stepped to the side. She'd drawn another line. Next to it read one name.

Saviors of the South.

Chapter Twelve

"The Saviors of the South effectively died with Marcus," Detective Foster said. "And even if it was some of the stragglers left over, that still doesn't answer why they want Lonnie."

Dane hadn't said a word. It was like Rachel had hit the mute button on the man. The sheriff was right there with him while Suzy and Caleb tried to disprove what she said. They were several minutes in and had gotten nowhere fast. Rachel hung out at her spot next to the whiteboard, trying to quietly piece together what the group was trying to put together aloud. After a volley of more questions between them led only in circles, she finally had an idea.

"If they are a part of the Saviors, then their interest in me is probably from what happened years ago," she pointed out. "The Saviors made me a widow and now this man Levi has, at least, some interest in getting me. Maybe Lonnie is somehow connected to what the Saviors did back then, too."

The silence that followed Rachel's words was swift and calculated. No one disputed her, but no one agreed, either. But Dane *had* asked for questions, theories, and even jumping to conclusions. Rachel believed her thoughts fell somewhere in the gray area of all three.

Sheriff Reed took off his cowboy hat, placing it against his chest in thought. Caleb wrote in his detective's pad. Suzy rubbed her pregnant stomach while her brow drew in. Dane looked back at the whiteboard, eyes—and maybe thoughts, too—focused on something Rachel would bet none of them could see. Trying to puzzle out what was *really* going on.

Then slowly but surely, Dane's gaze shifted to hers. Rachel had spent years of her life around the man before the years without him had fallen. In that time she had learned his expressions, mannerisms, bad jokes and even brand of cologne. By proxy she also had memorized the color of his eyes. Or, at least, she had thought that was the case. She'd once thought of them as dark chocolate. Rich and smooth. Now? Now she was changing her mind about that.

Soot. They were almost as dark as soot left behind after a fire had burned its way to and through life. Something that, once touched, stained skin. Yet in a comforting way.

The sheriff finally spoke. "Whether or not this Levi man and his friends are part of the original Saviors of the South, a new wave of them or in no way connected, one fact remains."

Rachel didn't look away from Dane as the sheriff continued. She couldn't.

"They promise consequences. And from what we've seen just in the past two days, I don't doubt they'll try to carry those out."

Dane broke eye contact.

"So let's not give them the chance," Rachel said, simply.

To her surprise, the sheriff smiled. He slipped his

cowboy hat back onto his head and addressed the entire room.

"You heard the lady," he said.

FIGURING OUT THE full motives, identities and whereabouts of Levi and Overalls didn't happen in the time spent in the briefing room. Not that Dane had expected them to magically find any answers just by talking about it. However, at least now they were all on the same page. Not to mention there were a few new leads to follow or already being pursued.

One of them being the possibility that the Saviors of the South were back. Which, Dane had to admit, wasn't too much of a stretch after listening to the broadcast loop as they drove out of town.

That didn't mean he had to like it. Just the possibility made everything in him pull tight, as if waiting to snap. When that snap happened, Dane had no idea if it would be his anger that came out in full force or his guilt. Either one was bad for his focus…and the woman next to him.

"I didn't know the sheriff's department had safe houses," she finally said, breaking their nearly half-hour silence. "I thought things like that were only in movies."

"This one isn't official, but we've used it a time or two in the past when we were in a jam. Do you know Suzy's husband?"

Rachel snorted. "Who doesn't know of James Callahan?"

Despite himself, Dane chuckled. James was the star of the smallest town in the county, Bates Hill. He was also the richest. Before Suzy, he'd also been the most sought-after bachelor. Even though they were raising several kids between them, and expecting one on the way, some women were still upset that James was off the market. Dane had seen the way James looked at Suzy, though. There was no doubt in his mind that he would only ever have eyes for the chief deputy.

An ache reverberated through Dane at the thought of their family.

He kept his eyes off Rachel.

"A while ago one of our own needed a place to lie low and he let them borrow a property he owned," he continued, gaze on the road ahead. "It was compromised, but he and Suzy saw the value in having a place or two that wouldn't be as easy to find. So he bought two properties and converted them strictly for hiding out. Only a couple of us, and I mean fewer than five, within the department know where they are."

"Is that where Lonnie is?"

Dane heard the worry throng through her words. It was intense and heartfelt. It made him answer without thinking. "Yeah. He's at one of them, but not the one we're going to. Even if both houses are off the radar, we didn't want to chance having too many targets together."

"But what about us?"

Dane tried not to tense. "What do you mean?"

"Well, aren't you a target now?" she said. "Doesn't that mean we shouldn't be staying together?"

Rachel had a point. The whole reason behind why they'd separated Lonnie and Rachel was to help curb the temptation to pool whatever resources Levi and his goons had to try to take both at once. But now Dane *was* a target, according to the broadcast. Which meant staying at the department might have been the best course of action.

Yet, even as he realized that, Dane knew he wouldn't have entertained the idea if it had been brought up beforehand.

He wasn't leaving Rachel.

He just couldn't.

Dane shook his head.

"That's different," he countered defensively. "We're different."

He hadn't meant the last comment, but it was true enough. He and Rachel were adults, for one. Second, Dane was a lawman. It wasn't like he was adding extra risk to the situation. He had a gun, knew how to use it, and would stop at nothing to make sure Rachel was safe if something did happen.

But that's not why we're different.

Dane opened his mouth to clarify but came up short. He didn't know how to explain something he couldn't make up his own mind about.

"We're friends," he decided to finally say. "And we stand a better chance of figuring this thing out if we work together."

Dane glanced over at Rachel. She took his explanation.

"Friends," she repeated.

"Friends."

Though Dane would be lying if he didn't like how final it sounded.

THE SAFE HOUSE was less of a house and more of a cabin. Small, cozy, and located at the beginning of several acres of old farmland, it looked like a page ripped out of a *Southern Living* magazine. From the pinecone and red berry wreath on the front door to the lone dining table's carefully arranged centerpiece to the hand-quilted throw across the bed, Dane felt like he'd stepped into his late grandmother's house. He resisted the urge to take off his boots at the door. Though he told Rachel how he felt about the small house. It made her laugh.

"Since when does Dane Jones read *Southern Living*?" she teased, attention going to the small bookshelf across from the only sitting area in the place. "I thought you only subscribed to magazines about college football and how to build things with your hands."

Dane rolled his eyes and looked into the pantry in the corner of the kitchen. It was open with the living area. Only the small bedroom and attached bathroom had doors between them.

"You learn a thing or two when you date Becky Carr," he said with a laugh. "She was a hoarder when it came to that magazine. Had stacks of them in her house *and* her car. She even had us make our own Christmas wreaths from an article in one as a date. It was…an interesting experience to say the least."

Dane went to the back door, opened it and looked out before shutting it and throwing the lock. He turned back to Rachel, wondering if she'd heard him. He was met with a raised eyebrow and a look he couldn't read. It turned into a grin as she dropped onto the love seat.

"You're dating Becky Carr? As in the Becky who runs the florist shop in Carpenter? The same Becky who nicknamed herself Hardy Carr-Carr?"

Dane threw his head back as a laugh came out uninhibited.

"I'd forgotten she called herself that," he said, dropping into a chair next to the couch. It was such a close proximity that he had to be mindful of his knees not touching hers. "But no, we're not still dating. That ended a few years ago."

"Oh, too bad." Rachel picked up one of the coffee table books. A picture of something craft-related was on the cover. "Was it serious?"

Dane couldn't help raising his brow at that. Then again, it wasn't unusual for Rachel to pry into his romantic life. She'd tried to play matchmaker for him multiple times when they were younger.

They *were* friends. They'd just covered that, after all.

Yet Rachel wouldn't meet his eyes.

"Not exactly," he admitted. "Suzy introduced me to her because she said I was becoming a hermit and it was 'alarming.'" Dane snorted. "We only went on a few dates. Honestly, I think she was more interested in the *idea* of dating someone in law enforcement and not actually dating someone in law enforcement. She actually tried to give an ultimatum when I had to cancel a date to go to a crime scene. Said it was either her or the job."

That earned a look of surprise from Rachel. "No, she didn't."

Dane laughed and held up two fingers. "Scout's honor."

"Considering you're now a captain at the sheriff's department, I'm assuming you let her down gently."

Dane nodded but winced. "I might have gotten overly defensive about it and come off a little too blunt, though. Said some things I'm not entirely proud of. To this day Suzy gives me guff about it. But Becky started dating her now-husband after that. Has a couple of kids running around and seems happy enough. I just can never buy flowers in Carpenter again."

They shared a laugh and, for a moment, Dane felt the walls he'd had up around Rachel start to lower. Could they really pull off being friends again? Did he want to? Was it even possible?

"How about you?" he asked. "Seeing anyone?" Dane had meant it to be casual, but somehow it sounded off.

Rachel put the book back on the coffee table and shook her head. "I haven't been on a proper date in almost two years." She managed to look sheepish. "Do you remember Tatum Rogers?"

Dane was already shaking his head. But not because he didn't remember the man. "Don't tell me you went out with Tatum Rogers." Dane was holding back a laugh the best he could. It was Rachel's turn to cringe. "Ha! How can you give me any flack about Hardy Carr-Carr when you went out with Tatum Talks-About-Himself-in-the-Third-Person Rogers?"

Rachel was off the couch and waving a hand at him.

"He didn't *always* talk about himself in third person," she proclaimed halfheartedly. "He only did it when he was really excited about something."

Dane got up and followed her into the kitchen. "Rachel, talking about yourself once in third person is too much already. Please tell me it was you who called it off."

She opened the pantry and went directly for a box of pasta noodles. He was suspicious when she didn't answer right away. "Rachel…?"

"Fine, he broke up with me."

Dane was afraid that he'd touched a nerve until she sighed.

"And he did it in third person, too."

Dane couldn't stop himself from laughing.

"Get it all out," Rachel said. "I'll just make us something to eat while you make fun of me. Deal?"

Dane just kept on laughing.

"I THINK IT's time to go."

Levi looked around the garage. He didn't want to

leave anything behind. At least, nothing they weren't *supposed* to leave. Making sure not to touch anything, he made one more sweep. The garage wasn't necessarily large, but it wasn't small, either. There was enough room to make a mistake. And he'd be damned if he'd be the one to make it.

"How long will this keep going?" Javier asked, motioning to the radio equipment. "How long will it keep playing?"

Levi rolled his eyes. He didn't like Javier, hadn't liked him from the start. But he was another set of hands and muscle. He'd already lost Wyatt that morning. Plus, Chet had been wounded. What had started as a well-manned group had shrunken in the span of one day. By the end of this thing, Levi might be the one holding all the strings.

"It'll keep going until it's manually shut down," he said. "*But* they have to find this place first."

Javier nodded and grabbed his bag. A semiautomatic was housed inside it. Levi hoped Javier was better at shooting than he was at thinking.

"What if they do? What if they find this place?"

"Then we better not be here. So let's stop yapping and get out."

Javier wasn't the least bit worried about double-checking his area, so Levi did it for him. Even though he had no problem with the dense man getting caught, Levi believed that if the FBI got Javier he would try and make a deal with them. Levi outranked Javier, Wyatt and Chet with what he knew but if Javier started talking he could still do some damage. Especially to Levi. He hadn't bothered hiding his identity from the ex-bouncer.

Levi was going to have to kill him when everything was said and done anyway.

The drive to the house was uneventful. Javier kept quiet in the back seat with his gun and Levi didn't try to start anything. They both knew what happened next. They'd certainly planned it long enough to be confident.

Levi parked the car and helped Javier take their gear inside. The house was cold. He hated the heat.

"Honey," he sang, high-pitched and mockingly. "I'm home!"

Javier snickered but was wise to stay quiet. He scooped up the cat and disappeared into the next room. The man in the office wasn't as amused.

"If he sees you acting like an idiot, he'll only continue to act like an idiot." The man looked up from his newspaper and gave Levi a look that said he wasn't impressed.

Levi turned and shut the door. "I think that ship has sailed already."

The man sighed. "Whether or not that's true, it doesn't matter now, does it?"

"Either way we get what we want," Levi said. "Well, if the plan works, that is." Levi tensed. He knew he was taking a risk, but he had to voice his concerns. He continued when the man didn't respond. "What if you can't get him? What if you can't grab the boy?"

Marcus smiled. "Then I'll grab her."

Chapter Thirteen

The steam filled the bathroom while tears filled Rachel's eyes. Thanks to Suzy and her husband restocking the house before they arrived, she and Dane had spent an hour or so eating homemade mac 'n' cheese and catching up like old friends. From disastrous dates to career moves and thoughts on gossip new and old, they'd found a way to make the cabin's kitchen into a time machine.

It had been nice.

And had made Rachel forget why they were there.

At least, until she'd gone into the shower.

There, beneath the stream of hot water, she had remembered the men. Remembered how they'd grabbed her. How they'd terrified her.

How one of them had almost killed her.

And how he had, instead, died in front of her.

Rachel had done what Dane had told her. She'd looked into his eyes and followed them until she had been no longer on the roof and safely inside Lonnie's room. But there had been the first moment after it had happened when Rachel had looked down at the man dead near her feet. His eyes had been open, staring at nothing.

Then there was the blood.

Rachel had cradled her cheek in the shower. The tears had been slow at first and then had walloped her. She'd held one hand over her mouth and used the other to hold herself up against the wall. Part of her was afraid that Dane would hear her and run in to comfort her. Part of her wanted that.

Which seemed to make the emotions spilling out of her even worse.

After everything that had happened, there she was, thinking about Dane, when less than two days ago just the thought of him had made her angry.

"Prioritize," Rachel told the mirror. She wiped the condensation aside and then scrubbed her hands beneath her eyes. They were red and swollen.

She sighed.

There was no hiding the fact that she had been crying.

She dressed quickly into the pajama set and underwear that, Rachel assumed, Suzy had purchased and put out for them. It was definitely a step up from the baggy tee and loose shorts she often slept in at home. It oddly fit like a glove, too.

Rachel took one last look at her too red eyes, pulled her hair into a quick, messy braid, and tried to pretend everything was okay as she left the bathroom.

Dane's voice was quiet but insistent. Rachel paused, worry starting to make her muscles seize up, but she never heard another voice. He must have been on the phone. She walked to the bedroom door. She'd left it open, not liking the idea of having two doors closed between them, and peeked out around the door frame.

Once again Rachel was met with an uninhibited view of Dane Jones. Sitting on the couch, he had a notebook open on his lap and the phone to his ear. The other hand held his chin, propped up on his knee. His brow was drawn and his jaw set hard.

He was in work mode.

He was so handsome.

The thought sprang up just as heat moved from below her waist. It started to travel upward, turning into a full-body blush. Rachel took a step back, worried Dane would somehow know what she was feeling. Instead, the quick movement alerted the captain to her presence.

Two dark eyes nearly swallowed her whole.

He smiled but held a finger up to tell her to hold on.

Rachel nodded. She swallowed when he looked back at his notebook.

"Yeah, Chance, thanks for this," he said into the phone. "I'll look into it… Yeah, should be no problem here… Yeah, just call this number." He laughed. "I guess I lucked out with this burner phone, huh? Good thing we had it at the department." Something serious must have been said on the other end of the conversation. Dane sobered. "I will, brother. Thanks."

Rachel went to the chair and sank into its fabric after he ended the call.

"Was that Chance the cowboy?" she asked. The burn from her blush was ebbing away. Dane nodded, his focus switching to the notebook. Rachel couldn't see what it said, but half the page was filled.

"I can't believe you even remember Chance," he said. "You two only met once or twice, right?"

"Hey, you never forget your first cowboy. Even if you just meet him in passing."

Dane kept his gaze on the notebook, but he snorted. "He's definitely something when it comes to first impressions."

Rachel waited for him to say more. When he didn't,

she continued. "Remind me to ask Suzy if she'd be interested in being a personal shopper. She guessed my size perfectly. Did she shop for you, too?"

Dane snorted again. "She didn't shop for us. James's friend and head of security did. Yeah, I know. It blew Suzy's mind that a man could find the—and I quote, 'perfect pair of jeans.' When she and James were in a tough spot a while back, he helped them out by buying some things she needed. Last I heard, Suzy was still begging him to help her out. Something about trying to find the perfect pair of boots to go with her jeans."

The whole time Dane spoke, Rachel could see his eyes scanning the writing on the paper. He was trying to solve their current predicament while keeping her entertained. It made her feel useless and stopped any normal response from coming out.

Dane noticed the hesitation. He looked up.

It must have been the first time he really looked at her. His gaze swept across her face and stopped at her eyes. Like a match had been struck, a look of such acute concern blazed across his expression.

It wasn't like she hadn't known he'd notice that she'd been crying.

It wasn't like he hadn't seen it before.

Yet he didn't say anything. At least, not about that. "Do you want some cookies?"

It was such an off-the-wall question that Rachel laughed. Dane's expression softened and an almost-wicked grin appeared as he rose off the couch. "I may have laid on the 'I'm a target' thing a little too thick with Suzy when I asked if she could add Oreos to the shopping list for this place."

"But the important question is, did you—?"

Dane held up his hand to silence her. She watched

quietly as he opened the refrigerator. He pulled out a small jug of milk.

"My hero."

Dane's grin grew. "When it comes to dessert, always."

She kept to her chair as he got out a plate and filled it with cookies. He placed it in front of her before fixing them two cups of milk. They didn't talk until they both were seated and had one milk-soaked cookie in.

"So, did Chance find anything helpful?" Rachel asked. "Are there any new leads?"

Dane let out an exhale that was long but didn't deflate his posture. He eyed his notebook before answering.

"Yes and no," he said. "He found out what happened to Tracy Markinson's van after he passed. Apparently it was given to a family friend who used it to help move a local construction company's equipment for out-of-town jobs. They ended up not using it as much as they thought they would, so never bothered changing the tag. The owner ended up letting a friend use it to haul things around his farm and his acreage for a few years. He didn't change the tag again, since the van only stayed on his property. *Then* one night it was stolen. It didn't reappear until it was spotted on security cameras leaving the warehouse in Birmingham."

"So, no lead but—"

"A mystery we can cross off the list," he finished.

Rachel dunked another cookie. She twirled it thoughtfully over the cup so it didn't drip. "Did he have any idea about why they took bubble wrap and dog crates?"

Dane shook his head. "He's still looking into that, but I'm not convinced it wasn't just a way to throw us off track."

"And Tucker?" Rachel felt a wave of anger at the man for leaving Lonnie behind when he had tried to run. "Any word on where he went after he left the house? Any change on his condition in the hospital?"

Dane shook his head again and put an Oreo in his mouth. It was the most thoughtful she'd ever seen someone look while eating a cookie before.

"No and no. Tucker still isn't conscious."

They ate the remaining cookies in silence. Rachel recognized that the captain had retreated into his thoughts. She joined him, trying to answer *something* with the limited information they had, but it didn't work.

"Have you ever had so many questions in your head you feel like you're going to explode?" she finally said. "Can you combust because of confusion?"

Dane let out another long sigh. A small smile tugged at the corner of his lips. "If you can, I think I would have by now." He flipped his wrist up to check his watch. "Okay, so I wasn't going to say anything, but I think it's high time I took a shower. This place is too small for me to wait until tomorrow."

Rachel stood with him and collected their dishes, waving him off. "Go on ahead. I've got it from here."

Dane gave her a slightly stronger smile and disappeared into the small bathroom.

Rachel cleaned up the little mess they had managed to make. She paused as she folded the blanket on the couch.

Really, it was a love seat.

And it was much too small for anyone to sleep on.

Rachel turned to look through the open doorway that led into the bedroom. A single butterfly dislodged itself in her stomach and continued to flutter around until Dane was clean and back to his notebook. It stayed flying around while she excused herself to brush her teeth and it kept up its flight path as she padded back to that same open door, but now looking out from the room.

"Hey, Dane?" she called, trying her best to keep her voice from giving her nerves away. "I think I'm going to call it a night, if that's okay?"

Dane looked up and nodded. The bags that had been beneath his eyes that morning had darkened considerably. Worry pushed aside her trying to remain nonchalant. She put her hands on her hips and narrowed her eyes. "And I'm here to tell you that it's your bedtime, too, Captain. You look like you're two seconds from passing out as it is."

Dane opened his mouth. Rachel wasn't having it. "You stayed up all last night to make sure I was safe. If you don't sleep here, it will only make me feel like even more of a burden. And you said it yourself. Not many people know about this place. Plus, I'm a light sleeper. If someone comes and breaks in, I should hear them."

Rachel fully expected to keep arguing. However, Dane surprised her.

"Okay." He put his notebook down and ran a hand across his face. "I guess sleeping a few hours might do me some good. Which might do this case some good. Who knows? Maybe some clue might shake loose in a dream."

Rachel laughed. "That's the spirit." That butterfly began an even more sporadic dance. She swallowed and pasted on a smile. "You can sleep in here with me," she said. "There's more than enough room and you've more than earned a comfortable place to rest your head after the past two days."

Dane must have been more tired than Rachel thought. After only a moment or two of hesitation, he stood.

"Okay," he said. "Thanks."

"It's nothing," she told him. "But let it be known, I get the right side. Otherwise that's a nonstarter."

Dane gave her a look that made the heat in her body start to pulse. When he answered, it was a deep, smooth sound.

"Yes, ma'am."

THAT HEAT OF the shower had pulled out whatever alertness Dane had had left. What made him sharp in the field or behind the desk at work must have dulled because of it. Not to mention, he *was* tired and not just physically. Trying to pull together the several threads of what was going on to make one cohesive piece had been draining. Especially when he had realized Rachel wasn't as okay as she had let on. Her swollen eyes were testament to that. But the heat of the shower, exhaustion and frustration couldn't account for why he was now in bed with the same woman.

No, that was something else.

Something Dane shouldn't have given in to. No matter how small the couch was.

"It's not like we've never slept together before."

Dane opened his eyes. He was on his side, facing Rachel. He hadn't wanted to sleep on his wound. The soft light from beneath the closed bathroom door was bright enough that he could see the shine of her eyes and the outline of her side beneath the covers but not much more. "When you helped me pick up that bed frame from my mom's house up north? And we had to stop in that crummy motel and spend the night because of the storm on the way back? Remember?"

Dane did. It had been almost a year after David had passed. Rachel had decided to get a smaller mattress and her mother had offered her a bed frame for it. Dane had offered to use his truck to help her haul and move it.

"Calling it 'crummy' is a lot more generous than what I would have described it as," he said. They had almost slept in the truck, but Rachel had been too nervous with the storm raging outside. So they'd slept in their clothes. Jackets and shoes, too.

"My point is, you don't have to be so tense," she added. "We're just two tired adults who have had one helluva weekend. Got it?"

Dane smiled even though he doubted she could see it.

"I'll try to loosen up," he promised. "Just as long as you try not to snore like you did last time."

A soft fist landed against his shoulder.

"Hey, now. I told you, I don't snore."

"Whatever you say."

Rachel laughed but didn't try to deny it any further. Dane closed his eyes as they both lapsed into silence. Slowly he tried to let himself relax, but their small trip down memory lane had had a polarizing effect on him. On the one hand, it brought back memories of the two of them before he'd decided to distance himself. Just like they had been earlier, back when they were good friends. Comfortable around each other and able to enjoy even the most mundane things together. On the other hand, it highlighted the differences between their impromptu motel stay and the impromptu sleepover they were having now.

Back then Dane hadn't noticed the freckles on Rachel's cheeks.

Now he could see them with ease just from memory.

Back then he had fallen asleep talking to her.

Now there was a silence that felt heavy in the room around them.

Back then there had been layers of clothes and jackets between them with a king-size bed giving them distance from each other.

Now?

Now Dane was doing his best not to think about Rachel's body so close to his that he could feel the heat from her pressing against the front of him. How she was so close he could smell the soap from her skin and the shampoo from her hair. How, even though his mind was saying no, his arms wanted to be around her, pulling her against him so that he could protect her even in sleep.

How another part of him pointed out he also wanted to *not* sleep with her at the same time.

Dane wrestled with his body and mind for what felt like hours, trying to figure out which was stronger, until finally something made his decision for him.

The sound of Rachel's even breathing filled the bedroom. She was asleep.

"Good night, Rach," Dane whispered.

And just like that, Dane followed her into unconsciousness.

Chapter Fourteen

Rachel awoke with a start. Not because of any noise or some other terrifying thing that had pulled her from sleep. No, instead, she'd figured something about the case out. Or, rather, remembered it thanks to a stress dream about being back in high school.

She opened her eyes as a jolt of excitement started to push the fog of sleep from her head. Even though she'd had a breakthrough, it still took her a few seconds too long to remember she wasn't in her bed. Not even in her house. Instead she was somewhere foreign. A pleasant heaviness surrounded her. It was soft against her cheek and radiated warmth down her front.

Rachel blinked several times until what she was looking at filtered in. It was Dane. And not only was it Dane, it was his collarbone she was staring at. Her cheek wasn't just on something soft, it was resting on top of his biceps.

Rachel froze as she took stock of the rest of her position. Not only was she lying on top of his arm, she was fully tucked into his sleeping embrace. As if she'd been drawn directly into his chest after falling asleep, forcing him to put one arm beneath and around her while the other was slung over her hip. Her hands were against her chest, but that did little to diminish the rest of their bodies' closeness.

Rachel's breath caught as Dane shifted the arm over her slightly. From one butterfly in her stomach the night before, hundreds had multiplied. Dane was just so warm, a detail that started a different surge of excitement within her.

Rachel tipped her head up as slowly as possible, trying to get a glimpse of his face. All she could see was the stubble beneath his chin and along his jaw. So she listened to his breathing to confirm he was still asleep and decided to take a moment to calm down.

And that was what being in Dane's arms was doing.

It was a place of comfort, of safety.

It was a place of longing.

It was unexpected.

Rachel closed her eyes and focused on the heat of his skin against her cheek. It was nice, sure, but it wasn't real. Just two people in a confined space who had gotten tangled together in their sleep.

It wasn't real.

Carefully, Rachel detangled from the man. Dane didn't wake up, so she retreated to the bathroom. Sunlight peeked around the blinds. Rachel sighed.

Now it was time to get back to their reality.

One where she'd hopefully come up with a new lead.

Suzy's personal shopper/head of security had done it again. Rachel slid comfortably into a pair of blue jeans and a long-sleeved blouse. Both were flattering but sensible. Really, she had half a mind to ask Suzy for the man's information when this was all over.

Rachel hurried through brushing her teeth, washing her face and rebraiding her hair before going back into the bedroom. To her surprise, Dane was awake and sitting on the edge of the bed. His head was bent over his phone.

"Anything new happen while we were sleeping?" she ventured, trying to keep the burn of a blush from crawling up her neck. Just thinking about how warm the man had been against her was toeing the line of keeping her cool and becoming obviously distracted.

"No. Everyone is still following leads." He cursed then apologized. "I was hoping sleep might help but—"

Rachel clapped her hands, cutting him off. Before she'd lost her mental footing by waking in Dane's arms, she had been on to something.

"It did," she exclaimed. "At least, I think it did. The man from yesterday who still hasn't been identified— Knife Guy? Right before Overalls showed up, when he was talking to Tucker, he mentioned that Tucker buckled under pressure. Especially at—"

Dane's eyes widened.

"Every football game," he finished. He jumped up, closed the gap between them in one fluid motion and picked Rachel up. She gave a surprised laugh as he spun her around, put her down and kissed her on the cheek. "They went to school together *and* played on the same football team. You're brilliant!" He dialed a number and was in the next room talking to whoever was on the receiving end in a flash.

Rachel touched her cheek.

It was a good thing Dane couldn't see her.

She had no doubt she was as red as a cherry.

CHANCE SHOWED UP just after lunch. The rest of the department was spread thin, and if Dane was being honest, he preferred working with the freelancing cowboy. At least, when he wanted to do something that Billy and his friends might shoot down. Chance rarely said no. He was more of a "how can we minimize the damage?" kind of guy.

Not that Dane believed their plan was all that dangerous.

"We checked every place we could think of online to see if we could pull up a yearbook of Tucker's graduating class," he explained again. "Nothing from that year has been digitized that we can tell and the principal was less than helpful over the phone."

"We also looked through the social media accounts of people graduating around the same time to see if they posted any throwback pictures, but came up short," Rachel added. "Tucker isn't that much older than us, but for whatever reason, finding even a candid photo from his class has been hard."

"We did find one picture of the football team from the same year, but it's from a newspaper and you can't make out many of the faces. Plus, no names."

Chance nodded between them. "So we're taking a field trip to…?"

Dane passed him a piece of paper with an address on it.

"Kipsy South Academy," he answered.

Chance whistled low.

"Not a cheap school back in the day," he said. "Heck, not even now for that matter."

"Which is probably why the principal is giving us a hard time over the phone," Rachel pointed out.

Chance looked between them.

"Okay, you've got me sold," he declared. Chance thumbed back at the front of the cabin. "I switched to an associate's SUV so we can all fit. How long a trip is it?"

Dane and Rachel had already plotted the route out.

The private school wasn't familiar to Dane, but he'd been there once before. "Forty-five minutes give or take."

Chance tipped his hat down. "Add a half hour of making sure no one is following us and we're square."

Dane smirked. "You sure you aren't interested in joining the department? You'd definitely fit in."

Chance waved him off. "You couldn't pay me enough to be stuck inside as long as you all are. Plus, I aim to never be pinned down." The cowboy sent a wink to Rachel. "I'm what you might call a rolling stone."

Dane rolled his eyes, but not in annoyance. He was grateful Chance had offered to take them to the school. Not only that, but act as backup. He had a gun permit, was a solid shot and had a good head on his shoulders. Plus, he was quick with his reflexes. When a situation turned on its head, he reacted swiftly and kept his cool. He was the only reason Dane had agreed to let Rachel come along, too. The last time they'd been ambushed, he was outnumbered. Even though Dane had killed the man they would *hopefully* find out more about, he liked having another gun on his side.

The drive to Kipsy South Academy was uneventful. Rachel used Dane's burner to call and check on Lonnie, while Dane and Chance reviewed the case. Again. He was starting to feel like Rachel had the night before. So many questions he felt like he was constantly on the brink of a headache.

"I think the lady should do the talking," Chance said. He parked in the private school's side parking lot and cut the engine. Kipsy might be a big city, but its private school was on the small side.

"It's easier to catch flies with honey," Dane said.

Rachel seemed to agree. "I don't know much about

this school, but I have heard about the man who runs it. Gerald Boyle is what one of the PTA moms at Darby Middle calls a man with a Napoleon complex, especially when it comes to being around other men." She gave them a wry smile. "Translation, don't try to assert any dominance, or not even my assurances that he's important will land."

Dane raised his eyebrow at that. It earned a deeper smirk from the woman. She leaned closer. "You're wondering if I have ever done that to you, aren't you?"

She winked. Chance laughed.

Apparently, Dane wasn't the only one starting to get excited at the prospect of a new lead.

Gerald Boyle was a short, stocky man in his early sixties. He wore a full suit and abruptly made it clear he wasn't fond of Dane. The PTA mom and Rachel had been right on the money. He'd started talking about them needing a warrant. Around that time Rachel had steered the man into his office, honey in her voice. Minutes later and they were laughing. He led them to a classroom in the back of the school. It belonged to the yearbook students and had a closet filled with at least one copy of each year since the school had opened in the seventies.

"Take your time," Gerald said, attention on Rachel only. "And let me know if you need anything."

Rachel said thank you, smiling for all she was worth.

When Gerald had gone, Dane couldn't help himself. "Fly, meet Honey," he whispered.

Rachel laughed. Then it was down to business. Chance stayed by the empty classroom's closed door, just in case, while Dane and Rachel divided and conquered searching for the yearbook in question. It took longer than he would have liked, but finally Rachel clapped her hands and pointed to the leather-bound book.

"Here's hoping Tucker and his friend weren't talking about playing football in middle school instead," she said.

The mood in the classroom changed as they flipped through the book to the football team spreads. Dane scanned the group picture, but it was too small to really tell many of the players apart.

"At least we know he was on the team for sure," Rachel said when he went to the next page. She pointed to the individual picture of Tucker. Even now Dane felt some residual anger for the man. He turned to the next page, not recognizing the man who had attacked Rachel. "Oh, look! There's Knife—"

Rachel stopped midsentence. Even out of his periphery, Dane saw her tense. He was a second from asking what was wrong when he saw two things. Or, rather, two *people*.

The first was indeed the man from the day before. Younger but with a smile that caused anger to erupt in Dane all over again, the teen staring back at them was Wyatt Hall. Their Knife Guy. A man Dane had felt no guilt about stopping before he could hurt Rachel anymore.

However, it was the teen's portrait *next* to Wyatt's that had stalled Dane out.

"What's wrong?" Chance asked, concern lacing his tone. He strode over, cowboy hat in hand. "Did you find him?"

Dane was the first to recover.

He nodded.

"His name is Wyatt Hall," he answered, phone already out.

"Then what's the problem? What's got you two stiff as boards?"

Dane didn't look at Rachel's expression, but not because he was worried what it showed. Instead he was worried what he looked like. He'd gone from trying to solve their present to *slam bam*, back in the past. Still, he answered. "The boy next to Wyatt is Marcus the Martyr." Apparently named Marcus Highland, something the department had never been able to figure out. "The leader of the Saviors of the South."

Chance whistled again.

"So Tucker, Wyatt and Marcus all knew each other when they were teens," he reiterated. "How much do you want to bet this Levi guy is in here, too?"

Chance took over searching through the yearbook. Dane texted Billy and Detective Foster Wyatt's name. Rachel remained quiet.

"Well, he wasn't listed in the football roster but—" Chance waved Dane back over. He pointed to a single class photo. The name Levi Turner was listed underneath it. "It's either a series of incredibly relevant coincidences or—how much you want to bet—this Levi is the same man tangled up with Tucker and the late Marcus and Wyatt."

"You think Tucker and Levi want revenge for Marcus's death? And that's what this is all about?" Dane ventured. It had been seven years since Marcus had been taken down by a SWAT sharpshooter on loan from the next county over. Exacting revenge now for their friend would be an interesting move. One that didn't make sense, especially when Lonnie was involved.

"I've seen men and women do crazy things," Chance said, picking up on his thoughts. "The reasoning behind waiting years before avenging a friend can boil down to a lot. Maybe they had to bide their time until they got the funds or the plan in place. Maybe they tried before and something went wrong. Heck, maybe Tucker decided he didn't want to be a part of whatever it was and tried to hide from Wyatt and Levi, but they found him now anyways."

"That could be why he tried to run," Dane conceded. Though it didn't feel right. Why not take Lonnie with him if he was bailing? And why did the men want Lonnie to begin with? Unless it was to use him for leverage against his uncle. Yet Wyatt had talked about keeping the boy safe.

It still wasn't adding up.

Dane was going to say as much when Rachel finally spoke. Her voice was even, calm.

"Maybe we're missing a key piece of the puzzle." She turned and met Dane's gaze. Sweet blues pulled him in. "And, maybe, Marcus isn't dead at all."

Chapter Fifteen

Chance left Rachel and Dane at the cabin like a dog homed in on a new scent. In the time it took her to watch the cowboy drive off, Dane wasn't that far behind. He set up shop at a small dining table with his laptop and phone. Rachel watched as he worked, calling what seemed to be an endless list of contacts, trying to make sense of the connection between Marcus, Levi, Wyatt and Tucker.

And also trying to track down Marcus's body.

Neither man had fought hard against Rachel's theory that the leader of the Saviors could still be alive. She'd fully expected pushback. Yet Chance had surprised her.

"The thought had crossed my mind," he had admitted. Then he'd shared a look with Dane that was loaded. One neither elaborated on out loud. On the way back to the cabin, they'd sidestepped the possibility to talk about slightly more plausible reasons why Tucker would do what he had done.

They'd also switched over to the broadcast, wondering if it was Levi's voice filling the car.

Rachel held back while Dane continued to thrive in his element. She picked a random book off the bookshelf and flipped through its pages, but the words blurred every time she tried to focus. What if she was right?

What if Marcus was alive? What if the man who had killed her husband was still causing chaos?

What if he was after Dane now?

Rachel's heart squeezed at the thought. Then she was angry. She fisted her hand against the love seat. One person shouldn't be allowed to take so much from another.

It just wasn't right.

Rachel sighed into the open book. Her emotions were all over the place. She needed a distraction. She needed a reprieve from her own mental torture.

"I need wine," she announced.

Dane looked up from his laptop, eyebrow cocked. Rachel jumped off the love seat and headed to the pantry without a follow-up. The small closet had cookies, chips, pasta, pancake mix, cereal and two boxes of fruit snacks. Surely, Suzy had added wine to the obscure list. Rachel continued to go through the kitchen when the pantry search proved fruitless. Dane watched her but kept quiet. Which was good; she was two seconds from picking a fight out of frustration.

"Eureka!"

Above the refrigerator was a lone bottle of Prosecco. There were even a couple of wineglasses.

"Do you think that's a good idea?" Dane had the gall to ask. Rachel ignored him until she found a corkscrew.

"What I think is that, as long as we're here, I can't do much to help," she said. The cork came out easily enough. "Other than do what we already have been doing, which is asking a whole lot of questions. Since I've already asked about all the ones I can think of, that leaves me thinking about either being chased by two men, having one almost shoot me the next day, seeing *his* dead body or…" She paused to fill her glass, then continued. "Or my least favorite, thinking that the man behind it all might just be the man who killed my husband."

She turned around, full glass in hand, and tried to ignore the invisible walls she knew had risen around the man. "So, I think the best route for me to take at this particular juncture is to sit on that love seat, try to read whatever book that is, drink that Prosecco we were lucky enough to find, and try to pretend that I don't feel as helpless as I did seven years ago when that son of a bitch Marcus Highland decided he needed to make a statement."

Rachel didn't wait for a response. She was close to tears, angrier than she thought she had been. She settled back in her spot on the love seat and took her first sip of the wine.

Dane, bless his heart, did the right thing.

He didn't say a word.

THE WINE WASN'T a bad idea, but it wasn't a good one, either.

Dane kept quiet as Rachel followed through on her plan for the next few hours. She sat on the love seat, drank her wine and read through a book about a city girl moving to a small town. In that time the acute worry of Marcus and his merry men dulled. The frustration and anxiousness were replaced by a warmth. Dane took calls outside or typed along his keyboard while the day crawled by. For a little while, Rachel forgot about their problems.

But then the city girl in her book ran into a problem that transcended the pages between Rachel's hands.

"You left me," he said. "Without a word, you got on a bus and came to this hick town. Why?"

Even though it was nothing more than a book and the situation was nowhere near the same, something in Rachel snapped. Helped, no doubt, by the wine she had once thought would work as a distraction. She put the book down, took a deep breath and finally asked the question she had avoided asking for years.

"Why did you leave me?"

DANE OPENED HIS mouth to say *something*, but Rachel kept on.

"And don't you deny that's exactly what happened," she said, voice rising as she stood. "One day you were there and then one day you weren't. Then you started avoiding me and, eventually, I gave up trying to connect. I gave up trying to *fix* whatever it was that had broken. I *let it go*. But now? After everything we've just been through? All I want to know now is *why*. Why did you leave, Dane? I want to know. I think I deserve that much."

Pretending he didn't know the woman a few feet from him well would have been a lie. Before David had died, Dane had already been friends with the woman, able to be around her with enjoyment and ease. After David passed, that friendship had only grown stronger, weaving together with something else in common. Tragedy. They'd become closer.

Too close.

That was how Dane knew that Rachel had reached the end of her grace toward him. Her eyes were shining, her body was rigid. Even from the distance between them, he saw her teeth gritting together after she finished talking. She was angry. She was hurt. She was looking for an answer.

One Dane still couldn't give.

Not after the way the case had possibly turned back toward the past.

So Dane took the easy way out and felt the fool for it.

"It was the guilt," he said simply. Not entirely a lie, not entirely the truth. "The anniversary of David's death was coming up and there I was, eating dinner with you. Talking. Laughing. It was too much." He shook his head slowly. "Being around you was too much."

The hurt was immediate. Rachel's whole body was seemingly affected by the sting of his words. Dane hated it. More than anything he'd always wanted to protect her from any and all pain. Yet there he was. The cause of it.

Rachel dropped her gaze and walked to the bedroom door. Dane watched her go, refusing to follow. It wouldn't do either of them any good.

"You know," Rachel started to say, pausing in the doorway and turning to face him again, "when you told me David died because of *your* plan, I was angry. But, like I've said before, never for one moment was I angry at you. Do you want to know why that is, Dane?"

It was his turn to become rigid. He didn't answer. He didn't think she expected him to, either.

"Because a man named Marcus was the one who killed my husband. *Our* best friend. While all you did was try your damnedest to save him. I was proud of you for that then and I'm still proud of it now. So whatever hang-ups or guilt trips you want to continue to feed, don't put any of that on me. I never forgave you, Dane, because I never blamed you."

And then she was gone.

RACHEL LOOKED UP at the ceiling and let her eyes adjust to the darkness. She'd been asleep, but for how long? A dim light filtered in from beneath the bedroom door. The spot next to her in bed was empty and cold. Not that she expected Dane to be there. She'd finally let him know that his abrupt abandonment and following absence through the years had left their marks.

Rachel sighed into the silence.

Now she finally knew why he'd done both and she didn't know how to process it. She had meant what she said, though. She didn't want the man spending any more of his days blaming himself and using her as an excuse to do it. Rachel wasn't going to have that, but at the same time, she didn't know how to make *Dane* accept that.

I guess that's not up to me, she thought. An ache of loss echoed in her chest at the sentiment.

Rachel rolled over and looked at the digital readout on her cell phone's screen. Not only had she retreated to the bedroom before she could *really* lose it earlier, but she'd managed to take a nap that had stretched well into the night. The emotional toll had been draining; the wine hadn't helped.

That same wine was making her feel the need to drink some water. She sighed, swung her legs over the side of the bed, and padded to the bathroom with her pajamas in tow. She had been so upset earlier that she hadn't changed out of her clothes. She had just wanted to close her eyes. Now she was better. She washed her face, brushed her teeth and nodded to her reflection in the mirror.

She wasn't proud that she had gotten tipsy and yelled at Dane, but it had been a long time coming. Now all they could do was move past it.

Rachel's stomach dropped.

How Dane had moved past it before was to cut her completely out of his life. After the case was solved, would he do that again?

Rachel felt like she was constantly sighing, but there another one was as she crawled back into bed. She wasn't tired anymore, but that didn't mean she was about to go get into Dane's personal space. Especially since he had admitted being around her was "too much."

Rachel felt another sigh about to escape when a knock on the door distracted it. She reached over to the bedside lamp and clicked it on.

"Come in," she called.

Dark eyes swept across the room and landed on her.

"I heard you moving around," he greeted. "I… Well…"

He rubbed a hand across the back of his neck. The movement made his biceps jump. Rachel tried to ignore it.

"Spit it out," Rachel said, surprised at how brash the command sounded. Still, it did the trick.

"I tried to sleep on the couch, and if there's one thing I'm certain about the two of us, it's that we're tall people." He managed to look sheepish. "I was wondering if, well… I know you're mad at me, but—Well, I—"

Rachel rolled her eyes and patted the bed next to her. "You can still sleep in here, Dane. I'm not going to kick you out."

Dane chanced a small smile. It, plus the promise of him being so close to her again, made Rachel's heartbeat start to speed up. It was annoying. Dane had hurt her, and just because she wasn't going to make him sleep on the floor, that didn't mean she couldn't stay grumpy. To prove this point to them both without saying a word, she turned the light off and rolled over, her back to the rest of the room.

Dane was smart not to comment. He moved around the bedroom and bathroom until she felt the bed dip beneath his weight. She tensed, making sure to not slide toward him. She just hoped her body stayed as vigilant while she was asleep. Waking up in Dane's arms after their short but brutal conversation wouldn't be ideal.

A few minutes went by without a word. The silence was almost too loud. Rachel waited for his breathing to even out to let her know he had fallen asleep, although after a few more minutes passed, it remained the same. She had half a mind to roll over and peek. But what would that solve?

"You awake?"

Rachel opened her eyes in a flash, worried for the briefest of moments that Dane had somehow heard her thoughts. She stared at the wall, trying to tamp down the spike in her adrenaline at his words.

"I am," she said after a moment. "What's u—?"

"It was your yellow dress. The one with daisies on it." His voice had fallen into an even lower than normal baritone. "We were supposed to meet for lunch and try out the new Italian place on Main Street. I'd already been in Darby that morning to talk to the chief, so I decided to stretch my legs and walk the park across from the post office. It being a nice day outside didn't hurt."

Slowly, Rachel rolled over to face him. He was lying on his back, staring up at the ceiling. She dared not speak.

"So I parked next to the post office and walked to the fountain," he continued. "There was some yoga class going on and I didn't want to seem like I was creeping, so I kept walking until I got to the other side of the park."

Even in the dim light from beneath the bathroom door, Rachel saw the man smile. "Then there you were. Across the road, parked outside Sadie's Bookstore, angry as a kicked hornet's nest. Your tire was flat, but by God, that wasn't stopping you. You already had the car jacked up and the bolts off the hubcaps. I instantly wanted to help you, which instantly made me laugh. I knew just about what you'd say if I tried to take over. 'I've done this enough times to know I can change this tire faster than you, Dane Jones.' After that you'd probably count off all the times you'd changed a tire since your mom had taught you how to do it when you were in high school." His smile smoothed out. Rachel nearly held her breath.

"And then I was looking at that dress, the one with the daisies," he said. "I'd never seen it before. I was sure I'd remember it if I had." Dane turned his head to meet her gaze. "That's when I realized I was in love with you. And *that's* why I had to leave."

Chapter Sixteen

The entire cast from *Game of Thrones* could have walked into the bedroom right then and Rachel wouldn't have even batted an eye. The moment Dane finished his declaration, all Rachel could do was stare.

"I should have told you," he said. "Instead of just going, but—"

Rachel's mind took a back seat as her body went into overdrive. She closed the space between them with little effort and pressed her lips to his with little thought.

Dane's reaction time was slow, but Rachel didn't care.

She needed to kiss him. She needed to touch him. She needed to let out some of the energy that had ignited within her at his revelation.

Because Dane saying he loved her hadn't irrevocably changed her. No. What he'd said was better. Because, Rachel realized, she didn't just want to be friends with the man next to her.

She wanted more.

Much more.

And apparently Dane still did, too.

He answered her kiss with force, pushing his lips against hers with a notable hunger. He rolled onto his side, deepening the kiss with a swipe of his tongue.

Rachel responded with her own exploration. Even at the odd angle, Dane threaded one hand into her hair. He was gentle with it, yet she still gasped against him.

His body tensed as he broke the kiss.

Dark eyes she had missed more than she had realized searched her face.

"Are you oka—?" he started, voice husky and raw.

Rachel didn't let him finish the question.

She was back to his lips and, like on the night before, she entered his embrace. The hand in her hair fastened her mouth to his while his other hand grabbed and pulled her hips closer. Rachel didn't waste any time showing she wanted more than his lips. She fingered the hem of his shirt and then slid her hands up and underneath it. They explored the hard surface of his stomach and abs. His bare skin electric beneath her own.

Dane made a guttural noise deep in his throat.

It was more than encouraging.

Rachel tugged up on the fabric of the shirt until Dane got the hint. He broke their kiss long enough to pull his shirt off. It was thrown across the room and out of sight. Rachel decided to join in. Or at least she tried.

Dane had other ideas.

He rolled over until he was straddling her and then bent over and worked the buttons of her pajama top. The task of getting her out of her shirt could have gone a lot faster, but apparently he was going for extra credit. Starting at her collarbone, Dane pressed his lips to her skin. The contact was dazzling and only became more pronounced the lower his lips traveled. With each new unfastened button, there was Dane. Trailing his lips and tongue down her newly bare skin. When there was nothing left to unbutton, Dane pulled her up and against him as she shimmied out of the top.

There was a moment when they sat there, bare chests pressed together, hearts beating, breathing, moving against each other, when Rachel felt like they were at some kind of precipice. An important one.

"You said you *were* in love with me," she whispered, breathless. "Are you still?"

Dane ran his hand across her cheek and tucked a strand of hair behind her ear. In the dim light she could see his smile.

"I never stopped."

Then his mouth was over hers and he was pushing her back on the bed. The rest of their clothes disappeared as their bodies, and hearts, finally intertwined.

DANE OPENED HIS eyes and felt the warmth of the woman he'd loved for years tucked safely within his arms. It was like a weight had been lifted from his entire body as he looked at Rachel's sleeping form. He'd finally told her the truth. The full reason he'd put distance between them.

In the year following David's death, he'd gone from being a friend to falling in love with her. Dane didn't know when it had happened or how—he definitely hadn't been looking for it—but there it was. He was in love with his best friend's girl.

David had once joked that if anything ever happened to him in the line of duty, Dane should look out for Rachel. Dane could bet he hadn't meant to fall in love with her a few weeks after the anniversary of his death.

An ache of guilt pushed through him at the thought.

It was like Rachel could sense his turmoil. She stirred in his arms. He pasted on a smile.

"Good morning," he greeted, eyeing the readout on her phone. It was just after seven. "Sorry if I woke you."

Rachel stretched her legs and arms out, her body vibrating against his. The movement plus the absolutely naked smoothness of her skin was jarring. Not in any unpleasant way, just not on the same wavelength as the guilt settled in his stomach. Having Rachel so close and in such a vulnerable position was teasing his more primal urges. He tried to focus.

"No, it's fine," she said, rolling onto her back to look at him. "I wanted to get up early today anyways." She smiled and then put a hand in front of her mouth. "But if you'll excuse me and my morning breath for a moment."

Dane laughed as the woman wasted no time in escaping from beneath the sheets. She grabbed his discarded shirt, threw it on, and sent him a quick wink before disappearing into the bathroom. He didn't like the empty spot next to him. However they weren't on vacation. He had a job to do and bad men to catch. Not lie around in bed, tormenting himself over a woman with denim-blue eyes and a set of lips that rocked his world.

No, he needed to focus.

He swiped his phone off the nightstand. No new texts or emails. No new calls.

Trying to exhume Marcus's body was a waiting game. One that couldn't be finished until a judge approved the request. Billy was going to work on that as soon as Judge Deal got to his office. Once they knew for certain one way or the other that his body was what had been buried under a single-named headstone in one of Kipsy's cemeteries, the lead on him, plus the men from the past few days, had hit a road block. At least, for Dane it had.

Finding Knife Guy, aka Wyatt, and Levi in the yearbook had been exciting. Yet that excitement had ebbed as the night before dragged on. Neither man was in the sheriff department's database and neither had a social media presence to follow. Everywhere Dane and the department had looked seemed to be a dead end.

It was like none of the men existed past their names and pictures in one edition of the Kipsy South Academy yearbook.

Which meant either they were really good at hiding their trails or they had the resources to help them keep themselves under wraps.

Or both.

There was also still the question of how Lonnie fit into everything.

Why did Levi want him?

What did Tucker know about it all?

Dane scrubbed a hand down his face. He could feel a headache start to form behind his eyes while the stress in his shoulders became heavier. It was hard to focus on a case that had so many questions but no answers. He rolled his shoulders back, trying to ease the building tension. What he really needed to do was to hit the gym. Work out some of the stress. Try to get his body and mind on the same page again.

The shower came on in the next room. Dane put his phone down as Rachel opened the door. She wasn't wearing his shirt anymore.

"I'm going to take a quick shower," she said conversationally. "I was wondering if you wanted to join me."

Dane couldn't help smirking.

His body and mind certainly seemed to get on the same page fast at that.

CHANCE SHOWED UP at lunch. He barely made it into the cabin before his hat was off and he was launching into a story.

"I was trying to figure out where Tucker went when he left the house the other night," he summarized for them, perching on the edge of the couch. "But I was coming up empty. So I decided to ask some different questions like who the hell this man is. If you know enough about a person, it's not hard to guess where he might go or do in any given situation. So, *who is Tucker Hughes*?"

Rachel didn't know if the cowboy wanted an answer, but *she* sure wanted one. "Who is he?"

Chance slapped his knee and snapped his fingers, excitement clear in his eyes. "He's a quiet man who has spent his life staying out of people's ways. He graduated from high school, got a manual labor job in construction, and has spent the past few decades maintaining a quiet existence." A wicked grin pulled up the corner of his mouth. "And, according to a high school sweetheart I managed to track down thanks to the yearbook, he's also an only child."

"Wait, what?" Rachel asked.

"He's raising his nephew," Dane pointed out. "I might be an only child, but I know you need a sibling to have one of those."

Chance put up his hands to stop them from continuing.

"Listen, believe me, I barked up that tree when she said that," he said. "But she said she was one-hundred-percent certain that he was a single child. So, without seeming like I was calling her a liar, I asked if she could direct me to anyone else who was friends with him back in the day. She said he was a total loner and he only hung out with her and one other person while they were in high school." The grin grew. "And that person was none other than Marcus Highland."

Rachel straightened her back. She felt her nostrils flare. She never would get used to hearing that name. Dane had a similar reaction but then was typing away at his laptop. Rachel couldn't see what he was looking up. She turned back to Chance.

"So what are you thinking?" she had to ask. "And what about Lonnie?"

Chance was practically beaming.

"I'm thinking that Tucker doesn't have a brother, but Marcus Highland does," he said. "Or did."

The cowboy turned his attention to his friend. Dane's brows were knitted together, his eyes narrowed and scanning the screen. Whatever he had been looking for was right in front of him. Chance must have sensed that, too. He waited until Dane caught on to his unsaid thought.

"Almost eleven years ago a John Highland was killed in his prison cell by a fellow inmate," Dane said, still reading the information on his computer screen. "He was there for felony drug possession, although his wife claimed the arresting deputy had planted the drugs. She tried to sue the department. The Riker County Sheriff's Department." He paused to finish reading. "She passed away in a car accident before it could go anywhere." Dane finally looked up. He only had eyes for her. "Leaving behind one child. A baby boy."

Chance nodded. "Now, I can't say for certain if John Highland is really related to Marcus, especially since we can't seem to find any trace of Marcus other than that yearbook, but when I went to look into what happened to that baby boy...well, I came up empty." Chance shrugged. Then he leaned closer. "But guess when Lonnie started showing up in Tucker's life?"

Rachel shook her head.

"No way," she breathed. "It can't be."

Chance nodded. "Two months after Jasmine Highland's death, Tucker Hughes became the legal guardian of Lonnie."

Rachel shook her head again, trying to come up with another explanation.

"That can't be," she challenged. "You can't just say you're related to some kid and take him in when it's not true."

"With the right papers, the right amount of money, and the wrong people, you can do just about anything."

Rachel had opened her mouth to try to attack that thought when Dane spoke up.

"Wyatt said Tucker was supposed to keep the boy safe," he said. "That's why. Marcus wasn't just coming for Lonnie for some kind of ransom or leverage to use. He was coming for him because Lonnie is *his* nephew. Not Tucker's." Dane fisted his hand against the tabletop. "And if this is all true, that's why Marcus was so hell-bent on the idea of corruption in the department back then." His expression softened. "And why he might have targeted a prison transport van to help make his statement."

Rachel's head felt like it was going to explode. "But why? Why do *all* this? Why not just raise his nephew himself? Why come for him now?" She threw her hands in the air. "I still don't understand!"

The sound of a phone vibrating made them all turn to the tabletop.

"It's Billy," Dane said. He scooped up the phone and answered it. Billy didn't say much, but it was enough. "I'm on my way."

Dane was standing taller when he hung up.

"I think it's about time we get some answers," he said. "And I think it's time to get some from Tucker himself. He just woke up and is ready to talk."

Chapter Seventeen

Rachel picked at the invisible lint on her jeans. Dane put his hand over hers to settle it but kept his gaze straight ahead. She took a deep breath and glanced around the small waiting room.

Chance was leaning against the wall, hat in his hands and eyes closed. Two local officers originally tasked with keeping a watch over Tucker were talking among themselves just outside the doorway. Detective Foster was pacing through the back of the room, head bent over his phone. Occasionally he would make a call, sometimes he would pull Dane over to talk to him.

Breaking out the theory that Tucker Hughes had adopted Marcus Highland's nephew had given the department a new direction to look into. It had also given the sheriff enough ammo to convince the judge that exhuming Marcus's body was the right call to make. Illegally adopting Lonnie was one thing. Illegally adopting Lonnie to keep the boy safe while Marcus continued to do devious things was another.

Rachel let out a breath, frustrated.

"Should Lonnie be in there right now?" she asked for what felt like the umpteenth time.

"We can't prove Tucker isn't Lonnie's legal guardian right now," he reiterated. "Even if we could, Lonnie has been with that man since he was a toddler. He wanted to see him."

"Tucker tried to leave him," Rachel muttered. Dane squeezed her hand.

"Don't worry. Suzy is in there with him," he reassured her. "She'll make sure Tucker doesn't say anything that could hurt Lonnie."

Rachel knew he was right, but still her nerves weren't happy. It was nice to have a theory that might get them answers to what was going on, but it was a theory she wasn't excited to entertain. Marcus had been shot and buried by the state. When no one could figure out his true identity, all he'd gotten was his first name and the date he died on his tombstone. The same date that was on David's, too.

What if he *was* still alive?

What had he been doing the past several years?

What was the endgame?

Dane ran his thumb across her wrist.

"I know," he whispered soothingly. "I know."

Rachel took a deep breath and then let it out, trying to rein in the excess anxiety making her feel even more crazy in their current situation. As much as he hated it, Dane had told her the truth during the ride over.

Right now was a waiting game. One the entire department was playing. Everyone had a part they were looking into.

"Once we get that first answer, the rest will fall in line like dominoes," Dane had said.

Rachel understood his confidence. He trusted the men and women in the department with more than just the case. He trusted them with his life. It was nice to know that, while Dane had left his original life plan after David's passing, he had still found his place in the world. One that included a job he loved and coworkers who were more like family. It was just nice to know he hadn't been alone for the past few years.

"Here we go."

Rachel looked up as Suzy rounded the corner, Lonnie at her side. Dane and Rachel stood. Chance started over. Suzy smiled and motioned to the drink vending machine in the corner. She handed the boy two dollars.

"Like I promised," she said with a grin.

Lonnie took the money and was off. It gave Suzy time to talk to them.

"Tucker is on some painkillers, so he isn't one-hundred percent there, if you ask me." She dove in. "But he knows where he is and what happened. I think he also is very aware that we know he left Lonnie. He looked nervous and guilty more than anything else."

"What did he say to Lonnie?" Rachel asked.

Suzy rubbed her stomach. Her expression hardened.

"Not enough, if you ask me," she said. "Lonnie did most of the talking. Told him what happened in the house the other day." Suzy looked directly at Rachel. "Talked a lot about you. Said you would die before letting him sacrifice himself to the man who was downstairs. Then he talked about your wound and how it looked under the bandage."

Rachel touched her wrist and smiled for a moment at the boy's earlier curiosity to see it.

Then Suzy turned to Dane. She lowered her voice. "I don't know how their relationship was before this all happened, but I don't think they're all that close. Lonnie didn't even try to hug him. Just kind of patted the bed. Tucker didn't try anything, either. It was almost like they were strangers."

"The rumor at school is that Tucker views Lonnie as

more of an obligation than family," Rachel said, matching Suzy's low tone.

"Which is in line with our new theory," Chance added. "He might actually be an obligation for Tucker." Rachel narrowed her eyes at the cowboy. He held up his hand and defended himself. "You know what I mean."

Rachel glanced over at the boy. Her heart squeezed at the thought of him living with a man who viewed him as some kind of job or chore.

"Can we go see Tucker now?" Dane asked. His voice was tight. He was trying to stay professional, but Rachel heard the anger beneath his words. "I'd really like to ask that man some questions."

Suzy nodded. "My advice? Don't press him too hard too fast," she said. "I don't like to make snap judgments about people I don't know, but honestly, I think he's one heck of a coward. You might break him before you get what you want."

Dane muttered some not-nice words. Rachel touched his arm.

"I want to stay out here with Lonnie," she told him. "I don't want to see that man yet. I don't have professional training in keeping my opinions to myself."

"I'm sure Lonnie would like that," Dane said with a small smile. "He seems to be a fan."

"While you all do that, I'm going to go call Billy and see how things are going with him," Suzy added. She looked over their shoulder to Detective Foster. "Then see what Caleb has going on. Deputy Mills is supposed to be on his way here soon to talk."

Rachel once again pictured each of the people around her with one piece of the puzzle. The anxiety of waiting settled back onto her shoulders. She would be happy when this was all over.

Dane and Chance disappeared down the hallway while Suzy went in the opposite direction. Rachel walked over to the vending machine in time to see Lonnie scowling at it.

"What did that machine ever do to you?" Rachel teased.

Lonnie looked over and let out a loud, long sigh.

"I wanted a Pepsi," he said. "This one doesn't have any. This week has sucked."

Rachel was going to correct him but decided to agree. "It *has* sucked, hasn't it?"

Lonnie looked surprised. Rachel snorted. It made him smile.

"Yeah, it has," he said, enthused. "They even brought me homework to do yesterday. But I told them I was too emotional."

His smile turned into a grin.

Rachel couldn't help laughing.

Despite everything, the boy had a sense of humor. It was endearing.

"Here, why don't we go look at the vending machines down the hall?" Rachel suggested. "See if they don't have a Pepsi or two. Maybe some candy while we're at it."

Lonnie nodded, eyes lighting up. He followed as she went to the two police officers watching the area.

"We're going to go to the vending machines down there," she said, pointing down the hall. They could see half of one of the machines just from where they were standing. It was probably the only reason they allowed them to go. Rachel turned to Detective Foster. His face was pinched, his attention narrowed. Whatever news he was getting over the phone was probably just as frustrating as all the other news they'd already gotten.

"So, do you like the place you're staying at?" Rachel asked as they meandered along the hall. She decided to avoid asking the questions she wanted to, like how he was doing and if Tucker had ever talked about *not* being his uncle.

"It's okay," he said with a shrug. "There's a pool in the back, but they said it was better to stay inside even though I told them I'm really awesome at swimming."

She didn't miss how his chest seemed to swell with pride.

"Tucker doesn't like the water, but I do. I taught myself to swim when I was in third grade. I'm really fast."

"That's impressive. I can swim but not fast. I'm really good at floating, though." They came to a stop at the first of three vending machines. Rachel smiled as she spied one had Pepsi. A man was standing in front of it, looking for money in his pockets. "And you know, I really like water, too. I even have a creek next to my house."

"Really?" Lonnie asked.

"Yep. It's *just* deep enough to swim in but not *too* deep. But my favorite part is listening to it from the deck. It's really nice in the summer."

That seemed to impress Lonnie. He opened his mouth to say something when the man next to them spoke instead.

"It really *is* a lovely feature."

He turned around so fast that Rachel didn't think to feel threatened. She figured it was just a man trying to make conversation. But then he kept talking.

"If you make any move or try to alert those cops down the hall, Marnie is as good as dead."

Rachel felt her eyes widen.

"And that means looking at me in fear."

Rachel adjusted her expression. She fought the urge to look back toward the police officers. All she had to do was yell and they'd come. Or run back to them.

But he'd said Marnie's name.

"What do you mean Marnie's as good as dead?" Rachel did the math in her head quickly. The last time she had talked to the young woman had been the day of the broadcast. While a deputy was there, she'd gone into the house and gotten June the cat, promising to take care of her until things calmed down.

Guilt, strong and fast, bulldozed into Rachel's stomach.

With everything going on she hadn't thought about checking up on her friend. Or her cat for that matter. She should have, plain and simple.

"Oh, don't worry," the man said. "She and June are still alive. Just as long as you listen to me." He titled his gaze down to Lonnie. "As long as you *both* listen to me." He took a dollar bill out of his pocket and held it out to the boy. "You take this and put it in that first vending machine. I want you to pretend you're trying to decide on what to get, got it?"

Lonnie didn't hesitate. He nodded. Without looking at Rachel, he took a step back and in front of the right vending machine. It kept Lonnie in the sight line of the officers. Rachel, however, was just outside it.

"Now, Ms. Roberts, here's the deal," the man began. "You and Lonnie are going to come with us, but unlike the last two times, you *aren't* going to cause any trouble." He motioned behind him. Farther down the hall a man she hadn't seen until now pushed his coat aside long enough so she could see he was wearing a gun.

"That man is the only one in the world who knows the right thing to say to another one of my associates *not* here. If he doesn't say that right thing in the next five minutes, that other associate will start the process of bleeding out young Miss Marnie." He steepled his fingers in front of him. "Now, *that right thing* will only be said when you and the boy walk out with us without any fuss. And let me point out that this associate of mine really doesn't have a taste for you. Considering you're the reason his friend was killed."

"Wyatt," Rachel breathed.

The man arched his eyebrow, but he smiled.

"That's right," he confirmed. "Wyatt was his friend and he's more than ready to kill yours. So let's get this show on the road, all right?"

"You're just going to kill us all anyways," Rachel pointed out, sure of her words. "Our chances at survival go down exponentially if we go with you."

She believed what she said and she hoped Lonnie heard that confidence in her voice. She was saying it for his benefit, not hers. He'd already tried to sacrifice himself when Wyatt was around. At the same time, Rachel couldn't damn Marnie just yet.

"Oh, as much as I wish we could, that's not the plan." He glanced at Lonnie. "The boy is off limits. You are on the fence. And Marnie? Marnie is just good ol' bait." He grinned. "And not to be a broken record, but whether she lives or dies is up to you. It isn't our decision at all."

Rachel's stomach twisted. She pictured the first time she'd met sweet, innocent Marnie. Awkward, talkative, and completely indifferent when it came to personal space. Since then the young girl had grown into a wonderful young woman. Rachel pictured her days ago, worried that something had happened to Rachel and distraught at just the thought.

Rachel took a shuddering breath.

Her heart sank.

The man's eyes narrowed.

Forgive me, Marnie.

Rachel spun on her heel and pushed Lonnie as hard as she could farther into the sight line of the officers.

"Help!" she yelled at the top of her lungs.

Then, before either of the men could react, Rachel ran.

This time, it wasn't away from danger.

It was toward it.

Chapter Eighteen

Her head was nothing but a throbbing ache. Rachel opened her eyes and tenderly touched her cheek. It hurt, too. Her fingers were wet as she pulled them back.

What had happened?

Where was she?

It was dark. Cool but not too cold. She tried to let her eyes adjust as she reached out on either side of her. One hand touched something hard. The other went through air.

"Lonnie?"

Her voice fell flat in the darkness. Like she was somewhere tight. She waited, listening. No one responded, least of all Lonnie.

The hospital.

The men.

Rachel's heartbeat started to gallop.

She'd managed to tackle the man closest to them in the hospital hallway, but after that things got hazy. The throbbing of her head was a clue she couldn't ignore. She'd been hit in the head. Hard. Someone had knocked her out.

"Marnie?" she tried instead.

No response.

Rachel took a moment to take stock of herself. She

wasn't tied up or bound. Her mouth wasn't covered, either. Aside from her head, there was no other pain. Still, slowly, she tested herself to see if there were any other limitations while also trying to figure out where she was.

She reached out to the spot where she'd connected with something hard and put her palm against it. Whatever it was, it was textured and firm. Rachel slid her hand up and then all the way to the floor. It was a wall. She put her palm against the floor and felt along it, hoping to find *something,* but came up short.

Rachel decided to follow that wall. She got up slowly and felt along it for a few steps before she hit another one. She did the same thing along the new wall until a foot or so later she hit another corner. Wherever she was, it was a very small room.

Alone in that very small, very dark, room.

Panic started to rise within her. Her breathing was becoming erratic. She traced the last wall back, hoping to find a door.

"Thank God," she whispered to herself. Her fingers wrapped around a doorknob. It turned but something caught when she pushed. Rachel turned the knob again and tried to push through. The door was blocked on the other side.

The panic in Rachel's chest quickly turned to fear.

"Help," she yelled, banging her fists against the door. "Help! Someone! I'm in here!"

Rachel beat at the door until the wound from her hand burned. She tried to open the door one last time. When it didn't move, she opened up her search perimeter. She moved along each of the walls again, this time with the intent of finding a light switch. When she came up empty, she moved backward, sweeping each foot out in an arc before she continued. Finally she felt something.

A string.

Rachel pulled it.

A fluorescent bulb came to life above her. She blinked against the new light. The room she was in *was* small. No windows, no furniture, just a cluster of boxes she was a few inches from tripping over near the middle. She turned back to the door and tried to open it again, as if seeing it would make some kind of difference. However, whatever was on the other side of it continued to resist.

Rachel turned her attention to the closest box. It was taped up. One name was written across its side in black Sharpie. The writing was familiar. So was the name.

"David," she read out loud.

Ice ran through her veins.

Slowly she looked around.

Rachel wasn't in a room. She was in a shed.

Her shed.

The one she had bought a few months back for behind her house. It had been too hot to move her excess boxes into it during the summer, so she'd only put in a few. The ones that were in there now were books. Rachel bent over and started to open the box closest to her. A book was better than nothing when it came to makeshift weapons.

A scraping sound made her turn. Movement shook the door. Rachel tried to claw the box open, needing to get her hands on *something*, but she ran out of time. A flood of light from outside came in.

Once again she blinked to get her bearings.

"Glad to see Levi didn't kill you."

A man filled the doorway. Tall, broad, and a mass of

muscles. He had a shaved head and a nasty scar across his right forearm. A smaller but still angry scar puckered the skin at his neck. He wore a dark navy blazer and a matching pair of slacks. His shoes reflected sunlight. So did the long knife in his hand.

"You're Marcus Highland," Rachel said, voice stone. It wasn't a question. She'd seen his picture and she would never forget it. So he really wasn't dead.

Marcus nodded and stepped inside. He didn't shut the door, but the man from the hospital with the gun came into view. After he flashed her a smile and turned around. He was the guard. Beyond him Rachel could see the trees that separated her house and Marnie's property.

Marnie.

Rachel began to feel numb.

If she wasn't in the shed, then did that mean…?

"You know, I'm impressed with you," Marcus said. He stopped and leaned against the wall. Rachel backed up until her back hit the one opposite. He pointed the knife at her. Its blade glinted in the light. "You're craftier than I thought you would be. Here I thought you'd just freeze up when my friends came after you and Lonnie. Maybe fight back a little, run a little, too, but nothing like what you did at the school. It was a surprise to say the least. But it was also a bad plan. One my deceased partner Wyatt decided to attempt a little too early. But when Tucker said Lonnie had Saturday detention and *you* were the teacher in charge?" He shrugged. "I could see how he thought moving the timeline up was a good move. When two pieces line up like that? Well, it's hard to pass up the opportunity that arises from it."

He smiled. It sickened her.

"But I guess you taught Wyatt a lesson. Or should

I say Captain Dane Jones did?" Marcus's eyes turned to slits for the briefest of moments. "Captain. I can't believe *he* made captain. I didn't think he'd have the stones."

The disgust that was clear in his voice made Rachel find her own.

"What's your plan?" she snapped. "Why do you want Lonnie now? Why come for him all these years later?"

Marcus didn't answer right away. Instead he studied her. It made her skin crawl, his brown eyes sweeping across her face like a machine trying to scan a code.

"You know," he finally said.

Rachel nodded.

"Lonnie is *your* nephew, not Tucker's," she confirmed. "But I don't understand why. You could have adopted him, but instead you started the Saviors of the South. Why? What was the point of it all? Why kill all those men?"

Rachel thought of David. Her voice broke enough to make her feel shame. She didn't want to give the man the satisfaction of her crying. The tears in her throat stayed down.

Marcus's expression stayed impassive. "Plans are hard to make and keep when corruption can take everyone and everything away from you."

"Your brother, John," Rachel stated. If Marcus was going to talk, she at least wanted answers.

"He was a good, God-fearing man. Much better than I ever was. Good husband, good dad. But that all changed when a Riker County sheriff's deputy decided he wanted to save himself by damning John."

"The deputy planted evidence and John was convicted," Rachel said.

She saw Marcus's hand tighten around the hilt of the knife.

"Never had a chance," he stressed, seething. "Especially after one of his buddies got up on the stand and praised him as an honest, honorable man. They took one look at my brother and decided he wasn't worth listening to. Went to prison in the blink of an eye. And if that wasn't bad enough…" He gritted his teeth.

If Rachel could have, she would have stepped farther away from him. His anger was almost thick enough to feel.

"If that wasn't bad enough, the people who were supposed to protect him while he was forced to be there? They let him be killed in his cell like he was nothing." The anger didn't dissipate. It transformed. From rage to a smile steeped in venom and dripping with violence. "So I decided to wait until I could punish the man who didn't save my brother."

Rachel was almost too afraid to speak.

Almost.

"You didn't just pick the prison transport at random because of opportunity," she realized aloud. "You targeted it specifically."

"After John was killed, Tracy Markinson went through an internal investigation. He was cleared. I knew it was only a matter of time until he was shuffled around. So I waited and waited. And then, *poof.* There he was, tasked with transporting some prisoners. It was like the stars aligned."

Rachel still didn't understand. "Why did you wait? If you were so hell-bent on killing him, why not go to his house? Or get him when he left work one day? *Why kill all those men?*"

Marcus shook his head. He had the gall to *tsk* at her.

"Because no one will hear what you're trying to say if you aren't loud, Ms. Roberts," he said as casually as could be. "And nothing is louder than kidnapping a van full of men and holding them hostage."

Rachel felt sick to her stomach. "You never planned on letting them go, did you?" Her voice was a whisper. "No matter what the sheriff did that day. You just wanted to punish one man. And then, what? Embarrass the department?"

"I wanted them to know what feeling helpless was *really* like," he said simply. "But I couldn't do that if they were all good men, now could I? *That's* why I waited for a transport. I needed someone who was good. Someone they would fight for. Someone like my brother."

Rachel thought she couldn't have felt any worse than she already had. But she was mistaken. Her face turned hot, her hands fisted on reflex, and the only reason she didn't cry was that the rage building within her was too quick. "You needed my husband."

Marcus nodded again. "Tracy was the target, but David was the message. They were both dead before you even knew they'd been taken." He shrugged. "Everything else after that? That was just for show, wasting time while I tried to get my affairs in order. That's when Dane showed up. Luckily, I'd planned ahead. Paid a doctor on standby just in case things—"

"Get out," Rachel interrupted.

It was like she was out of her own body, listening in from somewhere else. Her voice was unrecognizable even to her own ears. Menacing. Angry. Violent. She was seeing red. Blood red.

"Get out," she repeated. Marcus raised his eyebrow. He started to smile. Rachel took a step forward. "Get. Out."

His smile wiped clean. He studied her expression, her body.

"Listen here…" he started. It was his stance that changed now. He hadn't expected her to bite. He'd expected her to sit still and listen. To be the audience to his grand tale. To ask questions he wanted to answer.

He was grossly mistaken.

Rachel took another step closer. Every muscle in her body was coiling. Like a snake ready to strike. Then she was yelling. "Get out! Get out! Get out!"

With adrenaline coursing through her veins, she grabbed the box closest to her, lifted it and swung it around. It was too heavy to reach him, but it still sounded bad as it slammed to the floor in front of him.

"What's going on?" the man behind Marcus asked. His hand was on the butt of his gun. Rachel didn't care. She wasn't going to just stand around and do exactly what the man wanted. She couldn't. Not when he'd just admitted to killing her husband and then playing with their hope just to prove some kind of misguided point.

Not after he'd *used* David's goodness to justify killing him.

No.

She wasn't going to just stand there and take any of the man's madness.

Rachel opened her mouth to repeat her command, but Marcus held up his hand.

"We're going to leave Ms. Roberts alone for a while," he said, already moving out of the shed. "I think she needs some time to cool down."

Rachel felt all the sorrow and pain of David's death washing over her again. This time the rage of knowing his killer and the motive behind it was hot on its heels.

If Marcus stayed any longer, he would meet someone that even Rachel hadn't known existed.

A widow looking to avenge the man she'd sworn to love forever.

Or maybe Marcus did know exactly what was coming and how dangerous it was.

Without another word, look or evil little smile, he shut the door. The sound of scraping filled the shed as he put whatever had blocked the door before in front of it again.

For what felt like forever Rachel stayed in the middle of the shed, hands balled at her sides and rage pulsing through her body.

Then, slowly, it started to drain.

When it was gone, Rachel did the only thing she could.

She cried.

Chapter Nineteen

Tucker Hughes refused to say anything to Dane and Chance. He clammed up so fast that Dane was almost afraid he had passed out. But then he'd looked Dane in the eye.

That was when they both knew that *they both knew*.

Tucker had illegally adopted Marcus Highland's nephew and had been raising him for almost a decade.

The million-dollar question was why.

Dane didn't get to ask it, though. Not before chaos broke out. Not before two men were able to take Rachel straight from the hospital without any pushback. The only silver lining to the situation was that Rachel had managed to once again keep Lonnie out of harm's way the best she could.

Though, instead of pretending like he was okay, this time Lonnie had been shaken. He'd cried as he'd relayed the conversation back to Dane.

"It's my fault," he had said once a search of the hospital had turned up empty. If Lonnie hadn't been there, Dane would have hopped in his car and joined the motorcade of law enforcement that hit the streets. "I—I should have gone with them the first time. They wouldn't have taken her!"

Dane had been fighting anger at himself and anger at

the men who'd taken Rachel. He was fighting fear, too. Worry that they would hurt her—or worse—had nearly overwhelmed him, but he knew that losing focus would only make matters more difficult. He had placed his hands on the boy's shoulders and knelt in front of him.

"Rachel made a choice," he said sternly. "Those men, those *bad* men, wanted to take you. She decided she wasn't going to let them. It was the right choice and one I would have made, too. There was nothing you could have done contrary to that. So stop blaming yourself and let's figure this out."

Lonnie had calmed down enough to get the rest of what the man had said out.

"Marnie is the neighbor," Dane had translated for Chance. "She's Rachel's friend, too. But I don't know who June—" Dane had jumped up like he'd been shocked. "June is Rachel's cat! They're at her house!"

After that Dane had taken Lonnie to the lobby with Suzy and a local police officer. The former had her phone out and was rerouting available deputies to Rachel's house. It was a plan he'd called off once they were in Chance's car.

"Last time we were in a hostage situation with Marcus Highland and his group, we ended up trying to overwhelm them with our numbers," he had said once she picked up. "I don't want to do that again."

Suzy had trusted his judgment. "Tell us what you want to do and we'll follow you."

It was like a bad case of déjà vu, but Dane had told them what he thought would be the best plan.

Now, less than an hour later, Dane and Chance were at Marnie's house. Her green Beetle was in the driveway, but there was no other sign that anyone else was in the vicinity. Still Dane and Chance searched the house quickly and quietly. But only after they'd broken the front door lock off and let themselves in.

Dane would pay for it later.

"Marcus doesn't leave hostages alive long," Dane said, once they were done. He nodded toward the woods. "This cuts through to the side of Rachel's house. Maybe a three-minute jog. Once we hit the creek it'll be a hundred or so yards after that."

"Are we going to wait for backup to get here?" Chance had his gun out, checking it.

"No," Dane replied on reflex. "At least, I'm not. Wyatt made the decision to try to kill her the other day because she wasn't essential to their goal. They want Lonnie. Not her. I don't want to chance Marcus remembering that, either."

Chance nodded. "I'm not trying to talk you out of it, Dane. We both know how good a shot I am. I'm all the backup you need." The cowboy flashed a quick grin. Dane returned it.

"Thanks," he had to say. "I mean it."

Chance nodded again. His expression hardened. He looked to the woods. It was go-time.

Dane led the way, wordlessly going into the trees. He had walked the Roberts's property enough with David through the years to be familiar with the land that butted up to it. The woods weren't so dense that they couldn't pass through, but they were thick enough that they could use the surroundings for cover if needed.

Which meant so could the men who had Rachel.

Dane took the direct path between Marnie's house and Rachel's, deciding to cut down on time. He didn't know what the play was anymore. If the goal was to get Lonnie, would they use Rachel as leverage? Or was she bait?

Either way, Dane was done waiting around and asking questions.

A soft buzz in his pocket made Dane pause. He pulled his phone out. It was a text from Suzy. It made his blood run cold. He stopped in his tracks.

"What is it?" Chance asked at his side, voice low.

Dane cussed beneath his breath. "They can't find Lonnie." He said a few more *really* bad words. Chance joined in.

"There's no way they would already be at Rachel's house, then," the cowboy pointed out. "Which means, not only do we have a lead, but—"

"Not all of their men are at the house," Dane finished.

He didn't want to point out there was a good chance they wouldn't go back to Rachel's if they had what they wanted. *Who* they wanted.

"We need to hurry, regardless," Dane said.

"Don't worry, after we get Rachel we'll get Lonnie back, too," Chance assured him.

Dane nodded. He started forward again. "You're damn straight we will."

The two of them hustled until they hit the creek. Dane walked into the water, holding his cell phone and gun above his chest. He didn't think the water was deep enough to go over his head, but it had been a while since he'd swam there. The last thing they needed was to be soaking wet from head to toe and trying to be stealthy.

The water was cold but stayed beneath his ribs. Still not the best conditions for sneaking around, but he wasn't about to waste time trying to find a dry place to cross. Once they were on the other side, Dane kicked off as much excess water as he could and stopped within the cover of a group of trees.

"In a few more yards we'll be able to see the house," he said, nodding in the direction he meant. "It's the side of the house with an elevated deck that leads to a sliding-glass door that opens into the kitchen. If anyone is on that side of the house and looks out, we'll be spotted plain as day once we leave the trees."

Dane tapped the tree trunk with his index finger. "This is the house." He tapped off to the side. "This is us." He traced a half moon above both. "I'm going to use the trees we're in now as cover and run to this tree line that umbrellas the house. From there it's a straight shot to the back door. There's no cover between that tree line and there, but the only windows that have a clear shot of the space between are in the laundry room and a bathroom. Hopefully no one is in either one and looking outside."

"They won't be if I make them look somewhere else," Chance said with a sly smile. He tapped the bark that would be the front yard. "We should disable any vehicles just in case anyone tries to run. I can do that and also look out for anyone who might show up. I can also make some noise to draw their attention. It might be enough to get you in the house without anyone noticing."

"It also puts the spotlight on you," Dane said. "With no backup."

Chance thumped the brim of his hat. "Good thing I'm a great shot." He sobered when Dane didn't laugh. "If Marcus Highland is the one calling the shots and he has Lonnie now, then the window to get Rachel might be closing fast. This is our best plan, boss."

The last time Dane had made a plan, his best friend had been killed. Now there was more on the line. Rachel, Lonnie, Marnie and Chance. The woman he loved, the kid they'd do anything to save, a young woman who meant a lot to Rachel, and a close friend who meant a lot to Dane.

Worry and fear tried to push their way deeper into him. But this time Dane wasn't going to second-guess himself.

"At least it's not storming," he said, pulling his gun up.

Chance nodded. "There is that."

They shared a look that was their version of saying "good luck" and went in opposite directions. Dane followed the trees for a couple hundred yards before they started to thin out. He sprinted to the cover of the next tree line, following it until the back of the house was in view.

No one was in the yard as far as he could see. And even if they had been, a car alarm started going off at the front of the house. Chance.

Dane took a quick breath.

It was now or never.

He held his gun tight and started to run for the back door. The layout of the house in front of him was already pulled up in his mind. Once he stepped through the door, he would be in tight quarters. He'd have to shoot fast if anyone tried to attack. Then he'd have to—

A banging sound pulled Dane's attention to his left. A few feet from the corner of the house was a shed. He'd never seen it before. Rachel must have gotten it recently. It looked brand-new.

Dane switched gears, falling back enough to get a better view of the shed door. Or where the door should have been. A metal container was pushed against it, blocking the bottom half.

And someone was banging on the other side of the

door. Even from this distance he saw the force of it shake the structure.

Rachel.

Dane kept his gun high as he ran full-tilt toward the shed. He moved around the side, ready to shoot any guards that might be around, but came up empty. Whoever was in the shed was all-out throwing themselves at the door. Dane holstered his gun and focused on the container. It was an industrial toolbox. One he recognized as David's. The last time Dane had seen it, it had been in the garage collecting dust.

Dane didn't want to call out to whoever was inside for fear it would give away his location. Instead he planted his feet and bent to get a better hold on the toolbox. Even empty, the container was extremely heavy. Definitely a good makeshift lock for a door that opened outward. It took a few grunts and pushes before the toolbox budged, but once he had a good momentum, it was easier to clear the door. Though it scraped something awful against the shed's exterior.

The banging stopped.

Dane pulled out his gun again.

Slowly he opened the door.

"Ahhh!"

Something flew at Dane's head. He dodged to the side, barely missing it. Then Dane was looking at Rachel.

It was like every part of him had been reborn.

Rachel dropped the book in her hand and ran at him. He lowered his gun and pulled her into an embrace he felt in his bones.

"I'm so glad you're okay," he said into her hair. He squeezed once and then pulled away. "*Are* you okay?" Once again her eyes were swollen and red. She'd been crying. He caught one of her hands. Her knuckles were freshly bloodied. No doubt trying to get out.

Rachel nodded.

"Dane, Marcus is alive," she whispered. "He came to talk to me. There was a man with a gun with him. He was also at the hospital with... I'm assuming, Levi. I think Levi and Overalls are in the house, but I haven't seen either of them. Did Lonnie get away?"

Dane nodded but knew his expression had only soured. Rachel tilted her head to the side.

"He was okay, but a few minutes ago I got a message that he had disappeared."

Rachel tensed. "Do you think they're coming back here with him?"

"If Marcus is in the house, I have to imagine so."

Rachel nodded.

"Marnie has to be in there, too. We have to get inside," she said decisively. "We have to end this."

The car alarm stopped.

Dane shook his head. "It's too dangerous. Backup is going to Marnie's." He felt his jaw harden. "I didn't want to repeat what happened last time."

Rachel grabbed his hand.

"Dane, Marcus told me..." She hesitated.

"What?"

Denim-blue eyes bored into his.

"Dane, he said he killed David and the rest of the men before he ever even called the department. There was nothing you or anyone could have done to save them." She squeezed his hand. "They were already gone."

Dane knew he should have felt some small part of relief. His decision to storm Marcus's hideout when his gut told him something was wrong had plagued him for years. He'd gone over that plan thousands of times in painstaking detail. He'd worked through even more what-ifs and any and all plans he could come up with instead. He'd lost sleep, lost confidence, and lost some of his sanity since then. Just trying to understand what had gone wrong. Why he couldn't save his friend.

Now he knew why.

David had already been dead.

That should have made Dane feel some kind of closure, yet all it did was make him mad.

Livid.

Rachel saw it in his eyes.

"This time is different," she said. "This time will end differently."

Dane nodded, feeling the weight of the gun in his hand. "This time—"

Someone cried out behind them. It was a woman. Dane was barely able to keep Rachel behind him as he moved around the corner of the shed to look at the back of the house.

Marcus Highland had walked out the back door and was staring right at them. The only reason Dane didn't shoot him right then and there was the young woman he was holding by the root of her hair.

"Marnie," Rachel yelled out.

She was bloodied but alive.

Marcus smiled and pressed the gun to her temple. "I think it's about time we finally talk face-to-face, Captain."

Chapter Twenty

"Let her go."

Dane's aim was squarely on Marcus while the grinning man's was undeniably on Marnie. Rachel met her friend's gaze. She was in pain. That was clear. Her hands were bound at her side. She couldn't get hold of the hair Marcus was pulling.

"Let her go," Rachel repeated. "Please. You don't need to pull her hair to hold a gun to her head."

It was a crude point to make. It was also accurate. Marcus snorted but opened his hand. Marnie cried out as she fell against the ground. She rolled onto her side but kept quiet.

Rachel's heart squeezed at the sight.

"What's your plan, Marcus?" Dane asked. His voice wasn't chilly. It was downright arctic. "What do you want?"

A gunshot sounded in the distance. Marcus and Dane didn't flinch. Rachel and Marnie did.

"My plan is to finish what I started back then. Back before you ordered me to be shot."

"And what's that? Trying to get the Saviors of the South back into the news? Trying to grab some fame?"

Marcus let out another laugh. It actually shook his stomach.

"The Saviors of the South was a joke," he said. "I

wanted vengeance, but I needed help. And some people will do anything for a cause they believe in." He shrugged. "So I made a cause, gave it a name and gave it a voice."

"And then you killed those men and it wasn't enough?"

Marcus's mirth started to wind down. "I didn't expect you to come as soon as you did. It kept me from leaving."

"It kept you from getting Lonnie," Rachel proclaimed.

"I had a backup plan for being shot, for playing dead, for disappearing and living a life, the life my *brother* deserved, but—" He sucked on his teeth for a second. Like he was expressing mild annoyance at the weather or something as mundane as a traffic jam. "But I didn't expect you to come that early. I couldn't grab him. So I got my good, *useless* buddy to take him in. Keep him safe until I could finish what I started. Do right by his father. Make you all pay while showing the rest of the county y'all so-call protect that they're no safer with you than in the prisons you put them in."

"You should have done right by Lonnie," she snapped back. "You should have raised him, not erased yourself because you'd rather cause more pain than deal with your own."

Marcus didn't like that. He sneered at her. "You're so naive. That's why I wanted you, too. When I realized you were teaching Lonnie, it was like being given a second chance to repeat the past. But to do it *right*. The people might have changed, but our purpose didn't." He looked at Dane. "I can punish the corrupted sheriff's department by killing their captain." His eyes trailed to Rachel. "And we both know which part you'll play."

Anger so bright it nearly blinded her flashed behind Rachel's eyes.

"David," she breathed. "You want to kill me because I'm innocent. Like my husband was. You want to kill me because you can."

"It's poetic, in a way," he confirmed. "They'll feel bad because they couldn't save your husband and then they couldn't save you."

Rachel didn't need to know Dane that well to pick up on the fact that he was reaching a breaking point. Every part of him seemed to be keyed up, ready.

Which was why she placed her hand on his back.

She hoped it calmed him. At least, enough for him to remember there was more to the situation than revenge.

"Then you'll just take Lonnie and leave town?" she ventured. "You'll disappear to someplace far away and raise him? Take him to school? Take him to ball games? Teach him how to drive? You'll be done with vengeance and violence and live a happy, normal life? What about Lonnie? What if he doesn't want that?"

"If you think he'd choose to stay here, you're kidding yourself. Any life with me will be better than the life he has now," Marcus said. He was getting agitated again. "From what I've heard he's already angry at the world. Doesn't have friends. Even the teachers give him grief. He's already a lost cause. I can only make him better."

Rachel had been trying to keep Dane from going off on the man, but she reached her breaking point before she realized what was happening. Dane snagged the back of her shirt with his free hand as she started to run around him, fire in her eyes.

"Did you ever think sticking him with someone who doesn't love him for all these years might have had something to do with his outlook on life?" she roared. "*No!* You just treat all of this like it's some kind of game!"

"Rachel—" Dane complained as she tried to wriggle out of his hold. Marcus's eyes had gone wide like they had in the shed. She wasn't done, though.

"And don't you *ever* call him a lost cause," she yelled. "You don't even know him!"

Rachel was ready to kick it into high gear and destroy the man who had destroyed her family before he could spread his poison to his nephew, but another gunshot from the front of the house exploded. This time it wasn't alone. It sounded like the front lawn had been turned into a war zone.

Marcus and Dane once again stayed their ground. They didn't flinch, but there was definitely some concern. Rachel just hoped whoever was on their side was winning the fight.

And that Lonnie was nowhere near it.

Marcus's expression went blank. When he spoke, it was to Dane.

"You can still save one person," he said. He shook the gun over Marnie's head. "Tell me where Lonnie is and I'll make sure my men don't kill her. One soul is better than none."

Rachel froze. She hoped her face didn't give away her surprise.

If Marcus didn't know where Lonnie was, then who had him?

She glanced at Dane. His expression also gave nothing away. The gunshots ceased in the distance.

"Give me the girl now and I'll tell my men not to kill you," Dane countered.

"You're bluffing," Marcus said. Though a noticeable tremble shook his hand. He was getting antsy.

"I'll tell you what I'm not doing," Dane said. "And that's negotiating. We're past that."

Rachel's breath caught as the world around them seemed to get knocked out of focus.

In hindsight, she'd realize that everyone there knew Marcus was never going to give Marnie up. Just like he'd never planned on letting David live. He was a man who craved violence and wanted to inflict as much pain as possible. There was never any hope that he would do anything differently now than he had done seven years ago.

Yet, when he swung his gun around and pointed it right at her, Rachel was nothing but shocked. Then Marcus pulled the trigger.

Marnie screamed.

Another sound exploded through the yard and echoed through the trees around them.

Rachel waited, for the second time that week, for the pain that came with being shot. But all she felt was something heavy push her to the ground. Then she was staring at Dane's back.

"Dane?" she breathed. It was a whisper. Confused and quiet. "Dane?"

Then the picture around her focused.

Across from them Marcus had dropped to his knees. He was holding his chest with one hand, blood already staining his shirt, and trying to crawl to where his gun had fallen with the other. Rachel looked down at the ground in front of her. Dane was also slow to get to his feet. She didn't understand why until he tried to stand but could only rock backward.

Rachel reached out and caught his back and shoulders against her chest. She looped her hands around him in a one-sided embrace. She looked over his shoulder. That was when she saw the blood at his stomach.

"Oh my God, Dane!"

That was when she realized what had happened.

He'd taken a bullet for her.

"Get...get the gun, Rach," he wheezed, pointing. His service weapon was a foot too far away.

If Marcus got to his first, they'd all be dead.

Rachel tried to move out from under Dane, but his muscle mass and injury worked against them. Rachel tried to swallow her rising panic.

"Rach, I—" Dane started. It tore at her how pained the sound was. Her trying to push herself out from under him wasn't helping. Marnie tried to get to her feet to help distract Marcus, but he was already putting his hand around the butt of his gun.

Before Dane could finish his thought and before Marcus could finish them both, another flurry of movement rushed across the yard. However this time it came from behind them.

"Stop!"

Lonnie ran from the tree line and jumped in front of Dane.

"Lonnie!" Rachel pushed herself up against Dane, scrambling to get free. She felt Dane try his best to move. He managed to sit up enough that she slid out.

The boy ignored Rachel and stared at his uncle instead.

"I choose them," he yelled. "*I choose them!*"

Lonnie threw his arms out wide, blocking her and Dane from Marcus's aim. Rachel tore at the grass, trying to get her balance. Her legs didn't seem to want to work. Her adrenaline hampered her speed more than helped.

"Lonnie, run!" she yelled.

But it was like she wasn't there at all.

Marcus kept his gun up and spoke to his nephew.

"You choose them?" Marcus asked, sounding just as surprised as Rachel had been to see Lonnie come out of the woods.

Finally she was able to get up. Her heart was hammering in her chest. She stumbled but managed to jump in front of Lonnie. It was her turn to throw her arms out to block him.

Marcus looked between them.

Rachel braced for his next shot.

It never came.

"You choose them," Marcus repeated. He looked at Lonnie. "Okay."

Marcus Highland dropped his gun.

He died shortly after.

Rachel dove for Dane's gun and turned around, ready to use it without moderation on anyone else who decided they wanted to hurt the people she loved. Thankfully, when the back door flew open a few seconds later, the man in the doorway was wearing a black cowboy hat.

"Chance, Dane's been shot," she yelled, unable to revel in the relief of seeing a friendly face.

Rachel didn't know what Chance did next. She knelt next to Dane and lifted his head to her lap. Lonnie dropped down on the other side of him.

"Oh, Dane!" Unable to keep the tears from rushing out with her words, Rachel issued one concrete command to the man she loved. "You're not allowed to leave me again. You hear me? You're not allowed."

Sirens sounded in the distance.

Dane didn't move.

HOSPITALS.

Rachel had once thought there was nothing worse than being admitted into one. Now she stood corrected.

Watching someone you love flat-line in one was the worst. A million times so.

But hearing that same monitor come back to life?

That was a relief unlike any other.

It was that relief that only grew stronger over the next few days. After every surgery and close call passed, with Dane's chance of survival growing.

Now, a week later, staring at the captain from the end of his hospital bed, Rachel felt like she could finally breathe again.

"I'm sure glad you listened to me," she said with a smile. "I didn't like the past few years without you and I wasn't convinced I would like any more without you, either."

Dane snorted. Then cringed.

"Easy, now, Captain," she said. "You got shot in the stomach, you know. Might need to take things easy for a little bit."

Dane slowly waved his hand at her, dismissively.

"It's just a flesh wound," he said, an easy smile gracing his lips despite everything.

Rachel had worried she would never see it again.

"Do you remember talking to me yesterday?" Since the cavalry had come in and taken them to the hospital, Rachel hadn't left his room for more than a few minutes at a time. "You were pretty out of it with the painkillers."

Dane looked thoughtful for a moment.

"Yes and no," he said. "I remember you told me that I was shot, that I was going to be okay even though I'd been shot, and that the man who shot me was dead."

"So basically everything about being shot," she teased.

He snorted and then cringed again. She moved closer to him so she could grab his hand. He squeezed it.

"I also remember that Marcus could have killed you," he said, all humor aside. "And that he could have killed Lonnie, too. The same kid who ran away from Suzy at the hospital, stowed away in Chance's SUV and then followed us. I can't believe he did that."

Rachel nodded. "He told me, and I quote, 'It was my turn to make a decision and I decided to help.'"

Dane hadn't heard that part yet. She didn't miss the small smile that passed over his lips.

"He's a good kid," he concluded. "Even when he's trying to sacrifice himself for us."

Rachel laughed. "I can't argue with that."

Rachel recapped what she already said the day before. The gunshots they had heard were between Chance and three of Marcus's lackeys. He'd slashed their tires and then used the car alarm as bait. Levi had been the first one out. Chance had jumped him, knocked him out and then gone back to hiding. After that Chet, previously known as Overalls, had managed to get a shot off. Chance had been forced to shoot to kill. Then a man named Javier had gone toe-to-toe with the cowboy. Chance had won.

"He's a great shot," Dane said, not at all surprised.

They'd caravanned to the hospital. Marnie had been checked out and only had superficial cuts and bruises. Even though she'd been told to not go to the house alone, she'd forgotten June the Cat's favorite toy. June had already been showing signs of stress at Rachel being gone, so she'd brought the cat over while she'd looked for it—unaware the house had been taken over by Marcus. Now both Marnie and June were fine and at home resting. Though Marnie had spent two nights with Rachel at the hospital, waiting for Dane to wake up.

"How's Lonnie doing?" Dane asked. "Wasn't he with you yesterday?"

Rachel nodded. "For a little bit. He wanted to stay longer, but Billy and he needed to sort some things out." She felt a flutter of excitement in her stomach. She decided to wait until all the bad news was out of the way before she got into the good. "Right now, though, he's actually out with Suzy at the airport."

Dane's eyebrow went sky-high. "Why are they at the airport?"

"Someone had to pick up your dad." Rachel adopted what she hoped was a chiding expression. "Which, by the way…how am I just now hearing about some crazy guy attacking your dad a while back?"

Dane sighed.

"There's a lot we probably should catch each other up on," he said. "It's been a helluva year."

Chapter Twenty-One

Dane saw the cowboy hat before he saw the man.

"Well, if it isn't Sleeping Beauty," Chance greeted. "And here I was starting to get bored."

The man cut him a grin from the love seat against the wall. He motioned to the table next to him and then the side tables. All were covered in flowers. One even had a fruit basket. There had been two cakes, too, but those had mysteriously disappeared after Dane's dad left for the house.

"I didn't bring you any flowers, but I can pop out and grab some weeds I saw coming in that looked pretty good," he continued, grin growing. "You know, the ones that look like daisies."

Dane rolled his eyes and snorted.

"Your presence is always enough, Chance," he mockingly assured him. "Plus, you taking out three armed guys pretty much has you square in my book for life." Dane pointed to the fruit basket. "In fact, why don't you take that?"

Chance changed over to the chair Rachel had frequented the past few days. He shook his head with a laugh.

"We all know how fruit baskets are the worst," the cowboy pointed out. "Especially when there's not chocolate-dipped anything in it. If I wanted to eat healthy, I'd go to the grocery store myself."

The gesture was nice, but Dane agreed. He'd never been a fan of fruit, in his defense, but it had been a pleasant surprise to receive it and, really, all the gifts. News in Riker County traveled at the speed of light. He'd had people stopping by left and right. It had been all Rachel and the nurses could do to curb the attention. While Dane was expected to fully heal, he was still relatively fresh from the trauma of being shot. It still hurt to laugh occasionally and he was a fool if he thought he'd be doing his normal workout routine any time soon.

To prove the point to himself, Dane reached over to grab his water. He felt the soreness stretch and took it slow.

"So, how are you doing?" Chance asked after he was done. There was no denying there was concern there.

"I'm glad this is over," Dane admitted. He stopped what he was about to say and instead confided in his friend. "I feel like I can finally close the book on what happened all those years ago. Honestly, I already thought I had. I thought I'd moved on. But now...now it feels real. Now it feels *done*. Almost like I have a second chance."

"Or a new start," his friend pointed out. "One that I'm assuming involves a certain middle school art teacher. How's she doing, by the way? I haven't had a chance to really sit down and chat since you landed in here."

Dane let out a sigh. He was still tired even after spending half the morning sleeping.

"I've known that woman for years, and let me tell you, she still finds ways to surprise me." Even Dane heard the pride in his voice. "She's in damage control mode, trying to collect everything that fell between the cracks during the case and also deal with the aftermath of it. She has a habit of putting everyone before herself. She even flew in my dad to help out with Lonnie so she could stay near me." Dane snorted. "I think the toughest negotiation of my career was convincing her to go to lunch with Marnie."

"Not that I'm sure you mind having her around," Chance added.

"There definitely are worse things in life." They shared another grin before Dane became serious again. "Once things settle down, I think she'll finally start to process everything. She was really put through the wringer with this one. You should have seen her yelling at Marcus. I swear she would have attacked him with her bare fists if I hadn't grabbed her." Dane started to fist his hand as anger rose in his chest. He took a second to rein it back. "David, Tracy and the other men were dead before the prison van being taken was reported. There was nothing either of us ever could have done to save them. It's still a lot to process. For both of us."

Chance took off his cowboy hat and nodded. He gave Dane a moment to swim back to sturdier emotional ground. "So, part of the reason I haven't been around here is that I've been out trying to tie up loose ends and questions," he started. "I've learned a few things I thought might interest you."

Chance relayed information that Dane had forgotten to look for in all the chaos. He knew the FBI had found the radio equipment with the broadcast, but he hadn't heard anything past that in the bustle of his recovery.

"It was in the upstairs bedroom of a duplex out in Kipsy. There was bubble wrap covering the walls of one of the bedrooms, acting like makeshift soundproofing.

Turns out the duplex belonged to Levi's grandparents and was willed to him after they passed. It looks like that's where our motley crew of crazies was meeting until they took up residence at Rachel's."

"Then why soundproof the place if they just planned on moving?"

A disgusted look passed over Chance's expression. "Levi said that's where they planned on taking Lonnie after they grabbed him from the school. They were going to keep him there while they went after you and Rachel. Apparently, Levi and the others told Marcus they were concerned Lonnie might get loud. Marcus didn't want to gag the boy, so he decided to make a room where, no matter how loud Lonnie yelled, no one would hear him." Chance shook his head. "Me and Detective Foster tested it. I yelled my head off and Caleb never heard a thing."

Dane popped his knuckles, trying to get a hold on the new wave of anger pushing through him.

"Which brings me to the dog crates…" Chance continued. His expression lost its edge. His shoulder relaxed a bit. He smirked. "Turns out Wyatt was *really* into crime television shows. On one he saw this group of people confuse the cops by stealing a bunch of random things."

"So he thought he could throw everyone off their trail by stealing two things they needed and then one random thing?"

Chance made a finger gun. "Bingo."

Dane had to laugh at that.

Chance shrugged. "I guess it worked a little," he admitted. "I *did* take the time to go to every vet in the county asking anything and everything about dog crates. But want to know the kicker? I don't think I would have looked into it had they not taken *three* really bizarre things. Two? Maybe. But throw in the dog crates and I couldn't resist diving in."

"I'm sure Levi and Javier regret listening to Wyatt now. They'll be in prison for a very long time."

Chance smiled. "Music to my ears."

Dane knew the topic of Tucker Hughes wasn't far away, so he decided to address it now. "Tucker talked with Lonnie yesterday. I convinced the doctor to let me take a wheelchair in with him. Rachel was there, too. She convinced me that, even though we now know Tucker wasn't anywhere near a saint, he was the only family Lonnie had ever known and Lonnie deserved to ask his own questions."

"How'd that go?"

Dane's heart ached a little. "Lonnie tried playing it tough but did a lot of yelling. Tucker surprised us, though. He actually said all the right things, considering. And not once tried to defend himself. He also offered to answer any of Lonnie's questions about his real parents. He told me where he knew Marcus had kept all the photo albums of them, which I think helped Lonnie." He smiled. The look was genuine. "Then Lonnie did what he does best and surprised us all. He forgave Tucker right then and there."

Tucker might not have loved Lonnie the way he should have, but Dane knew being forgiven by the boy had meant something to him. He'd told Dane right after Lonnie and Rachel had left that if they ever had questions for him about Lonnie or his biological family, they could write him in prison and he'd respond without any ill feelings.

Tucker never said it, but Dane also recognized the relief in the man. The stress of being under Marcus's command since they were teens was finally gone. He was glad everything was over, even if it meant he was going behind bars.

"That kid's something else," Chance said after a moment passed. "But what happens to him now? Wasn't Marcus his last living relative?"

Dane nodded.

"But just because his biological family is gone doesn't mean he's short on people who care." Dane grinned.

Chance raised his eyebrow, but Dane knew the cowboy caught on to what he wasn't saying.

Then it was Chance who was smiling.

"Well, that boy definitely deserves a happy ending," he said.

Dane couldn't agree more.

RACHEL TOTED A slice of chocolate cake up to Dane's hospital room with a pep in her step and a song in her heart. She'd just gotten good news from Billy and had an even better talk with Lonnie. Now she had cake.

Her good mood only rocketed when she walked into the hospital room and was met with a wide smile from Dane Jones.

"Howdy," he greeted her. "You just missed Chance."

His eyes went to the container. It had a clear plastic top. His eyes widened. "Is that double-chocolate fudge cake?"

Rachel winked. "Good eye, Captain."

She crossed the room, gave him a quick peck and perched next to him on the bed.

"God, you're amazing," he breathed, taking the cake. "I'm going to save this for tonight, though. That's when my sweet tooth always punches me." He put the container on the side table.

Then he did what Dane Jones did best. He gave her a look that Rachel felt in her bones. It was quiet and perfect and real. It prompted her to finally say what she'd been trying to for days. She took a deep breath and put his hand firmly between both of hers.

Concern crossed his expression. She didn't give him a chance to ask why it was there.

"When you told me you loved me, I didn't say it back," Rachel started. "I should have, but then you gave me that look." She averted her eyes for a moment, searching for the right words. The ones that would make him finally understand.

The ones that would hopefully set him free.

"What look?"

Rachel ran her thumb across the top of his. She met his stare. "That one that said you felt guilty for loving me because of David."

Dane opened his mouth to say something but she cut him off. "Don't try to deny it. I know how you think. How can you be happy with me of all people when David can't be here? *But* I have something to say to that and I want you to listen, okay?"

For a moment she didn't think Dane would agree, but then he nodded.

She took another small breath and then said what was in her heart. "We have a lot of things in common, you and me. But one of my favorite things we share *is* David. You loved him. I loved him. But, Dane, he also *loved* us. Nothing will ever change those facts. Not even if we love each other. And, Dane, I do love you. I really do." She smiled. "And if David knew you were using him as an excuse not to be happy, well, then he'd kick your tail, Dane Jones. And you know that's the God's honest truth."

Dane surprised her with a laugh. Rachel loved the sound.

"You're right," he conceded. "He'd probably go find and put on those boots he got at the rodeo to do it, too. What did he call them again? The really terrible red ones."

"Ass-kickers," she supplied.

Dane chuckled. Rachel kept smiling.

"You see? Just because we can move forward and he can't doesn't mean we've forgotten about him," she continued. "It just means we're moving on. And David would have wanted that for us."

Rachel's eyes widened as Dane pulled his hand from between her own. But then he reached out and grabbed her chin. Gently he pulled her into a kiss.

It was warm and soft and wonderful.

However the most exciting part was everything else that would follow it.

Dane broke the kiss with a smile already across his lips. "One *helluva* year."

Epilogue

"This is madness."

Dane took a step back and ran a hand through his hair. There was no way they were going to be able to pull it off. It was crazy that they were even attempting it.

"I haven't been trained for this," he added.

Rachel rolled her eyes.

"This isn't madness, Dane. This is cake," she deadpanned. "The cake, I might mention, that we had to make and decorate last minute because you *dropped* the last one. Now stop your griping and hand me that bottle of sprinkles."

She might have had her grumpy face on but Rachel's voice let him know she was still amused. Still, he gave her the sprinkles and tried for the umpteenth time to defend his mistake. Or really, shift blame to someone else.

"It's not my fault Olivia decided she wanted to swandive off her high chair while I was trying to move it. I made a very valid decision to sacrifice the cake to keep our daughter from busting open her head. I'm sure Cassie will understand."

Rachel dusted the birthday cake with, in his opinion, too many sprinkles. The professional cake they'd bought had been perfect. Their new backup cake? Disaster. But he wasn't going to tell his wife that. Not after she'd been so excited to play hostess for the party.

"I'm not questioning you saving that wild child of ours," she pointed out. "I'm questioning why you moved the cake in the first place when I told you to *not touch it.*"

Dane looked away, trying to act nonchalant.

It made her laugh. "Can you tell me again why you moved it?"

Dane muttered the answer.

"Say again, Captain? I don't think I heard that."

"I was looking for the remote!"

Rachel tried to look stern but it didn't last long. She shook her head and continued to laugh. Dane rolled his eyes and was prepared to launch into another defense when the doorbell rang. Nerves flashed across Rachel's face. He laughed and dipped in to kiss her cheek.

"Everyone is going to love it," he assured her.

She let out a sigh but smiled. "You get that and I'll go get Olivia changed."

Dane complied with the instruction. He didn't stop as Rachel called after him, "And don't move the cake this time!"

It had been a little over three years since the Saviors of the South and their leader had been stopped. In that time a lot had changed and a lot had stayed the same. Dane had asked Rachel to marry him two months into dating and then moved in with her shortly after. He'd been asked if it was weird to live in the family home of her late husband, but Dane had been the one who'd suggested it. David had always wanted to keep the house and the land it sat on in the family, and that was exactly what Dane and Rachel intended to do. David's picture was proudly displayed on their mantel with the rest of their family, and they wouldn't have wanted it any other way.

Dane opened the front door wide and had to adjust his gaze down slightly.

"Hey, Mr. Jones!" Jude Carrington chirped, his red hair wild. He thrust his thumb backward to the car idling in the drive. "Did you see my new ride? Well, I can't technically drive it yet, but my mom said that I can have it when my brother goes to college. Isn't it cool?" Dane gave a wave to Mrs. Carrington and laughed. The car was dated but solid, a dream for a fourteen-year-old obsessed with cars. Which Jude definitely was.

"That's pretty cool," Dane admitted.

Jude nodded again and then yelled into the house, "Hey, Lonnie, come look at my car!"

Dane couldn't help laughing as Lonnie tore out of his room and rushed down the hall toward them like the building was on fire. Dane barely got out of the way as the two jumped off the porch. They were circling the car like sharks in chummed waters when Rachel appeared next to him on the porch. Olivia squealed in delight as Dane stole her from her mama.

"So I guess Patrice finally told Jude he's getting his brother's car when he turns sixteen?" Rachel asked with a laugh. Dane nodded. "He does remember he's not sixteen yet, right?"

Dane shrugged. "Jude rarely lets details like that stop him."

Rachel turned to try to fix the bow in Olivia's hair. It was a battle she lost every time, but that never stopped her from trying.

"Speaking of presents and getting older, are you *sure* we can't give Lonnie one of his birthday presents a little early this year?" She lowered her voice. "I mean, it's only a month away and it's not like he won't get others."

Dane raised his eyebrow. Rachel hurried to sweeten the option. "May I point out that his grades are great and he's been killing it at helping with Olivia? *And*— and this is a *practical* present for a growing artist."

Dane knew when there was a battle that he couldn't win.

"You want to go ahead and buy him the drawing table," he guessed.

Rachel smiled. "It might not be the promise of a car, but to him, it's more. He's been drooling over a professional drawing table ever since he saw his favorite comic book artist use one."

Olivia grabbed her bow and threw it on the ground. Rachel picked it up and put it in her pocket. Dane also lost his fight.

"Fine," he conceded. "You broke me down, woman."

Rachel winked. "I'm glad you feel that way. Because I already ordered it."

She smirked and tried to run away, but even with a toddler in his arms, Dane was able to catch her. Both ladies laughed as he kissed Rachel full on the lips.

"Eww, don't look now, Lonnie," Jude said as they walked onto the porch. "Your parents are making out. Let's get out of here!"

Lonnie laughed and followed his best friend into the house. Rachel looked after them with a smile clear in her eyes.

Tucker Hughes might have spent his life helping Marcus plan and commit crimes, but he'd kept his word to help Lonnie with any questions he might have. Not only that, he'd even helped Dane and Rachel with their own questions about Lonnie's early childhood. They would never fully forgive Tucker like Lonnie had, but there was enough good between them that they wrote to him and even sent a card or two. There was no denying that Lonnie had been shaken by what had happened, but he finally admitted to them that night after they'd talked to Tucker that he was relieved. He'd spent his short life up until that point thinking something was wrong with *him* and that was why Tucker hadn't showed him the love he deserved.

If Rachel hadn't already decided to try to adopt Lonnie, Dane was sure she would have right then and there. As it was, the business that the sheriff and Lonnie had to tend to while Dane was in the hospital was Billy setting up temporary guardianship with Rachel. She'd made sure to ask Lonnie first, though, promising him he'd always have a voice when it came to his future. Lonnie had immediately said yes. His adoption had been finalized right after Dane and Rachel were married.

Two days after that he'd asked if he could call them Mom and Dad.

They had also immediately said yes.

Now, for the life of him, Dane couldn't imagine his family without the boy in it.

A car honked, pulling their attention to the driveway. Matt and Maggie Walker parked and got out. Their son Cody had a present in his hands.

"Well, if it isn't the famous true crime novelist," Dane said by way of greeting Maggie. He mussed Cody's hair as Rachel directed him to Lonnie's room. "Does that mean we're famous by association now?"

Maggie waved him off with a smirk.

"One bestseller doesn't make you famous," she said. Matt hooked his arm around her shoulder.

"But that doesn't stop me from bragging to everyone about it." That made his wife laugh.

"He's endearing *and* embarrassing," she said.

"Ah, that should be the official slogan for husbands," Rachel said. She pulled Maggie into the house while Dane and Matt walked around to the side deck. It wasn't long before they were joined by a stream of guests.

Billy and Mara had brought their kids, along with Billy's mother. It was the perfect move, according to Caleb. He and his wife, Alyssa, had a toddler and a baby with them. Apparently he'd thought about asking their friends the Rickmans to come along just so they had an extra helping hand, but Alyssa had worried they would be intruding. Dane laughed that thought off. His dad had spent the first two months in town after Olivia was born helping them stay sane.

"Don't you even dare talking about kid madness," Suzy said, walking out of the kitchen with her own toddler on her hip. Her husband, James, was inside the house with their five-year-old. "We might only have two little ones, but don't let that fool you. We have a teenager and a college graduate."

Billy laughed. "But don't you have that live-in nanny?"

Suzy rolled her eyes but smiled. "If you're talking about Jensen, I wouldn't call him particularly helpful with this one." She motioned to her daughter. "Anytime there's a dirty diaper, he starts gagging. You'd think it wouldn't bother him as much considering he's had a drunk man vomit on him while he was running the bar."

"Oh, are we talking about kid war stories?"

Everyone turned to see Cassie and Henry coming up the stairs. Henry was wearing one of their twins across his chest while holding their toddler son Colby's hand. Cassie had the other twin in her arms. "Because we're late to my own birthday party because this one—" she pointed to Colby "—decided to put a popcorn kernel up his nose. We were two steps from going to the ER before he blew it out himself."

Henry shook his head.

"I'm not too ashamed to say I was more freaked out than she was," he said. "I mean one second it was there and then the next it was gone."

Everyone laughed and the next hour was spent talking, mingling, and swapping old and new stories. It wasn't until after the cake was served and they had all moved out to the seating area around the fire pit in the backyard that Dane felt it.

Really felt it.

Lucky.

Sitting there with the love of his life, the two pieces of his heart, and the closest friends he'd ever had, he just felt plain ol' lucky. He wasn't the only one. Looking across the fire, he caught Billy's eye. The sheriff took off his cowboy hat, smiled and stood. He used the hat to get everyone's attention.

"I know all of us here aren't for speeches, but sitting around and seeing us all has me feeling...well, emotional. And no, before you say anything, it has nothing to do with what I've been drinking."

The group laughed. Billy continued. "It's just that we've all come so far—together—that I can't help saying a few things." His smile grew. Dane leaned in.

"I remember when I started at the sheriff's department," he said. "I was young. I was determined. And I was as stubborn as a mule. I thought Sheriff Rockwell was too uptight, the break room was too depressing, and a certain partner of mine was too cocky." He sent a wink Suzy's way. She snorted. "I thought a lot of things in the beginning, but one thing I never thought was that the department would ever be more than a job. Certainly not become a family."

Billy took a second to look around. Dane didn't need to see their faces to know everyone was in agreement.

"But that's exactly what happened. Through thick and thin—a little too thin sometimes, if you ask me—we've stuck by each other, braved all the storms together, and done it while staying true to what we believe in. This county, the people who live within it, and the good fight for justice. I just wanted to say thank you to all of you for being exactly who you are. And to show how thankful I am, I'm going to embarrass each of you by singling you out." Everyone laughed. Billy turned to Suzy.

"Suzanne Simmons-Callahan," he continued. "When we first started at the department together, you once told me two things. One, don't ever for a second treat you any differently just because you were my best friend. Two, don't ever for a second treat you any differently because you were a woman. I think it's safe to say that none of us here has ever treated you any differently because of either. You have worked hard and true to be one of the best I've ever known in law enforcement all on your own. Nothing and no one has ever stopped you and we've been damn lucky to have you. To Suzy!"

Everyone raised their drinks and cheered. Suzy wiped under her eye. James gave her a big kiss. Billy turned to Caleb next.

Caleb groaned. "Oh boy, this is going to be brutal."

Billy laughed. "Caleb Foster, I remember your first week on the job. You complained more about the heat and humidity than anyone I'd met. It got to the point where I was worried you'd quit just to escape it all."

Caleb nodded. They all remembered that.

"And honestly, I wasn't too keen on you staying in the beginning. But then you proved everyone wrong. You stepped up in the best way possible and never stopped trying to fight the good fight. Once again, I think I speak for all of us when I say how glad we are that you decided to stay and I can't wait to see what you'll continue to do. To Caleb!"

They all raised their glasses and took a drink. Billy homed in on Matt. "Now to our other favorite detective, Matt Walker." Billy took a second to snort. "We've been through a lot. In fact, I think you've been through a lot with everyone here. Sure, it's your job, but I think it's safe to say helping your friends and this county is something you'd do even if you weren't paid to do it. From dropping everything to help those who need it, your time as deputy *and* detective has benefited us all in more ways than we can count. To Matt!"

Matt, closest to Billy, stood and clapped the sheriff on the back. They clinked their bottles together.

"And to the birthday girl and her husband," he continued. "Cassie Ward, we have said from the moment you started at the department that you were the heart of us all. Always a ray of sunshine despite times when work took us into darkness. You never once stopped trying to make us happy, even when it was at your own expense. I don't know where we'd be without you and I don't ever want to find out. To Cassie!"

They all cheered louder this time. Some of the children squealed and cried. Billy ruffled the hair of his son before looking at Henry.

"And then there's this guy." Everyone laughed. "Henry, you're just about the most impressive person I've had the pleasure of working alongside. Stubborn but in a good way. Clever but humble about it. However, I think the most impressive part is how, without a doubt, you're the only person we have ever thought was good enough for Cassie. You make her happy, which makes us happy."

He lowered his voice. "And believe me, we were waiting for her to give us a reason to tear into you."

Henry let out a hoot of laughter. Billy was joking, but was it a joke if it was also true?

"Thanks for being the solid, hardworking guy you are. To Henry!"

Dane raised his glass but skipped taking a drink. Billy's eyes were on him now. Rachel squeezed his hand.

"Dane Jones," he started. He was grinning. "In times of crisis you have told me that I keep this department together, but I just don't think that's true. There was a time in your life when you could have quit, left the department behind, and no one would have blamed you for it. But you didn't. You stayed and kept going, and I don't think you realize how much you've helped us all because of it. Late nights, long weekends, holidays… If there was one thing we could always count on, it was you being there. Even when we didn't realize it. You're the glue, buddy. Always have been, always will be. To Dane!"

Rachel yelled along with the people around him. Dane felt his chest tighten. But in the best way possible. He cleared his throat and stood.

"And now let's talk about the sheriff," he said, grinning at Billy. A second later he sobered. He wanted to make sure his friend saw that he was being sincere. "If Cassie's the heart and I'm the glue, then I don't think I'm being too dramatic when I say that Billy Reed is the soul of not only the department, but Riker County as a whole." A wave of nods spread through the group. "I'd like to think I love this place, but I don't think any of us has a love that compares to yours. You have never hesitated to help any and all of the people who are in our jurisdiction and you've never hesitated to help us, either, for that matter. You take pride in our home and it has showed through every good thing you've done for the department. In turn, you make us proud just to be your friend, never mind your colleague. *We're* the ones who are lucky to have you. Riker County sure is." Dane raised his glass. "To Billy!"

They all cheered. Billy's eyes were glassy, but no one called him on it. Instead they quieted as Billy stood one last time.

"I look around this group tonight, and as I said, I don't see friends or colleagues, I see family," he said. "We've been through a lot and we'll probably be through a lot more. But no matter what lies ahead, I can say without an ounce of hesitation, we will always make it through as long as we have each other. So here's to us and here's to our home." Billy raised his bottle. "To Riker County!"

This time everyone stood.

"To Riker County!"

* * * * *

COMING SOON!

We really hope you enjoyed reading this book. If you're looking for more romance, be sure to head to the shops when new books are available on

Thursday
6th September

To see which titles are coming soon, please visit
millsandboon.co.uk

LET'S TALK

Romance

For exclusive extracts, competitions
and special offers, find us online:

f facebook.com/millsandboon

◎ @millsandboonuk

𝕏 @millsandboon

Or get in touch on 0844 844 1351*

For all the latest titles coming soon, visit
millsandboon.co.uk/nextmonth

Want even more
ROMANCE?

Join our bookclub today!